DREAM OF LOVE

In a trance, he reached for her breast, needing to restrain his eager fingers. It took all his will to force them to trail slowly over the budding nipple.

The movement drew a tiny gasp of alarm. He pulled his gaze away, up to her face. "What is it? Have I hurt you?"

She shook her head, her hair rustling back and forth on the pillow. "I—I'm frightened."

He hated himself. What was wrong with him, taking advantage of a moment of weakness this way? Muttering an oath under his breath, he started to leave her, but a hand shot out to cover his. "Not of you. Of this. I—I've never . . . ever . . . I don't know what to do."

"You needn't do a thing." He laughed shakily as he smoothed the hair from her face. "For once, let someone else worry about what must be done. I've spent my life learning how to please a woman; trust me to put it to good use."

Other Leisure books by Barbara Benedict:

LOVESTORM
GOLDEN TOMORROWS

BARBARA BENEDICT

Carol Plater

LEISURE BOOKS   NEW YORK CITY

To Scott, as always
And to Jeannie, for all your help and support

A LEISURE BOOK

Published by

Dorchester Publishing Co., Inc.
6 East 39th Street
New York, NY 10016

Printed in the United States of America

1

Hudson, New York
Spring, 1878

"If I see another cow, I declare I'll spit."

Samantha Lynn Eggersley looked at her cousin Claire, in the carriage seat opposite her, with poorly suppressed amusement.

"You can laugh," Claire said with a pout. "You don't care about fun and excitement and adventure. With all the fabulous homes Lord Hoxton has all over the world, you get us invited to this backwater retreat. You must live to be boring."

Sam's humor faded. The accusation was patently unfair. It wasn't Sam's choice to be invited here; nor had she chosen the unexciting life that was hers. The sad truth was that there was no one else to shoulder the many responsibilities their grandfather, old Samuel Eggersley, had left behind.

"I've explained at length that Lord Hoxton is a recluse. We must respect his wishes and adjust to them for the next two weeks. Once we're in Chicago with Annie, things will be different."

"You adjust; I want to go to Chicago now. I'm dying to meet your friend Annie and find out if life as an actress is as glamorous as it sounds. I don't want to rot in some dreary hovel in the hills."

Sam folded her hands in her lap, knowing that if she did not, they would soon be about her cousin's lovely neck. How like Claire to make a scene. Fingers closing over her purse, she thought of the two letters inside. They were to blame for plunging her into this insane adventure when common sense insisted she could more profitably employ her time in Richmond, shoring up the sagging Eggersley finances.

But Anthony Rawlings, Lord Hoxton, had sent his invitation. Stiffly cordial, he had begged the pleasure of her company. He'd been thinking of her father, he said. He thought it was time the two people who missed Bill Eggersley most met and talked about him.

Tony Rawlings. Oh, but how Sam had wondered about that man. About her mother's wistful smiles each time his name was mentioned, and her grand-father's hateful sneers. About what could have happened so many years ago to send Tony Rawlings and her father on two opposing paths, so that one partner survived and proposed, while Papa . . .

With an uncomfortable ache, Sam thought of the second letter, from kind old Molly Malloy in far-off Colorado. Poor Molly was a widow now. Gus had been climbing up by the gold mine, Molly wrote, and just like Sam's parents, he'd fallen headlong from the cliff.

Mama! the little girl in her cried, her mind again seeing her mother's twisted body. She alone knew her mother's death had been no accident. Sam had seen *two* sets of footprints leading to the cliff. In the horror of discovery, though, she had never mentioned this to the sheriff. By the time she realized the implication of what she'd seen, she had been on her way to Virginia, where her grandfather insisted that she leave well enough alone.

Only now that Samuel Eggersley was dead was Sam free from his restraints. She hoped she wasn't too late to unravel the mystery. There was no way, now, to retrace those actual footsteps, but she could still ask questions. Far too many lingered, still unanswered. And behind most of them, somewhere, lurked the mysterious Lord Hoxton.

Claire gasped, bringing Sam's thoughts back to the present. Sam followed Claire's gaze. Directly before them, overwhelming the hill, was a most intimidating fortress. Awesomely large, its precise blocks of gray stone seemed to put a chill into the otherwise pleasant spring day. A tower perched on each of the four corners, and the casement windows were barred by iron. Down the hill and all around the mansion, a moat glittered in the sun, permitting access to the house only across a medieval-looking drawbridge. Not quite a hovel, Sam decided, but nor was it a welcoming sort of place.

Claire seemed to share her trepidation. Her blonde curls shook as a shudder passed through her body.

"I can't go through with this charade," she declared. "And you can't make me, Sam. Not even if you take away my allowance!"

Inwardly, Sam groaned. "We mustn't jump to conclusions," she managed with forced calm. "It might be quite pleasant inside."

"Know what I think?" Claire said accusingly. "I think you lied to me. You know exactly what Hoxton is like. He must be old and wrinkled and nasty—not to mention mean-tempered and tight with his money."

If Claire only knew how often Sam had wondered about him herself. . . . Aside from a brief, childhood encounter in Denver, Sam knew as little about him as the rest of the world did. A confirmed recluse since he'd gained his title years ago, Hoxton was a puzzle those far wiser and more desperate than Sam had been unable to decipher. In her mind, she liked to picture a tall, dark dream of a man, rather like the hero of her favorite stage play. But then, Sam was a dreamer. Her grandfather had told her over and over that if life continued to disappoint her, she had naught but her overblown expectations to blame.

"Think sensibly," she snapped, irritation coloring her tone. "If I'd met him recently, he'd know who the real Samantha Eggersley was. Then how would our deception ever work?"

"But why are we doing this? If there's nothing wrong with him, why are you so afraid to let him know who you are?"

"I am not afraid." Disconcerted by Claire's rare flash of insight, Sam shifted uncomfortably on the seat. "I merely hope to avoid an uncomfortable situation. From his letters, I fear the man appears to have marriage on his mind. Tidying up loose ends, he calls it. Understandably, I have little desire to be either a loose end or wed to a man I do not love."

What she didn't add was the deeper, more unsettling fear that it wasn't herself that he meant to pursue, but the memory of her mother, the beautiful, multi-talented Susannah Eggersley. Sam's grandfather had taken great pains to point out that she had inherited little of her mother's beauty. What she did have was the Eggersley brains, stubbornness, and a hearty sense of family pride. If Hoxton expected another Susannah, he would be sorely disappointed by Sam; she didn't want to face that disappointment.

Besides, she was not here for a husband, but rather to learn what she could from this man who had figured so largely in her parents' lives. Until she could resolve the past, she could not consider the future. She needed to unlock the mystery behind those unexplained deaths, and the key, she'd always maintained, was the enigmatic Tony Rawlings.

"Oh, pooh," Claire sniffed beside her. "As if love

has a thing to do with it. Why, if a man as rich as that proposed to me, I'd say yes so fast his head would spin."

"That's precisely why you are here. If you can't spin his head and distract him, no one can."

As she considered this, Claire brightened. Unfortunately, the entrance gate loomed before them and the drawbridge dropped with an ominous moan. Passing over it, the combined clattering of their carriage and the wagon behind them, carrying their luggage and Giselle, their maid, made an intimidating echo. By the time they entered a dark, narrow courtyard, Claire hovered at the edge of the seat.

"I can't do it," she whispered, her wide eyes darting to the drawbridge rising again behind them. "I don't like this place."

Neither do I, Sam thought, but knew better than to voice her misgivings aloud. Claire's cooperation had already cost a small fortune. All those gowns, lovingly wrapped in tissue paper, all for Claire. In her head, Sam could see an army of price tags, marching in time, taking away her own chance to ever own a decent wardrobe. "Just what do you suggest?" she hissed. "That we turn around now and leave?"

Claire turned to her in relief. "Oh Sam, let's. You can go home and marry Emery Blankfield, just as you planned before this silly invitation came."

Just as *she* planned? To her knowledge, Sam had never said she would wed the ambitious young lawyer, but her grandfather had, and even now, nearly a year after his death, Samuel Eggersley's word was law. "You go home," she told her cousin through clenched teeth. "I came to meet this Lord Hoxton and I won't leave until I do."

"Dressed like that? You look like a poor relation in all that gray."

9

Claire had the audacity to shudder. Did she forget whose fault it was that Sam wore her grandmother's castoffs? After Claire's demands had been met, one silly riding habit was all Sam could afford for herself. And that had been deliberated over for hours.

A spurt of stubbornness must have shown on her face, for Claire went suddenly pale. "Oh Sam, you're not going to do anything impulsive, are you? Think how foolish I—we—will appear. Granddaddy wouldn't like this at all."

If the reference to Samuel Eggersley intimidated her, Sam was determined not to let it show. "I won't leave until I've met him, Claire. And that's final."

The carriage stopped as her words did, jerking both to an unceremonious halt. Ignoring her cousin, Sam stepped down to gaze around her. A spacious lawn rolled its emerald green carpet down to the moat, broken only by the gravel driveway meandering toward the gray stone walls that towered behind her. While still ostentatious, the house, viewed up close, wasn't nearly as intimidating as the outer walls. Any man who would spend money on such masses of lilacs and azaleas, she reasoned, couldn't be all that bad.

As if to dispute this, a cavernous door opened silently behind her. Dressed in unrelenting black, a man with more years than pounds hovered at the top of the long flight of steps. His frown was as black and severe as his clothing. Hoxton? Fighting disappointment, and the urge to follow Claire's advice, Sam forced herself to the stairs.

A small boy, hair the color of carrots, crouched in the azaleas. As his eyes met hers, he brought a warning finger to his lips. Clearly, the lad was trespassing and not overly anxious to be caught at it. Sam's cautious nod was rewarded with a blazing smile and the most adorable wink.

"Miss Eggersley. Miss Farnstable." With a court bow, the man in black gestured indoors. He spoke softly, each word executed with precise British diction. Feeling like a child facing Samuel's displeasure, Sam winked back at the urchin in the azaleas and scurried up the steps.

"As for you, William MacPhearson," the voice continued, "may I suggest you get your silly bones back to your grandmother, before Ada descends upon us in all her wrath?"

There was a rustle and a flash of red hair, and the boy tore across the lawn. Glancing up, Sam was startled by the swift, involuntary crinkling of the man's lips.

"Young William has too much time and energy on his hands," the gentleman added to no one in particular as he directed them forward. "While Ada, his grandmother and only living relative, has far too much whiskey in hers."

"That poor little boy." Sam shook her head, angered by the frailness of the boy's frame, the raggedness of his clothes. "Can't you do something to help, Lord Hoxton?"

Another brief crinkling. "Forgive me. Apparently, I have not made myself clear. I am Stoddard, the butler. My orders were to inform you that his lordship has been detained. Pray, make yourselves at home in the parlor here, while I dispatch your maid to settle your belongings upstairs. Refreshments will be along presently, but I daresay Lord Hoxton will arrive before them."

As he left them in an odious little room full of dainty pink furnishings, Sam stifled the urge to grab for his sleeve. How quiet it seemed in this place, like a museum. Or a tomb.

Claire, apparently, did not see things in this light. With a gasp of sheer delight, she twirled in the center of the room, clapping her hands like the impressionable child she was. "I declare, isn't this the prettiest room you've ever seen?"

Sam shuddered. Nothing she had heard about Hoxton ever suggested a preference for pink and white. He must have hired a decorator, told him to do his worst, and then left town. As far as Sam was concerned, the only thing of worth in this display of rare collectibles was the unobstructed view of the Hudson. A marvelously comforting river, the Hudson. What she wouldn't give to be crossing it now, going west toward the sunset, back to Colorado again.

But she was here, in this cold, unwelcoming shrine to wealth. It was like a slap to the face, seeing everything her parents had dreamed of but never possessed going to their friend and partner. With every breath, her sense of injustice and indignation rose, until she was ready to smash the Dresden piece Claire so lovingly stroked.

"Miss Eggersley?"

The voice—warm, deep, and mellow—should have warned her. But as Sam turned, still as stiff as drying shoeleather, she was defenseless against the impact of that far-too-handsome face.

It was nothing as mundane as mere beauty, though he had that in unfair abundance; it was rather an air of being different, special, an entity all his own. Like the sun appearing suddenly out of the stormiest cloud, his boyish grin lit up that silly room, deep into the furthermost corners, until all was bathed in a special glow. That smile was a beacon, and Sam unthinkingly moved toward it, extending her hand.

He ignored it. With a long, leisurely stride, he crossed the room to Claire. His delight seemed to shelter the girl, leaving the two of them in a world all their own. Watching, hand dropping uselessly to her side, Sam felt a deep, sharp stab of envy, and did not like it one bit.

Speak up, instinct warned, but even as she opened her mouth, Claire giggled in that sickeningly adorable way she had and declared that yes, she was Samantha Eggersley, and she was just thrilled to death to be there.

"The thrill is entirely mine," he said softly, taking her hand to place a gentle kiss there. Sam's own fingers tingled alarmingly, as if they had been the ones to be so honored.

He was pleasantly tall. Not so large that he overwhelmed the room, but enough to take command of it. Not one hair was out of place; not a spot marred the smooth expanse of his well-tailored jacket. His eyes were as sharp and clear as the creases in his gray trousers, and his speech was as polished as the black leather of his shoes. Perfection personified. Still, there must be a flaw somewhere, Sam decided, determined to dig until she found it.

At the moment, however, Claire required her attention instead. "Never in all my born days," she simpered, deliberately prolonging the man's grasp, "have I seen anything like this castle of yours. Y'all can't know what an honor it is to be the first ever invited here. I wish I could stay forever and ever."

"May your wish be my command." As Hoxton gallantly bowed, Sam was struck by his grace. Executed with precise skill, each movement flowed effortlessly into the next, as if, it seemed to the uncharacteristically speechless Sam, he had been born with manners instead of having to learn them like anyone else.

Edging closer, Sam told herself that she must be

on hand to stop Claire from making a fool of herself over the man and thereby ruin everything. A skillfully delivered pinch could do wonders for keeping the girl in line. Since the chit had taken it upon herself to carry on with this charade, Sam would see to it that she did not disgrace them both.

"However can I thank you for inviting me—ouch!—er, us to this little hideaway of yours, Mr.—I mean . . ."

"The title is superfluous. Ignore it as I do. Do let's use Christian names. Samantha is such a lovely name, and I must say, it suits you admirably."

But I am Samantha, Sam nearly cried out, swamped by an inexplicable longing to have him gaze into her eyes that way. "I do not think," she said instead in a brisk, schoolmistressy tone, "that such premature familiarity is advisable."

Though he turned his attention to her, it was not with the gaze she had sought. Far from warm or amused, the too-blue eyes viewed her with wariness. She felt compelled to speak.

"We seem to have jumbled our introductions. I am—"

"No introduction is necessary. I knew you at once, Miss Barnstable."

"That's Farnstable," she said meekly. The scorn he failed to hide warned that it was already too late to admit the truth. "With an F."

His smile, a brief concession to courtesy, was swiftly redirected to Claire. "I meant no offense. If my familiarity is premature, then I must simply restrain myself. I can rely upon you, I trust, to keep me on the proper course?"

"Oh, Lord Anthony, you mustn't go changing your ways for lil' ole me. Besides, everyone says you and Un—er, Daddy was close as brothers. That makes us practically family. How can't we feel familiar when I just bet you watched me growing up?"

There was a quick, defiant smirk at Sam, before Claire treated their host to another dazzling smile. This once, though, he failed to respond.

"I'm afraid I remember precious little of those days. An accident"—he winced as he touched his head—"seems to have robbed me of my memory. Though I must say, I have never before felt the loss so keenly. Watching you grow up must have been a delightful experience."

"Why, I declare, you say the sweetest things."

"Ah, but the words merely match the subject."

"Are our rooms prepared?" Sam broke in before Claire could pour out yet another gushing tribute. "Due to the length of our journey, perhaps it would be wise if we both indulged in a short rest."

She might have gone unheard, so immersed were they in each other, but justice served Claire with an overpowering yawn.

"What a bore you must think me," Lord Hoxton said, then grinned, fully aware that they thought no such thing. "Come, let me show you to your rooms. You have time for a short nap before dinner."

Claire drifted to his side, the swish of her crinolines advertising her content. And what about me? Sam thought irritably as they waltzed off without her. How could a man of his reputation, his financial genius, listen to those inane giggles with a straight face?

Well, if the man wanted fluff, he had made a good choice in lovely Claire, with the world's emptiest brain. Nothing stayed long between those two ears of hers, but with a face like that, Sam conceded, a woman held court, not conversation.

15

And who was she to call Claire a ninny? It was too late to complain now. The time to prove her capability had been at the start. She should have asserted herself, let Hoxton know exactly who she was and why she was there. But no, she'd just stood there, tongue-tied and flustered, like a debutante at her first ball.

Drat. She had anticipated problems, but not to go weak in the knees at the mere sight of the man. It was . . . embarrassing. She was a solid twenty-four years of age, certainly too sensible to go about blushing and feeling faint merely because a man smiled. Hadn't experience long since taught her to be wary of those hands grasping for her wealth, while the eyes slid past to linger on Claire?

Yet as sensible as she knew herself to be, there was something in that casual saunter, in the devil-may-care twinkle of those eyes, that caught the breath in her throat. Damion, she had thought when she first saw him. Damion, the hero of her favorite stage play, *Marietta*. Ever since she could remember, Sam had dreamed of one day playing the title role, as her mother had so skillfully done before her. It was her preoccupation with this that had led her grandfather to burn all their copies of the play, swearing that if he caught Sam daydreaming again, he'd lay the switch to her himself.

By way of added reminder, Claire let loose a trill of her patented giggles in the hallway beyond. A low, pleasant chuckle followed. So much for her dreams. Her Damion was besotted, and it wasn't yet four o'clock. By dinner, Claire would have the poor man eating from her hands.

Hoxton's reaction, or lack thereof, had proved that she was no Marietta. It was this dress. Limp and formless, her grandmother's serviceable shirtwaist covered her with the charm of a shroud. Compared to the hoops and frills of Claire's latest confection, what hope had she of ever drawing his gaze away?

So be it. Setting her lips, Sam reminded herself why she was there. If she had truly come to learn what she could from this man, she would achieve far more if he remained unaware of her scrutiny.

To her ultimate indignation, when she reached the hall, it was empty. How typical of her little cousin! Leave Sam to fend for herself, while Claire went off to have a wonderful time. Vividly, Sam pictured the pair of them, heads bent close, laughing, touching . . . .

Hands clenched at her sides, she started up the endlessly winding staircase. As if Samuel Eggersley climbed beside her, ever lecturing, she knew where to fix the blame. She was dreaming again. Some people never learned. Dreams were what killed her parents, her grandfather had explained at length, yet Sam continued to waste everyone's time indulging in them. Imagine her picturing that unsuitable man as Damion. Her hero. Lord preserve her, he couldn't have run any faster, trying to get away from her. She couldn't even feel sorry for herself; she deserved to feel like a fool.

Suddenly, she saw gleaming leather shoes appear before her downcast eyes. Resolutions melting, she followed the sharp crease of the gray trousers up to the shirt, and by the time she reached the piercing blue of those eyes, she was a helpless lump of clay.

Head tilted slightly, his face mirrored her confusion. Of all times for him to surprise her like that, she groaned, knowing she must seem positively militant in her determined march up the stairs. Should she try a smile? Lord knew she wanted to, but what if he turned and walked away?

She hovered on the step, hesitant, and he continued to watch with a puzzled frown. From behind, sunlight filtered through a window, framing his auburn hair with a halo, making the gray streaks she had noticed earlier now seem silver, tinged with gold. The lean features of his face took on a similar glow, and it was as if the winged brows were set to take flight. The angel Gabriel would have such a face. Heaven help her, must he be so impossibly beautiful?

It just wasn't right. The man was her father's friend, for heaven's sake; a contemporary. This radiant good health should belong to someone closer to her own age. It was unfair, what all that money could buy.

"Tony, you darling." Down the hall, Claire's drawl went to an absolute purr. "I do believe I've died and gone to heaven."

If so, then Sam had gone in the opposite direction. "Tony darling" blinked quickly, as if waking from a bad dream, then smiled broadly as he watched Claire float off into one of the rooms. Knowing she had been forgotten, Sam trudged up the remaining stairs. She couldn't stand this. She would leave, she decided, the first thing in the morning.

"Miss Eggersley has laid claim to the pink room." Lord Hoxton's grin was indulgent as he forced his attention back to Sam. "Some notion of matching her wardrobe, I believe. Unfortunately, these are the only two connecting rooms."

"Unfortunately?"

Hands in his pockets, he made a little-boy shrug with his shoulders as he nodded toward the other room. "I'm sorry about all the green. If you don't mind being separated from Claire, please feel free to choose another room."

"I am hardly the sort to be affected by the color of my walls."

He looked at her then, with what she suspected might be pity. But before she could bristle, he covered

18

the awkwardness with a devastating smile. "The choice is yours. I wish you would both consider this your home. Normally, we dine at eight, but if this poses an inconvenience, we can easily rearrange our schedule."

The last was addressed to Claire, who was flitting amongst the treasures in her room—no doubt, Sam thought cattily, dreaming of taking up a permanent residence there—and did not reply.

"Eight will be fine," Sam answered automatically. "May I assume we are to dress formally?"

As he tugged his eyes from Claire, their temperature dropped a good twenty degrees. "When you've been with us longer, Miss Farnstable, you will learn that formality is not my strongest suit. Wear what you will; it matters little to me."

And that, most assuredly, put her in place. Turning his back to chat lazily with Claire, his thoughts anywhere but on the gray frump biting her lip behind him, Hoxton confirmed her suspicions. Sam could appear naked, and he would never notice. Or care.

"Lord Hoxton?"

To her surprise, he straightened. The lazy, little-boy pose was quickly abandoned as he spun around to greet the owner of that penetrating voice. "Oh, Riley. You startled me. Must you always sneak up behind me like that?"

"Sneak, sir?"

The upraised brow must be a permanent fixture, Sam decided, for it seemed quite at home on that otherwise unremarkable round face. Hairless, the head seemed to glisten in the light, drawing attention to the smooth, round dome and distracting the onlooker from the stiff, unyielding line of the man's lips. Not a comfortable man, this Riley; yet strangely enough, he seemed familiar. Should I know him? Sam wondered with an involuntary shudder. Thank goodness I do not.

"You know what I meant," Hoxton snapped. Whatever their relationship, there appeared to be little love lost between these two. "As you can see, our guests have arrived. Miss Eggersley is in her room, and this is Miss Farnstable. Riley is—er, my valet. I assume you have something to tell me, Riley?"

Impossibly, the brow rose even higher. "There has been a complication in the negotiations, sir. We did not think you would wish us to proceed without you."

"The—? Oh, yes. Of course. The negotiations."

Realigning his jacket, Hoxton threw a quick, nervous smile their way. "Forgive me, ladies, but certain . . . business details must be dealt with before I can indulge myself with your company. If you will excuse me?"

"Of course." Sam answered for both of them, Claire being lost in the wardrobe. "Take your time; we shall manage."

To make up for her earlier rudeness, Sam gave him her most gracious smile. If he noticed, or even heard what she said he gave no sign. Lips tightly pursed, he turned on a heel, glared at Riley, and ungraciously stomped away. Watching the controlled movement of those long, lean limbs, Sam sighed.

The sound was overloud in the near-empty hallway and clearly not something this Riley person would miss. Looking up, she found those intense dark eyes studying her, producing the most unsettled feeling in her chest. Dislike, disdain, and perhaps distrust, seemed to cloak her for a moment before, with his usual raised eyebrow, he abruptly turned and walked away as well.

And what, she thought, irrationally hurt, does one make of that?

2

Walking in front of Riley, "his lordship" missed the silent exchange between the prickly Miss Farnstable and his valet. It would have done little to better his mood. Questions, he would have ranted at Riley, were the last things they wanted to inspire in their guests. What they were attempting here was immoral, deceitful, and—unless Samantha Eggersley had a kind heart and rare sense of humor—involved a potential civil suit at best.

And at worst, prison. Shuddering, he knew he would sing and dance on his head rather than go back there. He did wish, though, that someone other than Charles Riley were calling the tunes.

Instinctively, he reached for the bronzed medallion on his chest to feel the lines of the falcon. Its wings were spread in flight, a symbol of freedom. Ever hidden, even from the hovering Riley, it was the one bit of his past, of himself, that was his alone.

Images flitted through his brain. He was laughing in a cheerful room, playing with a puppy before a large, roaring fire. A beautiful lady smiled lovingly as an elderly gentleman gave him the medallion. Health, wealth and good fortune, the man had said, belonged to whoever stroked its surface.

He had no idea what those images meant, but somewhere in the vast reaches of the British empire, that room still existed. It was where he belonged, he knew instinctively, and he would not rest until he found it again. Hell, he'd already spent half a lifetime in the attempt.

Pouring himself a drink, he flopped into the nearest chair. Where had it all gone wrong? Not long ago, his future had seemed bright. The money he would make playing Hamlet would further his investigation. So how the devil did he, Grant Barton, darling of London's stage and feminine elite, land in that jail?

It was an uncomfortable exercise, looking back. Unbidden, his mind returned to the day, nearly six months before, when this whole mad affair had begun.

He eyed the slime that seemed to be getting greener and thicker by the moment. He shuddered. How long, he wondered, before he went the way of old Mad Mortimer in the next cell?

Prison was a dismal place. At the start, assuming someone would step forward and prove his innocence, he had wiled away the hours running his lines. But as the hours stretched into weeks, with his name being removed, replaced on the playbill, and no doubt forgotten, he'd reached the inevitable conclusion. The only 'green room' he'd ever wait in was this cell.

He couldn't even snicker at the pun; the mere thought of green made him want to kick the bars that stood between him and his goal. To come so close, only to end up like this, farther than ever from that sun-filled room. How could he dream of having a family when he didn't even have a name to call his own? The fiend who'd bragged about buying him to work in the tin mines had called him Jimmy Clanton, after himself, but he'd changed that to Jamie the second he'd run away. By the time Sarah found him, scratching out an existance on London's streets, and suggested that the name Grant Barton had more drama to it if he wished to become an actor, he'd been beyond the capacity to object.

Especially not, starving waif that he had been, when faced with food. To this day, he could taste the sweet, melting miracle of the hot-cross buns Sarah had given him. She had seen the hunger in his eyes. She had known, all through her long tutorship, that sweets could make him behave. And so she had used them to teach him manners, diction, deportment, until he could play any role she chose to throw at him.

Hamlet was his choice, but time and again Sarah said no. That was serious acting, she would scoff, and he hadn't the least idea what the phrase meant. If he would spend half the time with Shakespeare as he did with the ladies, he would know that an actor must understand the complexities of life; he must suffer, endure and persevere to be able to play that great role. Self-discipline, she would demand, shaking her head in exasperation, before slating him for the pantomimes and the singing, clowning, and acrobatics at which he excelled.

You have no goals, no ambition, she would say, throwing up her hands in despair. Grant would shrug, loathe to explain himself. Experience had taught, early on, to give trust sparingly, to watch and wait and give as little of himself as he could.

He could have told her he had ambitions that day she had stormed in to deliver her 'I must do what is best for the theatre' speech. But it was not in him to plead. If Sarah, who had been like the mother he couldn't remember, failed to understand or believe in him, who on earth ever would?

How painful it had been, watching her face as she decided with cool precision that he was one liability her theatre could do without. Deep down, he knew he could only do irreparable damage to all she had worked to build, but here and now, where his mind functioned on a daily basis, he felt abandoned. Again. There was not one soul, in the entire world, who thought him worth a fight.

And that made dreaming rather absurd. Sarah knew. Men like the Grant Bartons of the world didn't have families awaiting their return. There was never a gentle, loving wife at the door, no children to bounce on a knee; no dog to fetch a bone, not even a bird to sing a jaded tune. His sort slipped through life on charm alone, and they always, *always* came to a bad end.

He paced the cell. Whatever his shortcomings, he was innocent, incapable of the crime he was accused of. Perhaps, as Sarah claimed, he had been too busy taking from life to develop the proper moral fiber, but for him to steal Amanda's necklace—Amanda, whose lavish party would launch him into greater success (and whose bed he had enjoyed on many an evening) —was nothing short of lunacy. Why couldn't anyone see that?

Damned waste of time, protesting. Only the slime would listen. And reliving the past merely brought into focus all he had lost. Oddly enough, it wasn't the luxuries, or even the women, that he missed most. It was the simple things, the roar of a well-laid fire, the crackle of bacon in the pan, the heady aroma of hot-cross buns . . .

He bolted back from the bars, appalled to find himself clinging to them. There's no time for weakness, he could hear Sarah say. Food was but another of life's generosities he must learn to live without. Dinner today would be the same as the meal before it and the one after, each of them about as appealing as the growth on the walls.

"Eh, Barton, make ye'self presentable. Ye've got guests."

Guests? What did the fool guard expect? That he would roll out a welcome mat, set up a tea tray of delicate scones dripping with butter, a row of dainty cakes, the hot cross buns . . . ?

No, dammit, with his luck, his visitors merely meant more trouble. They must content themselves sitting amidst the slime, with no cakes or butter.

Peering down the hallway, past the row of bars so like his own, he saw an approaching pair of lamps. Three men, it would seem, one readily identified as the night guard by the sneer that seemed more vicious than ever in the flickering light.

Instinctively tucking his medallion out of sight, Grant watched the other two. Each carried himself with an air of authority, not so much as flinching when hairy arms reached out between the bars to grope at their cloaks. Part of him—he couldn't stop himself—prayed that these were well-wishers, remnants of that vanishing breed believing in his innocence, and that they were here to devote their time, energy and wealth to his well-deserved freedom.

It took but one glance to dash that hope deeper than it deserved to go. Energy they had, yes, and money in abundance, but neither seemed inclined to waste it on relieving his plight. They burst into the cell as if they owned it, and if the cut of their clothes were anything to go by, perhaps they did. Lord knew the guard ran off with unaccustomed haste, all but scraping the floor in servility.

Not knowing what else to do, Grant gestured to the bed. "Pardon the accomodations, sirs, but I have little to offer in way of a seat."

Both stared at the molding mattress with disdain. *You haven't seen anything,* he was tempted to add, *until you've had a good look at the walls.* As they seemed remarkably short on humor, however, he took the opportunity to study them instead.

The first, closer to the lamp and therefore more easily assessed, was of shorter stature than his deep voice indicated. Using the latter sparingly, he clapped his hands and barked to the darkness beyond. To Grant, he seemed rather like a billiard ball, smooth and shiny at the top, but nothing rounded about his sense of purpose. Straight line, all the way.

And accustomed not only to giving out orders, but quite at home with having them obeyed. A legion of servants appeared, bowing and scraping like the vanished guard as they set the table they carried. Another clap brought three comfortable chairs, while a third produced baskets, brimming with more mind-dulling aromas than Grant dared dream could exist.

Another fantasy, he decided, sinking to the despised cot. Was that pork tickling his nostrils? Gravy? And oh, merciful heavens, potatoes—white, firm, steaming with butter! Nearby sat a treasure trove of vegetables, and not one of them green. And there, as if the good fairy herself had waved the wand, were the painfully anticipated hot-cross buns.

In sheer agony, Grant waited, itching, on his mattress, for an invitation. The servants dallied so long that he decided this was some elaborate torture, designed to wring out a confession. Indeed, he was prepared to admit to anything just for a nibble of that pork, when the last back retreated into the shadows.

"As you see," the stout man smirked, gesturing to the table, "the hospitality is on us. Please, enjoy yourself."

"Alone? I mean, won't you be joining me?"

"We have already dined." They exchanged what might have been grins. Their expressions were hard to determine, for the taller gentleman huddled behind a voluminous cloak and a broad-brimmed hat.

"Share this wine, at least?" He didn't know why he persisted. He'd likely starve before the ritual was done. "I have never been particularly comfortable with dining alone."

"So we have heard." Another swift, humorless grin. "Here, let me pour. I suggest you fill your plate, Barton. We want you properly sated before we begin the negotiations."

Grant had already reached for the pork. Though he hated betraying his eagerness, it was a good twenty forkfuls later before he could bring himself to speak. Not that the man's words hadn't been rattling around in his brain all that time.

"Forgive me," he said at last, eying the buns with glutonnous lust. "As grateful as I am for this feast—and I assure you, it just might have saved my sanity—I am not exactly in a position to be doing any negotiating at the moment."

"On the contrary."

As the man edged his chair closer, Grant fought the urge to push his own backward. "I must seem singularly dense, but I cannot begin to fathom what you want."

"You are an actor. Quite a gifted one, if Amanda Beckmorton can be taken at her word."

Grant's chair sprang back. "Knowing that lady's current opinion of me, I suggest you take your food and go. Contrary to public belief, I do not involve myself in unlawful schemes."

"Bravo, Barton. Is this how you play Hamlet?"

Grant glanced at the gravy-soaked napkin he must have tossed in the impulsive rise to his feet.

"You are misinformed," he protested, slumping into his chair. "I am not the man you seek."

"Admirable sentiments. But I assure you, we only seek an actor. To pose as an . . . acquaintance, for a brief period of time. The reward, I might point out, will be substantial."

"Might I point out the equally substantial bars behind you? They tend to be rather selective here as to who they let through them."

"We are acquainted with the workings of the law." Sleek hands waved the thought away. "Indeed, that is the least of our problems."

"The least of . . ." Grant had to audibly close his jaw. "You waltz in here, set up a table worthy of the Arabian Nights, and now you tell me that a minor consideration like solid iron cannot withstand your whim? I feel like Eve, talking to her serpent."

A deep-throated chuckle that did little to disprove the analogy came from within the dark cloak. As it rustled closer, a slender, gloved hand stretched forward to rest on the stouter man's arm. "Perhaps we do owe an explanation, Riley. Poor Mr. Barton must be confused."

"I wouldn't advise . . ."

"Your advice, as always, is noted, but since this is still my plan, we shall execute it as I see best."

The voice was cool, cultured, and coaxing, but behind the soft words, Grant could hear the crack of the whip. So, apparently, had Riley, for he sat back as if a hand had shoved him there.

None of which alleviated Grant's growing unease. He wished the man would reveal more of his features. All he could see was a mouth dawn into itself, its lack of generosity a complete contrast to the soothing voice. "Perhaps you will feel easier, Mr. Barton, if you know the identity we wish you to assume is that of one Anthony Rawlings?"

"Rawlings? Forgive me, but I don't recognize . . ."

"You might have heard of him under another name. Perhaps the recently acquired title of Lord Hoxton?"

All that delicious pork began to swim around in Grant's gut. Of course he had heard of Hoxton; who had not? Speculation was rife where this particular peer was concerned, for despite his meteoric rise to wealth and power in the past decade, few living souls could remember meeting the man. A confirmed recluse, his power augmented by anonymity, Hoxton had been the subject of more dinner conversations than religion or politics combined.

"You have to be mad," Grant sputtered. "Even supposing you can spirit me out, what will happen when Hoxton learns of it? Have you any idea what a man like that can do? He'll make this prison seem like Paradise in comparison."

They smiled indulgently, parents allowing a tantrum. Too late, Grant clicked his jaw shut.

The cloak leaned closer. "I am intimately aware of the man's reaction, Barton. You need have no fears on that score."

"Are you telling me you know Hoxton?"

"Actually, I'm telling you I *am* Hoxton."

The silence was appalling. Grant glanced about as if he could gain support in the shadows. "It's a joke. Gregory, down at the Brit, put you up to it."

"I realize this must be . . . a trifle unsettling, but I assure you, I rarely joke. If I say I wish you to pose as myself, you can believe that is precisely what I want."

And what Hoxton wants, Hoxton gets, Grant thought. Only why, in the name of sanity, did the man want him? "I don't understand. Can I know the why of it? Why—especially—me?"

The cloak seemed heavy on those thin shoulders. "You bear an astonishing resemblance to myself. I realized this the moment I first saw you on stage. I've watched you for some time, Barton."

Grant squirmed in his seat. He didn't like the idea of being watched—not the way Hoxton meant it. And for some time?

"Granted, you are a good deal younger, and according to Riley's careful research, unfamiliar with my world, but such superficial discrepancies needn't concern us. Any skilled actor can disguise them. No, to be perfectly candid, it is your skill with the ladies that attracts me most."

"My what?"

"Come now, there is no need for modesty. I am aware of why you were at Amanda's that night. Like most women, she seems to find you irresistible. It is my fervent hope that a particular female, a Miss Samantha Eggersley, might do so as well."

Grant raised a hand, instinctively wanting to stop this, here and now, but the men ignored him. Riley leaned forward, his grin in place. "Until recently, Miss Eggersley was safely esconced in her family home in Richmond, Virginia," he said, "caring for an invalid grandfather. A year ago, Samuel Eggersley succumbed to his illnesses, leaving Samantha free to pursue her own life."

"Riley, please. Let me explain." With a whisper of his cloak, Hoxton turned to Grant. "To understand my dilemma, Barton, you must realize that the relationship between Samuel and his son was strained. Bill dreamed of establishing his own fame and fortune by mining for gold in Colorado, and Samuel despised him for his refusal to take his traditional place in the family bank. Since I shared that dream, and worked hard at making it a reality, Samuel blamed me for their estrangement. Me and Susannah. Bill's wife.''

There was a cluck, and Grant glanced up to catch Riley's sneer. Samuel was not only one to dislike Mrs. Eggersley. Against his will, Grant felt his curiosity piqued.

''The long and short of it is,'' Hoxton said abruptly, ''now that old Samuel is dead, there is nothing to stop Samantha from coming to see me.''

''Ah, I see. You expect me to use my—er, skills to spin the poor girl's head so fast, she abandons her plan to become Lady Hoxton?''

''No!'' The crash was too loud to be made by that bony wrist. ''Can't you see? I want that girl to be my wife.''

''I don't understand.'' Grant glanced from one man to the other in his confusion. ''Then what is it you wish me to do?''

The silence stretched. Grant shifted his gaze to Riley, but the disdainful expression merely doubled his bewilderment.

''What I seek is simple. All I have ever wanted was Susannah's happiness.''

''Susannah?''

''I meant''—the thin lips folded inward, captured by perfect white teeth—''er, Samantha. The poor child has had a somber life, caring for an ungrateful old man and saddled with an impoverished cousin and a mountain of financial woes.''

Grant watched him work against some inner turmoil. An interesting study, this Lord Hoxton. Under other circumstances, he'd be intrigued by the myriad of emotions the man strove to conceal. At the moment, however, Grant was merely confused.

"She deserves far more. A handsome prince to waltz into her drab life, to charm and spoil her, to offer breathless romance. It is a role, I am assured, in which you are well versed."

Many things he'd been called in his time, but a handsome prince? Grant's suspicions grew with his discomfort. "I must seem terribly dense, but I can't see why you would spend all this time and money grooming an out-of-work—not to mention out-of-jail—actor, who however closely he might resemble you, could hardly court the girl as you would yourself."

Hoxton rose with an abruptness that had even his companion gasping. Grant grabbed for the tottering wine bottle, righting it as the man limped across the cell. Turning to Riley for an explanation, Grant was met with a frown. These two belonged with Mad Mortimer, he decided, whose eerie laughter had begun to drift through the cracks in the wall.

Hoxton never noticed. Swinging on a heel, he pointed a finger at his cohort. "What say you, Riley? Can we trust him?"

In the face of Riley's contemptuous snort, Grant's temper snapped. "If you two aren't the limit of endurance! You dig through my past with neither my knowledge nor my consent, and now have the gall to say you don't trust me? What in hell are you doing here then?"

"He's right, of course." Hoxton's words drooped beneath the weight of his sigh. "He deserves to know."

"No!" Riley reached for the bony arm. "Don't do this."

"I insist. He can accomplish nothing without the truth."

Riley returned his hand to the table, but the look

he shot at Grant was as black as the far corners of the cell. Mystified, Grant turned to watch Hoxton, whose gloved hands gripped the table's edge.

"Nothing would delight me more than to romance her myself. Unfortunately, it is not only undesirable, but quite impossible."

"Impossible? For the mighty Lord Hoxton?"

Another snort from Riley, but Grant's attention was trapped by the tense, trembling body in front of him. "Yes, impossible. I ask you, Barton, do you honestly think any woman could be charmed by a face like this?"

With dramatic emphasis, he ripped off his hat. The face revealed was so hideously pinched and twisted that Grant could not control the flinch. Livid pink scars pulled the eyes upward, nearly out of their sockets, and left no space for eyebrows to replant themselves. The hair had failed to grow on top of his head, and only a few long, white strands seemed at home there.

"There was a fire." The revelation over, Hoxton recovered quickly. His voice was cold and distant, as if this horror had happened to someone else. "I was trapped . . . too far from proper medical facilities. By the time I returned to civilization, it was too late. Nothing could be done."

Grant leaned back into his chair. That face, he had to admit, went a long way towards explaining the strange behavior. And the even stranger request.

"Don't waste time with useless pity," Hoxton snapped as he slowly replaced the hat. "I remember little. My doctor claims that amnesia is God's way of protecting me. And in all, the life of a recluse has suited me admirably. It has its, let us say, compensations. That is, until now."

Absentmindedly, Grant removed the napkin from

his plate. Someone, somewhere, wouldn't appreciate doing this laundry. "And so, you borrow my face to court Miss Eggersley. Good lord, man, have you thought this through? What if she should fancy herself in love with me?"

"Indeed, that is exactly what we hope."

"This prison must have addled my wits, but—"

"When the time is ripe, we shall stage an accident. Your face will be supposedly burned. When Samantha next sees you, I shall stand in your place. Do not fear I won't convince her. In my youth, I served my own apprenticeship in the theater."

The trouble with an actor, Grant realized, was that you could never be certain that the face he presented was the true one. He felt a swift, unwilling pity for the girl. "This Eggersley woman, just what is she like?"

The question surprised them both. For the briefest of moments, the lips relaxed. Grant could have sworn he saw a smile there. "Like her mother. A saint among sinners. Do not scoff; I am serious. Few women would sacrifice their youth to care for a cantankerous old invalid. And having gained her freedom, does Samantha turn her back on the waifs deposited upon her doorstep? No, she gives them a home. A future. Far more than she herself has. She's not had an easy life, my angel, but we shall soon remedy that."

Riley looked as if the speech were bad for his digestion. "Forgive the interruption, sir, but knowing Barton, I would assume he was asking more about her appearance."

"Oh, yes, of course. How do I begin? I have not met with the adult Samantha, mind you. I have seen her but twice, from a distance, but that is all I need to appreciate such treasure. Hers is a beauty that shines from within, do you understand?"

Ugly as a mule, Grant decided, but then, Hoxton was no gardenia either.

"Perhaps we should point out the benefits to Mr. Barton, sir. He will be interested in what he himself stands to gain."

Hoxton snapped his head toward his companion, as if he had forgotten the man was there. "Very well. Please do so."

Riley leaned forward, his head gleaming as bright as his eyes. "His lordship will be generous. With your earnings, you can do anything. Perhaps establish your own troupe in America. Think of it. You can choose your own roles, the very plays you shall perform."

"America?" Grant's mind, racing ahead, was tripped up here. His sunlit room wasn't in America. Why on earth would he wish to go there?

"You must go where Samanta lives. After that, well, London holds a somewhat limiting future for you, don't you agree?"

"As the future Lady Hoxton will reside here, it would be unnecessarily awkward explaining away two Hoxtons."

"Riley is right. But think, Barton. We offer a whole new life. A man of your talents can go far in America."

Grant was tempted. There was little use in lying to himself. An opportunity like this rarely came twice. The money would go far toward helping him find his past. If he were to later return to discreetly continue his search, he could easily assume yet another name and identity.

So why, for the life of him, did he hesitate? "Just like that, I am set free? What is to stop me from bolting?"

Hoxton focused on him. Grant could feel the

sunken eyes as if they reached inside his skull. "As you said. If I can't trust you, I wouldn't be here."

"And as added insurance, I shall accompany you."

Riley. Of course. He was merely to switch jailors, then.

"Think of Riley as your mentor. One that you will greatly need and appreciate. This is no easy task we've set for you, my boy."

"You talk as though I've already consented."

"Haven't you?" The smile stretched over the skeletal features, muscles pulling the spare flesh into the eye sockets. "You are intrigued, and rightly so. For an actor, this is the role of a lifetime. Clap your hands, and your every whim will be obeyed. And once our goal is accomplished, your future is secured. A more satisfactory future, I must add, than you will ever face here."

There was something wrong in all this, but it grew increasingly difficult to determine what or why. It was difficult to hold on to one's sense of right and wrong when faced with such do-or-die alternatives.

As if he could see the indecision, Riley pounced. "We can have you set free within the hour. Tomorrow evening, you shall set sail for America. We can begin our studies then."

"But . . ."

"Sir, shall I inform the guard? Very good. While I am about it, then, I shall summon the servants in to clear away this clutter. You are finished, are you not?"

As this last was addressed to Grant, he nodded dumbly. A whirlwind had swept into his cell, taking away both rational thought and appetite. Not even the hot-cross buns could tempt him now.

"Once I have dealt with the essentials here, I

shall make haste to your good friend, Sir Lockhart. I think this a suitable time to collect upon his debt, don't you?''

At Hoxton's nod, Riley clapped his hands. Grant rose awkwardly before the servant could pull the chair out from beneath him. All evidence of the feast vanished, as if his fairy godmother had returned to wave her wand.

It was incredible that he could rot in this hole for weeks, Grant thought in a daze, ranting and raving about the injustice of it all, and in strolls this Lord Hoxton, who just so happens to hold something over the man scheduled to hear his case. One snap of those bony fingers and the wheels of justice ran as smoothly as if they'd been oiled this morning.

But of course they'd been greased, along with a few palms along the way. He felt like a babe at sea, in the company of sharks. They'd be feeding off his naivete for weeks.

''Shall I order your carriage, sir?''

''No. I wish to stay and chat. I daresay Barton has a few more questions he'd like answered.''

Riley glared and, with the most perfunctory of bows, backed off into the darkness. Listening to the militant click of those boots, Grant wondered what on earth he could say to the man beside him.

He could almost hear the slime grow, snickering there in the farmost shadows, biding its time. His qualms vanished as he thought of it reaching out for him in his sleep. How humbling to learn that he was not as immune to temptation as he'd thought himself to be. But there was something overpowering about the prospect of a nice, clean bed.

''Doubts, Barton?''

For all his smiling, did the man have one humorous bone in his body? Why dally? Grant was going to do it, both of them knew that, so why carry out this farce of letting him protest? To assuage both their consciences?

If so, then he would speak out, just this once, and thereafter let it lie. "From what I've heard about you, sir, I find it hard to swallow this rot about your *angel* and your *treasure*. Pardon my bluntness, but I'd feel more comfortable knowing what you are truly about."

"Here, let us sit." The way the man's body radiated tension, it was no wonder he was so thin. It was hard to relate this Hoxton, Grant thought, to the one of society's gossip.

As if to reinforce this, Hoxton smiled pleasantly. "I can see I am not what you expected. Certain pretenses must be maintained, try to understand, to compete in the world of business. People will believe what they choose, and we never discourage them. Thanks to Riley's manipulations, I can be a tyrant, a womanizer, whatever seems necessary at the time. But the man and his image? I ask you, as one actor to another, are they ever one and the same?"

Now here was food for thought. Grant realized unwillingly that he and Hoxton might have more in common than bone structure.

"I was too young when I first met Susannah Myers. I wasn't as gifted as she. I turned to the stage only to defy the family that rejected me, so I couldn't help but be bedazzled. Heavens knows what I might have done had Riley not been there."

He shook his head, gripping the ends of the mattress. "Have you ever been in love, Barton? So deeply, you lose all control?"

"I doubt such a condition exists."

"Oh, it does. I am living proof. Even now, without my memory, I can still feel the ache, the longing. They tell me I was so caught up in my infatuation, I never saw the truth. To Susie, I was a younger brother, a friend in a lonely world. Fool that I was, I introduced her to Bill. I wanted my love and my best friend to like each other.''

His laughter was bitter. ''They say I tagged after them, hoping she would change her mind, that Bill would prove the cad he could never be, but they were perfect together. Not even I, apparently, ever denied it.''

Grant wished he hadn't started this. ''If you'd rather not talk about it . . . .''

''No, you need to know. Samantha will have questions and you cannot blame everything on amnesia.''

''But I don't understand. How do you remember so much?''

''Lawyers. As Riley will tell you, anything can be done with the proper funds. But enough; on with my tale. I must have had some pride, for it seems I stayed here when they sailed for America. Bill was determined to find his gold, you see. Years later, when I received an invitation to join him in Colorado, I knew I had to go.''

''To see Susannah again?''

''No! I had . . . well, my own reasons for wanting to strike it rich. And as far as I knew, Susie was to remain in New York. She didn't, of course, but by the time she surprised us in Denver, I had already prepared to leave. The Oh Susannah mine was worthless; everyone but Bill knew that. I couldn't afford to cling to the dream the way he did, so I sold my share of the claim to him.''

He winced. ''I had to go. Soon after I left, there was a cave-in at the mine. Bill was trapped inside and Susie went up to look for him. She never came back.

They found her body at the bottom of a cliff when they rescued Bill. Ever since, I've called myself a fool, a coward. Had I remained, might I have prevented her death?''

The man seemed to be pleading, as if the question were not a rhetorical one. Rising abruptly, he paced to the bars, facing out into the corridor. ''Bill died soon afterward. His body was never found but his hat and coat lay in the same spot where Susie had plunged to her death. The verdict was suicide. It was assumed that animals dragged the remains away.''

Grant felt suddenly uneasy. He didn't know any of these people; he didn't want to get involved.

''He did not—*could* not—kill himself!'' As if embarrassed, Hoxton lowered his tone. ''However deep his grief, Bill would never abandon his daughter. I was so certain of this that I went back to Colorado myself.'' The thin hands tightened around the bars. ''It was then, I am told, that I had my accident.''

Grant squirmed. Why was he being told all this? He'd been hired to impersonate him, not hear a life's story. Lord, the last thing he wanted was to feel sorry for the man.

''I saw Samantha. Just once, at the funeral, standing tall, proud, and refusing to cry.'' His cheek muscles flinched, as if the strange eyes strove to see the past. ''Do you see why I must make it up to her? Take care of her, spoil her rotten? I want that girl's happiness, Barton. Or I shall never have my own.''

''You expect me to swallow this?''

''I suppose it does seem incredible. Rivals call me Tony the Terrible, I'm told.'' His smile was convincingly sheepish. ''But even a tyrant has his vulnerabilities. I must say, it has been rather a relief to talk about mine. Admitting such feelings to Riley . . .

As you shall no doubt learn, he has his expectations, none of which includes my being a hopeless romantic. You see, I *want* to be in love with Samantha. I need to be."

"You should be telling her this. Not me."

"And subject myself to her scorn? Prison should have made more of a realist of you. Think of this not as deceit, Barton, but rather in terms of representing what I would have been, if not for a quirk of fate I can't even remember. It is not in my nature to beg, but please, help me. If I can't have Su—Samantha, I don't know what I shall do."

Vague though it was, the threat was effective. Once freed, Grant had no desire to return to prison. Besides, if this Miss Eggersley were even half as homely as he suspected, he might be doing her a favor. Being Lady Hoxton was nothing to sneeze at, after all.

Hoxton straightened, clearly ready to leave. Though not yet given, Grant's consent was taken for granted. "I need not add, I trust, that what was said was done so in complete confidence? Only a fool would violate it, no?"

It was a game, Grant decided, nodding stupidly. Blink an eye and everyone switched position, tilting the board off balance. Dizzily, he wondered what his next move should be.

"Good. And—well, good luck, Barton."

"Wait!" Grant scrambled to his feet. They weren't leaving him there? Now that he'd made the decision, he'd be damned if he spend one more minute in this hole. "But what about me?"

"Riley will be along shortly." Hoxton paused for a moment on the other side of the bars. "Forgive me. I have enjoyed your company, but from a purely practical point of view, we must never meet again.

Riley will accompany you to New York—the servants there have never seen me—and en route, he will tour you in whatever you need to know. Should problems arise, he will know where and how to reach me, but I think it best for all concerned if you do not."

"You must enjoy keeping people off balance."

"Riley will tell you it is the source of all power." Hoxton smirked as he disappeared into the dark. "When one can't know what to expect next, one treds carefully, no?"

"Get your shoes off that table. You've gotten scuff marks all over it."

Grant was scrambling to his feet when he realized where and who he was. He was Hoxton now, to all intents and purposes, and Riley was his lowly valet.

Not that the man seemed to think so. "Once a criminal, always a criminal. I tried to warn his lordship against hiring the likes of you."

"I've told you a hundred times I was innocent of those charges, dammit. When in hell are you going to listen?"

"Guilty or no, it hardly makes a difference to your present circumstances. You are being paid quite handsomely to do a job, and to take the money with any degree of conscience, one would hope a decent man would do it right."

"I was doing it right."

"Lounging in the doorway, taking advantage of the woman's pose to view her ankles, is not, I assure you, what his lordship had in mind."

"I was not—" Grant stopped, knowing that his tone was far too petulant. Riley somehow always managed to put him on the defensive. Besides, this time he was not exactly innocent. They were very fine ankles, too. A delightful surprise, our Miss

Eggersley had proven to be. Nothing like the miserable wretch he had imagined. That Farnstable woman, on the other hand . . .

"We are not amused by your antics, Barton." Even away from Hoxton's presence, Riley persisted in the use of the personal plural, a measure of how deeply immersed he was in the man's personality. Far more so than Grant, whose irreverent attitude irked the erstwhile valet no end.

"Must I remind you of what is at stake here?"

"I suppose so. You're overdue. Here it is past four, and I've only been warned eight times today."

The man's frown was as dark as the furnishings in this odious room. Riley was not, Grant had long since decided, the least bit prone to amusement.

"We cannot be pleased by your performance."

"I was marvelous. I had the woman eating out of my hand."

"Be that as it may, you are no longer a woman-crazed actor, young man. As his lordship, you have a position to maintain."

"Woman-crazed . . . ."

"Had you been less involved with your ogling, and more aware of your duty, you would never have made the faux pas of introducing a servant to your guests."

"A servant . . . oh, do you mean you? Oh, for heaven's sake, you're one to talk. You could have been a trifle less inventive. Exactly what am I to say I was negotiating?"

"I doubt the subject will arise. They're women; they haven't the capacity for business discussions."

True enough for Samantha, he thought, but the other one? Uneasily, he recalled the force of that initial gaze. Gray as the rest of her, the large eyes had produced a most unsettling sensation. Starting in the pit of his stomach, it had radiated outward, jangling along the nerves. She knows I'm a fraud, he had thought at the time, but he had since dismissed such fancies. No doubt she used that glare on everyone she met. The product of being an unwanted relation, instantly belligerent and twice as unyielding. An uncomfortable woman, this Claire Farnstable, and he could be thankful that she was not the one he had to court.

"Very well, Riley. In the future, I shall pretend you don't exist. Though I must say, I was impressed. You played the valet splendidly. You were so . . . intimidating, in all that black."

"I have worn many guises in my life, young man, and I shall no doubt don many more before I'm through."

Given their relationship, it was a remarkable thing for the man to say. Instantly curious, Grant probed for more. "It sounds as though you were an actor. Is that how you met Hoxton? Quite a coincidence, isn't it?"

"All coincidence, my dear boy, is merely the result of a wise man's planning."

"I beg your pardon?"

"It is late." Riley glanced at his watch and the moment was gone. The real Riley was as invisible as ever. "It is time you made your preparations for dinner."

"Now? Good lord, I have hours yet."

"You need to tint your hair. The gray is fading. And we want you to take special care with your appearance this evening; we can't have you looking the fop."

To Grant, who prided himself on his excellent taste, the words required retaliation. "In that case, what about my shoes?"

"Your shoes?"

"They stand in desperate need of a good polishing. As my valet, I believe that is *your* responsibility?"

"Careful, Barton. A wise man knows his limits."

"As well as his coincidences?"

He had thrown that out on impulse, thinking no more than to gain back a bit of his pride. He should have anticipated the dark, appraising glare directed his way.

"Just keep your wits about you, young fool. In life, remember, all is rarely as it appears."

And with that cryptic rejoinder, Riley spun on a heel and silently left the room.

Well, Grant was never one to kick a gift horse. Instead, he relished the respite from his mentor's hovering presence, using the time to think, to absorb the ramifications of his extraordinary good fortune. Samantha Eggersley. Damned if the besotted Hoxton wasn't right. An angel, a treasure; hell, the girl was an outright peach.

Yet oddly enough, it wasn't the adorable Miss Eggersley who invaded his thoughts as he stood before the mirror to comb the tint into his hair. Gray. Such an unusual color for eyes.

He hesitated, uneasiness swimming through his gut. On first glance, she had seemed the sort to ride a broom on the next available moon, but the more he looked, the less he could so readily dismiss her. In his mind, he saw all that gray coming towards him up the stairs. The woman could be related to Riley, he had thought as she trudged closer, but then his eyes had been drawn, almost against his will, to the soft, vulnerable gray of hers. For a swift, impossible instant, she had answered his loneliness with her own, and that had touched him, deeper than he had ever permitted anyone to do.

He'd had time to think, *why, she's lovely*, before she had hopped back on her broom and he had been left wondering if something at lunch had disagreed with him. It couldn't be disappointment he felt; it must be indigestion.

Whatever the cause, he was not about to let that witch get under his skin tonight. Riley's threats aside, it had been far too long since he'd had female company at a meal, and unless he misread the signals, Miss Eggersley's delightful surprises had just begun.

So you can glare at me all you wish, Miss Whatever-stable, he told his reflection with a grin. Do your worst, for I shan't even see you.

3

"Lordie, Sam, how can you stand all this green?"

Taking her gaze from the hideous decor, done in every possible shade of green, Sam abandoned dismay for pique. She'd been given no choice! If she insisted on another room, lord knew what mischief Claire might get up to in her absence. "It's only for two weeks," she replied. "I'm sure our hotel accommodations in Chicago will be less . . . colorful."

"Isn't he divine?" There was no need to embellish the pronoun; Claire's fatuous tone told all. "Why ever were you afraid to meet him? I must admit, when we first rode up to all that iron and stone . . . I was a teeny bit scared. But see how gorgeous it is here inside? Did you see those paintings in the hall? I just bet someone famous painted them."

The Rembrandt and the da Vinci? Sam shook her head. The man's wealth would be wasted on Claire.

"Here it is. I need to borrow this." With a triumphant gleam, Claire snatched Sam's riding habit, the only item in her luggage that wasn't older than the pair of them together.

"Wait a minute. I haven't even worn it yet."

"Go on, be selfish then. Only, you're the one who started this. I don't know how you expect me to divert his attention when you are the one with the pretty new clothes."

Sam shook her head, trying to clear it. Mixing up the facts for her convenience was bad enough, but the chit had also managed to remove the riding habit to the other room.

"Wait a minute!" Hurrying after her, Sam found Claire holding the soft blue velvet to her chest, frankly admiring the vision in her mirror. "Claire, think sensibly. What possible use have you for a riding habit?"

"Tony said we are to go riding, first thing in the morning."

"Lord Hoxton?" Sam didn't know which dismayed her more; the use of the name, or the thought of her cousin atop a horse.

"Don't be such a stick. He told me to use his Christian name, didn't he?"

"I imagine he expected you to use Anthony."

She should have saved her breath. Having tossed the habit on her bed, Claire was at the vanity table. Her hands, greedy little things, dipped into the box there, letting the jewelry rain through her fingers.

"Just look at this. And see this wardrobe? It's filled with clothes. Tony says I am to use whatever I wish and discard the rest. The gowns are a trifle long, but you're handy with a needle. Alter them for me, please? Oh Sam, have you ever seen such a room? You must be kicking yourself in the teeth for passing all this to me."

Sam could think of several other things she'd like to kick, but Claire didn't pause long enough for her anger. "This all could have been yours, but now it's mine, mine, mine. Have you seen these furs? They feel so yummy. Isn't my Tony frightfully extravagant?"

Frightfully mad, more likely. Being only human, Sam stepped closer to feel the fur, her anger softening with each stroke. "Claire, I'd be careful. Mr. Rawlings seems to be quite the one for the ladies. I wouldn't be surprised if he changed his women the way other men do their shoes."

Raising a brow, Claire let her eyes rest meaningfully on the fur Sam was stroking, before snatching it away. "If I didn't know better," she sneered with a toss of her blonde curls, "I'd think you'd been eating some sour grapes. Though I might be jealous too, if all I had was Emery Blankfield for a beau. I doubt he would ever know how to give a woman all these wonderful things." She stuffed the fur into the wardrobe and slammed the door shut.

Feeling rebuked, Sam straightened her back. What did she care about furs? She hated that those poor little animals had given their lives, just so a vain creature like Claire could strut about for a night or two. In her position, Sam could never accept such gifts. No female with any decency would be tempted by such an obvious ploy. Grandfather would explode in his grave.

Lofty sentiments, but her eyes remained on Claire as she paraded about, gown after beautiful gown hugged to her chest, until instead of feeling righteous satisfaction, Sam was swallowing her resentment like a loaf of stale bread.

Very well, so she *was* jealous. She had seen the way "Tony" had gaped, the way he still would have stared had they marched in under their true identities. How silly to worry about their deception. The man would happily believe anything they pushed off on him, as long as Claire was included in the package.

Looking up quickly, she found Claire studying her with an odd expression. "You're not bad looking, you know. With the right clothes, a different hairstyle . . ."

Sam's hands went self-consciously to her hair. It

was true that she took little care in her appearance. There had never seemed time. Or need. Not until she had come here, to watch Anthony Rawlings stride into the room . . .

"But that can wait until you're back home in Richmond," Claire hastily ammended. "It wouldn't do to make drastic changes now."

"I'm not certain I want to go back to Richmond. Perhaps I'll go out and see a bit of the world instead. I may become an actress, like my mother."

She had thrown that out in defiance, but once again, the effort was wasted. Claire merely shook her head sadly. "Oh, honey, not those dreams again. I thought Grandaddy cured you of them, once and for all."

Unbidden, the lean, dark features of Tony Rawlings flitted through Sam's brain. Only instead of the haughty Hoxton, he became Damion, down on his knee before her. *I love your eyes,* he purred. *I love your skin, your hair . . .*

"Well, whatever you do, I hope you will have the sense not to stay here." With a satisfied smile, Claire tucked her new silk undergarments into a drawer. "We will have better things to do with our time than entertaining unwanted house guests."

"We?"

"Most definitely *we*. Now that I've seen your Lord Hoxton, I fully intend to have him."

"Hoxton? Or his riches?"

"Why Samantha Lynn, what has gotten into you? What does it matter to you what I want from the man? It didn't in Richmond."

What had gotten into her, indeed. "You will be using my name, don't forget. I can't—*won't* have you tarnishing it. And even you must see it would be wrong to encourage him in any lasting relationship."

"Just because my mama hadn't the money—"

"Money has nothing to do with this. The man is a British peer. The position carries expectations. Oh Claire, you don't even know who your father was. What makes you think the man would offer marriage to a girl of so nebulous a background?"

"You heard him. He has no use for conventions. If he were to fall in love, he wouldn't care a fig about who my parents might be."

Sinking into the bed as if staking a claim there, the girl flashed the slyest of grins, all but declaring that if anyone could make him fall in love, it was she. Sam glowered at her for a moment but she had long since learned that when Claire was in such a mood, she might as well talk to the walls. That being the case, she would as soon talk to her own, however green they might be.

With a satisfying flounce, she swept into her room. The nerve of that chit—coming here, taking on her identity, and then having the poor taste to accept such outrageous gifts. Any properly reared young lady would feel affronted. Appalled.

Irritated, Sam paced across the limited expanse of the room. She had made a dreadful mistake in coming here. Claire's behavior was at her most impossible, that Riley person was downright hostile, and Hoxton . . . well, she thought, remembering that boyish grin, he might be the most dangerous of all.

Crossing the room for the third time, she noticed a floor-length window. On the other side, a small balcony beckoned. Forgetting her anger in her delight, she stepped outside to view the tranquil charm of the Hudson River.

This scene was likewise decorated in greens, but Nature had been far more skillful with her blend. Breathing deeply, Sam categorized the scents of the blossoming trees and grasses. A wonderful time of year, spring. A time for new beginnings, when even an old maid like Samantha Eggersley could dream of the future.

A horn sounded on the river, drawing her attention to the pinkish hue covering its surface. Beyond, over the hills on the distant shore, the sun was slowly slipping from view. Two boats passed, barely disturbing the current, the occasional voice hushed and indistinct. Abandoning their evening fishing beds, even the birds seemed curiously subdued. They were heading home, Sam thought wistfully; it was that time of night.

Below, a chorus of frogs stirred, proving that some were already nestled in. Papa had once said they croaked so for their nightly courting ritual. How many would find a mate tonight? Sam wondered, and was dismayed at the envy the thought provoked.

For wasn't that just the problem? Despite the feelings of guilt, despite Samuel's extensive training, Sam longed to be in love. With a real man, not Emery Blankfield. Someone with substance, who would wrap his arms about her waist, who could laugh and cry and yes, dream with her. Two lost souls, finding each other, making the world that much less lonely.

She sighed softly, like the breeze stirring her hair. Picking out pins, shaking it free, she let the dark curls fall to her shoulders. The breeze played with it, sending cooling drafts across her head. Enjoying the most satisfying moment of an otherwise frustrating day, she felt more like her old self, like the inner Sam, so secretly guarded that not even Samuel had known she existed. *Oh Papa*, she sighed hopelessly, *why did you have to leave me?*

As if he were in the room with her now, she could see Bill Eggersley's face as it had been that last day.

Standing by the window, so lost, all his hope, his love, dying with her mother. And Devon.

For the first time in years, Sam thought about her brother. How jealous she had been of that sickly baby, taking up her mama's time and all her love. That day, Sam had hidden under her bed when Mama asked her to mind the baby. How was she to know Susannah had had one of her hunches? A bad one, that drove her to take the baby with her, up the mountain to the mine.

Papa had been hurt bad that day, the tunnel collapsing on his leg, but the damage Mama's death had wrought on him had been so much worse. The few times he could bring himself to look at his daughter, Sam knew, he had seen only her guilt. He blamed her. He hadn't wanted to, but he couldn't help it.

And then he had died. He had gone to the same place she had found Mama and, according to the sheriff's report, jumped off the cliff to end his life.

Stiffening, Sam poked the pins into her head and stepped back onto the lime-green carpet. If she lived to be one hundred, she'd never be convinced that he'd killed himself. Not Papa. And until she saw the body, or some tangible proof of his passing, she refused to believe he was even dead. Deep down, she knew she would have felt his death, as she had with her mother, felt that same cold, black emptiness in her heart.

Maybe she was the fool her grandfather accused her of being by persisting with this crusade. She might even be clutching at her last straw, but she would spend every Eggersley penny to prove them all wrong! The day she relinquished her belief in her father, she would have nothing left to live for herself.

And that, she told herself sternly as she paced

across the room, was her sole reason for coming here. It was most certainly *not* to go dewy-eyed over a beautiful man. It was ridiculous to go soft now, merely because Tony Rawlings had the face of an angel, because, just for a minute there at the top of the stairs, he had worn that dreaming, wistful expression so endearingly like her father's.

Dropping to the bed, Sam imagined those blue eyes on her, but this time, instead of frost, there was an enveloping warmth in them. They held her gently, seeing past the gray to the real Sam, deep inside. And he was smiling. Tenderly. Reassuring her that everything was all right, that her father wasn't dead at all, only lost and wandering, and they would find him, together, always together . . . .

An overloud rapping on the door startled her back to the present. To her dismay, she found herself clinging to a bed post shaped like a gargoyle. She jumped up, dusting her gown, working to still the flutterings in her chest. Lord help her; had she been daydreaming again?

As she hurried to the door, she could hear the mutterings of her maid. *"Mon Dieu!* Run here, run there. And when at last I find time to unpack for my lady, my true lady, where is she? Off on an errand for that other one, I'll wager, as if she were too helpless to help herself."

Horrified that Giselle might be overheard, Sam pulled her into the room and smiled with exasperated affection. Ever since the tiny Frenchwoman had presented herself at Samuel Eggersley's door nearly ten years ago, Giselle Du Rambeau had begun her not always silent campaign to defend her mistress' rights. Sometimes, Sam thought, it might be easier if the woman's loyalty wasn't quite so fierce.

"I am here, Giselle. I was waiting for you. I know

how upset you get when I try to unpack for myself."

The woman was not one whit mollified. "There is nothing here worth the trouble," she mumbled, lifting the sorry garments from the bed. "I, who have worked with the finest couturiers in France, could create something worthy of that frame, but *non*, it is not allowed. Mourning, bah! For that old tyrant? And the other one, with her gowns to make you sigh, all lined up and waiting her whim. Who pays? Not she. Her allowance must be saved for her ribbons and trinkets. Some never know when they push too far. Me, I think it is time she was put back in her place."

Sam smiled weakly. "We've exchanged places, remember? If Lord Hoxton were to hear you now, what would it do to my plans?"

"*Your* plans?" Giselle wagged a slender finger. "She is using you, *ma petite*. Had you listened to me in the first place—but no, you let her coax you . . ."

"I've told you. It was my idea, not Claire's."

But Giselle was already launched. ". . . into taking your rightful place, as always. Have you seen what she has taken this time? The jewels, those furs? Him? And will she share, as you would have in her place?"

Sam stared at the animated face and felt weary. Giselle meant well, but the long journey from Richmond had been filled with her chatter, on much the same note, while Claire had been whining in her other ear. "Oh Giselle, must we go through this again? The decision has been made. It is too late to change anything now."

Dumping the pile of clothing on the bed, Giselle stepped closer, her eyes shining with a new purpose. "You poor lamb. Look how she has drained you. You must lie down."

Remembering the gargoyles, Sam shook her head.

"No. I mean—perhaps a bath, instead?"

"You are fatigued; I see it in your face. It is that girl, I tell you. I watched you on that train, trying to stop her, but no, she would make fools of us all with that Yankee."

"Do try to be discreet, Giselle. They are all Yankees here. And for all we know, Jeremy Lyte could have been a perfectly respectable businessman."

"Yes, and a cow, it jumped over the moon. *Mon Dieu*, are you blind? You saw how he touched her, the way she encouraged him."

"Hush! What if someone hears you?" Sam tried to sound firm, but her voice seemed betrayingly brittle. Lord, but her head ached. "Please, Giselle, draw my bath. And lay out a gown for dinner. Nothing elaborate. The gray stripes, perhaps."

The maid clicked like an outraged pigeon. "Stubborn girl. In your heart, you don't mourn him, so why not wear something cheerful for a change? Let me find something in the other room. I could alter it and *voila*, think how lovely you would be at dinner tonight."

Satan, begone. "And don't you think Lord Hoxton would notice that I've pilfered his clothes? Oh, Giselle, just do as I ask."

"I always do as I'm asked. Even when the orders make no sense. Why else would I be here, eh?"

"Please?"

Lips set in a tight line, the maid shook her head. "Very well. But me, I think you are a fool. To leave the comfort of that fine home, to abandon the benefits of your name, and for what? To turn that beautiful man, that enormously wealthy man, over to your trollop of a cousin without a fight? It is that old tyrant's fault, I tell you. Always taking from you, never giving in return. Cut from the same mold, that cousin of yours is. Why you let this go on . . .''

Giselle continued to mumble her way out the door. Holding her palms to her ears, Sam tried to shut the words out, shut out the doubts, but both had planted themselves firmly in her skull.

You are a fool, her brain repeated over and over. Two weeks—an entire fortnight of Giselle's badgering—she had committed herself to this. To two weeks of being on edge, wondering when her cousin's silly chatter would betray them both, to fourteen long days of watching the man of her dreams parading about, wasting his undeniable charm on a chit like Claire.

Irritated with her own whining, she grabbed for the gray striped gown. What she had, if she tried to be sensible, was two weeks to produce results—and for that, she must keep a clear head. If she let down her guard, let herself fall victim to wistful thinking, anything could go wrong.

Experience, and her grandfather, had taught her this. All those years, so close and tight-lipped, Samuel had guarded the one good lead regarding her parents' deaths. But one night, his pain had proved too much, even for the great Samuel, and he had dosed himself far too liberally with laudanum. Tony Rawlings had been poking around Central City, he had let slip then, right after Bill Eggersley disappeared.

Something must have happened to Rawlings then, Sam had since decided, for it was about that time that he had turned recluse—something drastic enough, perhaps, to result in a loss of memory?

She'd had a year to think about this, and to plan what to do. Hoxton would have medical records somewhere, detailing his injury. Where better to look than his current residence? If she had to tear the house inside out, or rampage through the local doctor's office, she would find them. And if they told her what she hoped, her next task would be to jog that fragile memory. Keep at him with questions, always probing, until that vital clue shook loose. It was ruthless, perhaps, but it was the only way.

She saw her frightened face in the mirror. It had seemed so clear-cut back in Richmond, before she had a face to go with the name. For the first time, she considered the man's reaction, his contempt when he learned who Samantha Eggersley truly was.

It didn't matter, she told herself. With any luck, she'd be gone before he stumbled onto the truth. Gone to Chicago to visit Annie, and then on to Colorado, back to the Oh Susannah mine, where it had all begun. Perhaps where it all should end.

She had a sudden longing to be back there. So much of her father's hopes and dreams, of his life, was tied up in that mine. And though it had been abandoned all these years, what if Bill Eggersley had been right? What if there *was* something worth saving in the ruins? Wasn't it the duty of a child to see to the finishing of her father's dream? And considering the father—well, Bill Eggersley deserved no less.

So for the time being, Sam told herself sternly as she gathered the gray dress close to her chest, her own dreams would have to wait. After all, there would be other Damions.

Wouldn't there?

Jumping from his horse, Charles Riley struggled to contain his irritation. Wretched female. It was time to report to his employer, only what on earth was he expected to say?

Since there was no telling the man's reaction, he felt a strong reluctance to tell Hoxton the truth. All their carefully laid plans could be ruined. At this stage of the scheme, Riley could ill afford to allow that.

With a deepening frown, he stomped into the house. He would make his report, he decided, but for now, he would say nothing of this. In truth, it might be interesting, even amusing, to see what the chit would try next.

With a rare smile, he acknowledged that it might not be all to the bad, having another Eggersley against whom to match his wits.

You think yourself so clever, dear Samantha? Well, we shall just have to see about that!

4

Central City, Colorado
March, 1861

Limping to the window, Bill Eggersley had an awful, crawling feeling along his flesh. It could be the result of last night's overindulgence with the bottle, but he didn't think so. It felt more like a hunch, a bad one, drumming against his skull like the loose shutter out back.

But just what did he expect to see out there? Some monstrous dark thing, hovering over the cabin? Hell, the only thing hovering hereabouts was his sense of failure. With his wife and son dead, the mine collapsed, and his dreams in shambles, all he had left was a heart and head that hurt so bad, he wondered if the pounding would ever go away.

He stared out the window, hating the snow, hating his life, but most of all, hating his father for being right. Failure. That's all he'd ever know. He should accept it by now, he'd had it drummed into him often enough. Pounded into him.

"Dammit, Sam. Can't you do something about that shutter?"

A soft *meow* warned him that she'd crept up behind him. He hated when she did that. Nowadays, Sam seemed as silent as an Indian and twice as withdrawn, more like that stupid cat she hugged like a shield against her chest. A matched pair, they were, both flinching if you stepped too close.

Dumb cat. It should have rolled over and died months ago, only Sam had found it and dragged it clear up from Central City under her coat. She had scratches all up and down her arms from the ungrateful animal, but that was Sam, hands always feeding the mouth that bit them.

What kind of father was he, letting the poor kid break her heart over ungrateful strays? She needed to laugh, one of those those low-pitched, all-over body giggles that had so charmed him in the past. They had raised the girl on laughter, he and her mother, only Susie was gone and even a smile seemed beyond him now.

"There's nothing wrong with the shutter," Sam said softly.

Damn, did she have to hunch her shoulders so? Wincing, Bill wondered what he could have done last night to put such a look on her face. God help him, it was getting so he couldn't remember a thing, once the whiskey got the best of him.

"Maybe you're hearing a stamp mill, Pa."

"In this storm? The only mill in operation around here any more is the Warrens' and we both know Jim's too cussed lazy to be mining on such a day."

"Yeah. Besides, Gus said the Warrens sold out, too. To that Mr. Bavoure."

"Jim's gone?"

She nodded, far too solemnly for a kid. "Pa, sometimes, don't you get to feeling like someone's out there, creeping and circling around? Like someone's waiting to get us? I mean, the way the mine collapsed, and then Mama—"

"Stop that nonsense right now! Gad, girl, where do you get these ideas?" He refused to look at his hands. He knew they were shaking, and he couldn't blame the whiskey this time. "I don't want you visiting with the Malloys any more. You're starting to sound as crazy as Gus.''

"What are you saying? You'd trust Gus with your life and we both know it.''

True enough. If not for the Malloys' coming over here with meals and encouragement, Lord knew how they would have managed. Sam was a good girl, and a capable one, but losing her mother had hit her hard. He'd seen the way she looked at him. With Sam, you could see every emotion she owned in those soft, gray eyes, every hurt, fear, and disappointment. Bill Eggersley was her biggest disappointment. Even Sam blamed him for Susie's death.

"Go get me my bottle, will you?''

"Whiskey, Pa?''

"Pa? Know what your grandfather would say if he heard you calling me that? He'd say you sounded ignorant, that's what. And he's right. Maybe it *is* time I sent you back east to school. Someone's got to teach you how to talk and act properly, now that your mother's . . .''

Four interminable months and he still couldn't force out the word. Dead? How could anyone so strong, so vibrant, cease to exist? Snatching the bottle from Sam's hands, Bill sent the fiery liquid down his throat. When would it go away, this bone-deep aching, this looking over his shoulder to catch a glimpse of her?

"I can speak properly, when I have to—I mean, must.''

Sam squared her shoulders. Fighting for pride, she looked so much like her mother, Bill feared he might bawl, right here in front of her. "I mean it, Sam,'' he barked as he stared out the window instead. "There's so much you don't know. So much I can't teach. Look at you. Wearing trousers, and a shirt older than I am. If your Mama could see you now, she'd up and die."

They both winced. Amazing, how tomblike the room seemed. Every hiss and pop from the fire behind him accentuated what a fool he was to stay here. A cold and heartless land, these Rockies. At least back in Richmond, the damned snow knew better than to show its face after March.

Sam's hand seemed so small on his shoulder. Tiny, yet so warm. Thinking of the strays she had saved with it, he wondered if, given time, she could work one of her miracles on him.

You're weak, he could hear his father accuse him. Sam deserved the miracles, not him. He'd let his dreams die with Susie.

"You know," he said slowly, as if the idea had just occured to him, "with the money Mr. Bavoure is offering, I could set us up in real style back east."

"No!" The hand withdrew. "The money would run out and Grandfather would find us. He'd make you go back to work in the bank. That's not what you want, is it?"

"You think life cares about what I want? Or you? It doles out what *it* wants and you gotta make the best of it."

"All right. Then let's make the best of what we have, right here. As soon as you're on your feet again, we'll rebuild."

"With what? That shaft collapsed completely. We don't have that kind of money, girl. Everything we had was sunk in the Oh Susannah."

"Wouldn't Mr. Rawlings help? Mama said he was your friend."

"Tony gave up on the mine months ago."

"He wouldn't need to buy back his share, just offer a loan."

"Not Tony." He hated to squash her eagerness, but how could he explain that Tony's feelings for her mother ran as deep as theirs, that Tony couldn't bear the memories this place evoked? Besides, with his grandfather's death, and a missing cousin clouding up the succession, Tony would need all his spare cash for court battles. Bill knew what being Lord Hoxton meant to Tony—how it felt to be always proving yourself to an unloving family.

"He has money troubles of his own. I won't be taking advantage of a friendship by bothering him now."

"But you can't just give up. What about your inheritance?"

"How would you know about that?"

"I heard you and Mama one night. Oh Pa, make Grandfather give it to you. He has to, if it's rightfully yours."

"You don't understand." His father was a wily, tight-fisted miser and the years had merely tightened his grip. He had that trust from his grandmother so tied up, there was but one way Bill could get his hands on it. He could be rolling in capital, if he sent Sam to Richmond. Bill could have his dream, yes, but at what cost? He pictured his girl, imprisoned in that great empty Eggersley mansion, living the same, sterile youth he had once suffered through, learning life's rules according to Samuel Eggersley. Would Sam learn, any better than he, how to "be tough, fight rough, and give no quarter?"

"But you can't sell out. That's exactly what he wants. You always tell me to follow my own dream. Well, yours is here, Pa, not in that stuffy old bank."

A hundred emotions rallied inside him and he felt a sudden, overwhelming urge to see the Oh Susannah, to learn where everything had suddenly, irrevocably gone wrong. To know, for certain, that all hope was gone. He looked at his bum leg, wiggling his toes. Doc had told him to stay off it, but then he'd also advised moving to a warmer, less hostile climate. He meant well, the doctor did, but he didn't know beans about Eggersley stubbornness.

As he reached for his hat, he heard Sam's gasp. "Pa?"

"Be a good girl and straighten up. Molly'll be here soon to fix dinner. I can't listen to her scolding again."

"Where are you going?"

"For a walk. I need fresh air."

"You're going up there, aren't you?"

He could pretend not to know where she meant. Not much sense in it though, since Sam wouldn't let up until she had an answer. She had her own share of Eggersley stubbornness.

"But you can't. The tommyrockers—"

"You still obsessed with that rot? I thought once the miners left, their Cornish nonsense would go with them. Face facts, girl. What happened to your—er, to the mine, has nothing to do with imaginary creatures from the bowels of the earth."

"Then what, Pa? What *did* kill Mama and Devon?"

The question, beating so long unanswered against his brain, seemed an accusation to his sensitive ears. "Carelessness. Isn't that what they say? The mine caved in because I risked too much, digging for a lode that isn't there. And your ma, well, she was in too much of a hurry trying to get to me to watch where she was going. Even you, daydreaming under your bed when you should have been . . ."

She went as white as the world outside and twice as still. As if squeezed too tight, the kitten leaped to the floor with a meow. Sam watched it scamper off, deliberately avoiding her father's gaze. Angry at himself, yet not knowing how to take the words back, Bill snatched his jacket and jammed his arms into the sleeves.

"I could go with you."

"No!"

"But Pa, what if your leg gave out? I swear, I won't say a word. We could just walk together, like we used to."

Didn't she know how it hurt to look at her? "Dammit, girl, didn't I tell you to stay put? Can't you ever do as you're told?"

She clearly wanted to cry. Lord knew, there was pressure enough behind his own eyes. So they stood there like weakened warriors, battling emotion, eyes not quite meeting as their lips fought to smile.

"Relax, Sam," he offered lamely. "I'll be back soon."

"Pa, please?"

"I said no, didn't I? Now get this place tidied up."

She bit her lip to keep the protests inside. "Don't forget Molly is making Irish stew. You wouldn't want to miss that."

He knew what an effort it took, smiling at him when she so clearly wanted to cry. For a weak moment, he considered staying. The growls in his stomach were nearly as persuasive as her strained smile.

"Won't be but an hour," he flung over his shoulder, knowing he had to go but not having what it took to face his daughter. He knew she'd look just like her mother, the day of the accident—erect and proud, eyes glistening with unshed tears. Susie hadn't wanted him to go that day, either. "Go on," he told Sam. "Go play with your kitten."

He slammed the door behind him, but he couldn't

Barbara Benedict

shut out the guilt. Stooping to buckle his snowshoes,
his eyes strayed to the window. Sam stood where he
had left her, skinny arms hugging each other for dear
life, eyes as wide as the gulf between them. Part of
him longed to go to her, to hold her close and let her
cry. But he was too afraid he might let go himself and
his father's training was ingrained too deeply ever to
allow that. A man must never cry.

So he swallowed the ache in his throat and turned
toward the path. One more failure, one more example
of weakness. It seemed the only way he could deal
with grief was to run away from it.

5

There they go, Sam thought, watching Claire tug her precious Tony toward the stable. Moving from her post at the parlor window, she sighed in relief. She should have plenty of time. Claire and Hoxton were sure to be gone for hours, and Riley had taken himself off to the village.

Just what "business" had taken him off this time? she wondered. They were a close-lipped pair, Hoxton and Riley. The last time she had questioned her host about his "negotiations," all she'd gotten was an amused smile and a don't-worry-your-pretty-little-head-over-it. As if she had bubbles for brains like her cousin.

She left her pique in the parlor, knowing it was silly to complain of being underestimated when it suited her purposes so well. For had they suspected her true motives in coming here, they'd never have left her alone.

For thirty minutes, Sam roamed about the lower floor, making certain no one else was home. She wasn't stalling, she told herself, simply being cautious. Yet, as she found the house depressingly empty, caution gave way to resentment. Sure, leave Sam to her own devices. Who cared what she did with her time? Marching to the staircase, she made up her mind that it would serve the man right if she rifled through his belongings.

Halfway up the staircase, she heard footsteps on

the back steps. She froze. Hoxton must have seen in her eyes what she planned, or heard it in the pounding of her heart. And now . . .

How absurd. The man was too involved with her cousin to notice anything else. However similar the sound might be to the oft-listened-to graceful step, it couldn't be Hoxton. He was with Claire and men never left her for less than a vital cause.

Considering the hour, it was more likely Stoddard. This was when he took the mail to Hoxton's study, Sam knew, for she had collided with the butler yesterday, just as he left the room. Squinting over a letter of his own, the poor man had tried to claim failing eyesight, but Sam slowly learned the true reason he needed her to read to him. Arrogant beasts, these Hoxtons, not to have seen to his education so that that proud old man would not be forced to seek help from a stranger to read of his family in England.

Stoddard was a victim, like the boy, that Willie MacPhearson. Sam worried about that child. He was too thin, too alone, for one so young. Reaching the top step, she decided to kill both birds with a single diplomatic stone. She would tell Stoddard that to instruct the boy, she needed someone there to inspire trust. Then she could teach them both without sacrificing anyone's dignity.

The sense of satisfaction vanished as she looked up to see Hoxton's suite not ten feet away. Setting her shoulders, she told herself it would be foolish to succumb to nerves now, that Tony Rawlings was a self-gratifying snob, and any harm her investigation might inadvertently do was clearly deserved. With a stiff nod, she forced herself forward.

The door was not locked, as she had almost hoped. A sliver of sunlight beckoned from the crack. *Stop being a ninny*, she told herself firmly. *Do what you came here to do and leave.*

With a glance backward, she slid inside the room. She listened, back hugging the door, to every creak in the house. Was that . . . ? No, she mustn't be silly. No one had followed and no one had seen.

She scanned the room. Bookshelves stretched to the ceiling across two entire walls. A single window, heavily draped with burgundy velvet, wedged its way between them, permitting only that sliver of light to enter the room. Dark furnishings crowded the remainder, huge, cumbersome pieces that hovered like sentinels. And every last cabinet and drawer, she discovered as she tried their knobs, was locked tight.

No wonder Riley had seemed so smug as he strolled out this morning, that dark glare almost daring her to try something foolish. Eyes leaping to the door, she thought again of the footsteps on the back stairs. It would be just like Riley to pretend to be called away, just to lie in wait for her. What could she say, or do, if he should suddenly burst into the room?

Frantically, she rifled through the papers on Hoxton's desk, but it was meaningless drivel. There were no medical records, no clues to the accident that had taken Hoxton's memory, no letters, no photographs or mementoes from his time in Colorado.

A board creaked and her heart bounced clear into her throat. It had to be Riley. Any moment, he would open that door and pounce. She waited, but the door stayed shut. Gad, she was a silly, useless woman. The way she behaved, she might as well let Claire conduct the search.

She had to laugh at that. Imagine her cousin giving up her daily rides with their host. Or Sam's once-new riding habit. They might have switched names, Sam thought with a sigh, but nothing else had changed. How nice it would be, just once, if she could forget her responsibilities, just hop onto one of those very fine horses to gallop through the hills. As in those long-ago days in Colorado, she could taste the fresh air, the freedom and innocence of childhood.

Yet it wasn't her youth she imagined, nor was she alone on the steed. From behind, firm hands gripped her waist. They held her close as the horse galloped through a meadow so green, so fragrant, she could taste a blade of grass between her teeth. As the strong thighs tightened, she leaned back into a broad chest, to feel the heat of his body. She turned her head, lips drawn to his. She saw blue eyes, the aristocratic nose, the mouth even now crinkled in humor, as the beautiful face approached . . .

A soft thud brought her back to reality. She found herself sprawled across the desk, a pile of books glaring up at her from the floor where they'd fallen. Hands fumbling, she reached for a few travel directories and a dog-eared copy of Shakespeare's plays. In her mind, she could hear Samuel say that one could tell a man by the books he read. But Shakespeare?

Clasping the battered volume to her chest, she approached the shelves. While there was a veritable treasure of volumes, intricately bound in the finest leather, each looked as if it had been purchased yesterday. Closer inspection of several titles proved that to be the case. From their crispness, their scent, she knew they had yet to be opened by human hands. Glancing at the Shakespeare, she wondered about this paradox named Hoxton.

The silence was shattered suddenly. "Someone must polish these boots, Riley. I feel like a fieldhand with all this mud . . ."

Dropping the book on the desk, Sam wheeled to face her host. He had halted as abruptly as her

breathing. She couldn't tell who was more flustered—
she, caught in his rooms, or he, standing there with
nothing but a towel to cover him.

Her first instinct was to run. Too late, pulling up
only inches away, she realized the man had his legs
planted before the door. To get past, she must take
those firm, brown arms in her hands and move him to
the side, for he seemed in no hurry to move himself.
On the contrary, the lazy grin most expressively
revealed how much he was enjoying himself.

Something huge lodged in her throat and Sam
wondered if it were her tongue. Never had she seen,
much less been so close to, a man's naked chest.
Evenly tanned, perfectly proportioned, its broad
expanse was covered by a soft nest of chestnut hair.
Sam envied the medallion dangling there, its bronze
adding to the blatant virility of all that firm flesh.
How nice it must be to roost there, to lay down one's
head against it and listen to the steady beat of his
heart. Her fingers itched, longing to slide along that
glistening skin. She had this sudden, insane urge to
know how it would taste beneath her tongue . . . .

As if her thoughts could touch him, the muscles of
his chest tensed, rippling erotically. Her stricken
glance shifted to his face. Blue eyes held her,
warming her flesh wherever they strayed. He's like
this with all women, common sense warned her, but
her body refused to listen. Wickedly, it wanted to pull
him back to that tub, to slide into the soapy, silky
water beside him. She pictured the bubbles, tickling,
dissipating slowly. Blood running like syrup through
her veins, she forgot her mission, even her name, in
the sheer pleasure of her fantasy. I could love this
man, she thought weakly.

Perhaps this showed in her gaze, for something
flickered in his own. "I—er, excuse me," he blurted

out. "I was just changing out of my riding clothes."
Before Sam could reply, he was gone.

She felt extremely foolish, standing in the middle
of the room like that, but she was unable to move. *I
could love him*, her brain was stupidly repeating, while
her body trembled from the reprieve it hadn't
wanted. He could have done anything with her—
dragged her by the hair to his bed, if he wanted—and
she'd have happily complied.

But he had run away, like every other male in her
life. It was embarrassing that she had never had the
sense to do the same.

Preparing herself to do so, she was stopped in her
tracks as he reappeared in the doorway. Hastily
garbed, he still fumbled with the buttons of his shirt.
"Oh, good. I thought you might have left," he said
with an adorable grin as he took five long strides to
her side. "Forgive the abrupt departure, but I
suddenly realized you might prefer it if I were—er,
decent, before we continued our discussion."

Decent? Discussion? Facing that magnificent
chest, still revealed by the half-buttoned shirt, how
could she speak? If she opened her mouth now, all
that would emerge was a moan.

"Is something wrong?" He tilted his head, clearly
confused, before straightening into a businesslike
pose. "Rest assured, Miss Farnstable, it was not my
intent to impose any *premature familiarity* on you."

"I know. I mean . . . nothing is wrong. Nothing at
all. I was just admiring your . . . your medallion.
What is it, an eagle?"

"A falcon." He eyed her suspiciously. "It's a good
luck piece. Good things happen when you rub it."

"Do you think I could try?" As she reached for
the bronze, she tried a smile, wishing he would return
it. "I could use a bit of luck . . ." She broke off, hand

dropping uselessly, as he tucked it under his shirt.

"I fear not. I was told never to remove it from my person."

Sam felt as though a door had been slammed in her face. Hurt, she stammered out an apology as he hastily buttoned the rest of his shirt. "I only meant—that is, I—I was merely joking. I suppose I don't do it well. Joke, I mean. I'm a bit out of practice."

He stopped to look at her, clearly puzzled. Sam knew she was babbling, but she felt compelled to explain. "I assumed you were teasing me, so I thought I should, well, fall into the spirit of the thing. Especially considering where I am . . ."

An eyebrow shot up. "Indeed. In telling you to make yourself at home, I had not dreamed you would choose my rooms in which to do so."

Too late, Sam remembered the telltale mess on the desk behind them. Had he guessed her intentions or was he merely fishing? It might be wise to divert his attention elsewhere. "Forgive me. I seem to have interrupted your bath, so perhaps it would be best if I leave."

"My bath is finished. But I might have lingered longer had I anticipated company."

"I beg your pardon?"

"That was a joke, Miss Farnstable, though not a very good one, it appears. Like you, I seem to be out of practice."

She couldn't help but smile. "You can't expect more, under the circumstances. After all, it's not every day a woman barges into your private quarters."

"Only every other." They spoke in unison. Pleasantly surprised by it, they both grinned.

"There," Hoxton added, "I do believe we've

found the knack."

"In that case, I do hope you will forgive me. Actually, I had no idea this was your room. The door was open (that, at least, was true) and when I saw the shelves, I thought this must be the library. I do love to read and since I've already exhausted my private supply . . ."

"Books, you say?" He gaped at the shelves as if seeing them for the first time.

"Well, yes. I'm a prodigious reader."

"Are you? How completely lowering. Most women have an entirely different motive for visiting a man's bedroom."

The blue eyes, dancing with mischief, watched for her reaction. She tried not to respond, but she felt suddenly giddy, half with laughter and half with the need to run her fingers along the tanned muscles of his neck, through the dampened tendrils of his reddish-brown hair . . . .

"My goodness, what happened to your hair? Where is all that gray?"

A hand shot up to run his fingers through it. His smile was tight. "Ah, you've discovered my guilty secret. I wash this concoction into my hair in a vain attempt to deny the passage of years. I suppose you think me a silly old fool?"

"Of course not. Anyone can see what fine form you keep yourself in."

The lips twitched. "Why, thank you."

She bristled. "I'm not very good at this. Flirting, I mean. I think I should leave."

He grabbed for her arm. "Without your books?"

His grip was firm and warm. Sam could feel his heat radiating up into her. "I—I feel positively dreadful. I'm so sorry. I've no doubt disrupted your entire daily routine."

"Do you always apologize so profusely?"

"I'm sor—" Realizing what she'd been about to say, she smiled. "Very well, no apology, but I do promise this shan't happen again."

"No." His gaze was so warm, Sam could have melted, right there to the floor, had his hand not grasped her arm in support. "I want you to use this library. After all, what is the sense in having all these titles if they merely gather dust?"

As he gestured, the scent of his soap wafted between them, enhancing rather than disguising his deep virility. Swamped by sensual revelation, Sam wondered if Mama had felt this lost, this delirious, when looking into her father's eyes. As Hoxton's gaze traveled to the bedroom door, she knew that should he ask, she would follow him through it unquestioningly.

"All I ask," he was saying, as if from a long way off, "is that you make arrangements with Riley beforehand. He becomes so irrational when his—er, routine is disrupted. And I do hate to upset him; good servants are so very hard to find."

She was happy for the reminder, she told herself. She had not come here to melt into a puddle on the floor. "I have no idea where you found him, but I doubt you could do worse."

There was a restrained smile. "He's quite the character, isn't he? Actually, I met him in the theater."

"He was an actor?"

"I was. Or rather, I fancied myself one. Riley arrived in time to talk some sense into me."

"There's nothing wrong with acting. My—my aunt was a fine actress."

"Ah, but Susannah had talent. I did not."

He needn't sound so wistful, she thought. But this

was the opening she'd been waiting for. "Oh? So then you weren't with her at the time she and my—my Uncle Bill died?"

He dropped her arm. "Apparently not."

"Apparently?"

"Amnesia. I can't seem to recall much of my past."

"Oh yes, so you said. But what could have happened, to cause such a loss?"

He shrugged, clearly not wishing to pursue the subject. "An accident of some sort. In the mountains."

"In Colorado?"

"I suppose."

"But when?"

He looked at her with suspicion. She gulped, hoping she hadn't pressed too hard. "You see, Uncle Bill and Aunt Susie were special to me. No one ever talks about their deaths, not even Samantha, and I—well, I always wondered what could have happened in Colorado. I'm sorry; I didn't mean to pry."

"Apologizing again, Miss Farnstable?"

"I suppose it's a habit."

Looking deep into her eyes, he took her hands in his own. "I'd tell you everything, but I have less idea what happened than you. So don't apologize. Not to me."

He couldn't possibly be sincere, she tried to tell herself. He was a libertine. A thousand other females could easily and immediately step into her place. If she had any pride, she would snatch back her hands and walk away while her heart was still intact.

But he was so close, enough to feel his warm breath on her cheek and see the widened pupils of his eyes, his awareness equal to her own. Close enough that if she leaned forward just an inch more, there would be nothing to stop him from taking her into his arms and kissing away every last doubt she owned.

And just as she gave in to her folly, her brain dreaming up all the ways he could take advantage of it, Riley burst into the room with all the drama her earlier fears had predicted.

His brows were all but joined and his cough was as forced as his entry. As the dark eyes settled on Sam, the reproach in them so like her grandfather's, she wondered if the constant disapproval was what made the man seem so familiar.

"Begging your pardon, sir. Miss Eggersley . . ."

He paused and Sam went rigid. Why had he called her that? "Miss Eggersley is my cousin. I am Miss Farnstable. Claire."

"Of course you are." The brows separated, one rising slightly. "I came to advise his lordship that Miss Eggersley has returned from the stables and has been seeking his company."

His scowl went to their hands. Hoxton dropped hers as if burned by them. "Samantha and I had a spat," he said.

The brow rose another notch. One more surprise, Sam thought, and it would pop right off his head.

"I believe her intention was to talk about that spat. Perhaps you should go to her?"

"I am busy at the moment."

Sam didn't dare look at Riley's brow now. "I was just about to leave," she told him.

"No!" Hoxton blinked, as if his outburst had startled him, too. "You must take your books, Miss Farnstable. Which do you prefer? Classical literature, modern novels? Perhaps poetry?"

Sam watched him go to the shelves. Curious. He seemed on edge, as if Riley made him nervous as well. As if they both had something to hide from him.

"What about plays? There's a wonderful collection of modern comedies somewhere, with all my personal favorites. Ah, here it is. *"Love's Bite, Run If You Can*, and best of all, *Marietta.*"

"Oh, I love *Marietta*." Taking the volume from his outstretched hand, Sam beamed as she hugged it close. So he liked the play, too. Surely that meant something.

Apparently not. As Riley hacked out another meaningful cough, Hoxton stepped back and his tone and expression turned chillingly polite. "Then I hope you enjoy these as I have enjoyed your visit. If you would be so kind, please inform Samantha that I shall be along shortly to escort her to dinner?"

And that, quite neatly, put Sam back in her place. Run along, dowdy little prude, your allotted time is done. Next, please.

Smile tightening, she mumbled a thank-you and marched from the room with shoulders squared. She would take her pride, thank you. It was better than nothing at all.

Once in the corridor, she leaned against the wall to regain her bearings. What in glory's name had just happened to her? What of her search, her questions? All she had to show for her efforts was a time-worn book of plays and a silly heart that would not stop its absurd pounding.

Hugging the volume tight to her chest, she cursed her cousin. That beautiful man should be hers, by right of birth, but Claire had placed her stamp on ownership everywhere, so that even Riley, that obnoxious little man, thought Hoxton belonged to Claire.

"What was the meaning of that little scene?"

She froze as Riley's voice drifted through the

crack in the door. Eavesdropping on one's host might be a social sin of the first order, but Sam lingered a moment longer to hear the reply.

Grant watched the door with longing, wishing he too could escape through it. What, in truth, could he answer? Of them all, he had the least idea what any of it meant.

"What was that female doing here? She is hardly the sort to encourage a dalliance."

You'd be amazed, Grant thought as he considered the depth of that gray gaze. Had she actually . . . ? But no, they were talking about Claire Farnstable here. The prudest of prudes.

Annoyed at himself, and at the probing Riley, he barked out a denial. "Dalliance? Where on earth do you dig up these words? For heaven's sake, man, the woman wandered in for a book."

"Oh? And what were you doing?"

"Teasing. I couldn't resist. It isn't every day you catch Claire without her composure. I wanted to penetrate that stiff skin of hers."

"And just what did you learn from this—er, penetration?"

Damn the man and his insinuations. "All I learned, as if it matters, is that the woman likes to read."

Riley glanced from the shelves to the door. There was a thoughtful crease between his brows. "I don't like it. She would never barge into a man's room for less than a crucial motive. I hope all was secured?"

"You have the keys, not I." No doubt he sounded peevish, but from the start, Grant had not hesitated to voice his derision of Riley's elaborate precautions. One couldn't get a bloody handkerchief in this house without the proper key.

"She has no reason to be in your rooms. We can't be pleased by this. Not at all."

"You can't think I spirited her in here?"

"Did I say you were the culprit? On the contrary, you seemed quite successful at diverting her attention. In another minute, spying would have been the last thing on her mind."

"Spying? Are you serious?"

Stroking an imaginary beard, Riley glanced at the door again. "Hmmm. Not a bad idea, should she prove susceptible."

"What are you talking about?"

Hands clasped behind his back, Riley paced the carpet. "With her lack of beauty, she will have had no experience, and therefore little defense, against such strategy."

"Strategy? Are we engaged in battle? We *are* talking about the all but invisible Miss Farnstable, aren't we?"

Riley frowned at him as he would at the village idiot. "The quiet bear the most watching. Should she prove as innocent as she seems, it will hurt no one to carry on a flirtation. It will throw her off balance and make certain she can't think clearly in your presence. Let her try to discover anything then."

"Oh for God's sake. Even supposing the girl is a spy, a prospect I find ludicrous in the extreme, how do I do this? I thought I was to dazzle her cousin."

"You've been known to juggle more than one relationship in the past. What of that circus performer and the—"

"Hardly the same." How on earth had the man known about that? "These two are under the same roof. Being cousins, they must tell each other everything."

"I doubt Miss Farnstable is the sort of young lady

who would kiss and tell.''

Grant felt the starch go out of him. Partly because he recognized the futility of pitting his scruples against Riley's schemes, but primarily because the prospect was not an entirely unwelcome one. There had been a moment there . . .

''You needn't make a cake of yourself, of course. A discreet compliment, an occasional lingering touch, and I daresay a man of your talent can turn the poor woman into a dithering idiot.''

Ah, the chase. Grant found himself grinning. Not that the woman was likely to surrender as easily as Riley predicted, but it was enticing to imagine. Claire with that brown hair loose and flowing about those softened shoulders, the gray eyes smoldering as they had, all too briefly, moments ago. Enticing indeed. Instinct insisted that a passionate woman lay buried beneath the layers of propriety, and if he understood his mentor correctly, he'd just been given license to excavate for her.

''Did you hear that?''

He looked up to find Riley at the door. ''What is it?''

''Nothing. For God's sake, finish dressing. I shudder to think of his lordship's reaction, should he learn you've been entertaining in such a state. Or, God forbid, Miss Eggersley's.''

Riley specialized in timely reminders. Remembering Samantha, Grant imitated his shudder. Not that she'd be distressed by his bare skin—far from it, as she'd already proved—but she would expect his lustier thoughts to center on her. From the way she had stomped from the stable, merely for being denied the horse she wanted, he could imagine her rage if she found her cousin in his room.

But no, Samantha was the softest, most pliable

creature he'd ever held in his arms, the ideal female and the complete antithesis of her cousin. The tantrum must have been a quirk.

Yet as he struggled with his cuff links, brushing aside Riley's attempts to help, it wasn't Miss Eggersley who brought the smile to his lips. So she read prodigidously. In bed? Should he teach her what other pursuits could be conducted under the sheets?

It must be spring and his enforced celibacy that addled his mind. Imagine taking a shrew like that to bed! He might as well put a noose around his neck.

He felt a flash of—what? Disloyalty? Whatever it was, he denied it instantly. He owed the woman nothing. Certainly nothing to make him question his own worth. If she denied what was likely her last opportunity for a little pleasure with an experienced and skillful lover, then it was her loss, not his.

Furthermore, he had a job to do, the next part of which was to charm Miss Eggersley into matrimonial bliss. Smoothing down his coattails, Grant reminded himself of how fortunate he was to have such charming company for dinner.

Oddly enough, though, the prospect didn't seem nearly as attractive as it had the night before.

Snow. Pristine white, wherever the eye could see. Tiny, delicate crystals danced in the winter air. One, beckoning like a star, was so pretty it made Samantha cry. She followed, but it flitted forward, then up, always out of reach. Stretching for it, she fell face-first into a pile of snow. She giggled as the fat flakes tickled her nose.

Sitting up to brush herself off, she laughed at the sight of her boots. So big. Too big, always tripping her.

"Sam?"

From far off, she heard her mama's voice. A horrible pain settled in her chest as she remembered whose boots they were. She had borrowed them from her mother when she could not find her own, when she knew she would have to go out in the snow. When she realized that someone must stop Mama from taking Devon to the mine.

She began to run again, but this time it was the voice she chased. "Mama!" she cried out, the voice becoming as elusive as the snowflake. "Mama, where are you?"

With each step, the boots seemed to grow longer. Tell lies, another voice hissed in her ear, and your feet will grow. *But I'm a good girl!* she protested.

A dark silence bounced back to mock her. All around, the snow seemed scarred. Blackened timbers reached for her with long, gnarly fingers. Here and there, with increasing frequency, the ground was stained with red. Blood red.

Mama! she called out frantically. Her answer was a chuckle, so low, so menacing, it drew the breath from her lungs.

She stopped then. With frightening certainty, she knew she was lost. Above, the trees stretched up, then reached down with curling fingers for her hair. *Tie it up*, her grandfather hissed; *act like a lady.*

Even as she reached for her head, laughter erupted across the air. In the midst of the trees, she saw tiny forms emerge from the ground. Tommy-rockers, she thought with an indrawn breath, the nasty little gnomes that guarded the inner mines and laughed so viciously. She clapped her hands over her ears to shut out the sound.

She saw a taller form wriggling in the center of them. *Mama!* she called out again, but her mother stopped struggling and dropped the bundle from her arms. Devon. The laughter grew louder than ever.

Too frightened to move, Sam saw them now pointing at her. But it was not at her, but behind her that they gestured. Nearly too late, she heard the footfalls, smelled the evil.

Her feet moved without her. Her mind might reach out for her mother and brother, but those gigantic boots carried her deeper and deeper into the gathering dusk. Behind her still, she heard the footfalls, heavier with every step. She could feel all that anger, that hatred, as if it had already touched her.

Glancing back, she tried to identify him, this king of the tommyrockers, but she could see little in the gloom. He was not overly tall, or graceful, or much of anything that she could identify. All that was the least remarkable was the sudden glow of his domelike head.

The appraisal cost her dearly. He gained a few steps, then a few more. Running, following the footsteps imprinted in the snow, she saw a vast opening in the ground, a yawning chasm waiting to swallow her whole. She was trapped. All around her, tommyrockers whooped with laughter. *Mama!* she screamed.

"Mama?"

Sam opened her eyes to a strange, dark room. Twin monsters glared from the bedposts. Whimpering now, she groped in the covers for her teddy bear. She wanted her mama. And papa.

Never again, came her grandfather's cold, uncaring rasp. He had made her leave the bear behind in Central City, and he had torn the memories of her parents to shreds.

Breathing slowly as Giselle had taught her to do, Sam fought the aftermath of the nightmare. It always happened this way. Even after the dream was done, she had trouble leaving that part of her childhood. Once, a few years back, she had wandered in her sleep to wake at her grandfather's bedside. For a strange moment, staring across the years, she thought she saw compassion in the old man's eyes, even remorse. But then she had come fully awake, and he had ordered her out of his room.

Focusing, she now saw gargoyles. Where on earth had the sleepwalking led her this time? Slowly, she remembered she was no longer in Richmond, but here, in Hoxton's palace. In the hideous green bedroom.

She swung her legs from the bed, purposefully avoiding the bedposts. Small wonder she'd had the nightmare again. Strange, that she could never remembering the details when she woke. Only the fear. She was still trembling with it.

Crossing the window, she stepped out onto the balcony. A whiff of pipe smoke hung on the air. She looked over to the neighboring balcony, saw the vacant chair, and wondered if Hoxton had been having trouble sleeping, too.

Like the smoke, wisps of an overheard conversation lingered to haunt her and humiliate her. It served the wretch right, if his conscience would not let him sleep. If he had one.

Invisible, he had called her. And Riley, that odious little man, thought her so plain, so desperate, that a mere word would turn her into a grateful puddle. That the assessment was near to the truth only made matters worse. Puddle? Two minutes more with the man and she'd have been a pond.

Annoyed, she left the tranquil scene for the more

appropriate atmosphere of her bedroom. Did they fear she would disrupt their silly business negotiations? Good lord, the man had only to ask. He certainly needn't force himself to kiss her.

Plopping down on the bed, she punched her pillow. He didn't seem to follow Riley's advice, anyway. His rapt attention to Claire tonight had convinced her of that. Prettier than ever, her consciously confident cousin had begged for, and gotten, yet another dress. The man must have a seamstress waiting in the wings, happy to answer his whims. No doubt she was in love with him, too, and devastated to learn that his whim, for the moment, was Claire.

Well, Sam Eggersley was no seamstress. If Hoxton and his infuriating valet wanted to engage in a battle, she would give them the fight of their lives. After all, she had come here to clear her father's name, not to go weak-kneed at the flash of a lopsided grin. How lucky that she had overheard them. She would have humiliated herself, had she taken his flirting seriously.

Pounding the pillow into a ball, she swore that she would be the one to do the kissing. She would be cold and hard, just like them, and there would be no more dreaming. As pleasant as fantasy might be, she could not control her destiny with it. Once she slipped into the stream of mindless fancy, she lost control. Tony Rawlings could then stroll up, deliver one of his "compliments," or dear lord, a "lingering touch," and God alone knew where her imagination would lead her.

But two could play the game. She had watched Claire often enough, had she not? And she had always wanted to be an actress. Quite a role, flirting with Tony Rawlings. Playing Marietta to his Damion, just as she had imagined. With one distinction. In this scene, her heart would be as false as his own.

And that, she insisted, would give her immense satisfaction. To laugh in his face, to call him at his own game, to see if he thought her so amusing then. She would show them all she was made of sterner stuff, that she as a worthy representative of the family name. Samantha Lynn, the last of the proud Eggersleys.

It was an ominous prospect, being the last. Shifting uneasily in the bed, she remembered Riley's gloating tone.

6

Sam sighed and flopped onto her back on her bed. The daily reading lesson had been cut short because Willie had to clean chimneys for Ada, and Hoxton, via his sour-faced valet, had ordered Stoddard to oversee the spring cleaning of the upper floors.

Yet even without the interruption of lessons, most of each day left Sam with nothing to do. She had walked over every inch of the estate, and there was no sense in returning to the village. Why subject herself to those queer stares when no one would tell her a thing anyway?

The local doctor had raised his brow, before stating firmly that he had never treated Hoxton. His lordship, everyone knew, traveled with a retinue of physicians. As his house guest, surely she knew this? Equally dampening, the pharmacist had sneered that even had Hoxton an account there, which he unfortunately did not, such information would never be released to a stranger. It simply was not done.

Sam flopped onto her stomach. No wonder she was so edgy and restless. A week and a half she'd been there and other than the reading lessons, she'd yet to accomplish a thing.

She needed to move, to be out in the breeze, wild and free. In her youth, up on the family's horse, she had climbed the hills, feeling the wind whip against her face. And later, in Richmond, she had often taken a mount from her grandfather's stable without permission.

The grin spread with her thoughts. Why not? Hoxton had even finer horses. Claire had commandeered her new riding habit, but she still had the split skirt she'd worn years ago. Digging through her clothes, she grabbed the burgundy plaid. What memories it invoked! Hours of joyous escape and unhindered daydreaming on her grandfather's horse, where her imaginary Damion had kissed her. Then he had swept her down, cradling her tenderly as he lowered her to the soft bed of pine needles beneath him . . . .

None of that today, Sam told herself as she buttoned the habit. The jacket was a bit tight about the bodice, pushing her breasts up out of the simple white blouse, but how heavenly it felt to move about without those hampering skirts. Watch this, Claire, she silently challenged. See if I don't have some fun of my own, for a change. Let's see who lives to be boring.

Whistling and jingling the keys in his pocket, Grant sailed down the stairs. He felt so good, so in control of things that he could well be the over-blessed Hoxton. Heaven knew, he spent the man's money with unwarranted ease. That little filly, for example, waiting in the stable . . .

He grinned. Riley would spit nickels when he learned of it. No matter. Samantha wanted a proper mount. Hoxton could hardly begrudge the girl, or her erstwhile protector, the fun of having such a horse. Not when he was as rich as French cuisine.

Not that Grant felt the need to justify his actions. Indeed, the more time that passed without discovery, the more comfortable he felt in his role. Over a week had gone by, with Miss Eggersley being as much charmed as charming. Even Riley's complaints seemed to have dwindled.

Grant shifted uneasily as he remembered Riley's recent insinuations. How he resented the sly digs with the elbow, as if Claire were a pawn to be used at a whim. Or himself, for that matter. What did Riley think him, another stud in the stables?

His stomach growled. Empty, again. Sniffing, he caught the sweet aroma drifting from the kitchen. Miss Harmony was baking hot-cross buns. Though it drove the poor cook mad, he would sneak in, pilfer one, and be off again before she could complain.

Before he could make the turn, there was a trill of laughter upstairs. He stopped, the emptiness shifting lower in his anatomy as he relived last night's farewells. How had that delightful, pink-frocked child matured so rapidly into a wily, seductive temptress? Whatever the little minx had been up to since her grandfather's death, he'd wager, hadn't a thing to do with balancing Eggersley's books.

His skin still tingled where her slender fingers caressed him. She had wanted another gown, for an evening out. Riley would be livid, but when Samantha batted those lashes, it took a far stouter will than Grant Barton's to resist her. A sultry seductress, our Miss Eggersley, and he had been a veritable Hercules, not to mention a damned fool, in resisting her lures thus far.

Willfully shutting out the sound of her laughter, he forgot the buns as he stomped to the front door. How much longer would he—could he—resist? Urge her to stay longer, Riley insisted daily. Was the man blind? One night, and one night soon, those long, involved partings at her door wouldn't end with Grant walking honorably away. And what then? It didn't take a genius to guess Hoxton's reaction. Grant would be blamed, no matter how freely, how insistently, the woman had given herself.

There was an alternative, of course. Slamming the door behind him, he wished Riley would leave off badgering him about it. Using Miss Farnstable to ease his baser needs was a scurvy thing to do. Not that she seemed in the least amenable to the prospect. Indeed, on the few occasions she had let their gazes meet, there had been something this side of frost in hers.

Strolling across the huge span of lawn to the stables, Grant tried to regain his earlier euphoria. It was a grand day, he reminded himself, too fine to spoil with introspection. Beneath his feet, the grass felt as soft as the satin quilt on his bed. He twirled on it, the lord and master surveying his grounds with unabashed admiration. It was quite a showplace. The poor gardener must slave night and day to maintain it. Grant had to credit Hoxton for getting the most from his staff.

Then again, as far as the staff was concerned, *he* was Hoxton. It might be Riley, invisibly prodding, who got things done, but Grant would always take the credit—or the blame—as lord and master.

Dammit, why couldn't he remain blind to, and therefore happy with the situation? There was no denying the place was run with military precision, but it was a lonely life Hoxton had cut out for himself. The staff might be efficient and inconspicuous, but Grant couldn't remember ever feeling so lonely. No one returned his smiles. Wherever he turned, he was met with that distant, touch-me-not-stare, so like Miss Farnstable's. Did his staff watch him, too, judging his actions only to find him forever lacking?

He kicked a stone at his feet. Take the way she had glared at him at breakfast, as if his head had grown so swollen he couldn't remember to thank Stoddard on his own for what the man did. Guilt stirred now as it had then. Perhaps he should go after the gardener—no, the man had a name, didn't he?—to praise Foote for this jungle of azalea blooms. Scanning the grounds, he saw him slaving at the iris beds. How like an English garden it seemed. A wave of homesickness, powerful in its unexpectedness, froze the words of praise on his lips.

Home? And just where is that, Barton? Newgate Prison? Or perhaps the workhouse? For even had the charges against him been dropped, he would never find work on any stage in England. No, if he ever wished to find that cheerful, sunlit room of his earliest memories, he must earn his fortune here in this vast and impersonal America. And since his future hinged upon Hoxton's favor, Grant must continue to play the haughty lord, supervising this huge estate with the firmest of hands and ignoring the backs he broke in the process, as well as Miss Farnstable's contemptuous glares.

Jamming both hands into his pockets, he strode to the stable. All pleasure in the new horse was gone. It was all a sham, anyway, a stupid fairy tale that couldn't possibly come true. How could he expect to play the prince when he more aptly fit the role of the villain, breaking the spirits of the peasants, robbing the countryside blind. And now he had taken to seducing innocent young maidens as well.

He was what life had made him, he protested. If Fate continued to deal him a losing hand, he had no choice but to play it. If only an occasional bad card could go Hoxton's way! Somewhere in this world there must dwell a being capable of defying him, of proving that he and Riley were no more invincible than anyone else.

A commotion on the bridle path below stopped him where he stood. Riley had decreed that no one was to use that path, or take a horse without his permission. And my good lord, was that his new filly, intended exclusively for Miss Eggersley's use?

Someone was doing a rather neat job of managing her, though. A female, by the look of the long, brown hair that bounced in time with the horse's rhythm. With open admiration, he watched the woman take the fence. She flew through the air as if bodily joined to the animal and, with athletic skill, dropped gracefully on the other side. Grant whistled. She was riding bareback, for heaven's sake, the distinctive burgundy and gray plaid of her habit hugging the filly's flanks with an almost masculine determination.

She turned the animal, her pose declaring her satisfaction with the day's outing, and headed it back to the stable. Without conscious thought, he stepped forward, hand upraised to hail her. A female who could ride so wantonly, so the reasoning went, should be as wild and free in bed. Inside, he could feel the pressure gathering. His fingers itched to touch the velvety sheen of those dark, flying tresses. He ached for the magic of a woman's soft flesh. This woman's.

Yet before he could finish the thought, or even consider the insanity of it, there was an ungodly howl from behind, a compelling, not-to-be-ignored plea for help. Irked beyond belief, he turned to answer it. Not that it mattered. It was too late anyway. The girl, and any hope of meeting her, had already vanished. Reluctantly, belligerently, he started back, to the house.

From the ruckus emanating from the kitchen, it seemed nothing short of catastrophe was upon them. Visions of the cook writhing on the floor, arms burned to the elbows, ran through his mind, all because he had requested—no, demanded—hot-cross buns for his tea.

One glance into the vast caverns of his kitchen proved his cook was not the victim. A stout woman of miserly cheer, she huddled in the corner with a timid undermaid, all four eyes as large as the ham steaming on the table in front of them. Momentarily distracted, Grant stared at the roast, its spicy aroma tickling his nostrils. Just beyond, scattered across the table, were a dozen hot-cross buns.

A series of barks drew his gaze to the right. Tied to a table leg, a disreputable mutt was yelping with puppyish enthusiasm as its tiny legs dug at the kitchen floor. Peeking out from the mangy tangles of golden fur, its large brown eyes watched the pair just out of its reach. Following its gaze, Grant saw at once why the mongrel was so upset.

Bending over the far end of the table, buttocks as bare as the day he had been born, was an equally scrawny lad. Ugly red stripes streaked up beyond the soiled material of his shirt. Towering above, strap raised and ready, was the ubiquitous Riley.

"What in heaven's name are you doing?"

Appalled, Grant lunged for Riley's arm. The dog began to yelp in earnest, its dirty feet digging at Grant's trousers as if recognizing rescue. It was an optimism the boy failed to share, for both his eyes and mouth were rounded in a most astonished O.

Riley alone retained his composure. "This does not concern you, sir. This is a domestic matter."

"I believe it is my domecile, is it not? Good lord, Riley. Is a beating necessary? He can't be more than ten."

"I'm twelve, come next month." With a defiant shake of that dirty head, the boy snatched the opportunity to scramble from the table and refasten his trousers.

Grant recognized him as Willie MacPhearson,

orphaned grandson of Ada, Hoxton's former house-keeper of many years. The bottle had gotten the best of the woman, Riley had sneered, and she had to be let go. Bitterness had since turned her cold efficiency into equally frigid rage. A good many of the stripes on the boy's back, if rumor were right, had been there long before Riley could make his own imprint.

"This is my affair, Lord Hoxton." The name was sharply pronounced to serve as a reminder. "I caught the boy stealing. As you can see, he left a trail of hot-cross buns."

"That ain't true. I told you what happened."

Arm poised, the valet plainly itched to use his strap. As the dog growled from deep within his throat, Grant was reminded of the only pet he'd ever had, a mongrel much like this one, only Salty had too quickly fell victim to a set of carriage wheels. At the time, Grant had vowed never again to let any animal so unman him, but he found himself leaning down to soothe this one. The mutt's response was immediate and energetic.

"Get that filthy beast off his lordship, boy. You know the rules. Lord Hoxton is allergic to animal hair of all kind."

"He don't seem allegic to Gus."

"Insolence. If I were you, I'd watch how you speak to your betters. As it is, you're already facing one night behind bars."

Grant was sickened. Was Hoxton so tight-fisted, so jealous of his possessions that he would seek retribution from a twelve-year-old child? A boy whose largest crime was to pilfer a few sweets, a treat so obviously denied that spare frame?

"I won't have it, Riley," he pronounced through his teeth.

"Do not concern yourself, sir."

"As they were my buns, I am the one to deal with it. I think I am capable of handling a sweets-thief by myself."

"Perhaps, if that were his only crime."

"Don't tell me he stole a glass of milk to go with them?"

"It might seem less humorous once you learn he has charged a considerable bill at Anson's market in your name."

"Hey, wait. I told you. The lady said I could."

"Ah yes, this mysterious lady." Riley's sneer went back to Grant. "He has yet to supply a name. As far as I can see, it is but another of his fabrications."

"If he means I'm lying, it just ain't so."

"Isn't so."

Willie shrugged, grammar plainly not a priority. Riley's snort revealed similar impatience. "His lies merely compound the crime. I fear we must go to the local magistrate with this."

"Are you serious? For heaven's sake, Riley, I said I will deal with him. And without an audience, if you don't mind."

As this last was directed toward the two trembling ladies in the corner, they shuffled out with grateful haste. Left alone, the three males glared at one another. "I am warning you," Riley said at last. "This could have drastic repercussions. Sir."

"As long as I an nominally in charge, I am willing to take my chances."

Bowing, Grant held the door open. As the disgruntled Riley bustled out of the room, the dog sat down, its tail brushing the floor as if in applause. Grant could have sworn the silly mutt was smiling.

"What does he mean, drastic reper-russians?"

"Repercussions." Grant squatted beside him, his efforts to untie the dog hampered by its enthusiastic licking. "In essence, I suppose Riley was trying to warn us both that stealing, no matter how unimportant the object, is a serious crime."

"I didn't steal nothing. I came in here to get the scraps the lady's been saving for Gus."

"Ah yes, the lady. The same one, I assume, who bought you food at Anson's?"

Willie nodded enthusiatically. "Me and her, we found Gus, in the ditch, beat up something awful. She cried and cried. Said he reminded her of a friend that just died so could we name him Gus? I said sure. She fixed him up and said he would stay in the kitchen until he got better, out in the back pantry. I told her you didn't like dogs, but she said fiddlesticks. Said it wasn't fair to make me go running halfway around the world when the scraps was right here."

"Scraps I can understand. But what about the market?"

"That was for me. Couldn't have me going hungry, she said, and that if you was any kind of a landlord—well, I mean, she practically ordered me to buy the stuff. She promised to pay for it later."

By now, Grant had an idea who this woman must be. "At the risk of agreeing with Riley, this sounds rather mysterious. Could you describe your lady to me?"

"Not the silly one. The taller one. With the pretty eyes. The—why, that one there, sir."

Grant followed the grubby finger to a very disarrayed Miss Farnstable. With the dark curls hung about her shoulders, prim face softened into dismay, he nearly didn't recognize her. It took the gray eyes for positive identification. As his stunned gaze slid down the distinctive plaid habit, resting on the creamy swell of her blouse, he felt again that tightening of his mid-section. *Claire Farnstable?*

There was no denying the boy's pleasure at seeing her—nor the puppy's, who was yapping excitedly at her heels. Grant shook his head. Claire, the female who had stolen his horse and turned the household upside down? He had this most untimely, and equally unsuitable, urge to throw back his head and laugh.

She dropped to her knees, hugging the dog. "This is all my fault. Down, Gus. Oh Willie, can you ever forgive me? I thought Cl—I mean, I forgot . . . ." Words trailing away, she firmly shut her mouth. Gus, likewise, stopped barking long enough to adequately dampen her face.

"Ah, Miss Farnstable. I'm told you've been feeding the native populace with Hoxton funds?"

As she looked up, her spine visibly straightened. "I had meant to reimburse you. I was afraid the local grocer might not extend credit to the Eggersley name."

"Is it your habit, then, to run up bills others must pay?"

Two bright spots of color showed on her cheeks. "My cousin would have understood. As any decent human being would."

She glanced meaningfully at the spare frame of Willie MacPhearson. As always in her presence, Grant found himself having to defend his actions and resenting it fiercely.

"But that still doesn't explain your actions, Willie." She turned to the boy, ignoring Grant entirely. "Why steal from the kitchen, when you have carte blanche at the market?"

"I didn't take no carts."

"Any carts. It's an expression, son. Miss Farnstable means that you had a free rein, a do-what-you-will."

"Oh? Yeah, well, that didn't work out."

She shot an accusing look in Grant's direction. "Regardless of his lordship's insensitivity, you should have come to me. I'd have managed something. It was wrong to steal from him."

"Apparently he didn't. The dog did. He mentioned something about scraps?" Grant was beginning to enjoy these blushes. Color did wonderful things for her face.

"Such a fuss about nothing," Willie sneered, drawing both their gazes to him. "What should it matter who takes what, when he owns everything in the world anyway?"

It wasn't until after she had pulled her gaze back to the boy that Grant realized how they'd both been staring. And how peculiar he suddenly felt.

"It happens to matter a great deal, young man. Why, if everyone took your philosophy, his lordship would soon have nothing left, now would he? Those hot-cross buns happen to be his favorite, and I'll wager that if you'd worked as hard as he for what he has, you wouldn't like being robbed behind your back, either. Even by such a charming rogue as Gus." With a silly grin, she roughed up the animal's fur.

Fascinated, Grant watched them, wondering how she could know the buns were his favorite, and wishing, strangely enough, to be included in the affection she was doling out so freely.

As her finger went to the boy's lip, the smile faded. "Gus might have been the primary culprit, but what is this sugar on your mouth? Oh Willie, why didn't you tell me the truth? You know how I detest lying."

And how would she feel about his own deception? Grant wondered. He rather doubted she would wipe his lips so gently. More likely she would land her fist square in his gut.

"Don't you see," she continued. "A man caught lying can never be trusted again. How many times must I tell you this?"

The boy twisted away. "I don't need no lectures."

"Any lectures," Grant corrected, flashing back to that first harsh winter after escaping the clutches of Michael Clanton and the horrors of the Cornish mines. How tough and belligerent he'd been, too, until faced with Sarah's overladen table. It was amazing, how hostility could melt in the face of good, hot food.

Feeling as Sarah must have felt those many years ago, he stifled his grin. "Believe it or not, I was once much like you, Willie. Trust me, grumbling never gets you what you want and though stealing might, it's a sad fact that nothing in life comes without its price. Sooner or later, we all have to pay it."

"And you do the collecting, right? You just sent old fatso away so you could beat me yourself. Aaah, you're all the same." He spat on the glistening tiles.

It was getting harder and harder not to smile. "The man's name is Riley; I think you should use it. And please, don't spit. Not only is it a disgusting habit, but the poor maids will need to mop the floor again. They are overworked enough as it is. Here, take this chair instead."

"You want me to sit? What for?"

"For negotiating. A great deal more can be decided if we are comfortable. I always sit when I discuss the pros and cons."

Siding three chairs to the table, he turned to a skeptical Claire. "Miss Farnstable, please. Won't you join us?"

What a pair. Willie folded his scrawny arms defiantly across his chest; Claire's gray eyes darting from Grant to the chair and back to Grant again. Gus alone seemed to trust Grant, watching with remarkable calm as he sliced the ham.

"What's a con?" Plopping into the adjacent seat, Willie made a good show of indifference, but his eyes never left the fork. Nearly drooling, he watched as Grant popped the juicy meat into his mouth. Claire silently slid into the chair opposite.

"Never mind. Let's concentrate on the pro. Speaking of which, my cook has outdone herself. I don't suppose you would like to try a bite?"

Willie snatched the meat and chewed on it noisily. Amused, Grant grinned at Claire. "How about you, Miss Farnstable?"

"It does look delicious, doesn't it? Though I suppose it was meant for dinner."

"Ever proper Claire. Your parents can be proud; you must have been the model child."

"My parents are dead."

"I'm sorry." Grant softened his tone. "But I was merely teasing, you know. Lord, what is the sense in paying for all this if I can't choose when, what, and with whom I will dine?"

Popping the ham into her mouth, she sported a surprisingly naughty grin. Fascinated, Grant saw her, really looked at her, for the first time. Smiling like that, she didn't seem half so prickly. Or so plain.

He had begun to think her downright pretty before he realized that it was his gawking that caused the attractive pink on her cheeks. He forced his gaze back to the boy. "Slow down, son. If you can chew like a gentleman, I'll fix you a plate of your own."

One would think he'd been offered Buckingham Palace. Amused, Grant risked a glance at Claire, hoping to catch a trace of approval, only to find her sneaking scraps to an ecstatic Gus.

"As charming as that scamp might be," he

snapped, annoyed that even the damned mutt got more attention than he did, "I will not have him fed from my table."

"I told you, he don't like dogs."

"Doesn't. And this has nothing to do with my dislikes. Basic deportment requires—oh, here. Put this plate in the corner and let him eat it there."

He saw the grin before she could hide it, so she hastily changed the subject. "What happened at the market, Willie? Did Mr. Anson refuse to fill your order?"

"Ain't likely." The boy shook his head as he returned to the table to attack his own plate. "Not when it come from the big house. No, t'was Gram. Swore I must've stole the stuff, that Ole King Midas would never be giving out hand-outs. You see, then it made it all right for her to sell the stuff and use the money for whiskey. Since all I got from it was a whipping, plain didn't make sense going back to Anson's."

He could see that Claire ached to hug the boy. Still, she had the good sense to respect his pride. And respect drew respect.

"Well, we can't have a growing boy going hungry," Grant heard himself mutter. "Perhaps I can speak to your grandmother."

All chewing stopped. Four eyes stared at him in disbelief. "Heck," Willie blurted out, his mouth still half-full, "you forget what she's like? Gram would as soon chew off your head as speak to you. Wouldn't she?"

As both their gazes focused on Claire, she smiled weakly. "Ada doesn't take kindly to interference in family matters."

"I'll say. But Miss Claire didn't back down, not for a minute, not even when Gram raised her whip.

Shoulda seen how her hand was bleeding when she took that strap away."

"It was merely a scratch, Willie. I had mistakenly hoped to deter your grandmother from ever beating you again."

"But when the whiskey's in her blood, she can't help herself. Heck, she didn't beat me nearly so hard or long this time."

Grant was impressed by the worship in the boy's eyes. Turning to Claire, though, he was stumped by the appeal he found in hers. What on earth did she expect him to do? Wrestle with the old lady himself?

"I was just thinking," he said finally. "As invaluable as Riley is, the man can't manage a decent shine for my boots. I don't suppose you know the intricacies of shoe polishing?"

"Beg your pardon?"

"I wouldn't be able to pay you in coin, at the start, but I suppose I could manage a payment in meals."

"Meals? You mean, like this?"

"I would include potatoes and vegetables. And if you prove industrious, perhaps even dessert. Cook has several other items in her repertoire besides the hot-cross buns."

Wiping his mouth on his sleeve, Willie leaned down for a closer look at Grant's boots. "Ain't nothing to it. I can have them gleaming like brass in two minutes."

"Splendid. Though I warn you, I wear anywhere from two to ten different pairs a day. Think you can manage the position?"

Willie snorted. "With my hands behind my back."

"No necessity for that. Very well, my footwear shall be placed by the kitchen door each evening.

Complete your task and you shall receive dinner, as well as the following day's breakfast and luncheon. Cook will see that you receive a schedule for the appropriate times.''

The boy nodded solemnly. ''And Fat—I mean, Mr. Riley, ain't he gonna be miffed about this?''

Without a doubt, Grant realized, but the devil take him. ''Leave Riley to me. I have ways of getting around him.''

His smile faded as he glanced into the corner. ''But it might be simpler to revise the arrangements for Gus. I daresay Miss Farnstable can continue to save her scraps, but it might be best for all concerned if you fed him on the sly. Outdoors, where Riley need not come in contact with him.''

''Of course,'' Claire said. ''Gus has recovered sufficiently to stay outdoors. Don't you agree, Willie?''

''Right enough.'' Willie jumped up, stuffing the last piece of ham in his mouth. Wiping his hands on his trousers, he extended one in Grant's direction. ''Wouldn't do anything to risk me new job. You won't mind, will you, if we say nothing about this to Gram?''

''Consider my lips sealed.''

''I don't care what the others say. I think you're a right regular one. Well, I'd best be getting along, before Gram starts wondering why the fire's not been laid.''

What others? Grant wanted to ask, but was afraid of the length of the list. Instead, he reached for the hot-cross buns. ''Here, take a few of these for your journey. I can't have my bootboy going about hungry, now can I?''

Like a squirrel, cheeks puffed out, Willie grinned his assent. Brimming with confidence, he turned to

Claire. "Well ma'am, now that everything's worked out to a peach, do you reckon you can still show me how to ride one of them fancy horses?"

Grant nearly choked on the bun he was chewing. The lady in question, as he glanced at her, seemed no less uncomfortable. "You're getting ahead of yourself, young man. Suppose we concentrate on my footwear for now, and think about the horses later on."

Willie smiled sheepishly as he edged backwards toward the door. Claire, Grant noticed, was doing likewise in the other direction. Feeling torn, not knowing which to go after first, he blurted out, "Wait! Both of you."

Surprisingly enough, they both did, with a jerking, almost guilty motion. "It's getting too dark for the boy to be about by himself," he said with his most encouraging smile, hoping to convince Claire to wait. "I won't be but a minute, so if you can spare the time, I'd very much like to speak with you."

From the way her eyes darted to the door, he held little hope that she would find the time. Not that he blamed her. Sneaking off on his new horse, stealing from his kitchen, running up unpaid bills . . . she must feel guilty as hell.

Walking Willie to his cottage, Grant chuckled to himself. All this time he had thought of her buried in her room reading, yet she had been battling with Ada MacPhearson, saving strays and hiding them in his kitchens. Just what, he wondered as he remembered her taking that fence, had she used to pressure his groom?

It had probably taken not much, he conceded. Look how she manipulated him into offering the boy a job. Uncomfortably, Grant wondered how to explain the new arrangement to Riley. The valet would be jumping up and down on his floor for a week. Served him right, Grant huffed defiantly, for doing such a sloppy job with his boots.

But it wasn't his valet's reaction that preoccupied him as he returned to the house. Considering the many faces she'd already presented, how would Claire act on their next encounter? Would that glorious hair be refastened to her head? The scowl firmly back in place?

He chuckled again. With a little care, he'd learned, he could coax a smile from those lips. Absentmindedly, he rubbed the medallion at his chest. Marvelous smile, that woman had. Marvelous lips. And perhaps, with just a little luck, he could coax a bit more than a smile from them.

All in all, he looked forward to testing his theory.

7

Leaning against the doorframe, Sam tapped her foot. She could as easily be waiting for Samuel, so familiar was the scene. She had been stupid, to be caught riding that horse, and then to charge in here, dressed so disreputably, because she heard Willie's cry. It was no one's fault but her own, this lecture. Stupid, stupid, stupid! So much for turning the tables on him. How could she hope to tempt the man if he treated her like a naughty child?

But then, Claire managed it all the time. She merely batted those long lashes, looked pathetically contrite, and in no time at all, had her would-be lecturer eating from her hands.

Practicing with her lashes, Sam decided this might be a perfect opportunity. Preoccupied with his anger, Hoxton wouldn't know what she planned until she had him too flustered to know what he was saying. Then she would fire her questions at him.

Smoothing down the front of her riding habit, she grinned as she considered the possibilities. The two of them, here alone—why, anything could happen. Let us just see who becomes the puddle now, Mr. Riley.

Hoxton strolled into the hall, halting her thoughts with her breath. He stopped suddenly, as if amazed to find company. He, who had asked her to remain. What a confusing, exasperating man he was!

Head tilted, he studied her. "I have this feeling there is more to you than readily meets the eye." His grin was likewise tilted. "Tell me, with what did you bribe my groom?"

Drat the man. Must he always catch her off-guard? Smiling tightly, she answered in her sweetest tone. "I'm afraid Todd had no idea I would take the horse. I often stroll in to admire your collection, but today the temptation was more than I could resist. It's been ages since I rode an animal of that caliber."

"I do have saddles, you know."

She smiled with Claire's honeyed charm. "Beautiful ones. But I'm afraid I'm not very comfortable on a sidesaddle and Todd would have insisted I use one."

"I must have a talk with him. Frankly, I can't see why women insist upon torturing themselves so. Take your cousin, for example. She does try, valiantly, but I live in fear of her one day sliding off the horse."

"It's the skirts. So difficult to manage a horse in them. I spent years trying to coax my grandfather into going against convention, but in the end, I designed this split skirt myself. So you see, I was not the model child at all."

As expected, his eyes slid down to view her handiwork. But though the invitation had been deliberate, her reaction was not. Claire could accept such boldness, such frankly admiring gazes; Sam could only tremble. To cover this, she tried to poke the pins back into her wayward hair.

"Don't," he said softly, grabbing her wrist. "I prefer . . . that is, leave it. It looks . . . nice."

Somehow, she had stopped breathing. When she tried to remedy this, the sound she made was a huff. Frowning, Hoxton released his hold to gaze at his hand, as if wondering how it had gotten there. The silence stretched.

Sam fidgeted with her hair. Claire would never let such a compliment pass. "What I meant," she said, tension making the words too stuffy, "was that I was wrong to take the horse without permission. It won't happen again."

"But it should. I want you to feel free to use whatever horse you desire. That is—oh damn, I feel frightfully stupid about this, you know. Had I the least idea you enjoyed riding, you could have accompanied Sama—Miss Eggersley and myself."

"Do you always apologize so profusely, Lord Hoxton?"

"Touche." He grinned. "But in this instance, what else can I do? Surely it must be a crime to waste such talent. Help relieve my guilt. Do me the pleasure of joining us tomorrow."

Us? Sam failed to picture her cousin sharing his pleasure. Just where would she ride? Tucked in the middle, with Claire sulking on one side and Hoxton ignoring her on the other? "In truth, I rarely ride. I haven't the time."

"Oh?" He leaned back on the doorframe, casually assessing, his expressive features dancing with amusement. "Tell me. Just what is it you do with all your time? We only seem to see you at dinner and the occasional breakfast."

We again. Wasn't that just how it was, he and Claire, indelibly paired? "That, sir, is my own affair."

That took care of the grin. The arms uncrossed, going stiffly to his sides. "True. Unless, of course, your affairs extend to my stables. Riding for your own pleasure is one thing, but teaching that young ruffian—"

"Willie is not a ruffian! And you're one to talk. You, who promised three square meals, just for polishing a pair of boots."

113

"Several pairs of boots."

"You quibble. Grand gestures are permitted only if made by yourself? Not that you seem to make that many of them."

"You don't like me very much, do you?"

The question surprised them both. He winced; Sam cringed. She wasn't managing this well at all. Flirt with the man; don't bite off his head. "I'm afraid I tend to say things without thinking. My grandfather swore it would be the ruin of me."

"Is that an apology?" He grinned, his face lighting up with it, and she couldn't stop herself from responding. He was no less nice to look at, up close like this. Enough to forget the many reasons that she should be wary.

"I suppose, though I'd say the antipathy is more on your side." She fluttered her lashes. "You rarely have anything nice to say to me."

"A thousand pardons, then, for the false impression. Just at this moment, I can think of a dozen nice things I might say."

Not bad, for a discreet compliment. Was the lingering touch next? Waiting for it, her midsection fluttered like her lashes.

"You're skeptical. How can I blame you, the way we banter back and forth? But quite frankly, you intrigue me. You must be the most complicated, unpredictable female I have ever met. And that," he added hastily, "was meant as a compliment."

He was so close, so beautiful, and his eyes seemed to swallow her whole. "I—I have a beastly temper," she managed at last. "I lost it when I shouldn't have."

"On the contrary. You should do so more often. Pardon the cliche, but you are deuced attractive when you are angry."

That did it. Any semblance of composure

crumpled. Her voice, she was distressed to note, quavered badly. "D—do you truly think so?"

Leaning closer, he brushed the hair from her face, trailing a finger across her cheek. "I do. Although I might as well admit to being partial to smiles. There, that's more the thing. While we're at it, don't you think we might stop this verbal sparring and become friends?"

Friends? Taking a mental step backward, she recognized the tactic. The man must think her a complete fool. What would a rake like Tony Rawlings have in common with a female like her? "Friends? Like you were with my—my Aunt Susannah?"

He muttered something under his breath. She thought it was an oath. "I've told you. I recall so little of those days."

"By choice?"

"I beg your pardon?"

"For a man of your resources, it seems odd that you would never try to recover your past."

He was annoyed. She could tell by the darkening blue in his eyes. "The doctors are quite adamant. The shock of remembering, they claim, might do more harm than good."

"And you've never questioned this? Don't you want to know what happened in Colorado to cause this amnesia?"

"Just what are you trying to say?"

In too deep, she decided to plunge ahead. "Samantha claims to have seen footprints in the snow. Two sets, leading to the cliff where her mother died. But only one set returned."

"You can't think I had something to do with that?"

No, she didn't. Looking into his eyes, she would have sworn he was innocent. "No. Of course not. I was only trying to help you remember."

"And I want to help you. We must get you out of that green bedroom, Miss Farnstable. I fear you spend too much time in it."

"Oh, no. I sometimes take walks to the village, and—"

"—and steal my horses, wrestle nasty old women, and turn the household upside down. Do you think if I were less lax in my duties as your host, you might land in fewer scrapes?"

"Why do I suddenly feel like Willie?"

His smile seemed to stretch from one end of that magnificent body to the other. "That seals it. You, my dear, will accompany me in the morning. That filly will be desolate without you. Yes, the filly. I watched you take that fence, you know. I doubt I know anyone with whom I could better trust her."

"I don't know what to say."

"Why not try, 'thank you, Grant'?"

"Grant? But I thought your name was Tony?"

"Well, yes, it is." He pulled back, jamming a hand in a pocket. "But I ask you. Do I look like an Anthony? Or even, God forbid, a Tony?"

The shudder, as well as the face he made along with it, made her laugh. "I must admit, every time my cousin uses it, I have the hardest time figuring out who she means."

"Exactly." With a hesitant glance over his shoulder, he gave a sheepish smile. "Do you think, though, we could reserve its use for when we are—er, just the two of us? The name's from my mother's, not my father's side of the family, and well, Riley is quite the stickler about such things."

"Of course." She returned his smile, perhaps more warmly than the part might call for, and when she added the 'Grant,' she realized she was positively purring.

One arm above their heads, he leaned against the

doorframe, his eyes again holding hers captive. His voice was soft and coaxing. "Do you think, then, that I might call you Claire?"

Tingling as he uttered the name, Sam wished she could lay claim to it. Coming off his lips, Claire sounded so soft, so desirable. Enviable, too, for as the real Claire Farnstable, she would have no need to fight this most delicious sensation. She could—and would—grasp the moment, not to mention the man, and make every second count.

Standing so close, it seemed impossible that he did not share the attraction. Deep inside, there should have been corresponding magnets, pulling them closer, until their faces were inches away. A thousand scents drifted between them, from both of the stables and the kitchens, yet Sam smelled, heard and saw only him. Though her brain listed all the nouns and adjectives Samuel would use against her, her body didn't heed in the least. It wanted him to kiss her, quickly and thoroughly, before an objection could be raised. She stared at that expressive mouth, silently willing it to approach her own before the moment was lost.

Something stirred in his eyes. She closed hers and licked her lips nervously. Careful. She must remain in control. Be the one to decide when and if they should kiss. First, she must tempt him, lead him just so far, and then leave him trembling in frustration. That was how Claire managed her men.

Cool and electric, his lips brushed hers. Pleasure rippled through her body, concentrating in and buckling up her knees. If he hadn't already encased her in his arms, she would have fallen to the floor. Stop him, caution warned. But it was too late. Passion now called the tune.

As if searching, his lips moved over hers, the contact sending sharp little spurts of fire through her veins. Dazed and weak, she clung to him. No wonder

Claire was forever involving herself with a man, she thought. Especially this one.

Engulfed in sensation, she abandoned all thoughts in the miracle of his freshly shaven face. Touching it with reverence, she had some vague notion of needing rescue, but she couldn't imagine why this should be so. His lips were an artist's brush, swirling colors and emotions, spiraling in dizzy succession to cloud her brain. Lost, and deliriously happy to be so, she felt his hands press into her back, tightening the pressure, easing her closer yet. She was swamped by the need to throw herself upon him, wildly, wickedly. With a desperation she refused to question, she lifted her hands to his neck. His response was immediate and dramatic. Another indrawn breath and his fingers were buried in her hair, cradling her head as he molded her against his taut frame.

He used his tongue well, sliding it along her lips, teasing, driving her to distraction. Of their own volition, her lips parted slightly. He answered by thrusting that facile tongue inside.

Stunned by so intimate a touch, she drew back. He breathed heavily, struggling for words. "Claire, I'm sorry. I—I don't know . . ."

Heels clicked behind them. Sam stepped back, crimson with guilt. It could only be Riley. How mortifying to be caught like this, yet again.

And then, much too late, she remembered. This was exactly what they had planned. Had Riley been listening, to appear the moment the touch lingered a trifle too long? Or did he merely wish to judge for himself if she were flustered enough? Stealing a quick glimpse, she caught Hoxton's scowl. Was the frown for his valet, himself, or—and here she cringed—herself?

She made a great show of consulting the hallway

clock. "It—it is l-late," she stammered, groping for dignity. "I won't abuse any more of your time, my lord, but I, uh, would very much enjoy a bath and since my, er, cousin's maid will be with her, do you think I might borrow Angelica to draw my water?"

While Hoxton stared with blatant bewilderment, his valet cocked the inevitable brow. "Certainly Miss Farnstable. She will see to it at once. If that is all right with you, sir?"

Hoxton gave an absentminded wave. "Yes, of course."

She squared her shoulders. She couldn't see why he was so flustered. She was the one caught acting like a ninny—Still acting that way. "I, uh, suppose I had best hurry, hadn't I? I mean, it's nearly dinner, and well . . . thank you. I mean, for the filly. For letting me ride her."

Knowing his eyes followed, it took all she had to leave gracefully. How positively humiliating, kissing that womanizer right there in the hallway where anyone could see. Did see. For there was no denying the triumphant smirk on his valet's face.

Once out of sight, she fled to her room. If only there were some place to hide from herself! She had let him gaze into her eyes and see how badly she wanted him. One skillful kiss, and Hoxton had managed what no other suitor, no other person, had ever accomplished. There were now cracks in the painfully constructed facade of Samantha Eggersley, openings through which the fragile inner being, so long encased, might now emerge.

But how on earth had he known she was in there? More importantly, what did he intend to do with the creature he'd unleashed? What did she mean to do?

Throwing her boots across the floor, she cursed soundly.

There was no denying it; round one had gone to Hoxton.

Nice ankles, Grant thought as he watched her climb the stairs. She carried herself well, with poise and pride, and she made it damned difficult for him to drag his gaze away.

"I must say, you were quite cozy with that woman just now."

Riley's leer nabbed his full, if irritated, attention. "Being cozy, as I remember, was your idea."

"Not at the risk of indiscretion. What is this about a new filly?"

"I meant to tell you earlier. I've acquired a new horse for Miss Eggersley. She had raised numerous objections against the mare Todd selected for her, so I thought . . . I decided she should have a proper mount."

"Then why is her cousin riding it?"

Why indeed? "When Miss Eggersley claimed she could ride, I mistakenly took her at her word. I have since learned that Todd knew exactly what he was doing when he put her on a tamer mount. Oh, for heaven's sake, Riley! Miss Farnstable is admirably capable. It is as simple as that."

But listening to the footsteps tapping on the floorboards above, Grant wondered if anything about the woman was simple. Quiet, unobtrusive Claire, who had an uncanny knack of slipping under his skin. Ears attuned, he heard the muffled slam of a door and pictured her letting down her hair.

Not once had she complained at that hideous room, had she whined about being excluded, her only entertainment long, lonely walks to the village. Solitary walks, in which he had a curious wish to be included.

"Miss Eggersley has been looking for you. Something about an appointment you failed to keep?"

"Oh, hang Miss Eggersley."

"Where do you think you are going? I am not finished yet."

Grant halted obediently, his irritation deepening. Was he a trained bear, then, told when to dance and when not? He couldn't even carry on a harmless flirtation, for heaven's sake.

Or was it so harmless? He thought of the way the gray eyes had sparkled at the promise of a morning ride, how ingenuously she had laughed at even herself. A good sport, Claire Farnstable.

And what a cad he was to take advantage of her. Her reaction to their kiss sprang from sheer innocence. A woman like that would never manage the sophisticated battle of sensual wills Riley expected them to conduct. That she would make the battle exciting, Grant didn't for a moment doubt, but unlike her cousin, who plainly understood the rules of flirtation, a woman like Claire would give her heart completely, permanently, before she gave her body. It would be kinder to stop this now, before it began.

"You're acting queerly, Barton. What happened? Did the woman say or do anything suspicious?"

"She held a gun to my head and demanded I spill all my dark secrets. What do you think happened?"

"Lower your voice!"

Grant was sick to death of his charade. It was a horrible way to live, always on guard, never himself. Except for those few moments with Claire. Lord, had he truly offered his name? To a woman who'd already warned him how she felt about liars?

"I want to know what you discussed, Barton."

"Nothing important. She was asking about Colorado and Susannah Eggersley's death. Seems

Samantha saw two sets of footprints going up to that cliff.''

"Nonsense," Riley scoffed.

Grant heard Riley pattering behind him and wished rather ungraciously that his valet would disappear. But the man hovered behind, trudging up the stairs, and Grant had an uncomfortable vision of Riley riding his back for the rest of his life.

"I am off in search of Miss Eggersley, to apologize for missing an appointment I cannot remember ever having made. Why don't you find something else to do? Unless you prefer to make the apology for me?"

Riley wore his smugness like a new suit. "If you were to glance at the clock, you would see that at this hour, Miss Eggersley is deep into her dinner preparations. She will hardly take kindly to being interrupted. Might I suggest, instead, that we repair to your suite where we might do likewise?"

Grant felt the now familiar tightening in his throat. It was a deuced uncomfortable sensation, being trapped and not knowing how to break free.

Stepping ahead, Riley held open the door, grinning like the cat cornering its prey. The thought of those hands touching him turned Grant's stomach. "You must have better things to do than buttoning my shirts," he growled, storming into the room. "I am perfectly capable of dressing myself."

"I have my job to do, Barton."

"Don't we all? I am serious, man. I wish to dress alone. To *be* alone."

As Riley assessed him, Grant refused to squirm. Better to show exasperation than this sudden urge to run.

"Careful, Barton, this is no simple game we play."

"Lord, is that what this is to you? A game?"

Riley flashed a secret smile, brief but dazzling, before resuming the stiff and somber pose. "All life is a game, boy. A giant chess board, filled with pawns to be moved at our whim."

"Ours, or Hoxton's?"

"Moot point. At present, they're one and the same. And I warn you, your king seems to be in danger from the opposing queen. Until you can divine her strategy, exercise caution. One never knows which direction a female will take next."

The man was insane, Grant decided as the valet finally left him. Was he doomed to be sorrounded by lunatics? In view of his own recent behavior, of course, he might be inquiring about the current rates at Bedlam himself.

Lying on the bed, he stared at the ceiling. Claire. What was it about that woman that had him alternately wishing to flee for his life, then wanting to bury his head in her lap?

Riley had called her the opposing queen. Did the man, with those hawklike eyes, see a trap where Grant did not? Then why, by all that made sense, did he insist upon pushing them together?

Remembering his impulsive offer of friendship to Claire Farnstable, Grant felt his uneasiness deepen. He hadn't been playing one of Riley's games then. He had meant every word. He had felt he could depend on a woman like Claire, could trust her. Couldn't he?

Damn Riley and his insinuations. Claire wouldn't know the first thing about his particular brand of chess. Innocence was written all over her face—and her body.

God, but he had wanted her. He still did, if this ache in his loins was anything to go by. All that hair, the sweet taste of her . . . . It was a heady sensation, being her tutor. She had already proven what an apt and eager student she could be.

His smile drooped, then vanished. Did he want the girl as a friend, or a lover? In his experience, the two rarely sat comfortably together. Nor, if he chose to be frank, did he and the prickly Miss Farnstable.

Besides, there was a little matter of deception here. He was not so far gone that he didn't know what her reaction would be when she learned of his part in it. A stickler for the truth, was our Claire, and while he might somehow be able to accept her contempt, how could he ever deal with the hurt he would see in those deep gray eyes?

Far wiser, and kinder, to let her be. Better to devote himself to the more accessible Samantha, to drown himself in the inane chatter, knowing the best would come when he shut her mouth with his own. Women didn't make good friends, as Amanda Beckmorton had so callously proven, and all doubts about Claire Farnstable's feminity had evaporated the moment he touched those lips. A remarkably jolting experience, that kiss.

Unconsciously rubbing his mouth, he jumped off the bed to dress. At this stage in life, he couldn't afford such jolts. He had more than enough troubles without adding an unpredictable female to them. Call me Grant, he had said. Grant Barton, of Newgate Prison.

He felt the chill engulf him. Hadn't he learned yet to trust in no one but himself? A sport she might be, but Claire Farnstable was first and foremost a woman. A woman scorned, everyone knew, hadn't an understanding bone in her body. One word to the right sources and he could easily find himself back where he started.

Out, out, damned woman, he paraphrased, and like

Lady Macbeth, refused to acknowledge that he might already be doomed to failure.

8

Central City, Colorado
April, 1861

Failure. How keenly he felt it, here where his dreams had taken root. Poised at the crest of the hill, his cabin in one valley, the mine in the other, Bill was reluctant to take another step. His leg was bothering him, just as the doctor predicted, but that was not why he hesitated. It was a damned hard thing, facing up to the mess he'd made of his life. About the only thing pushing him on was the memory of his daughter, standing where he'd left her, wondering and worrying.

And still believing in him. On that realization, a bit of the gloom receded. Sam might be a kid, but she was a smart one, with more soul than his father would ever have. She knew he'd selected those timbers himself, that he had used his own hands to erect them. The only reason she had let him go tonight was because she knew that until he inspected those tunnel walls, saw the breaks, he'd never stop wondering how the hell they had collapsed on their own.

No matter what they told him, or he told Sam, he knew Susie hadn't just stumbled over that cliff. In looking for him, had she seen something? Some*one*?

But who would do such a thing? Bill had few illusions left, but if he had such an enemy, the man had yet to introduce himself. Had Tony, in all his business schemes, crossed someone desperate enough to commit such a vicious, criminal acct? But why? Tony had stopped being his partner months ago. Lord, he hated these suspicions. They wore him down, and he didn't much like the man they'd made of him, seeing threats in every corner and mistrusting everyone.

Not liking his train of thought, Bill shied away along a different track. Thing was, everyone else insisted his deed wasn't worth the paper it was printed on. Since men simply didn't kill for a useless claim, there must be some other explanation. A less sinister one. As soon as the grief let go of him, he'd undoubtedly find it.

But to formulate any answer, he had to see the mine. He'd had sufficient schooling, been to enough mines in Cornwall, to recognize sabotage when he saw it. Sabotage? Murder? Obscene words, here in so peaceful a land.

With a sigh, he glanced back at his cabin, snug in a nest of pines. It wasn't grand, like the family home in Virginia, but it had its own charm. With those white puffs of smoke, the golden glow of lamplight at the windows, how inviting it seemed. He'd built it himself. The moment Susie surprised him by coming to Denver, he had stopped working his claim to cut those logs. He could still see his wife's delight, that very first day he'd brought her here to view it. Like a girl, she'd run down the hill, hair bouncing on her shoulders.

Willfully, he shifted his gaze to the left, where tall pines gave way to an alpine valley. It was this very dip in the mountains that had been calling to him in Virginia, those many years ago. Damn, there was gold there; he knew it like he knew his own name.

Straddling the two centers of his existence, Bill remained reluctant to approach either one. Beyond the cabin, he saw the dark patch of road winding down to Central City. That's where he should be going, taking Sam all the way back to Richmond.

Had it come to this? To ache to be going home, his tail between his legs, crawling to a father who would curtly tell him "I told you so" before putting him to work? "Idle hands," the man would taunt, delivering homilies in place of sympathy. No, he couldn't go home.

Breathing in the crisp, cleansing air, Bill let the snow's gentle rhythm work on his jangled nerves. Big fat flakes dotted his jacket, soothing him. God would live in such a place, he'd always thought. Sell this? Relinquish the dream for which so much had been sacrificed? Sam would never allow it.

Maybe the damage was minor, he hoped, setting one foot before the other. The model for the new smelter he'd been working on, to turn all that stubborn rock into profit-making ore, could still be sitting in the tunnel, waiting for him. By summer the Oh Susannah could be producing. The local miners would return and the "richest square mile on earth" would be humming with activity again. Bill Eggersley would save them all, prove everyone else wrong.

The wind whistled through the pines, making an uncanny, unsettling sound. It was perfect accompaniment, he thought bitterly as he slowly approached the mine through the drifts of snow. A requiem for a dead dream. Even from a distance, he could see that the only one who'd been wrong was Bill Eggersley—wrong for believing his luck would change, that fortune would ever smile on him.

The destruction couldn't have been more complete. Both sluices lay in pathetic heaps, their darkness making ugly scars against the snow. Up above, where the tunnel had once yawned, sat a pile of stone and rubble, so dense it would take an army years to clear it away.

The breeze wafted through the trees. Bill would have sworn he heard it sigh. Then again, maybe it was just the air he had released from his lungs. Nothing left. All that back-breaking labor, all the worries and fears, the hours stolen from his home and family. Defeat hung on his shoulders like a heavy load.

And there, far to the right, loomed the most frightening spectre of all. The cliff. The breeze whispered, beckoning him there, to the spot where . . .

Slowly, hypnotically, he answered its call.

9

Gingerly lifting the material from the tissue wrappings, Sam set her lips. This was mad. She readily acknowledged it, but she was tired of being ignored. He will notice me in this, she thought defiantly, holding the peignoir against her bare skin. Now all she need so was think of some way to "inadvertently" present herself to him.

She was only doing this to jog that stubborn memory of his, she insisted as she removed the last of her undergarments. Eggersley pride was at stake. She would show Anthony Grant Rawlings that she was not about to be stopped by a simple little kiss. No indeed, she was not to be stopped at all. Not until she had every last one of her many questions answered.

As she gazed in the mirror at the snowy folds draping her body, she suffered misgivings. She had brought the garment impulsively. It had been the only item in her grandmother's trunk that was not black or gray, but she had never realized how perfectly it suited her. All that virginal white was so colorless, it made her feel untried and unwanted. Twenty-four years of age and she didn't even know how to kiss right.

But there was color enough on her cheeks now—as there had been all evening, each time their host glanced her way. His gaze had been enigmatic, as if he could not even see her. Clearly, he still thought her invisible.

It was better so, she sniffed. A man like that
kissed hundreds of women. Women who knew how
to kiss back. She could picture him shaking his head,
wondering how anyone could reach her age and still
be such a ninny. She wondered the same thing.

She felt suddenly uneasy in the peignoir,
embarrassed. Just what had she expected to do?
Waylay him in the hall? "Excuse me, but I was
looking for a book and couldn't find the way back to
my room." Or did she plan to wait here, as if any
moment, he might suddenly tire of Claire and stroll
through that door?

The door suddenly opened and she gasped. Her
hand went to her chest to cover herself, but it was
only her cousin. Sam had time to register
surprise—she had thought the two of them would
settle down to a long, intimate evening. Claire
slammed the door with a bang.

She's in a snit, Sam marveled, though her cousin
took great pains to conceal the fact. With a weak
smile pasted to her lips, Claire strolled into the room,
fingering an item here and there in her slow, circular
route to Sam. Now what did she want?

Her destination won, Claire put extra effort into
her smile. "New nightie? Where on earth did you dig
it up? You look like Gramma."

"Don't you ever knock?"

"My, but you're grumpy tonight. We never used
to bother with such things. Whatever happened to all
our cozy little chats?"

You discovered boys, Sam nearly snapped, but
her eyes were arrested by Claire's own revealing
laughter. "Speaking of new clothes, where did you
get that negilgee?"

"Don't look at me like that. I paid for it myself. I
wouldn't let Tony buy something like this, silly."

"And where would you get that kind of money?"

"I used the money you gave me—oh!" Eyes wide, she covered her mouth with her hands. "I forgot. You wanted me to take it to the market, didn't you? I kept trying to remember what that money was for, and then I saw this, and well, Hannah—she's the seamstress—swore it must have been made just for me. It's awfully pretty, isn't it?"

As Claire twirled before her, Sam fought the childish urge to yank the blonde curls. Of course it was pretty. Did the girl wear anything that wasn't? Stealing a glimpse in the mirror, she wondered if she truly did look like a grandmother.

Claire prattled on about the sum involved, about the bargain that couldn't be passed up, but Sam barely heard. If she removed the pins from her hair, perhaps she wouldn't appear quite so staid. So safe and tame.

"I declare, wasn't Tony in the strangest mood tonight?"

"I didn't notice." There. Yes, much better. And if she brushed it full, out around her shoulders . . .

"So—I don't know, distracted maybe. I've never known him to miss a single word I said before. You don't think he has money worries, do you? Oh Sam, aren't you listening either?"

"Huh?"

Claire slammed the brooch she had been inspecting on the table. "About this riding. You're not actually planning on accompanying us in the morning, are you?"

"I'm sorry, what were you saying?"

"Tony said you would be coming with us, you and that dirty little boy, but I said no, Sam would never do that to me."

Sam slowly placed her brush down, her full

attention captured now. "And why shouldn't I go riding?"

"You are! I hate it when you spy on me."

Did everyone in this house think they were being spied on? "I'm hardly spying. You know how I enjoy a good ride."

"And just what do you plan to wear? That trouser thing? I hope you haven't forgotten you gave your riding habit to me. Hannah altered it, you know. It won't fit you any more."

In truth, Sam hadn't given a thought to her wardrobe. Grant had approved of her "trouser thing." Hadn't he?

"Why are you doing this? You won't enjoy yourself. All we do is laugh and tease and have fun."

"And what makes you think I wouldn't enjoy some fun?"

Claire made a very unladylike snort. "Because you don't know how. You'll give one of your glares and everything will be quiet and sedate and—and dull. *Boring.* You're only going because you're trying to be polite, like Tony."

"Claire—"

"Oh don't spoil it for us, Sam. Those rides are the only fun we ever have in this prison. The only time we can be alone. Wouldn't you feel uncomfortable, coming between us like that?"

Once more, Sam pictured herself between them, Claire pouting and Hoxton staring off into space. Much like dinner, in fact.

Only a fool would persist in thrusting herself into such an awkward position, or at a man who clearly had no interest in her. Vaguely depressed, she sat on the edge of the bed. There was nothing she could accomplish here. He'd never answer her questions, no matter how she pried or what she wore. She should just leave. She ought to be getting on with her search, and the next stop was Chicago.

"Claire," she began, "I've been thinking . . . we're not accomplishing anything here. Perhaps we should go on to Chicago right away."

"Chicago! But we can't! Any day now I expect Tony will ask me to marry him. He's all but declared himself. You wouldn't stand between me and my happiness, would you?"

"He . . ." Sam swallowed hard. "He's declared himself?"

"Well, as near as. Honey, how can he ever make that proposal if we leave so soon? You do want to see me settled and happy don't you?"

This was criminaliy silly, feeling so close to tears merely because Claire "thought" the man might ask her to marry him. It didn't matter in the least. It wasn't as if Sam would ever have him.

"Sam honey, are you feeling ill or something? You look dreadful."

"No. I mean . . . Actually, I do feel rather tired. It's been an exhausting day."

"And what a beast I am, bothering you so." Claire glanced over her shoulder, toward the hallway. Sam could almost hear the calculations. Tony, perhaps, would be more receptive to the charming picture she presented in her new nightgown. "Poor dear, I won't bother you a moment more. You have sweet dreams, y'hear?"

As Claire flitted off, Sam rose from the bed and began pacing the room. Was the girl imagining things? The man couldn't be fool enough to actually marry somone like Claire. But if he were, someone should warn him that he was chasing the wrong woman.

And what purpose would that serve? Perhaps his original intention had been to woo Samantha Eggersley, but chained to her mother's memory or not, Hoxton clearly had found a new face to worship. Claire might know little else, but she knew how to make a man mad to have her. Sam only knew how to make him mad.

Smiling sadly, she lifted up the ragged volume he had given her. It was ironic that she was all but living that play. Just like Marietta, she had stupidly let herself fall in love with the wrong man. Damion, blinded by the wiles of the scheming Rebecca, failed to see what treasure could be his. Until that fateful night he had stood beneath her balcony. Gazing up to see her silhouette against the moonlight, he had been suddenly struck with the painful truth. All along, he had pursued the wrong woman. All along, it was Marietta he loved.

As Sam mouthed the lines, the book fell unheeded to the floor. Drifting outside, she let the magic of the words overtake her, until she was no longer there in Hoxton's mansion, but on a faraway balcony, in despair of ever winning her poor, confused Damion from the Lady Rebecca. She could almost see him, down there below, dazed and bedazzled and wanting her.

"Your lordship," she whispered. "You shouldn't be here . . . ."

Entering his suite, Grant went straight for the brandy. He needed a drink. He felt as though he'd taken a blow to the head. Or the gut. Had there been something in that ham? Lord knew, Claire had behaved oddly, too.

But then, Samatha had acted peculiarly, too, and she hadn't shared in their raid of the kitchen. It had been Claire. How lovely she had looked with her eyes merry with conspiracy, her lips smiling her delight in the unexpected treat. Where, by all that made sense, had that delightful female gone? At first, coming upon her unexpectedly in the parlor tonight, he had been struck anew at how lovely and gentle she could be, his resolution about forgetting her vanishing into the air. But then Samantha had waltzed into the room, and Claire became the stiff-skinned Miss Farnstable, leaving Grant bewildered, disappointed, and feeling as empty as this glass.

Unbuttoning his shirt, he poured with his other hand. What was happening to him? Nothing seemed right any more. Or real. With an oath, he stopped undressing to take a gulp of brandy. Facing the library shelves, he thought of the day he had found her here. Was she curled up with one of her books this very moment, on the other side of that wall? So close, yet further away than ever?

She had been in an unflattering hurry to say goodnight. She couldn't have run any faster, trying to escape. Not that he blamed her. Samantha had been transparently rude. But then, he realized that had been the trend of all their dinners. Samantha taking the mistress' chair and with it, control of the conversation. She had been manipulating him, grabbing at him, as if their intimacy were a settled thing.

Like a caged animal on a wild summer's eve, he prowled about the room. Pacing from one wall to the other, he tried to erase the day's images from his mind. None of it made sense. Had he actually kissed the woman? Or had he merely dreamed it?

Riley and his absurd plots. Grant felt like the victim of some elaborate scam who still hadn't the least idea how he'd been hoodwinked. Somehow, someone had turned the tables until he now found himself lusting after the wrong woman.

It was this house; he was losing himself here. He needed fresh air, lots of it, to blow these cobwebs from his brain. Dragging a chair to the balcony, he plopped himself down in it and took a deep breath. How bloody typical, he sneered at the frantically chirping frogs. Here he sat, tortured by these hopelessly erotic fantasies, while everything else in the world mated.

He flung his glass at the noisemakers. After a slight splash, there was blessed silence. Yet, as the chirping resumed, he decided it was rather nice to know some things couldn't be controlled, even with all of Hoxton's money at his disposal.

He leaned back, letting the night work its magic. Swirling above the river, a soft haze shimmered in the moonlight, its distinctive perfume wafting up to soothe him. The fresh, healthy air seemed to have a hundred fingers, all massaging his brain. He drew it into his lungs, as if the earthly scent could save him.

Feet propped on the railing, he studied the dark, upwardly rolling Catskills across the river. There was something enticing about them. On the other side of this vast continent, he'd been told, there were "real" mountains, great, massive peaks to touch the clouds. A place where a man could battle the elements and prove himself worthy. Hoxton, for all his frailty, had gone there. In a spurt of envy, Grant wished for the same chance.

Like one of those dime-novel cowboys, he pictured himself climbing the rugged terrain atop one of Hoxton's admirable mounts, Britania perhaps, with the sterotypical sixshooters at his hips. And seated before him on the saddle would be a graceful female, a dark-haired, gray-eyed woman with long, slender limbs. He could feel every bouncing curl slide through his fingers. Should he pull one, ever so gently, he could tilt her head backward and slowly lower his lips . . . .

A soft click shattered the image. As the door on the next balcony creaked open, Grant held his breath. Definitely a dream, he decided, this wraithlike vision with the flowing hair. How could it possibly be Claire?

Behind her, the moonlight diffused into a silvery spray. Framed by it, her hair seemed to shimmer as it danced in the breeze. Her diaphanous gown billowed out and then draped her, revealing every alluring detail. Awed, he drew in a deep breath.

His mind couldn't accept what his senses told him. He was mired in a dream, it insisted. Any moment he would wake, the gray-sacked shrew would return, and he would wonder what the devil he had seen in her.

But no matter how he mentally shook himself, the vision would not go away. So he sat back in his chair and let himself admire her. A strange pastime, surely, for out of all the females he had known in his life, even those with whom he'd fancied himself in love for a moment or two, not one had ever inspired admiration. With such a woman at his side, a man could go a long way. All he would need was one of those gentle, warming smiles.

Intrigued, he watched her glide to the railing, looking down to the bushes below. As she shivered, defensively wrapping her arms around her slim frame, Grant fought the urge to vault the twenty or so feet between them. Lord help him, but he longed to use his own arms to warm and shield her, to erase that worried, almost haunted, look deep in her eyes. To take her chin in his hand, tilt her head back, and bring his lips . . .

"You shouldn't be here," she muttered softly,

and the sound seered through him. "Should Rebecca find you gone, there will be the devil to pay."

Rebecca? Edging forward, he searched the bushes below. He could see no one. Had the woman lost her mind, as well as her inhibitions? Yet there was something in the cadence, something familiar.

Of course—the balcony scene from *Marietta*. It was at this point that the newly smitten Damion presented the fragrant rose, comparing its softness to hers. "Let the devil take her, then," he would reply. "I would far rather take you."

At her gasp, he prayed he hadn't spoken aloud. "Good evening," he managed with surprising calm as he lazily rose to his feet. "Lovely night, isn't it?"

"My goodness, you startled me. I—I had no idea you were there. I didn't see you."

A cue the actor in him couldn't resist. "I am devastated, dear Marietta," he said giddily, as if the brandy had gone in a rush to his brain, "for I can see nothing *but* you."

On the other balcony, she struggled for composure. Outlined against the night, the seductive swell of her breasts rose and fell with every difficult breath. "How long have you been there? Oh, this is so embarrassing."

"Yes, it is, rather. I mean, here it is, the climactic moment, and I have quite stupidly forgotten the rose."

As she almost smiled, Grant's heart seemed to leap to his throat. "But you have other things to distract you, my lord. Rebecca waits; you must go to her. Give her your . . . your . . ." To his relief, she giggled. "But how silly of me. You don't have a rose."

"Hang it. From the scent, there seems to be an adequate supply of lilacs, however. I don't suppose you'd accept a substitute? After all, a rose by any

140

other name should smell as sweet."

"That, as you well know, is from an entirely different balcony scene. Besides, the Damion I know would ride to the ends of the world to find that flower."

Damion was a fool, Grant scoffed, fighting the urge to go down and forage through the garden for the unlikely bloom. "It sounds as if you know the play well."

"Every syllable. When I was younger, I dreamed of one day playing the part of Marietta."

Claire, an actress? The actresses of his experience were hard-boiled, reality-tested businesswomen, any of whom would make mincemeat of this girl. Yet, that this was as close as she would be likely to get to realizing her dream, talking to a cad like him across separate balconies, made him wish, more and more, that he could find that damned rose.

"I've outgrown the dream, of course. Except on nights like this one." She sighed, the sound cutting through his chest. "It's silly, I suppose, but it does seem terribly romantic, don't you think?"

He followed her gaze, out toward the river, and felt an odd contentment. "Yes, it does. You know, I love it here. Here, on this balcony. I guess it's the only place I can see past the trap I've built around myself. This house is . . ."

He glanced back with a shudder, then shook his head. There was no way he could explain. ". . . awfully ostentatious."

"Why live here then?"

If you only knew, he thought, and then prayed she never would. "Sometimes, no matter what we do, circumstances get the best of us. Besides, it has its compensations. Take this view. It's rather soothing, that river, even with those silly frogs. I sit out here most every night, and sometimes it's as if that chirping actually makes sense. Music, almost.''

"Yes, I know what you mean.''

"I thought you might.'' The words came out soft, barely audible, and when she laughed, he felt like a boy again, with the whole world before him—Scared and exhilarated at the same time.

"My mother used to tease me that I sang like a frog. I always thought I sang splendidly, but thinking back, I suppose I did tend to croak a bit.''

Strange, that he had never before noticed her voice. But then, with Samantha chattering in his ear, Claire's deep, rich tones would never reach him. "I find that hard to credit. If you sing half as beautifully as you speak . . .''

His words withered away as he watched her straighten her spine. "I see,'' she snapped. "You obviously think I am my cousin. Forgive me, I should have spoken sooner.''

"Dammit. I might be considered eccentric, but I have not yet reached my dotage. If I can't tell the difference between you and your cousin, Miss Farnstable, I deserve to be sent back to—to— London.''

He stared across the space between them. The physical distance he could surmount, but what of the lies he'd told her? He had this crazy urge to tell her everything, to hold her close and confide how he'd lied and cheated.

"I should be going in,'' she said quickly, her smile as weak as her excuse. "I hadn't expected to meet anyone when I undressed—er, dressed this way.''

"Wait!'' He wanted to tell her she looked lovely to him, but the words stuck stubbornly in his throat. What was wrong with him? Such an affliction had never struck before. Watching her gaze stray to the door, he sensed her desperation to escape. A nasty little pattern was being set here.

"I want . . . That is . . ." Good lord, what he could he say to keep her? "We never settled on a time for our ride in the morning."

The directness of her gaze struck him square in the chest. "I meant to explain at breakfast, but I might as well tell you now I can't go. I can't imagine what prompted me to say I would."

"What do you mean you can't go? Does Samantha have anything to do with this?"

"No." Another frantic glance at her door. "I—I merely realized, later that is, that I—well, I have nothing to wear."

"Oh, for pity's sake, what is wrong with what you wore today? Or have Hannah whip up one of those skirted things. She'd likely enjoy the respite from sewing for your cousin."

"Neither alternative is acceptable. Or proper."

His spine went as rigid as hers. Who was she to lecture him on propriety? "I suppose you consider changing your mind at the last minute more the thing?"

If she was confused by his persistence, he was no less so. Why should he care if she buried herself in that horrid room? Being enticed by the dreamlike Claire was one thing, but now it was back to the witch on her broom.

And then, just as he was arming himself, she turned those wide gray eyes on him, looking so like an injured, neglected child that he could feel her hurt as if it were his own. Damned if his heart didn't defy his brain by going out to her.

"Do come," he coaxed. "The outing will do you good."

"I know you mean to be kind, but truly, it would be best if I rode alone. My cousin should have a chance to ride Britannia. I have reading to do, anyway."

She edged back, leaning towards the door. Grant could feel the threads of his dream unravel. His voice was so tight, he feared it might betray him.

"How can you sleep in that room? You can't possibly be comfortable with all that green."

"It's not so bad. I've grown accustomed to it."

"Are you always so adaptable?"

"I am what I have to be, Lord Hoxton."

He was at the edge of the balcony now, all but leaning over the railing, while she clung to her door. He had the sinking feeling that he could squeeze his eyes shut with all his might and still the dream would slip from his grasp. He didn't know which irked him more—the loss, or the inexplicable need to recapture that vision.

"So it's back to Lord Hoxton, is it? I thought we had settled on Grant?"

"It's better this way. Why cause any more unpleasantness?"

"Damn!" His fist came down hard on the railing. "My name, if nothing else, is mine to do with as I choose. If I ask you to use it, then you bloody well—"

He broke off, as unnerved as she seemed to be. He laughed somewhat shakily. "My, but I seem to be in a beastly mood tonight. I suppose my feelings were hurt. I truly thought we were going to be friends."

Her fingers slipped down a notch or two. He watched, waiting, hoping she might relent. But her fingers resumed their position and he saw that she had no intention of even facing him. "I think it unlikely. There is no room in your life for a . . . a friend like me. At the risk of sounding poetic, I fear our paths will always remain too divergent to ever sustain friendship."

"Is that your idea of a risk? To be caught talking like a poet? What an exciting life you must lead."

She flinched. There was no mistaking the slight movement. "I repeat, I am what I have to be."

Aren't we all, he thought bitterly, wishing he could take the peevish words back. Yet even as he was formulating his apology, she was slipping through the door, its soft click merely adding to the reproach in her words. He stood there, cursing her and hating himself for not having the courage to call her back.

Pushing himself away from the railing, he muttered an oath. As much as he might have preferred kicking something, he contented himself with the over-loud commotion of dragging his chair inside.

Impossible woman. Rejecting him, Grant Barton, owner of a good hundred British hearts. He, the Don Juan of London's stage, had let the unpredictable fishwife make him look and feel the utter fool.

Damned if she wasn't right, though. They had nothing in common. He had plans for his life, plans that held no room for a "friendship" like that. The moment Hoxton released him, he would take his poetically divergent path and good riddance to her. He shouldn't be complaining; he should be rubbing his medallion in gratitude. A man might as well face the gallows as involve himself with a female like that.

Pouring another drink, he pondered the mystery of the word 'involve.' For someone who prided himself on always avoiding such a state, it was harrowing to think how nearly he had landed in the midst of it. Not he, thank you very much. He'd never allowed a woman to burrow under his hide before, and he was not about to begin now. Involve himself, indeed. With the unstable Miss Farnstable? He'd have to be out of his mind.

Yet he kept seeing her, soft red lips slightly parted. How he ached to explore them, delving in where she had been too untutored, too untried, to welcome him this afternoon. For as he had watched from the balcony, she unaware of his scrutiny, he had seen through her disguise. There was quite a woman under all that gray. Why, he wondered, did she insist upon hiding her?

A wave of intense longing washed through him. He could picture her, standing as she had the last few nights in his dreams, waiting at the door of their home—nothing fancy, a tiny cottage would do—her gray eyes lighting with anticipation as she watched his approach.

An overloud knock brought his loneliness into focus. Grant set his glass on the table to hurry to the door. Being who she was, Claire would have realized how rudely she had snubbed him. In her artless way, she'd come now to make amends.

His feet moved faster than his brain, his body not hampered by pride. It took him to the door, wanting nothing better than to pull her close and kiss her silly.

But it was not Claire. Samantha glided past with a smug smile, all invitation. Numbed, he let her tug him with her into the room. The wrong woman, his body insisted as those tiny, skillful hands caressed his shoulders.

"Darling, I know it's late, but I feel so dreadful about how I went on at dinner and I do so hate you being angry at me.

"The devil take it, Rebecca—"

The pink hands dropped. "What did you say?"

"Just an expression," he muttered as he lowered his mouth to hers.

A woman was a woman, he decided as the kisses

deepened, and quite frankly, he'd been too long without one. He would take what Samantha so clearly wanted to give and forget this nonsense about dreams. Claire, waiting at his cottage door? If ever she were, she would be clasping a skillet, aimed for his skull.

Smiling grimly, he steered Samantha toward the bed. Here was the adoration he craved, the eagerness he deserved. Only a fool would refuse it, and for what? A baseless fantasy neither he nor that fishwife wanted to fulfill? Sheer lust prompted these yearnings, and he knew but one way to exorcise it.

But when his tongue touched hers, both brain and body protested. Not the right feel, they insisted; not the taste he wanted. Not the right anything. He couldn't do it. Lord knew his body craved the release, but for the first time in his life, physical gratification wasn't enough.

Cursing himself for seven times a fool, he pulled away, mumbled some drivel about respecting her far too much, and all but shoved the girl back into the hall.

Damn you, Claire Farnstable, he muttered at her closed door as he slammed his own. You, and these unwanted dreams about you, can both go to hell.

On the other side of her door, Sam suffered similar sentiments. How dare he offer friendship! How dare he give her that long, sorrowful face, make her feel guilty for behaving as she had, when all the while he had been expecting Claire!

She blinked rapidly, tightening her grip on the knob. A good dozen errors she'd made this day, but there was no mistaking the smile as Hoxton opened the door to her cousin. His smile of welcome, of anticipation, had frozen the apology on her lips.

If Samuel were here, he would poke her in the ribs with his cane. "Where's your pride?" he would rant. Clearly, the man was using her. That kiss this afternoon had been planned, while tonight . . . What a touching little scene, the lonely little boy trapped in a world of hard business—but that had been only the actor in him, so skillfully playing his part.

A tyrant he might have been, but Samuel Eggersley had known better than to let emotion betray him. He had hidden his own feelings in secret niches where they could not touch or hurt him. He could have gazed at that pair, so blatantly lovers, and felt only contempt. They deserved each other. Claire was a slut, always had been, and Hoxton was spawned by Satan himself. Sam could be glad her lesson was so cheaply learned. It was time to stop snivelling, pack her bags, and hop on the next available train.

All very sensible, but Sam, fool that she was, would never be a Samuel Eggersley. After the reception Claire had just received, that marriage proposal took on threatening proportions. Were they making their plans this moment? Hoxton, the besotted fool, would leave the decisions to Claire. And she would insist Sam serve as her witness, wearing some silly pink thing. They'd expect her to stand on some monstrous altar, watching, smiling, as her cousin drifted inexorably closer, the Lady Rebecca leading poor Damion into the trap.

She couldn't stay here. Not one more day. Running to the wardrobe, Sam flung its contents on the bed. She'd go to Chicago. To Annie. She wouldn't wait another day, no matter how much Claire begged.

It was time to put the second part of her plan into action. She had arranged it all months ago with her childhood friend, Annie Singleton. Annie had begun

148

performing in the rugged mining camps of Colorado. To Sam, it seemed the ideal way to get herself to Colorado and fulfill her childhood dream of becoming an actress. When she'd written to Annie, her friend had responded with an invitation to join her in Chicago and a promise to use her influence to help secure Sam a place in one of the lesser known troupes, where her lack of experience wouldn't be a problem.

Yes, she decided, it was time to move on to Chicago. Turning her back to the balcony, she insisted that the last thing she wanted was to spend another day in Lord Hoxton's company. He'd already proven that he could give her no answers, only problems. And she had better ways to waste her time than spinning hopeless daydreams about Anthony Grant Rawlings.

After all these years, she was going home, to Central City.

Stroking his chin, Riley paced across the monastery-like room, deciding what to divulge in his next report. Sooner or later, he must tell the truth, considering the persistence the chit showed in prying information from Barton. That was an unsettling piece of news, about those footprints.

Ah, but didn't he love the challenge! His laughter rang out, echoing against the stone walls. They had quite a game going here. She was no match for him, of course, but quite diverting all the same.

All at once, he knew what he must do. Barton had been awfully cheeky this afternoon. Imagine his having the gall to order him, Riley, from the room! It would take the insolent pup down a peg or two to learn he'd been making a cake of himself over the wrong woman. What a pleasure it would be, watching his face when he learned who Samantha Eggersley truly was. Perhaps the girl's face would bear watching as well.

I do believe it is your move next, dear queen, he chuckled quietly. And I do hope you make it a good one; I would hate to see the game end so soon.

10

"What do you mean, you've known all along?" Grant felt the sun's heat collect beneath his collar. He wanted to punch Riley, right in his oh-so-smug leer.

"Had you paid the least heed to the details with which I so lavishly provided you, Barton, you would have recognized the real Miss Eggersley yourself."

"Details?"

"For one thing, height. None of that extensive wardrobe we prepared could possibly have fit Miss Farnstable. For another, I told you Samantha had brown hair, not blonde."

"You never mentioned her hair."

"No? Well, no matter. The damage is done. What we need to decide now is what you intend to do about it."

"Me?"

"Don't sputter. We're disappointed, Barton. You've made his lordship look extremely foolish. As a consquence, you must now repair the damage done to the Hoxton's honor and reputation."

Grant refused to sputter again. His *honor*?

"If the man's reputation was so bloody important," he blurted out, "why the hell did you wait until now to tell me about her?"

Riley shook his head sadly. "We had hoped you might unearth the reason she felt such a deception was necessary."

It was a good question, Grant had to admit. She

hadn't seemed the dishonest sort, but perhaps she was more of an actress than he had thought. Had she merely been acting out a role every time they spoke? The melting glances, that virginal kiss . . . was it all illusion?

No man enjoyed being made fool of, Grant Barton least of all. Battling the urge to jump on his horse and gallop off, he wondered how his instincts could have been so wrong. "All right, the damage is done," he snapped, wanting to end this quickly. "What am I expected to do now?"

"Continue as before. Delay the confrontation."

"What do you mean, continue as before?"

"Simple. You must lay the groundwork. Provide little hints. When you confront her, Miss Eggersley must be convinced that you knew all along."

Grant felt sick. If he went along with this, how could he complain about her deception? On the other hand, how could he refuse? Thwarting Hoxton, he had learned, was not a wise thing to do.

As always, Riley seemed to read his mind. "I trust we needn't remind you what is at stake here. For yourself most of all."

"What the hell do you want me to do?"

"I'd have thought that was clear. Discover her motives. Learn more about this preoccupation with Colorado. What she means by those footprints."

"Footprints, again? What aren't *you* telling me?"

"Try ot to be so dense. The girl's parents died in Colorado, remember. She is apparently deeply scarred by the experience. Unfortunately, these questions deal with a period Hoxton's doctors stress should not be resurrected for him. Therefore, you must convince her to forget that which neither of you can change. Use that oft-touted charm. Do whatever you must to see that his lordship's marriage will not be adversely affected by this ill-founded obsession of hers with the past.''

"You mean, lie to her?''

"Don't be squeamish, Barton. Didn't she lie to you? For all we know, she may be attempting to blackmail us.''

"What the hell for? She's an heiress, isn't she?''

"Was an heiress. The Eggersley Bank is in serious straits.''

"Why wasn't I told of this?''

Riley waved his hand. "It wasn't releveant to the task at hand. Rest easy; you weren't alone in being kept in the dark. Not even her fiance knows of her financial difficulties.''

"She has a fiance?''

"Do you ever listen to anything you are told? We were most concerned about that union, especially as it was fostered by Old Samuel himself. It was our hope that you might supplant Emery Blankfield in her affections. However, it seems Miss Eggersley has only been amusing herself at your expense.''

"Are we finished?'' Grant had heard enough. So there was another man. So she was amusing herself, was she?

"Yes, I suppose that will be all. Do take your time in riding back to the house. We want you to have ample time to absorb and accept all this. There is no sense in ruining everything with an ill-timed spurt of temper.''

"Oh, for heaven's sake, is that why I was dragged out here to the edge of beyond? To cool my anger?''

"Partially. Also, we run no risk of being over-heard here.''

"What the hell is going on, Riley? There's a lot more to this situation than you or Hoxton have told me.''

The man gave him a measuring look, then an ill-concealed smirk. Damn him, he was enjoying this. "Look lively, Barton. We both have our jobs to do. If you will excuse me, I have to report to Lord Hoxton."

Grant watched him climb into his carriage, hating him, hating all of it. So Hoxton was nearby? He could follow behind Riley, storm into Hoxton's room, and declare to anyone within earshot that he was sick to death of these games.

But Riley's smirk told him, as the carriage rattled off, what would happen if he did. Nothing would give his valet greater pleasure than to see Grant once again behind bars. To give Hoxton his long-awaited I-told-you-so.

So be it. He would go back to being Hoxton, but he'd be damned if he'd delay the "confrontation." Throwing himself on the back of his horse, Grant dug his heels into the animal's flanks and charged off down the road. If nothing else, at least he would have a few hours alone with her. As he saw it, Samantha Eggersley had some explaining to do. He had no idea how he would get this information, but whatever she told him, Riley wouldn't be there to hear it.

Sam poked the key in the lock, wishing she were miles away. On the other side of the door, she could hear her cousin and her maid arguing. Did they never cease? Jiggling the key—the dratted thing never worked—she wondered how long it would take the hotel manager to come up and complain again.

For the hundredth time since their departure, she wished she had not been so hasty in her flight. But when Hoxton and Riley had gone off together that morning, it seemed the perfect moment to make her escape. There would be no need for embarrassing excuses or explanations. Unfortunately, there had also been no time to make new hotel arrangements in Chicago, and the only room available was decidedly second-rate.

To her surprise, Claire had not renewed her objections to their early departure. Had she and Hoxton fought? Sam wondered. Whether they had or not, Claire had insisted on coming to Chicago.

The lock finally clicked. With a sigh of relief, Sam turned the knob. The door jammed. From the din inside, she knew neither Claire nor Giselle could hear her frustrated attempts to get in.

Annoyed, she put her shoulder to the door and gave it a good shove. This time it burst open, plunging her into a scene she might have preferred to avoid.

The commotion halted at her entry. Arms braced across her chest, Giselle stood glowering like a military general. Most of her disdain was directed at the red-faced Claire, who was seated in front of a writing desk, pen still in hand.

"I found her writing to Lord Hoxton," Giselle announced.

"Claire, how could you!" Sam exclaimed. "You promised—no letters."

"I warned you." Giselle used her most self-righteous tone. "This girl will bring us nothing but trouble."

"Giselle, please. Claire is my cousin; let me deal with her. Go back to your room and get some rest."

"I have no need for—"

"Giselle!"

The maid opened her mouth but Sam's stance warned her not to say another word. As she left the room, Sam felt a familiar throb at her temples. If only she could run and hide.

Giselle left an inordinate silence in her wake. On the street below, Sam could hear the horses clip-clopping, the shouts and din of the early evening traffic. She wished she were anywhere but here. For a moment she let her mind wander ahead to her audition. Incredible, that by late next month, she could actually be in Central City.

Playing Marietta, of course. The stage of the Montana Theatre would glow with a thousand lamps. As the audience waited with breathless anticipation, she would enter from the wings, a true actress, with all her mother's poise. And when she whirled, facing her Damion, he would have auburn hair, melt-you-to-the-spot eyes, and the face of an angel. He would take her hand and the audience would draw a collective sigh, sensing at once how perfect they were together. They would be stars, legends in their own time . . . .

"It's all your fault, you know," Claire pouted. "If you hadn't insisted on switching identities, none of this would have happened."

Not this again. Sam refused to let her cousin goad her into a guilty conscience. "You could have stayed with Lord Hoxton. I never expected you to accompany me to Chicago under the circumstances. I certainly didn't mean to ruin your wedding plans."

"But you did. How could I stay behind and explain how we tricked him? If only he'd proposed before he found out what I really was! You're all but ruined my life with your silly schemes. And now you won't even let me explain to Tony. How can he forgive me if he doesn't know where I am?"

"Don't worry," Sam said bitterly," he'll find you if he wants you. A man of Hoxton's resources won't be stopped by a simple disappearance. It's just a matter of time."

Taking the steps two at a time, Grant told himself that he couldn't wait to get his hands on that female.

Far from calming him, the thunderous ride home had given more time than he needed to think. His ears still rang with Riley's taunts. Amusing herself, indeed!

Entering the darkened hallway, he was spoiling for a fight. He didn't care in the least about the footprints Riley kept harping upon; he would ask the woman pointblank why she had lied to him. Her and her pious sermons to Willie. She wouldn't know the truth if it bit her in the face.

What a gullible fool he felt. To think he had felt sorry for her. All the while that he'd been fighting this need to defend her, the ungrateful wretch had been using that gray exterior as a shield. Riley was likely right there, too. She had been a spy, Lord, she made Amanda Beckmorton seem like an angel of mercy.

He stopped at the foot of the stairs, doubt niggling at his brain. Even in his rage, he found it hard to believe she could be as cold-hearted and calculating as Riley had led him to believe. He should at least give her the chance to explain.

He caught sight of a piece of notepaper on the mail tray. Sick inside, he snatched at it. What was this, the ultimate proof on the woman's insincerity? The final insult?

No, he protested, some perverse part of his nature refusing to believe she could be such an unfeeling coward. Surely the Claire—no, dammit, the Samantha he had known—would make her explanation to his face.

He fingered the paper, curiously reluctant to open it. First, he would have a drink. He called for Stoddard, reasoning that if anyone could restore a sense of order, it would be a proper British butler. He shouted twice, but the house remained oppressively silent.

Where the hell was Stoddard? Bellowing for a

servant, any servant, Grant marched through the massive hall to the kitchen. Somebody would do his bidding around here. He'd get an explanation if he had to wring it from their necks.

Halfway to the kitchen, he collided with Stoddard. Clearly, Grant was not alone in losing his composure. The man must have wriggled into his coat only seconds ago, for it sat most awkwardly on those frail shoulders. Furthermore, perhaps worse, there was too strong a whiff of brandy about him to pass unremarked.

Grant had time to wonder if all the world had lost its senses before Gus came bounding into the hall. He dropped a leg of mutton on Grant's already scuffed boots to yap eagerly at him.

Stoddard turned a deeper shade of red. "Er, good afternoon, sir. We had not expected you home so soon."

"Obviously."

"I—er, will put the dog outdoors at once."

Staring at the wreck that had once been his rock of a butler, Grant lost what little patience he had left. No doubt Miss Eggersley was behind this breach, as well. "Forget the dog. Summon the ladies instead. Ask them to meet me in the parlor within the hour."

"I beg your pardon, sir, but that is impossible. The ladies are no longer with us."

Grant battled several emotions, foremost of which was dread. If Riley had been displeased before, he would be absolutely livid now. "They're gone? Good God, man, how could you let them out of the house?"

"I was under the impression that guests, even female ones, are free to come and go as they wish."

Though Grant was vaguely aware that his butler should be taken to task for such sarcasm, he was too stunned to do so. Gone? Hoxton would have his head. Fingering the note in his hand, he wondered what lies it would contain. A dying relative? A sick friend? "All right, so you were forced to let them leave. Where did they go?"

"I did not ask."

"Then who made their arrangements?"

"Miss Farnstable dealt with everything, sir. Quite efficiently, too."

I'll just bet she did, Grant sneered. And without telling this poor old man the truth. For no matter what name Stoddard used, there was no doubting who did what. The thought of the real Claire making intricate plans was ludicrous. With all the money he'd lavished on her, he'd bet they'd had to drag her bodily from the house.

"Think. Did either lady mention a destination?"

As Stoddard eyed him, he realized two things. Whatever the butler knew, Grant would be the last person in whom he would confide. Worse, no one else would tell him the truth either. Having played the tyrant with such zeal, how could he blame his servants for enjoying his predicament now?

"Please," he pressed. "Are you absolutely certain that nothing was said? No messages left?"

"I quite forgot." With sudden animation, Stoddard dug into a pocket. "Yes, here it is. Miss Eggersley expressly asked that you, and only you, receive this the moment you arrived."

Grant stared at the second note, more bewildered than ever. Could it be that his first instinct was the right one? That Samantha Eggersley, the real Samantha, wasn't at all like the Amanda Beckmortons of this world? That she was basically good, intrinsically honest, and that this note was proof that she had the best of reasons for what she did?

Snatching it from Stoddard's hands, he compared it to the one he had found earlier. Clearly, he had made a mistake. The first note, with its strong, bold strokes was a request from a tenant farmer, perhaps, or an invitation, or—or, heavens, nearly anyone could have penned it.

His euphoria, fragile at best, withered as he scanned the lines. A sick aunt, just as he feared. The second note was possibly harder to endure. The curlicues, the heart-shaped dots over the 'i's, the distinctively heavy perfume; he hardly needed a glance at the signature to know it was from Claire. He didn't even bother to read it.

"You fool," he raged at Stoddard. "Are you blind? This isn't from Miss Eggersley at all. Didn't you see the name?" Stoddard's next words were dignified, yet dripped reproach. "Even had I the inclination to read your note sir, which I assure you I never did, I do not have ability."

Grant gaped at the man. Samantha Eggersley was behind all this, he would wager. How like her to make everyone feel either guilty or put upon, and then waltz away with casual disregard for the disaster she left in her wake.

"Forgive me," he said, moderating his tone. "I had no business barking at you that way. It's no excuse, I realize, but this Eggersley nonsense has me rattled. She lied to me, dammit. To all of us."

"Lied, sir?"

"For some reason, the women exchanged identities. I haven't the least idea why either felt such deception was necessary, but I aim to find out."

"She tried to warn me," Stoddard muttered, running a shaky hand through his thinning hair. "Whatever I learned, she begged me not to judge her harshly. She had her reasons, she said."

She could have stayed to explain those reasons, Grant thought with peevish resentment. Running his own hand through his hair, he exchanged a bewildered expression with Stoddard. What a pair they were. Duped by a heartless woman, their lives turned inside out, they both refused to believe her guilty. "Hell, man, where is that bottle you've been tippling?"

"B-bottle, sir?"

"It's a bit late to play coy, Stoddard. I could smell it on your breath the moment you walked through the door. Now I think we could both use a drink."

"This is highly irregular, sir."

"It's been a highly irregular day."

Their gazes locked for a moment, the look of one man measuring another. A reluctant, though no less pleased smile transformed the normally straight line of Stoddard's mouth. With a curt "very good sir," he led Grant to the kitchen.

After filling two glasses in ceremonial silence, he raised his like a seasoned professional and tossed its entire contents down his throat. Grant followed his lead somewhat more sedately, eliciting another rare grin. "Might I suggest, sir, that you read that note with infinite care? Miss Egg—Farnstable has proven less than discreet in the past. She would be the most likely to reveal their whereabouts."

With a low curse, Grant picked up the note. He should have thought of that himself, but then again, he hadn't been thinking straight since the whole abysmal affair began.

It took Claire several paragraphs of sheer nonsense to get to the point. When she eventually did, Grant wanted to fling the note in the fire. It was all Sam's doing, she swore. She would never willingly do such a thing, but Sam controlled the money, and his poor little Claire could only do as she was told.

They were not, as he had supposed, returning to Richmond. Instead, Sam was dragging her to Chicago, to meet a Miss Anne Singleton. Claire didn't know where they would be staying, but she promised to write again as soon as she could.

Though she continued for several more paragraphs, Grant had read enough. He turned to the butler. "I need to get to Chicago. Immediately."

"I beg your pardon?"

"Don't be dense, man. I need you to make the necessary preparations."

"Mr. Riley should do this. I doubt he would be pleased to have me usurp his position."

Damn, he had forgotten Riley. For some reason, it seemed more vital than ever that he speak to the girl alone. How long before the man returned? Hours, surely, for he couldn't hope to keep Grant's pace in a carriage. "Riley is elsewhere. I need you to fill in for him."

"Perhaps if I understood what it is you wish to do?"

Looking up quickly, he saw the butler's skepticism. Shared drink or no, Stoddard was reluctant to do anything that might harm Miss Eggersley. And until he proved otherwise, Grant was the enemy.

"I'm going after her," he told him, trying not to clench his teeth. "The real Miss Eggersley. I promised to look after her. I can hardly do so with her wandering about unescorted."

"Harm, sir?"

Odd, but when Stoddard said the word, it became real. Grant thought of Sam and those huge gray eyes of hers, and he felt an itching impatience to be in Chicago with her. "You know the woman. Forever landing herself in scrapes. We can't have that, can we?"

"Most assuredly not." All that moved was the butler's neatly clipped mustache. So the old devil had a soft spot for Sam Eggersley. Would wonders never cease? "I suppose I might manage something."

"I'd need to leave at once."

"I will do my best."

"I'm sure you will." Grant felt a tightening in his chest and denied that it was excitement he felt. He was going after the chit, dragging her back by the hair, if necessary. He was going to confront the real Samantha Eggersley, if it was the last thing he did. And to hell with Riley and his arrogant demands.

"Oh, and Stoddard? Thank you. For everything."

There was a tightening of his lips, which Grant took to be another smile, and then the butler was gone. In the ensuing silence, Grant had time to wonder if he had lost his mind. Was he truly sneaking off without Riley? Risking everything?

All he could see was huge, lost eyes, gazing up at him. He had to be certain she was safe, didn't he?

Something damp touched his hand. Looking down, he saw Willie's mutt. Feeling an embarrassing affinity with the animal, he leaned over to stroke the dog's fur. Like Gus, he was begging for affection he would never receive, following someone who clearly wished him lost. Dammit, she could have left him something, anything besides these lies. Or didn't she think him worth the trouble?

Taking a gulp of the brandy, he denied those feelings of betrayal. He'd been so careful, so miserly with his emotions. How could he, rogue that he was, possibly feel lonely?

"Morning, cap'n. Where's your boots?"

The gruff little voice snapped him back in the

opposing direction. Self-pity be damned. He hadn't been deserted; he'd been rescued. Sam was no better than any other female. She was worse. His pity should be reserved for the poor soul she was visiting now, for she was no doubt stirring up trouble there. He could not, did not, miss her chilly glares.

With a puzzled frown, Willie repeated the question slowly. "Your boots, cap'n. Can't be getting my grub if I don't do the work, now can I?"

"Oh, my boots. Completely slipped my mind. My lord, they do look rather scruffy, don't they? But it can't be helped now; they'll have to do. There's no time to polish them."

"But it won't take long." The boy's smile drooped, fading inward. "Oh. I see. You ain't satisfied with my work."

"Aren't satisfied." The correction was automatic, but as the young face fell another notch, Grant's conscience was bruised. He was doing to Willie what Sam had done to him.

But it couldn't be helped. She had seen to that. "Of course I'm satisfied," he tried to explain. "My boots have never looked better. The moment I return, I promise to personally deposit any and all footwear at your door."

"Yeah, sure. C'mon Gus, we don't belong here." Shoulders slumping, Willie dragged the mutt to the door.

"But wait. You haven't eaten."

"I ain't—I aren't no charity case. No work, no food."

So that was why the boy had been so happy to see him. It seemed that his pride, as well as his conscience, was taking a beating today. Grant had to admire the boy's reasoning though. No boots, no food. And lord knew how long those boots would be gone.

How had he let this boy grow so dependent on him? Sam Eggersley, that's how. One more crime to lay at her door. She had started this, then waltzed away with heartless ease. His anger fed upon itself. all that hogwash about responsibility. How many hours of sleep had she lost worrying about him? Had Willie gotten an explanation? A good-bye?

"Who said anything about charity?" Grant barked, angry at himself for not walking away. "Polish the boots right now. I can't be going anywhere looking like a tramp."

He sat down, wrestling with his boots and fighting a similar battle with his emotions. Damn that infernal female for disrupting his life! For leaving him with these unwanted emotions and responsibilities while she flitted off on some lark to Chicago.

"Here, let me help." Willie could have been his parent, for all the amused exasperation in his tone. "So. You're going to Chicago after her?"

"She told you where she was going?"

"Nah, I make it my business to know things." A grin crept up the right side of Willie's face. "Weren't hard. I went down to the depot and asked Old Herman where their tickets were for."

The boy grunted as the boot shot off. As he tackled the second, though, his grin faded. "Me, I think it's good you're going after her. I mean, why would she take off like that, without telling anybody why?"

So she had abandoned the boy, too, even knowing it was likely that he and his silly mutt would starve. "I imagine she grew tired of all this rural peace and quiet. She craved the excitement only a big city can give."

"Not Miss Claire."

"Wake up, son. Sometimes people wear masks.

The person underneath is not always the one they let us see.''

"Like you?"

"I beg your pardon?"

"At first, I had you pegged for a hard one. As tough to get into as this place of yours.''

"But you've changed your mind?"

"I can see you're just as worried as me. If she's in trouble, she's gonna need someone like us looking out for her.''

"Rubbish. I've never met a more self-sufficient soul in my life.''

"Like you said, sometimes there's more to a body than they let us see.''

"All I see is that she fled without looking back. I can't believe you don't resent that.''

"I ain't saying I wasn't hurt, some.'' As the second boot flew off, Willie landed on the floor with a thump. "I mean, I sure will miss those reading lessons she was giving me and Stoddard. But if you think about it, she don't owe me nothing. I ain't her kin. 'Sides, people are always taking off when you least expect it.''

A valid point. And if this chase went on indefinitely, the boy would likely starve without Grant's boots. Then he'd be drawn back into the petty theft that had brought him to Grant's attention in the first place. "Tell me, are you always this good at ferreting out information?''

"Depends.''

"Oh? On what?"

"On what ferreting means?''

The boy needed a tutor, Grant rationalized. A few lessons in grammar and deportment, and with that smile, those mischievous eyes, he would go far. Since the task had already been started, wouldn't it be a waste of effort not to finish it? "You don't happen to be free for the next few weeks?"

"Free for what?"

"There is the ferreting, of course, but then again, my boots must be constantly polished."

"You want me to come with you?"

"If your grandmother agrees."

The boy's face fell. Grant knew he should be relieved. Now that he'd made his offer, he could graciously, and without guilt, escape alone. "I could talk to her," he heard himself blurt out. "If that girl can wrestle her strap away, I daresay I can, too."

"Nah, I couldn't ask that of you. You're not one of Gram's favorite people right about now."

Too late, Grant remembered how Hoxton had dismissed Ada. Go there, and she would expose him as an imposter.

"I know," the boy said suddenly. "I'll get her to sell my services. Got a spare bottle of whiskey we can use?"

Chuckling, Grant roughed up his hair. "Willie, my lad, I do believe you will be a positive asset."

"Ass-it?"

"A bonus. I expect you'll be a great deal of help to me."

"You bet I will. I'll be your right-hand man. Or is Fats—I mean, is Mr. Riley coming?"

"Riley will be detained. It's only the two of us."

"Truly?" As if embarrassed at betraying too much emotion, Willie grabbed for the boots. As he did so, the dog gave him a lick. "Aw heck, I forgot about Gus. I guess I can't go with you, after all. I—I have responsibilities."

No doubt he would regret this, but Grant had gone too far to back down now. "What the devil. Bring the mutt along, too. Who knows? Perhaps there's a hound somewhere in his lineage.''

The boy flashed a smile so brilliant, Grant knew that he would not regret his decision after all. ''We'll find her, cap'n. But first, I reckon I'd best polish these. Hey, does this new job include meals?''

''It most certainly does,'' Grant chuckled, ''and God alone knows what else.''

Daunting, that statement. Did even God know what the wily Miss Eggersley had in store for him? This wild chase could cost dearly. It could lose him his job, the chance to find his past, and perhaps even his peace of mind.

So why do it? It made no sense. There was no use telling himself it had anything to do with the job, or some vague sense of duty to Hoxton. Nor was it even remotely connected with common sense. Something dragged him along in that wretched woman's wake, like a fish fighting the pull of the line.

Oh, and he was good and hooked. All those questions, dangling in front of him, luring him on. Important questions, that Riley would never answer. Was Sam Eggersley a frightened girl wading through a dangerous past, or a hardened adventuress looking for money? A great many inexplicable motives were involved here—Sam's, his employer's and not least of all, his own.

All at once, he felt a frantic impatience to be off. Telling Willie to polish the boots later, Grant hurried him out the door. He didn't want time to think things over rationally; he wanted—needed—to act. Now. Any moment, Riley might come racing across that drawbridge and all hope of ever again reaching that girl he'd dreamed about would be gone.

With an oath, he crumpled the two notes into a ball. Dreaming—where did that get him? Angrily, he tossed the wad into the trash, wishing he could throw his imagination there too.

Dreams, bah!

Storming through the room, Charles Riley hesitated at the whiff of a familiar scent. Perfume had dripped off the silly chit, she used so much of it. He sneered.

The sneer faded as his brain jumped to the logical conclusion. Claire Farnstable would never waste her time in a kitchen. Tracking the scent down, he saw the bright white wad on the top of the trash.

He tried hard not to laugh. There was no sense celebrating until he was certain. But as he smoothed the creases of the heavily scented note, the corners of his lips began to rise. Thank heavens for stupid women.

Barking for Stoddard, he stuffed the notes into his shirt. Chicago, eh? Anne Singleton? Not a good move, my queen. I have the Hoxton resources behind me. Don't you know how easily I can find you?

11

Central City, Colorado
April, 1861

Bill stood at the edge of the cliff. How easy it would be to slip, he thought. One quick motion and he could let go of this aching loneliness, leaving the burden of failure on someone else's shoulders.

Sickened by his thoughts, he leaned against a rock well away from the cliff. After the bank had foreclosed on his house, poor Pat Singleton had taken a gun to his head. Bill remembered Susie's anger, as she sat rocking his daughter in her arms. She had wanted to give up, too, did poor little Annie, but Susie wouldn't let her. She'd stayed up all night, convincing the girl that life was glorious, that it was an adventure to set her sights on a dream worth pursuing, and then to have fun skirting around the obstacles life set in her path. Nothing got done with self-pity, Susie would have said. Your destiny lies in your dream, so you might as well go out and follow it.

Turning away from the cliff, Bill was shamed by the memory. Heck, Annie was barely older than Sam, yet she hadn't given up. He'd heard she was making a name of herself in the local theater circuit. If a mere child could make sense of a busted life, a grown man could do no less.

His gaze was caught, and then trapped, by the ugly shack in which he'd stowed his tools. Funny it should be the only thing still standing. Back braced against the side of the mountain, it stood out amongst the white rock like a dirty mule—short, squat and determined not to budge an inch. Bill smiled grudgingly. They had a great deal in common, he and that shack. Right down to the rickety appendages.

Gazing around the site, his heart swelled with pride. It might be hopeless, yes, but wasn't it his? It was his dream and his destiny. How could he ever let it go?

Half smiling, he moved toward the shack. The wind had picked up some, he noticed. It was whistling now, making a body cold enough to shiver. His mood shifted and he felt as if that hunch had crept up to touch his shoulder. "Don't go in the shack," the wind whispered.

Superstitious nonsense. As if he could go in, anyway. The place was locked. He'd secured it himself, that long-ago day before he'd gone in for that last look at his smelter. The key sat home in his top dresser drawer.

Yet he kept approaching, as if he could clap his hands and say "Open Sesame" to it. As if he could just turn this knob . . .

It opened easily in his hands. Was this his destiny, then, to go inside? His fingers seemed frozen to the knob, the sense of foreboding stronger than ever.

Something *was* wrong. It wasn't just the knob; anyone could have jimmied the lock any time in the past. But the thing was, he'd all but needed a crowbar to gain entry in the past. Today, the door swung open with silent ease. Bill shivered again. He thought he felt a draft, but it could as easily be nerves.

Removing his snowshoes, he rubbed his bad leg. He should rest it; he didn't want it seizing up on him. Not in the dark, though. The way that wind was whistling . . .

His fingers groped along the shelf he'd kept the lanterns on, to find only dust. Damned vandals, was nothing sacred? Digging into his pocket, he found and lit his next-to-last match. It hissed into the darkness like a snake.

The match burned his fingers before it burned itself out, but the light produced vital, if meager, impressions. A sole lantern sat on a table in the center of the room, and behind it, stretching along the far wall, hung a massive black curtain. It rippled slightly, and Bill shuddered. Every instinct he owned shouted for him to get out of there.

But he was an Eggersley, stubborn and proud. This was his shack, his land. Nobody else on this earth had a better right to be on it. Certainly not to erect a curtain of those proportions to . . . to do . . . what?

Hobbling through the dark, he went straight to the lamp. He spent his last match on it, but soon a golden glow spread over the room. Like Pandora approaching her box, he inched toward the black curtain, half hoping someone would burst through the door to stop him.

Coward, he swore at himself as he yanked the cloth aside. Expecting an entire gamut of horrors, he was taken aback by the somewhat prosaic hole in the hillside that he had revealed.

Bewilderment delayed his acceptance of the obvious. Braced by beams for as far as his light could reach, a tunnel loomed into his mountainside. As the whys and wherefores came clear in his brain, his feet carried him forward. He was inside and walking forward before he could reconsider.

It was hard not to be impressed by the size of the thing, tall enough for a man of even his size to walk comfortably upright and wide enough for a pair of him abreast. It had been four months since his accident, possibly enough time for a healthy crew of men to blast through this rock. But as the passage stretched deeper into the mountain, here and there branching into the direction of his own diggings, he knew a good year would be required. They must have come digging in from the other side of the mountain. With all the blasting going on back then, he'd never have noticed.

But he would have noticed when they hooked into his claim. Was that why his tunnel walls had collapsed? he wondered in a daze—to stop him from noticing?

He paused at a fork in the shaft. As if to mock him, laughter echoed eerily against the stone. Not singular laughter, but vastly in the plural. Bill stopped in his tracks. If he continued along this branch, toward that laughter, God alone knew what he might find.

He took it nonetheless. Creeping forward, he broke into a nervous sweat. He should take off his jacket. Best be prepared, in case it came down to a fight. Slinging the coat over his arm, he took a deep breath and pushed himself forward. He had no wish to brawl, but he couldn't go back until he had proof enough to show the sheriff.

Rounding the second curve, he found his proof. Blasted from the rock, *his* rock, was a room the size of an army barracks. Locked behind a heavy iron gate, gathered about a pot-bellied stove playing cards, sat an army of men.

Shielding the lamp behind him, Bill slid closer. He recognized the dialect from his university days. It was a business, locking these poor Cornish devils underground. It was the only way to keep a major claim secret, some mine owners maintained, but Bill could never believe anyone could be that cold-hearted. Not until now.

GOLDEN DREAMS

But his pity was lost to a sense of betrayal. Not four months hence, these men had huddled about his stove, gambling away the wages he had paid. Now, someone else was doing the paying, and judging from the impressive rack of tools, the shelves lined with provisions, they must be doing so handsomely. He knew these men would not be sitting so calmly, locked away from their families, without the promise of riches to sustain them.

Yet, as angry as he was, Bill couldn't find it in his heart to blame them. With so many mouths to feed, a man couldn't be waiting around for the boss's bum leg to mend. Not with a carrot the size of this being wagged beneath his nose by another man.

Though he itched to rush in and demand the man's name, Bill knew he had to get out of there. Alive. There was no sense trying unnecessary heroics. He'd let the law deal with it. In his mind, only that mysterious Mr. Bavoure and his unknown backers could be behind this. Why else would they have bought up all the neighboring property? Obviously, they meant to seal up the operation, tight and secure.

Even if it meant murder.

12

How does anyone manage in these big cities? Sam wondered as she stepped from the curb to cross the street, nearly being run down by a cabby who shook a fist at her as she jumped back. It could take hours to wade through this traffic to Annie's hotel. If she missed her audition with Jack Langrishe, what would Annie suggest she do? Start her own troupe?

With a half grin, Sam bullied her way back into the street. Gumption. According to Annie, nothing got done on this earth without it. Gumption got you what you wanted. Discretion, propriety, duty—those virtues had their place in a neat and tidy world, but if your world tilted, you had no one to rely upon but yourself. To unlock the past, Sam must depend on pluck, not luck.

"Sam, there you are! Oh my, you certainly are—gray . . . ."

Blinking, Sam stared at Annie's revealing burgundy silk and lace frock. "I'm afraid everything I own is gray."

"And you look lovely in it. Be a love and hail a cab. I want to leave word at the desk where I can be reached."

As Annie rustled away, Sam turned to the busy street and gulped. How did one go about hailing a cab? Shake a fist of her own? Or step in front of the horse?

"Gumption," she could hear Annie say. Stepping

to the curb, she raised a hand to call to a passing cab. The miserable thing sped past. She was ready to admit defeat after three more attempts, when a hand clamped down on her shoulder. She wheeled to face burgundy silk.

"My goodness, Annie, you startled me."

"Any luck?"

"I was thinking. It's such a nice day, why don't we walk?"

"Your grass roots are showing, sweets. No one walks in the city if there's a cab around. Besides, I'm not about to hike clear across town just so you can stall your audition."

"I'm not stalling. You said the theater was a block away."

"Whoa, I was just teasing. Did that grandfather of yours take your sense of humor away, too?"

"I'm sorry. My nerves seem to be over-stretched."

"Don't you go apologizing again. Not to me. Not when my news is just gonna stretch those nerves tighter. I'm afraid there's been a change in plans. Jack won't be auditioning you because the Montana Theatre burned down. The whole town near did."

Burned? Going back to the Montana in Central City had been part of the pilgrimage. Sam could still picture every detail, just as it had been when she had sat backstage watching Mama weave her spell. That's when it had been born, this dream to create a little magic of her own.

". . . will do just as well," Annie was saying. "though I'll grant you, Cyrus isn't half so good looking."

"Cyrus?"

"Cyrus Wynecote. He won't for a minute admit how desperate he is, but don't let his blustering fool you. With his train leaving at four o'clock, he must complete his troupe in the next few hours. Wait a minute. I see a cab."

Sam stopped listening to glance at her watch. There was so much to do and too few hours to get Claire packed, convinced, and onto a train to Richmond. It couldn't be done.

But Annie had already grabbed a bellhop and was gesturing to the street. Clearly, that was how to hail a cab. Sam should have known better than to flag one down herself. Heavens preserve her, how would she manage on her own?

Her anxiety deepened as it became apparent that not even Annie was invincible. The more empthatic her gestures became, the more the man shook his head and pointed inside the hotel. Any moment, Sam feared, those gestures might come to blows.

She saw a cab pull to a stop on the other side of the street. Hoping to end the threatening scene, she took advantage of the lull in traffic to go and hire it.

Part of her saw it move forward, but another part saw an irate Annie step into the street. The cab picked up speed. Sick inside, Sam knew what would happen. She propelled herself forward, and as her weight slammed into the actress's shoulder, they toppled to the ground together. They landed hard, the wheels narrowly missing their feet as the cab sped away.

Annie stood up again immediately, shaking her fist. "Where did you learn to drive," she shouted after the cab. "Hicksville?"

Sam couldn't move. Her heart, she felt certain, must be embedded in her ribcage. It was thundering so, she could barely hear Annie's grumbling.

"It's criminal to let such a dolt on the road. You all right?"

Taking the offered hand, Sam said she thought so,

but Annie was already off to test their luck again. Planted in the center of the road, she held up a hand. Sam eyed the curb with longing, thinking that Richmond had never before seemed so like home.

"Are you coming?" Seated in a cab, Annie's black eyes danced with mischief.

"How can you smile? That cabby tried to kill you."

"Me?" As Sam climbed in next to her, Annie chuckled. "Oh, honey, this sort of thing happens all the time in the big city. Consider it one of the hazards of modern life. Speaking of which, I can't believe how quickly this town recovered from the fire."

"There was one here too?"

"Town-burning seems to be an epidemic these days. This one was so bad, folks swore Chicago would die. Hard to believe now, the way the buildings are going up, but you should have been here in '71. I was scheduled to play here that October, but the theater was just a pile of bricks. The whole town looked like a cemetery. Dead stone for as far as the eye could see. You'd never know to look at it now, would you?"

Gaping at the tall buildings, Sam agreed. Solid and secure, these ornate structures could have been there for centuries.

"They blamed it on a cow. Claimed no self-respecting Chicagoan would be stupid enough to knock over a lantern in a barn full of straw. You've got to give them credit for spunk, though. Before I left town, they'd already hauled the stone in from the quarry over in Joliet. Never missed a day of business."

"All these buildings are new?"

"All except where we're going. The fire never touched across the river."

Following Annie's outstretched finger, even at that distance Sam could see the stamp of the less prosperous side of the river. There were graceful buildings there. Dark, squat wooden structures huddled together, unable to shake off an air of abandonment. Naturally the fire had shunned that part of town. They might be prudent to do likewise.

Annie read her thoughts. "Sorry. I guess Cyrus isn't quite a Jack Langrishe. But if it's getting to Colorado that you want, he's your best shot."

As they stopped before a tottering remnant of a theater, Sam wondered about that. She had a nasty suspicion that this was but the first of many dilapidated structures in which she would perform. Not quite the stuff of which dreams were made.

Still, she kept her doubts to herself. Annie had worked hard to arrange this and Sam wasn't one for complaining, no matter how unlike her fantasies this might be.

"Coming?" The black eyes held an amused glint. "Trust me, it's better to get it over and done with."

"I know, but . . ."

"No buts. You're a natural. You have one of the most intriguing voices I have ever heard. Cyrus will be scratching his beard and wondering what made him so lucky."

"But . . . Oh, Annie, I can't help it. I keep thinking of what my grandfather would say. Or the people back in Richmond."

"The very same people who looked down their noses at a sweet and loving actress named Susannah Myers? Your mama didn't let their shortsightedness stop her."

"Mama didn't have to live with them."

"Neither do you. Honey, there's a whole world out there. Go out and enjoy it. Unlace the old corset and set yourself free. That's what your mama would say. She told me I was wasting time, moping and feeling sorry for myself. If I dreamed of being an actress, she said, nobody but me could make it come true. The trick was to follow my heart"—

"—but letting your head lead the way. I know. She said the same to me."

"There you go, then. A smart lady, your mama, and I sure am happy I followed her advice. Did you ever think, back in Central City, that your playmate would grow up to be a big-time actress?"

"Remember how being actresses was our favorite pretend game? You were so good at it. I always thought that if anyone could be one, like Mama, it would be you."

"And here I always thought you would. Ain't it funny how life works out? After all this time, you're getting your chance, too. Question is, are you going to take it or are you gonna keep making excuses?"

"I guess you're right." The smile spread slowly across Sam's face. Linking Annie's arm in her own, she propelled them toward the theater. "Let's go, then, and corsets be damned."

Annie's approving grin buoyed her for the few seconds it took to enter the building, but it took less than a minute for the gloom inside to infect them both. Stirred by the breeze, litter of every imaginable sort danced in through broken window panes to line the walls. They sidestepped it to read a tattered sign warning that the theater's days were numbered. Sam prayed the structure would remain upright for the brief time they required it.

At a touch, the inner door squeaked, then flew flat against the opposite wall. A hollow echo was quickly lost in the cool darkness. As they inched forward, papers clung to their feet, fighting the tug of the wind. Sam felt the tiniest shudder pass from Annie's arm to her own. She answered in kind. Arms linked, they made their tentative way down the aisle.

A single lamp flickered on the stage, a good fifty miles away. "Mr. Wynecote," Annie tried, her voice scratching at the dark. "Are you here?"

Few seats remained in the large auditorium. One of these squeaked, like the door, as a portly gentleman with a massive brown beard rose to greet them.

Sam's remaining optimism died as he scrutinized her with a frown. "This her? Gad, Annie, but she's a skinny thing. Didn't I make myself clear? I need a woman with color. Someone with a little meat on her bones."

"Pooh." Breaking away, Annie tossed back her head. "You already have more cows than the state of Texas. Look at her. She'd be perfect for the Principal Boy in your pantomimes."

Principal Boy? Pantomimes? Sam searched her cluttered brain. Were they dramas? No, now she remembered. They were musical comedies, where men often played women and women played men. Samuel would squirm in his grave. An Eggersley, his heir, carrying on in trousers on some sleazy stage?

"I don't know," Cyrus whined, echoing her own doubts. "How can I do musicals if I don't have a leading man who can sing?"

There went another dream. Annie continued to argue, but a resigned Sam walked up to the stage. Looking out at the empty seats, she felt the full stab of disappointment. How close she had come this time, only to learn, again, that dreams don't really come true. If they did, she wouldn't be here at all, but back in New York, with—

"Don't just stand there," Cyrus suddenly barked. "Let's see what you can do."

Flustered, she turned to Annie. At her nod, a rush of stage fright clogged Sam's throat. Seeing this, bless her heart, Annie spoke for her. "Miss—Malloy will perform the love scene from *Marietta*. First she will sing the solo, and when Damion enters, I will read his lines to her."

They had acted this scene a hundred times, yet Sam could remember none of it. This side of panic, she caught the sneer on Wynecote's face. Her grandfather had worn the same insulting expression when delivering his "women belong in the home" speech.

She found her voice. She would show him, show all of them, that she was capable of more than being Samuel's puppet. "I wonder," she began a bit woodenly, gradually sliding into the role, "if he will ever know how I truly feel . . . ."

Listening in the darkness, Grant remembered the day he had first stepped onto a stage. They had called him skinny, too, had glared with the same hostility. Poor Claire—no, Sam. Oh, damn, how could he possibly feel any sympathy for her, after the chase she'd led him? If Claire's note hadn't mentioned Annie Singleton, he'd never have been able to trail them hee to this middle-of-nowhere. It had cost a small fortune in bribes, just so he could gaze up at that stage and wish himself a million miles away.

Seeing her again, he realized how unprepared he was for Riley's aptly-termed "confrontation." If she were to shout, or worse, snub him, others would hear. Better to return to his hotel and wait for an opportunity to get her alone.

As he went for the door, Miss Singleton began to speak. He stopped in his tracks. Sam meant to audition with a complex role like Marietta? He turned to watch them, wondering what sort of friend would let her make such a fool of herself. Then again, perhaps Anne Singleton knew this was the only way to convince the stubborn wretch to remove her head from the clouds. A quick, swift blow, with only three to witness her shame. Four, if they caught him hiding in the shadows.

Which they would not. He was at the door, inches from escape, when the strident voice attacked the dark. He cringed. She sounded more like an irate schoolmarm than the young, blossoming Marietta. Oh good lord, was she going to sing?

Against his will, he turned to the stage, squinting as he silently coached her. *Relax*, he pleaded. Let your emotions out, Sam. Let them show. Think of someone you care about and sing your love to him.

And somehow, he would never afterwards remember how, she got to him again. She spun her magic so tightly that his feet were rooted to the spot. As the stridency melted into a soft, clear lament, its poignancy tugging his own emotions into play, he heard the frogs chirp. Around him, he felt the velvet caress of a summer night, smelled the sweet, intoxicating fragrance of the rose clasped in his hand. Before the song was done, he was the cocky Damion, happy to humble himself at her feet.

Vaguely aware of passing Miss Singleton, whose jaw dropped open in a most unattractive way, he strode down the aisle. He leaped up onto the stage, his eyes on Marietta alone.

Her surprise and embarrassment proved that she had been singing to him. He could feel it. He could see it in her wide, bewildered eyes.

Grinning, Damion took his time, using his voice, and a circuitous approach, to seduce her. Playful banter, his words and hers, but the heat rising between them was in delicious earnest. Electricity sparked. He could taste the tension as Marietta reached up to touch his cheek. "Don't you see," he rasped as he brought her fingers to his lips. ''I love you.''

And then he leaned closer, the moment right, his need drawing her trembling body tight to his chest, and as his lips paused, inches from branding her as forever his own, a rude, commanding voice bellowed out for him to stop.

''I say, sir, who do you think you are, barging into our audition this way?''

Grant cursed, far too audibly, as he realized what he had done. Sam gaped at him with those huge, luminous eyes, as if she, too, had been too rudely jolted back to reality.

She drew in a ragged breath. She seemed to shrink behind the gray mask, eluding him once again. ''Damn,'' he repeated, the oath this time muffled by the fat man's grumbling.

''I will not have your fans disrupting this audition, Miss Malloy. Dismiss him at once. Why, one would think you were married, the way he was groping at you.''

Grant knew his jaw must be as slack as Miss Singleton's had been. Miss Malloy? Sam Eggersley seemed to change identities the way other women did their wardrobes. With a tight smile, Grant reorganized his emotions. Two could play this game.

''My silly darling. Didn't you forget to mention I would be joining you? I know I'm a trifle late, but we're a team, now that we're wed. I'd never make you attempt an audition alone.''

Sam now gaped at him, mouth opened, which tickled him no end. Tackling his new role with relish, he strode forward with hand extended. ''Barton's the name. Grant Barton.''

There was suspicion in the gaze directed at his hand. ''Not by any chance *the* Grant Barton, of the

Britania Theatre? The one arrested for pinching some lady's diamonds?''

Grant stumbled, then kicked away some imaginary debris to cover it. ''Dreadful affair,'' he mumbled, leaping from the stage to take and pump the man's hand with forced enthusiasm. ''All smoothed over, of course, with apologies flying every which way. But after such scandal, I must say I find it far more comfortable on this side of the Atlantic.''

''So tell me Barton, what brings an actor of your stature to my troupe? I never thought this sort of thing was your, as you British say, cup of tea.''

''Normally, no. But my marriage brought me to this part of the country, and I've this yen to test myself as you westerners do. Pit myself against the elements and all that. I rather think I'd make an elegant cowboy, don't you?''

''We won't be stopping at any ranches. Our destination is the mining camps.''

Mining? Memories flashed. Ugly ones, of black, enclosing walls and Michael Clanton's leering face. Heartbreaking moans of lost souls who never saw the light of day. I can't go back, he thought in sudden panic; I won't!

The man stared at him queerly. ''Of course I realize that,'' Grant snapped, embarrassed. ''The rugged life is what I seek.''

He risked a glance at Sam. She watched him warily, no doubt plotting her next move. Why is she doing this? he wondered. Why all the subterfuge? If Riley was right, and Hoxton's money was what she sought, wasn't there an easier way?

''Actually, my wife was as dubious as you when I first mentioned my plans, but she must now see the possibilities or she wouldn't be here. Isn't that right, darling?''

"You're always right"—if she had a knife, he'd be wearing it in the ribs—"darling."

Securing an arm around her waist, Grant felt her rage. A pity, for his hand felt surprisingly at home there. "Such an arrangement would be temporary, but the salary could reflect that. We shall, however, require separate rooms. My wife—sorry, darling—has a tendency to chatter in her sleep. I simply must have a good night's rest if I am to perform well."

Loose jaws must be in vogue, Grant thought, watching Wynecote sputter. "Hey, now, I said nothing about hiring *her*."

"Didn't you?" Pinching Sam to forestall an outburst, Grant swept his other hand in a grand gesture to portray magnanimity. "No matter, I can overlook the omission this once."

"Wait just one minute, Barton. I run a small troupe. I can't be hiring every Jack or Jenny who walks in off the street."

"Every Jack or Jenny, eh? Come, darling, we've wasted our time. Let's join that other troupe instead." Sam, as he nudged her, was as tight as a coiled snake. And no doubt twice as dangerous.

"Barton, wait." Glancing at Sam, the man winced. "I—well, we misunderstood each other. Of course I'll hire you both."

"Splendid. Our son—by my wife's first marriage—shows precious little talent, so we won't expect employment for him. My mother-in-law, on the other hand, is quite adept with a needle, so if you require a seamstress . . ."

"What have you here, Barton? A menagerie?"

Grant didn't know who looked more outraged, Wynecote or Sam. The latter required another pinch. "A menagerie. I like that. Quite a wit you have there, Mr., er . . ."

"Wynecote. Call me Cyrus. But be warned, I can't afford to feed your zoo. Rooms I'll pay for, if you double up, but your meals will be your own responsibility."

"Could you wait here a moment, darling, while Cyrus and I have a tiny chat? Business details, you know."

Sam glared, as if suspecting his intent. But just what did she expect him to do, leave her cousin behind? There was but one way he knew to make Wynecote include her. Taking the man aside, Grant spoke into his ear. "You married, Cyrus?"

He nodded stiffly, proving that for him, such a state was not designed in heaven. "Good. Perhaps you understand my dilemma. I have a—er, a friend who generally accompanies me. I am prepared to pay all her expenses, naturally, unless you can use her as well. She can't act to save her life, but she's quite an ornament, my Claire. I imagine she can draw a bigger crowd than all your billboards combined. But then, you shall have ample opportunity to judge this for yourself."

From the grin, Grant imagined he had gone up a good ten notches in the man's estimation. With a hearty slap on the shoulders, he led Cyrus back to the ladies. "So tell me, when do we leave?"

"The train departs at four this afternoon."

The clipped tones came from Sam. Unless he missed his guess, there was a major explosion ahead. Ungrateful wretch.

Her glare deepened. As Cyrus shuffled off, Grant wanted to urge him to stay, for she made him feel like a boy caught at a naughty prank, waiting to catch hell for it.

"How the devil did you find us?" she burst out finally, when Cyrus had disappeared backstage.

"Don't be so rude, honey," Annie interrupted. "Introduce us. I take it this is your Lord Hoxton?"

Grant glanced at the dancing, sparkling eyes. "I am. And you must be Anne Singleton. I can't tell you how I relish this somewhat contrived introduction. I've been a fan for years."

"You, my dear sir, are a charming rogue."

"Charming?" Sam demanded. "Did you see how he avoided my question?"

Grant glared back. "A mutual young friend was worried about you. Needlessly, it seems."

"Can I assume you mean Willie?"

"Clever lad. Says that if you grease enough palms, you can learn anything. I think you will find the desk clerk at Miss Singleton's hotel has a slippery grasp."

"How could you? You've ruined my dream."

"Dream? My dear Miss Eggersley—"

Her eyes went wide, her voice correspondingly small. "You know who I am?"

He ignored that. "Even in your wildest dreams, you can't have imagined the realities of barnstorming. Didn't you hear the man? We will be playing in the worst hovels the circuit has to offer. I ask you, what on earth was there for me to ruin?"

To his utter astonishment, she burst into tears and flew down the aisle. Grant stared after her, scratching his head and wondering if he would ever know what to expect next from her.

"I'll get the lantern," Miss Singleton offered. "Hate to see the town burn again. You go on along after Sam."

Only the hope for her good opinion propelled him down that aisle. Rage he could deal with, but never a woman's tears.

But by the time he reached Sam, however, she'd

more than adequately recovered. Perched high on the carriage, iron firmly propping her spine, she was every inch the lady. Her haughty glare was ready to set him down where she felt he belonged. "With all your vast concerns, Lord Hoxton, one would think you had better things to do with your time than chasing after us. Or is it an obsession with you, arranging other lives to your satisfaction?"

"My satisfaction?" Tears might have been better after all. "I convince the man to take on not only you, but an entire pack of tagalongs, amongst which I beg you not to number me, and you now have the gall to think I wanted it that way?"

"What makes you think *I* wanted it that way?"

That stopped him. Why did he persist in believing she cared a fig for anyone but herself? "You were going to leave them stranded here? Abandon them, the way you did Willie and m—er, his mutt?"

She sniffed, turning away. "You don't understand anything."

"Explain, then. God knows why, but I have an unhealthy curiosity about this."

"I'd have thought it was obvious. I sought employment."

"People of your social class rarely call acting a job."

"My mother was an actress, if you will remember."

Irked that he had forgotten who she was, he spoke sharply. "However talented a parent might be, it hardly guarantees a child's success. Regardless of heritage, one does not simply go out to *be* an actress. It takes practice and hard work."

Her chin went up several inches. "I've had practice. Several weeks of it, in fact. Go on, I dare you to claim you knew who I truly was."

Oh hell, another lie. But Riley, and pride, demanded it. "My dear woman, you're not the only one with theatrical aspirations."

"I have a great deal more than aspiration."

"Do you? Have you a sense of propriety, then? Surely, premature familiarity must pale beside playing a bit player in a traveling troupe."

She turned a gratifying shade of pink. "It was hardly a 'bit' part. I was to be the leading actress."

"I can't help but notice you use the past tense."

"Naturally. It's all ruined now."

"Faint-hearted?"

"You needn't be so smug. How long will it be before Mr. Wynecote realizes it is not notorious Grant Barton he has hired, but an imposter?"

She didn't know the half of it. "I've done my stint on the stage. I can hold my own."

"Without a memory?"

"Amnesia affects the past, not the present."

"How convenient."

"Yes, isn't it? It certainly facilitates taking on a new identity. You know, I find I rather look forward to our joint venture, Miss—er, Mrs. Barton."

If she were anyone else, she would have slapped his face. He could see her fingers itching to do so and silently blessed that rock-iron control.

As if knowing she had rescued him, Miss Singleton stepped into the carriage with an ear-joining grin. Whatever Sam might have said was locked, with an audible click, inside her jaws.

"Everything settled between you?" Anne was either an incurable optimist, or criminally blind. "Splendid. Then let's get Sam back to the hotel to pack."

"There's no need. I'm not going."

Grant snorted. "Coward."

"Don't be silly, Sam. Of course you are." Signaling the cabby to drive off, Ane squeezed Sam's arm. "But who else is going? The mother-in-law must be Giselle, but who is this son?"

"A young lad named Willie MacPhearson. Since Claire—forgive me, Sam—promised to keep him from starvation, I assumed she wouldn't wish to abandon him now."

"I never abandoned anyone. I left money with Stoddard to take care of Willie."

"Remind me to discuss my butler later. As for Willie, how remarkably short-sighted of you. Even you must realize his pride would never allow him take what he terms charity."

"Of course I realize that, but . . ." She looked away, down the street. Her voice was as tight as the hands clasped in her lap. "Considering how *thoughtful* you've been with everyone else, I wonder how you neglected Claire in your arrangements."

"Who said I did?" He watched her go a gratifying pink. "I let Wynecote believe she was my—er, special friend. How the devil else could I explain her presence?"

"You could have claimed *her* as Lady Hoxton. I daresay she'd be far more pleased with the role than I."

"The distaste is mutual. And for God's sake, from now on, do try to remember your name is Barton."

"How appropriate, that you should share the same Christian name with a criminal. And what a coincidence that you have the same character deficiencies, too."

He wanted to throttle her. Damned, infuriating baggage. "There's a saying, I believe, about who should be the first to throw stones?"

"From what I've heard," Annie piped in

anxiously, "this Mr. Barton stole far more hearts than jewels. My current maid once worked in the London theater. She claims that even as a lad, Grant Barton had a way with the ladies. A real charmer, but a gentleman, too. Can you handle such a role, sir?"

"I shall do my best."

"Yes, I imagine you will." She grinned, making Grant wish his bogus wife could be more like Anne Singleton.

"You're my friend, Annie. Stop swallowing everything this—this libertine tells you."

"Libertine?" Exasperated, he turned to the more sympathetic audience. "Miss Singleton, does your conscience allow setting this utter innocent loose in the world? Mine doesn't. There is a minimum of five dozen more important tasks in which I can involve myself, but unfortunately, circumstances have made her my responsibility. What else can I do but follow after her?"

"Did you rehearse that speech? What a pity you had poor Cyrus so flustered; you could have auditioned with it."

"Ah, but I did audition. Or were *you* too flustered to notice?"

Score one for him, but it was a point he didn't much enjoy. After the initial wince, Sam retreated, backing into the cushions as if hoping to hide there. He couldn't have been more unfair, especially considering the state of his own emotions at the time. It made him feel guilty, which in turn irked him no end.

"My goodness," Miss Singleton chirped beside him. "Here we are at Sam's hotel. We'd best hurry if we hope to have you packed before your train leaves."

From the moment he had learned about Sam Eggersley, Grant decided, irony had followed him around. Typical, that she should be staying at the same hotel he had checked into only a few hours before. Had he and Willie not been combing the city, she would no doubt have walked straight into his arms. Disturbing thought.

As a matter of course, he stepped down to offer his arm. Tossing back her head, she ignored him entirely.

With a muttered, "fall and break your neck then," he turned to assist Miss Singleton. She, sensible woman, knew how to behave. Taking his hand and squeezing it, she gave him a reassuring smile. "Come, you and I can slip inside while Sam pays the driver. No, let her; she'll only make a scene otherwise."

"What's wrong with that woman?"

"Try to understand. Sam's been forced into the habit of doing most things for herself. When someone offers help, she no longer knows how to react. It's not that she means to reject your gallantry. She's simply not accustomed to it."

"Come now. At her age, she must have had suitors."

"You've met her cousin. With Claire around, how much attention, much less gallantry, is left for anyone else?"

He didn't want to understand Sam Eggersley and her myriad pesonality quirks. He wanted to hate her, as she so obviously despised him.

"Where do you think you're going?"

He spun on a heel to face the gray eyes, as sympathetic as granite chips. "I believe packing is on the agenda?"

"I am perfectly capable of packing my own bags. Or do you need to rearrange them as well?"

"I have my own packing to do. As it happens, I

am lodged in the hotel as well.''

"I see. In that case, I won't keep you from your packing. If you will excuse me?''

"Not just yet. As long as you're here, we might as well talk.''

"No. You may own half the world, Lord Hoxton, but you don't own me.''

"Quite frankly, I can't think of a more alarming prospect.''

Annie clucked her tongue. "If you two don't stop bickering and discuss your differences in a more civilized manner, how can you hope to survive the weeks ahead? For heaven's sake, Sam, go with him. Hear what he has to say.''

"I have to pack. The train leaves soon.''

"I'll go up and get the others started. You go with him. Then, when we're all done, we'll head over to my place for a drink. With all this excitement, I could do with a bit of a boost.''

Grant braced himself for the lecture on the evils of alcohol, but Sam's nod was surprisingly obedient. Almost stupidly so. As he bowed, pointing the way, he felt like an executioner leading his victim to the gallows.

This time, he knew better than to offer his arm. Walking beside her down the lengthy hall, he stole a glance at her face. She was biting her lip so viciously, it was a marvel that any remained. A crime, surely, for they had been the most delectable . . .

Hell no, he wasn't going that round again. The woman lied habitually. She used people, then threw them aside when she was done. Had she repented one inch? Or made an attempt to explain? No. Only a fool would swallow this little lost kitten pose, and Grant Barton had long since proven himself immune to kittens.

Ignoring the muffled yelps emanating from his suite, Grant steeled himself for the confrontation ahead. No more playing the gullible fool. Sam Eggersley was going to give him some answers or he would throttle her lovely neck.

13

Swearing silently at Hoxton's unrelenting back, Sam scrambled to keep pace with his long stride. A few more ticks on the clock and she would have been safely away. Why was it that she alone never got away with anything? One error, the tiniest thing wrong, and retribution was waiting to pounce.

How had Hoxton found them? she wondered.

She thought she had been so clever, registering under the assumed name. The man clearly had spies everywhere, or he'd never have tracked them down so soon. She didn't want to think it had been an overwhelming need to see Claire.

He paused suddenly, and Sam nearly ran into his back. His expression was positively leveling. As he slid the key into the lock, Sam heard a whimper on the other side of the door. Hoxton's features darkened more as it mushroomed into a very distinctive yelp.

Another howl and Gus was bounding out the door, jumping, licking and barking. The stiffness on that dark face deepened into a scowl. "Willie!" he bellowed as he strode into the room beyond. "I thought I told you to keep your mangy mutt quiet."

Doors opened along the corridor. Sam smiled her reassurance at the owlish faces, hoping they would feel no need to alert the hotel staff, while grabbing Gus and dragging him into the room.

Shutting the door behind her, she dropped to her knees. "Gus, *shhh*! Down, boy. Oh, you silly animal, how I missed you."

A red head popped into view, freckles joined in a grin. "You found her, Cap'n? At the hotel, like I said?"

"Not quite. It took nearly every cent I had to bribe the desk clerk into telling me where they went."

"Gus is sure glad you spent the money." Willie beamed as he turned to Sam. *He's furious*, she tried to project silently, but the boy either didn't heed, or didn't care. "He missed you, Miss Claire. We all did."

"Her name is Samantha." Hoxton spoke quickly, as if to prove conclusively that he did not include himself in that "we." "Though I suppose you should start calling her Mama from now on."

"Mama?"

Hoxton intercepted the questioning gaze. "I'll explain later. At present, I need you to go down to the desk. Inform them that Miss Eggersley's—that is, Miss Malloy's—entourage will be leaving this afternoon. Arrange to have their luggage delivered to Miss Singleton's hotel."

"We switching hotels, too?"

"We're switching towns. I believe the next stop on the itinerary is St. Louis."

"Ooo-ee, I knew this was going to be fun."

"Fun?" Even Gus went still at the sound. "Of all the words describing this fiasco, I daresay fun must be the most unlikely. Oh, stop gaping and just do as I ask. And take that mongrel with you."

"Down to the desk?"

"Tie him up outdoors. We'll meet you there within the hour."

"You're the cap'n." Winking at Sam as he reached for the dog's collar, Willie giggled. "Reckon it's up to you and me to show him how to relax and have a good time, huh?"

Grinning, Willie hustled through the door. Sam took a deep breath and squared her shoulders as she realized that the boy would take the diversion with him.

But Hoxton didn't pounce. Instead, he went directly to the brandy decanter. "Care to join me?"

"No, thank you, I don't drink." The upraised eyebrow made even that seem like a fault she had better soon remedy. Well, she would not be intimidated. Moving to the sofa, she decided she could at least appear relaxed and unruffled. Unfortunately, the leather upholstery swallowed her whole. She felt, and knew she looked, smaller and more insignificant than ever.

He didn't notice. Against her will, she watched as he circled the room. She loved the way he moved. Each step seemed to flow into the other effortlessly. Power and strength was softened by grace, as if each muscle had been trained for a specific task, the lot of them orchestrated into one grand movement to soothe the senses. He must dance marvelously, Sam thought, just like Damion. Damion, who had been just about to kiss her when Mr. Wynecote so rudely ended the audition.

She wriggled on the cushions. The man must have done far more than a "stint" on the stage. Look at how skillfully he'd suspended reality. For that brief, magical moment, he had her believing that it was she he chased after, not out of duty, but out of the desire and the need to see her again. How his gaze had warmed her! For the first time in her life, Sam had felt lovely, desirable, alive with the knowledge that he wanted that kiss as much as she. Only the two of them existed. Only they mattered. She had been prepared to die, right there on the spot, for nothing else life held in store could ever surpass that moment.

A superb actor, indeed, capable of spinning a thousand illusions. She had been so completely taken in that when reality reared its unwelcome head, she had refused to accept it. It had taken those damned tears, streaming past her guard, to convince her she was a pathetic fool.

It had to have been deliberate. He must have had some idea of retribution, for there was no other reason to humiliate her so. She would have told him where to find his precious Claire. He didn't need to bring her here, where her eyes were doomed to follow his every movement, while he seemed to forget that she was even in the room.

She watched him remove his jacket, then absent-mindedly tug at the buttons of his shirt. How dark his throat seemed against the stiff white collar. How finely sculptured. Sam held her breath, wanting those fingers to go further. She hated herself. Hated him. Or tried to.

"If you had the least regard for propriety, sir, you would wait until I was gone to disrobe."

"Disrobe?" He swung to face her, expression incredulous. "My dear woman, I have simply unbuttoned a deuced uncomfortable collar. Considering your own behavior, I wonder where you find the gall to lecture me on propriety."

She tried to sit straighter. Ridiculous cushions, she couldn't get a grip on them. "I haven't the least idea what you mean."

"No?" The muscles tensed at the open collar. "Correct me if I am wrong, but you were a guest, not a prisoner, in my home. Surely common courtesy dictates an explanation for your hasty, and I might add, unseemly departure?"

"I—I left a note."

"Ah yes, Aunt Emily. I assume she is here in

Chicago for treatment? I wonder, shall she accompany our menagerie, too?"

Guilt stirred. "How dare you ridicule me!"

"Oh no, the shoe is on a much smaller foot, I fear. Why did you do it? Did you enjoy making a fool of me?"

Defiance seemed the only defense, so she stood up to face him. "Yes, as a matter of fact, I did. Tremendously."

Still as a statue, he stared into her. Sam tried not to cringe, but she found herself edging backward.

"As I recall, my original invitation was quite explicit. I thought it made my intentions painfully clear. Didn't you realize that I meant to ask you to marry me?"

"I knew you planned to ask Samantha Eggersley. Who she actually was didn't seem to make much difference."

"That's because . . . ." Running a hand through his hair, he looked away. "Oh, damn. There's so much you don't understand, so much I can't possibly explain."

Was he pleading? Or was this just another pose, aimed at the soft touch he knew her to be. Lord help her, but she longed to respond. To lay her head down on that magnificent chest and hold him close, to tell him everything, from the bottom of her soul on upward.

"All vanity aside, most women would jump at the chance of linking themselves with the Hoxton name. Why not you?"

"It was all rather sudden. I—I didn't even know you."

"I suppose that's true enough. Listen, Claire—"

"My name is Sam."

"Sam then. If you snap every time I utter a word,

this will be a hellish few weeks for us both. Good lord, woman, what can I have done to make you so consistently miffed at me?''

"What have you done? For one thing, what about using my friends to spy on me? And, a twelve-year-old boy at that?''

"Mentally and emotionally, Willie is older than the pair of us combined.''

"He is nonetheless a child. You should be ashamed.''

"*I* should?'' His eyes rolled upward in disbelief. "And what of you? How have you been sleeping at night, knowing you jeopardized poor Stoddard's employment?''

"You didn't turn him out?''

"I should have, the way the man barked at me in your defense. Is it innate, or did you cultivate this talent for turning my life inside out?''

"What did you do?''

"I tortured him.'' He leaned closer, blue eyes dancing with mischief. "I dragged him to the dungeon I keep for just such occasions, and stretched his brittle bones until he broke. Easy enough, then, to learn where to find you.''

"Y-You're teasing.''

"Of course I am. We both know Stoddard would never tell me a thing. Even on the rack.''

Sam couldn't stop the smile as she thought of the old man, trying so hard not to be affected by Gus's antics. "He is a wonderful man. I know you won't believe this, but I did hate dividing his loyalties. That's the major reason why I never told him where I meant to go.''

The eyes went sober as he studied her. She knew Samuel would expect her to say nothing, to make a quick, insincere apology and be gone while she still had a chance. But Sam couldn't have moved if she wished to. Which she didn't. Rather, she had this insane urge to prove she was not the wretch he thought. "I never meant to turn anything inside out. I truly thought you'd be happy to see the last of me. If I'd the least idea you would follow me—I mean, us—oh drat, how on earth *did* you track us down?"

The right side of his face curved upward, as if he were trying hard not to smile. "Claire."

"I am not Claire."

"So I've learned. But what I meant was your cousin told me. In a note. It's strange, but hers didn't mention Aunt Emily."

She'd been stupid not to have suspected this. The little traitor. Her hand went to her temples. "There is no Aunt Emily and you damned well know it."

"Was that an oath? Miss Eggersley, I am shocked."

"Continue with this charade, and you will hear a great deal worse. Why don't you just take Claire and go home," she snapped, none too thrilled with the pleading note in her tone. "You can't want to get involved in this."

"What, and miss all the fun?"

She broke away from his gaze. He had no right to laugh at her. Angry and hurt, she went to the window, blinking her eyes furiously to control them. She would not cry. She would not.

"Miss Eggersley—Sam—I acted on sheer impulse at that audition. I meant well, but I've obviously upset your plans. I'm sorry for that, but since it can't be undone, why not band together and make the best of things?"

"And be friends?"

She had meant to mock him, but he didn't seem to hear the sarcasm. "Well, yes. It's not so novel a concept, you know. We have already proven to everyone's satisfaction how well we—er, work together onstage. Perhaps we could manage it on a more permanent basis?"

Avoiding his eyes, Sam turned her gaze outside the window. Perhaps he was trying to be nice. Should she trust him? Could she? He had spoken in this vein before. Right before she had seen him welcome Claire into his room. No, he was not to be trusted.

As if to support her suspicions, a familiar carriage rattled to a stop in the street below. The gold of the Hoxton crest glittered accusingly in the noonday sun. Watching the bald-headed occupant emerge, Sam sighed. At least she'd been spared the humiliation of softening toward him. There would be one less thing for them to chuckle over tonight.

"I see we must add another member to our menagerie," she sneered. "But I suppose we couldn't expect you to muddle through without the services of your valet."

"Riley? Here?" He was behind her instantly, his arm resting on her shoulder as he pushed the curtain aside.

It was a casual touch, nothing more. Absurd, to feel such tingles running up and down her spine. "Just what is his role going to be? I warn you, I refuse to claim that man as my father."

"Damn! How the devil did he find me?"

"Ask Claire. She's quite fond of penning notes."

It was her tongue she should be biting, not her lip. He would think she was jealous, that she cared a hoot what he and her cousin did. That she wanted, even now, for that hand to slide down her arms, twist her around, and . . .

"Let's get the others." And if that were not enough to slap her back to her senses, he pushed roughly away to cross the room. "We can't stay here. He'll have my room number from the clerk in no time."

Disoriented, Sam leaned back against the window, watching him yank open the door. Not wanting to kiss her was one thing, but this panic to leave? "I don't understand. You don't wish to see your valet?"

"I do not. Nor do I wish him to see us. Damn, I haven't time to explain. This once, can't you do as I ask without an argument?"

It had nothing to do with the pretty plea, she insisted as she slipped past him into the hall. She had no wish to confront Riley, either.

Hoxton's feet could not move fast enough, dispelling any remaining illusions about his desire to be alone with her. The sense of betrayal, irrationally enough, was further enhanced when the door to their suite flew open and an ecstatic Claire fell into his arms. "Tony, darling! I knew you would come for me."

Where was the urgency now? Sam sneered as he took overlong to disentangle himself. To be fair, though, she had to admit that her cousin could cling like wisteria when she chose.

To their right, Sam saw Annie shake her head as if the scene did damage to her digestion. "As much as I hate to interfere with so touching a reunion, we are a bit behind schedule. If we want those drinks . . ."

"Tony, why is she being so mean to me? First I have to pack all my things and now you barge in with Sam, of all people, and—what did she tell you? Why are you looking at me like that?"

"We have encountered . . . difficulties." Pulling free from her grasp, Hoxton strode to the window. "My valet seems to have followed me here."

"So?"

Sam watched him grip the still. Was this was Hoxton, surpreme commander, so furtively evading a servant? If he didn't want Riley tagging along, why not just tell him so?

He flexed his fingers before turning to them. His smile was clearly forced. "This must seem melodramatic. But you see, Riley has been with me so long, he's thinks and acts like my father. Though most often he does know what's best for me, this once, I'd like to conduct an adventure alone."

"Adventure?"

His smile was a trifle tight, but his tone was jovial enough. "Sam will provide the details. At present, we must hurry away. You are ready, I hope?"

Behind Claire, Giselle grinned fatuously. "Ready and waiting, *monsieur.*"

As his eyes went to the pile of luggage, his pretense at humor died. "All this?"

Sam felt sorry for him. It would certainly be hard to execute a stealthy escape, loaded down like a pack animal. But since it was primarily Claire's wardrobe, let him be the one to plead with her. If he could.

It seemed beyond him. One melting gaze and he was picking up one satchel after another. She should feel nothing but contempt, Sam knew, but she found herself reaching instead for the heaviest of the lot. The poor man couldn't be expected to carry everything, could he?

"Let me." Their eyes met as he grabbed at it. "If I can manage your cousin's, I can certainly carry yours."

"That's not Sam's," Claire sneered. "Good heavens, hers is that ugly brown thing."

There was a ridiculous moment as they struggled over the bag. Unnerved by the intensity of his gaze,

Sam relinquished her grip. Hoxton sagged, but his eyes never left her face. They seemed puzzled, almost questioning, as if searching for what made her tick.

"I thought we were in a hurry," Claire whined from the doorway. "Are we going or not?"

Sam snatched at Claire's bag. "Here, let me. You won't be much use to anyone with a broken back." He wanted to argue, she could see it. "Oh, for once, *you* do as you're asked."

"Touché!" Releasing the bag, he studied her, clearly bewildered. "And thank you."

With a huff, Sam struggled across the room, feeling like the proverbial beast of burden. Behind her, Annie insisted that Sam was right, that they could all take at least one sachel. Giselle enthusiastically followed her lead, but Claire had already escaped, sailing ahead down the stairs.

"Let me take that. You can try one of these others."

Catching up with her on the stairs, Hoxton exchanged loads, and gave Sam a lopsided grin. "What on earth does she have in this thing? Stones?"

"Shoes, I imagine," she giggled, feeling not only lighter in load, but in spirits as well. "From your expression, one might think you've begun to regret taking on my menagerie."

"Regret, Miss Eggersley? Don't be silly. Not with all this *fun* you and young William are providing for me."

"Speaking of whom, where exactly were we to meet him?"

"At the . . ."

As he paused, and Sam's mind followed the logical sequence, there was a telltale bark in the lobby below. "Damn," Hoxton muttered, hurrying down the few remaining stairs. "Must that man anticipate my every move?''

Annie stopped Sam with a puzzled frown. ''Where is he going? Shouldn't we be using the back door?''

With a nervous shrug, Sam hurried down to the partially opened door where Hoxton stood peering into the lobby. ''There's another complication,'' she whispered over her shoulder to the others. ''It seems Riley has Willie.''

''That dirty little boy,'' Claire whined, materializing behind them. ''I swear, Sam, the fuss you make about the brat is ridiculous. I've had enough of you playing Lady Bountiful while I am forced to travel third-class everywhere. You won't involve us in any more of your schemes. We have better things to do with our time, don't we, Tony?''

He gestured impatiently for silence. ''We need a diversion,'' he muttered, returning his attention to the lobby. ''Willie is bright enough to scamper away, if he gets the opportunity.''

''Tony!''

''Any ideas, Sam? Miss Singleton?''

Claire performed her prettiest pout, but no one paid any attention, Hoxton least of all. Sam watched in bewilderment. Here he had ample opportunity to escape both Riley and Claire's threatened tantrum, yet he stayed. He seemed to genuinely care what happened to the boy. Sam was surprised, yet pleased at such an unselfish act.

''He would not recognize me,'' Giselle whispered next to her. ''Perhaps if I yelled *fire*?''

Annie shook her head. ''Not in this town. We'd cause a panic and likely land ourselves in jail. I don't suppose he'd believe a fake message?''

''Riley? Not a chance.''

''What if a crochety old lady delivered it?'' Sam

heard herself say. "Men of his ilk are allergic to them. If she were obnoxious enough, he'd do anything she said, just to get rid of her."

Grant turned to her, a slow grin replacing his frown. "I like it. And we have just the actress for the job." Sam felt herself inflate, almost preen, but his eyes slid past her to Annie. "What say you, Miss Singleton? Can you out-bully a bully?"

"Oh for pity's sake, Tony. No one in his right mind would think Annie was an old lady."

"You'd be amazed what an actor can do with greasepaint."

"Look at her. That red hair, that dress. Oh, it's lovely on you, Annie, but an old woman would never wear anything cut that low. I say we just go. The boy won't mind; he's accustomed to fending for himself."

Sam almost felt sorry for Claire, the way he scowled at her. "I suppose I could do it," Sam said.

As all eyes switched to her, Sam realized she had volunteered. Was she serious? She thought of failing, of the dark glittering in Riley's eyes, and shivered.

"You? Are you serious?"

Claire's nastily expressed doubts erased all sympathy. "You can hardly find fault with my dress. Or hair. If Annie will help apply the greasepaint she gave me . . ."

Blue eyes probed into her. "You don't have to do this, Sam. We can think of another way."

He offered a chance to retreat. To play the helpless female as Claire always managed to do. It was tempting, but Sam knew how she would feel if caught in Riley's grasp. "I'm afraid I do. Let's face facts. We have few options and even less time. Don't worry, I'll do my best."

His smile, surely, was worth whatever happened. "I never doubted that. Very well then, in which one of these bags will we find the greasepaint? I don't suppose you have a wig tucked away in there?"

"Claire has a generous supply of face powder," Annie offered. "And Sam has this perfectly horrid hat—sorry, love, but it is a tad out of fashion."

Everything Sam owned was. She would look horrid, but as Annie so tactlessly pointed out, she almost always did. Riley would see nothing new. He wouldn't see her at all.

Digging into the bag for both the make-up and the hated hat, she muttered under her breath. No glamorous roles for Sam. No, she played dowdy, unwanted cousins and nasty old ladies. Who could blame the man for choosing her cousin?

"There must be a mirror in one of these rooms." Annie said, tugging at her arm. "Come, let's make an old crone out of you."

As they ducked through the door, Sam risked a quick peek at Hoxton. She shouldn't have. He was back at the door, with Claire frozen to his side. Having gotten what he wanted, why waste any more charm? Good old Sam, throwing herself to the wolves, and no one bothered to watch.

Well, she huffed, stiffening her backbone; this would be the absolutely last time.

Grant would have bitten his nails if Claire had released his arm. Twice he had tried to shrug free, but her grip merely tightened. A third attempt, he feared, might cut off all circulation.

He wished Sam would hurry. Riley was clearly using the boy as bait, but for whom? Himself or Sam? And how the devil had the man known they were there?

He didn't like it, but he didn't know why. Somehow, the persistence and patience involved held an ominous note. Though inwardly Grant knew Hoxton would never allow his henchman to harm Sam, it was nonetheless unnerving how Willie stopped wriggling in the man's grasp, how even Gus now sat obediently silent.

"Well, here she is!"

As he whirled, he broke Claire's grasp. Her protest went unnoticed as he approached Sam. What he saw made him want to laugh. She was perfect. From the horrid hat down, she as every inch the autocratic bully. All she lacked was a cane with which to poke him.

"Just what are you laughing at, young man? If you had the least sense of chivalry, you'd see I was in need of a cane. Look lively now, and find me one."

He had this silly urge to kiss her. "Well done. I am impressed, ladies. But I must warn you. Riley looks just this side of murder."

A tiny ripple passed through the slender body, the only sign of nerves. "At my age, sonny, murder is more a treat than a threat. Come along now, I need that cane."

"There is an umbrella tree, two steps from the door. Will one of them do?"

Favoring him with a sniff, Sam brushed past. He grabbed at her elbow. "You don't have to do this."

"I know, but regardless of what you think, I would never abandon that boy willingly. So you just go on and take the others to Annie's hotel. We'll meet you there as soon as we can." She flashed a weak smile before hobbling into the lobby.

"You heard her, Tony. Let's go."

This time, he happily yanked his arm away. The boy was one thing, but how could Claire consider leaving her cousin behind? He certainly couldn't. "I want to be here, in case there's trouble."

"I can't believe this. After all the time we've been apart, you can't prefer to look after Sam. Come on, I want to leave."

"Go ahead. I'll meet you at the hotel."

Annie slipped between them. "Lord Hoxton is right. There's no sense in cluttering up this hallway. You ladies can come with me, and he will join us later. I'll have the drinks waiting."

He glanced at the clock. "I'm afraid we must forego those drinks. The train leaves within the hour. I hate to impose, but could you take the ladies straight to the depot instead?"

"Tony—"

Whatever Claire had to say was cut off by the thud of the satchel Annie thrust into her arms. "Here, take this. We can't have your poor Tony trying to escape with all this luggage." Lifting a bag and handing another to Giselle, Annie smirked at him. "Right, Tony darling?"

"I don't know how to thank you."

"Just take care of Sam. She's always so busy worrying about others, she never takes time to look out for herself."

"So I've noticed."

As Annie followed his gaze to the pouting Claire, she smirked in satisfaction. "I like you, Hoxton. Barton. Or whoever you are. I feel much better, knowing Sam has someone like you at her side."

"Quite honestly, I'd feel better too, if I knew what she's planning next. Why is she joining this down-and-out troupe?"

Annie shook her head. "That, my dear sir, you must ask Sam. Just do me a favor and look out for her." She kissed her index finger and lightly touched his forehead. "That's for luck. And now, as I see you are anxious to return to your post, I will take these distractions and go. Coming, ladies?"

"To-ny—"

There was a squeak, as if Claire had been abruptly yanked out of sight, but his attention had already focused on Sam. She was poking the pilfered umbrella into the valet's ribs. Her voice, Grant thought, could surely be heard back in New York.

"Must you remain so disagreeable, lad? I told you, I merely need the boy for a moment."

Gus sniffed at the hem of her skirt. He whined and enthusiastically wagged his tail. Groaning, Grant saw that the silly mutt could ruin everything.

"If you will recall, madame, I told you the boy's services are required elsewhere."

"Fiddlesticks. I see him sitting here, twiddling his thumbs. Call this blasted dog off me. Filthy animal. Get. Get away." She stepped back, just out of sniffing range, and the bewildered Gus sat, his floppy ears hanging low.

"Well," she said, resuming the attack by flinging up the umbrella to pin Riley to the wall. "What are you waiting for, boy? Come with me."

Willie looked from one to the other, obviously ill at ease. It was all Grant could do not to chuckle out loud.

But he should have known by now that the valet was not so easily vanquished. Taking the umbrella by its tip, Riley slid it off to the side. "As I have repeatedly told you, I have other plans for the lad."

"Plans, huh? Tell me boy, is this rude lout your father?"

"No, ma'am."

"Hmmm. Your employer, then?"

"No ma'am. Fact is, I never seen him before in my life."

Bless the boy for his quick wit. And Sam, for hers. "Then why the devil is he so all-fired anxious to make me mad? How about you, sonny? Do you enjoy seeing an old lady hobble along burdened down with luggage? Or does a heart beat somewhere in that ill-fed chest?''

"I—I'd be happy to help."

"Good lad. Follow me."

Grant held his breath as Riley made another grab at the umbrella. "Wait one moment, madame. That boy belongs with me. I am taking him to his grandmother."

Sam fixed him with her haughtiest glare. Grant wondered that Riley didn't recognize it, but couldn't blame him. In his place, he'd have dropped his hand too.

"His grandmother, eh? Then I doubt she'd mind him helping another old lady in trouble. Silly man, I'm only asking to borrow the boy, not kidnap him. What would I want with a mewling brat anyway? Just as soon as he gets my baggage into a cab, I'll leave you both to your buisness. Whatever it may be."

"They have porters for that very purpose, Madame. I'll be only too happy to find you one."

She stopped him with the umbrella. It would have to hurt, Grant thought, the way it jabbed into his arm. "If one was available, sir, don't you think I'd have fetched one myself? They're all busy. Some filthy millionaire named Hoxton. Sickening, the way they bow and scrape and scurry to obey his every whim. He'd better be leaving a decent tip, too, with all the luggage he's accumulated. That lady friend of his . . .''

Clucking and shaking her head, Sam jammed the umbrella into the floor. Both Riley and Willie jumped, ever so slightly, taking a step backward. "But that's none of my affair, either. I want to know if you'll lend that boy to me, or must I kick up a fuss?"

Riley was cornered, and therefore dangerous.

Don't push, Grant wanted to warn Sam, and unconsciously poised or action.

"For pity's sake," Sam growled. "If it makes you feel better, come with us. I don't care, just so long I get out of here some time today. I can't abide hotels. They're always trying to take your money for services you don't want and don't even get."

Clever. Convinced of Hoxton's imminent departure, Riley couldn't leave his post, but the empty offer left him feeling less trapped and more agreeable.

"Very well, take him. But I want him back in ten minutes."

"I said I'd have him back, didn't I? Some people . . . " She grabbed poor Willie by the ear and dragged him in Grant's direction.

Just before she reached the door, inches from success, Sam stunned them all by wheeling around and pointing the umbrella again. "You. Yes, you with the sour face. See about fetching me a cab. I'll need somewhere to put my luggage once I'm done with the boy."

As the exasperated Riley shoved through the door, Sam pushed Willie forward. Over her shoulder, she hissed, "run for it," and swung back into the lobby for Gus.

Heart in his throat, Grant prayed as Sam struggled with Gus's rope, and the damned mutt's wriggling hampered her efforts. She would never finish in time. Sam's quick thinking wouldn't help her, even with the umbrella, if that bald head popped into view.

As the front door opened, Gus came bounding free. Willie had to call him, for both adults focused on the door. They both breathed a sigh of relief as an elderly gentleman strolled into the lobby. With a broad leer, he approached Sam, but her frosty glare made him veer quickly off toward the stairs.

"That was quite a chance you took," Grant snapped as she ran through the door and inadvertently into his arms.

"I happen to know that it takes forever to hail a cab in this town," she bristled as she broke away, the old lady again. "Which reminds me, what are you doing here? I told you to run."

"Sam, you were magnificent. Remind me to kiss you when you take off that grease paint."

"Sam?" Willie looked from one to the other of them.

"May I introduce the intrepid Miss Eggersley. The lady with a thousand faces."

"Do you mean to stand around jabbering all day, or can we go?"

"By all means. If that paint makes you such a shrew, I can't wait to get it off you. Follow me. Since you sent that poor man into the street, I suppose we should go out the back. I, for one, would hate to run into him now."

"I don't believe this," Willie chanted as he followed them out the door. "You two never do what's expected."

Grant chuckled as he consulted his watch. "We'd better hurry. It won't take him long to discover why Gus is gone."

"Where are the others? And the rest of the luggage?"

"They went on ahead. Willie, you're familiar with the neighborhood. What's the quickest and least conspicuous way to the train depot?"

"This way. Are you gonna tell me what's going on? I can't be much help if I don't know what the heck we're doing."

GOLDEN DREAMS

Following the boy through a narrow alley, carrying the bags over his head, Grant refused to admit that he knew less than anyone. "Miss Eggersley has decided to become an actress. We're all tagging along. Our destination, I believe, is the Rocky Mountains."

"Whew, I didn't know she could act."

The umbrella shot out in front of the boy and halted him accordingly. "I don't see how you can stay that, young man, considering how taken in you were by my performance. Oh, no." The old lady's voice melted into Sam's again.

"What is it?"

"The umbrella. I forgot to return it."

Grant threw back his head and laughed. "Sam Eggersley, you must be one of a kind. My dear woman, you have involved yourself in a series of crimes, not least amongst them being kidnapping, impersonation, skipping the bill . . . ."

"The bill will be paid."

"And now you're worried about pinching an umbrella?"

"Stealing is abhorrent to me, sir."

"Oh? I seem to remember you saying the same about lying."

For a moment, he thought she would jab him in the ribs. "How can I expect *you* to understand? You, who so easily assume the identity of a thief."

"An identity far easier to assume than that of your adoring spouse."

The look in her eye was one Grant had learned to recognize. And regret. "Oh yes, my wonderfully considerate husband, who brought along a mistress to throw in my face."

"Oh, for heaven's sake, what did you expect me to do? I could hardly leave Claire behind."

"No, of course not." Her voice was tight as she looked away. "Here is the depot. I will look for the others and meet you inside."

"Sam, wait."

But she was already gone, swallowed up by the crowd. Grant felt the strangest discomfort, as if something inside was warning him not to let her out of his sight.

"So the other one's coming, too? Her highness?"

"Not you, too." In exasperation, Grant turned his attention to the boy. "Look Willie, Claire—Miss Farnstable, is my friend. Show some respect."

"She the mistress Miss Sam's complaining about?"

"What would you know about mistresses?"

"I ain't no baby. I've been around. Enough to know which are worth the chase, and which are just wasting your time."

"Do you honestly think being barked at by that shrew is anyone's idea of a love life? I'd rather be celibate."

"Suit yourself. Just don't come crying to me when you wake up kicking your teeth 'cause you wasted your time on the first available skirt instead of grabbing quality when you found it."

"Quality? Rubbish. That woman has lied and cheated and God knows what else."

"So have we." Willie planted his feet squarely on the sidewalk, arms folded across his chest. "If she's done wrong, she has her reasons, same as us. I only know she put herself out to free me from Fatso. A friend who's there when you need her, that's quality."

"What are you, a child, or a ninety-seven-year-old sage?"

"Looks to me like I'm your little boy, huh, Pa?"

He flashed a mischievous grin. "Which reminds me. When we gonna eat?"

"Just as soon as we get our things—" With a groan, Grant realized he'd left everything they had back in the hotel room.

"We ain't got no money?"

"Haven't. And no, unless Sam does, we won't eat until Wynecote gets around to paying our salaries. With the way my luck has been running, we just might starve."

"So we tighten our belts some. We'll make it, Cap'n. I mean, Pa. Don't you worry."

Grant envied those people free to hug their children whenever the urge struck. Affection had come too rarely in either his or the boy's life for them to feel uncomfortable with the gesture, so Grant contented himself with roughing up his hair instead.

"Mr. Barton?"

"Miss Singleton. What is it?" Wheeling to face the actress, Grant felt that strange discomfort again. "What's wrong? Where is Sam?"

"Sam is fine. Relatively, that is. I just thought you might appreciate the warning that there's been a change in plans. It seems that Cyrus took one look at your—at Claire and decided to use her as his leading lady. Nothing I have said holds much sway, but perhaps if you were to intervene?"

"Me?" Inwardly, Grant felt relief. It was too intimidating, the idea of playing opposite Sam. On that stage today, he had lost control of his emotions. God only knew what he might do if it happened again. He thought of Sam, of the disappointment she must feel, but dismissed such weakness swiftly. Self-preservation, after all, was his way of life.

"Don't you think I've antagonized the man enough for one day? Casting is his job. He must know what he's doing."

"Lord Hoxton is right." Sam materialized behind them. "I asked you not to make a fuss about this, Annie."

"But Sam, you—"

"I appreciate your loyalty." A hand shot out briefly to touch the other woman's arm, before Sam resumed her stiff, unyielding pose. "But nothing will be served by kicking up a fuss. In fact, it is most likely better this way. I, uh, can learn, gradually, what is expected on the stage. One does not go out and *be* an actress, remember?"

"How sensible of you," Grant said.

Sam shot him her blackest look. "Yes, that's me. Sensible Sam."

"I don't know what I'm doing hanging around here, then." Annie looked from one to the other of them. With a heavy sigh, she threw her arms around Sam. "Honey, you've got to know I wish only the best for you. I hope you find what you set out to do."

"Oh, Annie, I'm going to miss you."

"Then you come visit. And bring this husband of yours along. I'd hate to think this is the last time I'm going to see him."

"I'd hate that too, Miss Singleton."

"Call me Annie." Breaking away from Sam, she took his hands. "Remember what I said. You take good care of her."

Watching her walk away, Grant slowly became aware of the stiffening form beside him. Things could get sticky, indeed, without Miss Singleton to act as arbitrator.

"What was that all about? When were you two discussing me?"

In the old-lady guise, Sam seemed more than ever the shrew. Grant felt his exasperation build. "She

222

didn't like the idea of you being alone. I said I'd watch over you. Nothing more."

"Watch over me? Of all the nerve! I will have you know, sir, that I have been taking care of myself adequately, thank you very much, and even if I had the need for a protector, which I do not, I can't imagine why I would ever choose you."

"Oh? Have you another choice then? I must say, I don't exactly see them lining up at the door."

She had provoked him, he knew, but that was unnecessarily cruel. Her face crumpled, as if he had slapped her. Grant wondered if he could somehow snatch the words back.

"As plain and uninspiring as I might be, Lord Hoxton, I am not as stupid as you and your valet chose to believe. Indeed, the only protection I have ever needed was against you and your nefarious plots."

"Nefarious . . ."

"Come now, you know what I mean. A few discreet compliments, a lingering touch or two?"

Suddenly chilled, Grant searched through his memory. My lord, what had she overheard? Had there been anything to reveal his true identity? Was that why she had run away?

"What? No quip? Don't tell me I have you thoroughly flustered for a change."

"Claire—I mean, Sam—dammit, let me explain."

"Tony!" Claire's shriek could be heard from one end of the depot to the other. "Darling, I have the most wonderful news. Guess who's going to be your leading lady?"

Oblivious to the tension around her, Claire sidled up to take his arm. "Oh, you already knew. You devil, I bet you asked Cyrus to do this, didn't you?"

His eyes stayed with Sam, who was staring

fixedly at his feet. "No. I swear, I didn't . . ."

"I need your protests less than I need your protection." Though barely audible, Sam's voice was ice cold. "You and your—your leading lady can go about your business and I'll go about mine. Just leave me alone."

"Pooh Sam, you always spoil everything. We don't have to stand here watching her scowl. C'mon Tony, let's find Cyrus. Wait until you see the script he has for us."

Grant's locked his eyes on Sam. "What happened to us being friends?"

He hated himself for the almost pleading note, but he hated her more for not responding to it. "I'm sorry, Lord Hoxton, but friends don't lie to each other."

"You would know best about that, I suppose."

She blanched, before her cheeks filled with a dangerous red. Her gaze focused on her cousin's grasp. "What I do know, sir, is that I'd rather have nothing to do with you. With all your other entertainments, you should have no further need to annoy me."

"Nor desire."

"Exactly. As long as we understand each other."

"We do."

"Then you will leave me alone?"

"With pleasure."

"Good. If you will excuse me, I must oversee the loading of our luggage."

"Make certain they don't crush my hat box," Claire chirped. "Oh, and have my little pink bag put by my seat. I shall be sitting next to Tony. We have so much to discuss, don't we, darling?"

Claire turned to him, but his eyes followed Sam. The woman had the shoulders of an army officer, he thought in disgust. When he thought of all he had risked, just to accompany her on this escapade, he would have spit. Annie was wrong; Sam didn't need a guardian. Any protection should be from her, not for her.

Willie apparently didn't agree. With a contemptious snort, he followed behind Sam. Grant raised a hand to stop them, but pulled it back. He had better ways to waste his time.

Yet he felt increasingly depressed as he followed where Claire tugged. This was an adventure, he tried to tell himself, not an ordeal. Claire was beautiful, and she adored him. He should be ecstatic.

But as he passed the small group around Sam, he badly wanted to be in their number. How quickly they had rallied to her side. Watching Sam hug the boy, soft and gentle now, Grant thought the shoulders seemed to slump in a betraying manner. If she were hurt, surely he . . .

She looked up then, straight into his eyes. Pure frost blanketed him as she deliberately turned away. Her head, as she moved toward the train, seemed to be held three inches higher.

Hurt, my foot. Gloating, that's what she was doing. Very well, if she wanted nothing more to do with him, that was just fine. More than fine. Goodbye, unwanted responsibility. He could forget her and all her problems and enjoy the less complicated fluff her cousin so lavishly provided.

Yet even as he told himself this, he was overwhelmed by a sense of foreboding. Urging Claire onto the train without him, he stepped down to take a last look around the depot. Tension crawled along his nerves. He didn't know what he expected to see, but something seemed to stalk them. Danger?

It was a fanciful notion, an altogether too absurd

one, but it convinced him of one unpalatable fact. No matter how he felt, no matter what she said, he shouldn't let Sam out of his sight.

Damn you, Sam Eggersley, he cursed silently as he jumped onto the departing train. Damn you for complicating my life.

Charles Riley watched the train pull away, fury building inside. It wasn't their escape that enraged him. A man of his intelligence could easily find them again. No, it was the manner in which they had managed it.

He knew, now, who that old woman had been. What could she have promised, to make a cad like Barton take up her cause? He certainly wasn't working for Hoxton any longer.

His fingers flexed as he thought of them laughing at him. Together, Barton and that Eggersley chit had made a fool of him, a feat about which few men lived to boast. They might laugh now, but they wouldn't for long. They would pay for their nonsense. They would pay dearly.

Returning to the street, Riley barked at his driver to return to the hotel. He had to think, to revamp his plans. Retribution was in order, and he wanted to relish every moment. Next time he encountered that pair, he would be the one laughing.

They could lay a wager on it.

14

Central City, Colorado
April, 1861

Back hugging the wall, Bill made his way along the tunnel, wondering where he might have gone wrong. He could have sworn he should take the right fork, but he should have reached the shed by now. He was hobbling rather badly and his stomach echoed its earlier complaints, nagging about Molly's stew. Why the hell did these things always have to happen at dinnertime?

The half-smile died as he suddenly faced a vast opening in the stone. As he approached, he realized that it was the darkening sky that he saw. Could this be another way out? The blackguards must have dug clear through the mountain, making a front and a back entrance, and for all he knew, maybe a good dozen others!

Anger churned within him. No man enjoyed being played for a fool, but this went beyond games. Unless he missed his guess, this was suspiciously close to where his wife and son had plunged to their deaths. Though the hole was camouflaged with branches and leaves now, had poor Susie seen something in it worth killing for?

Trembling inside, he stepped to edge, willfully looking away to the right. What he saw enraged him further. A primitive road embraced the ledge. A good way down it, a heavily laden wagon wound its way down the mountain to town. That was quite a load it carried, too. Damn them all to hell if that was his gold!

His first instinct was to run along behind it, screaming and hollering all the way to Central City, for he knew he'd get help there. They'd likely lynch the culprits, the good citizens would, and he was just about angry enough to let them.

Two things stopped him. One was his lantern, even now flickering from lack of fuel. He could break his neck on that ledge with no light. And to be painfully honest with himself, he would never make it with this damned leg. The way his knee wobbled, he'd be lucky to get back to the cabin.

He ducked back into the tunnel, determined to find a way out of the mine. Once home, he'd send Sam for Gus, who in turn would fetch Tony. Whatever their other differences, his former partner would stand behind him on this. Criminal, that's what it was, and Tony would help see to it that the guilty were punished.

Unfortunately, he had pushed his stamina too far. Before he could go twenty yards, his leg collapsed. As he fell, he concentrated on holding up the lamp, letting his coat fall and his body go sprawling in a spasm of pain.

Spitting out gravel, he dragged himself into a sitting position. Wasn't so bad, he tried to deceive himself. Not so bad he couldn't get home. He flexed his leg, trying in vain to bend the knee.

Staring blankly ahead, it took him several seconds to focus, several more to accept what his eyes told him. A doorway, they insisted. Could it possibly be another, easier way home? He snatched at the failing lantern and held it high, but he couldn't see much of anything. He brushed against iron posts—another gate?—but he pushed himself forward anyway. The way he figured it, his only other hope was to tackle that ledge.

As faint as it was, the light revealed a storeroom, its floor littered with empty burlap sacks. Tiny golden flakes clustered around them. He nearly laughed. Here was his proof, all that he needed!

But he couldn't laugh, not while the anger kept building in him. To think he and Sam had been living off the charity of the Malloys, while God knew how much ore was sitting here! He grabbed a sack, planning to take it home to show Sam they were right, that all this time, there had been a bonanaza waiting for them in the Oh Susannah mine.

But it was too late. Though he was angry enough to brace himself against the pain in his protesting leg, his rage was powerless against the metal bars that clanked shut behind him. A key grated in the lock.

"Who's there?" he demanded of the darkness. Only a rasp of laughter answered him. "Talk to me, dammit."

"Oh we'll talk, Billy-boy." The voice grated, as the key had done, tauntingly familiar but impossible to identify. "But not until you're ready to say what we want to hear."

Dragging himself to the gate, Bill battled panic. "Let me out of here, dammit. You can't hope to get away with this."

Another rasp of laughter. "But I already have."

"My girl knows where I went. She'll send a search party. When they see the lock off the shack, they'll go inside and see your useless curtain."

"Thanks for the warning. I'll go see to it now."

The laughter mocked him as it vanished down the tunnel. See to what? Bill asked himself desperately.

The lock? The curtain? Sam?

No, Molly would be with the girl by now. Not even a maniac would risk touching the girl with Molly Malloy's buckshot aimed at his gut. No, what should concern him was his own immediate danger. He'd been left with no food or shelter from the cold. All he had was a lantern that wouldn't last the hour.

Hell, he tried to tell himself; there were worse ways to go than freezing to death. Hunger might be bad, but the chill should put him away first. Perversely proud of his stoicism, he sank down against the wall.

Besides, none of this was real. It had to be some crazy dream, conjured up by his fears for the future. Any minute, he'd wake to the aroma of Molly's stew, laughing at the zaniness of it all. Cornishmen living in his mountain? A hole in his shack that led to a vein so tempting men would buy up all the land hereabouts just to break along the side of a treacherous cliff to spirit the gold away? Next, he'd be seeing Sam's tommyrockers!

The thought of his daughter eased his giddiness. He pictured her, soft eyes going hard and cold as she wasted her youth searching for him. First Susie, and now . . . hell, how could he let such a thing happen? For Sam's sake, if nothing else, he had to survive.

If only it wasn't so damned cold. Where in tarnation was his coat? Brightening, he remembered dropping it in the tunnel as he fell. It couldn't be far from that gate. He should be able to reach it through the bars. Yet when he lifted the lantern, sending its light first one way down the tunnel and then the other, his coat was nowhere to be seen. His jailer must have taken it away.

Defeated, he leaned his shoulder against the bars. Their chill stripped away the little warmth left in him, and he shuddered convulsively. How long could a man last, even one with Eggersley stubborness, in such bone-numbing cold? Hell, the snow might just as well be blowing through that opening to pile up beside him, right here on these . . .

His hand rested on burlap. The sacks. Wool might make a better blanket, but since there didn't seem to be any sheep available, he would make do with what he had.

By the time he had dragged the lot of them to his corner and wrapped himself in relative comfort, his lamp was sputtering, a chilling forecast of his own slow and inevitable end.

He huddled in darkness, thoughts revolving in helpless confusion. Primarily, he thought of his daughter, of how he had failed her. He had seen how Susie's death had affected the girl, how thin she was getting, but what had he done? Selfish beast that he was, he let his own grief stop him from sitting down and talking to her. He had firsthand experience with the pain, the guilt, yet he had let that poor, bewildered kid suffer alone.

Just one more chance, he prayed to whoever might listen. Just one more opportunity to hold her close, to tell her how much he loved her.

He could hear his eerie, mirthless laughter echo off the walls. What beautiful irony! Here he was, sitting on a mountain of gold, the supreme justification of all his claims and sacrifices, and all he could think of was a scrawny kid and how gladly he would trade it all away, just to see Sam smile again.

A valuable lesson, that. Shivering in the dark, he could only hope it wasn't too late to put it to use.

15

"Look at her. Do you not see how she pushes herself at him?"

"Giselle, please." Sam didn't want to see. Or hear. Her head pounded in time with the engines of the train, grinding out the miles with neither Claire's giggles nor Giselle's caustic comments ever ceasing.

"How much before you say no more?" As if the words were not enough, Giselle punctuated each with a flash of her fan. "*Mon Dieu*, she takes your name, your job, and now she makes a fool of you, misbehaving with your husband."

"He is not my husband." Giselle's wince annoyed her. What did she care if anyone heard? It would be a relief to be done with this farce.

"These actors, they do not know he is not. Have you no pride? Can't you see how they sneer at you?"

Sam jumped to her feet. The rocking motion of the train nearly thrust her back, but she was determined to escape. If Giselle went into details, if she said one word about how he had managed to bring Claire along, too, there was a good chance Sam might scream.

"Where do you go? Soon we will be in Denver."

Sam slipped at the restraining hand. "I need to be alone." Her whining embarrassed her, so she tried again. "I don't feel well, Giselle. It's all this travelling, and the heat. Maybe I just need fresh air. Or quiet . . ."

The dark eyes flashed with hurt feelings. Sam knew she should stay, as her conscience urged, but the giggles from across the aisle seemed even louder now. "I won't be a minute," she promised. "I'll be back to organize the unloading long before we stop."

She left Giselle grumbling. Too late, she saw she could not reach the back of the train without passing by the two she most specifically wished to avoid. There was no help for it, though. One glance at her maid convinced that retreat was impossible.

Weaving along the aisle, she tried not to look, imagining her cousin draped over that long, lean, and far too often dreamed about body. Better to concentrate on keeping herself upright. With her luck, the train would round a curve, just at the right moment, and she would land with a thud in their laps.

Fortune smiled, more or less, by keeping the train on an even course. Claire still giggled, Sam couldn't help notice, but Grant had slumped in his seat, his head at an uncomfortable angle against the back of it. With his eyes in a perpetual wince, Sam thought smugly that he might look worse than she did.

No one stood on the rear platform, she was relieved to find. Hugging herself, she relished the unaccustomed quiet. No "Mrs. Barton, mend this costume." No "Sam, fetch me this or that." Fanning herself, encouraging what little breeze there was, she watched the rising plains and sighed, the sound stretching over the chug of the train. They could likely hear her frustration clear back to Chicago. She thought of Annie, packing them in and making bundles of money. Not like this tour, which had been mismanaged from the start.

Cyrus Wynecote was an irresponsible fool, she told herself, hiring the face and not the talent. As long as Claire simpered up at him or batted her long, silky lashes, he didn't care that she couldn't act worth a lick, that Grant had to work like the devil to save each scene from ruin.

Momentarily unaware of how she championed him, Sam raged at the injustice. She had spent her childhood in the wings watching the best American actors. She could recognize an artist when she saw one. Grant Barton was as brilliant as the lamps illuminating his magic each night, and twice as effective. The unfairness of saddling him with Claire, of wasting him in this two-bit troupe, made Sam want to spit. If she had her way . . .

Her thoughts hit a painful snag. He was really the high-and-mighty Lord Hoxton, she kept forgetting, not Grant Barton, the actor. But whatever his name, the man avoided her with insulting ease. Each time he took Claire's hand, every smile he gave to someone else, was a reminder of how out-of-reach he would always remain for her. In the nearly three weeks they'd been with the troupe, he hadn't said more than two words together to her, and neither one meant a thing.

Sam watched him constantly. Dammit, she hadn't expected to actually *like* the man. Watching him pore over the grammar books with Willie, sneaking snacks under the table to Gus, or coaxing a performance from a weary colleague, she wondered more and more why her mother had never fallen in love with him.

Then again, he had changed in the intervening miles, as if he had shed the skin of the overbearing Lord Hoxton. That was just more of his artist's magic, perhaps, but in her mind, he had somehow become the heart-stealing actor, Grant Barton.

Not for the first time, she wondered about the actual Grant Barton. She pictured him, rotting in some jail cell, his fine clothes slowly turning to rags. He would be joking, always grinning, no more sincere than his impersonator.

But, oh, didn't the ladies love a rogue! Ask "Tony." There wasn't a one amongst them he couldn't charm. Even Emma, Cyrus's shrewish wife, bent her harsh rules for him. Talented, adorable; he had them all eating out of his hands.

Yet, through it all, he remained aloof, as if playing the rogue were but another role and he focused his inner, secret thoughts elsewhere. On Claire? Sam doubted it. Sometimes, when he thought she wasn't looking, she would catch him staring at her long, hard, and wistfully. The trouble was, she knew he saw not her, but Susannah Eggersley.

Drat the man. It was a dreadful thing, to be jealous of one's mother. She was as bad as all the others combined, for no matter how fiercely she denied it, more than anything, she wanted him to look at and see only her. And not scowl.

Not that she could fault him for that. Not after how she had behaved in Chicago. He had tried to be nice—oh, she could admit it now—but all Sam had seen was her cousin's smirk as she claimed his sleeve. Claire, with her mountains of pretty gowns.

With an abrupt motion, Sam brushed at the ugly gray cotton. Another dream gone to waste. All her hopes for a new life had evaporated when she learned her meager funds must feed them all. Sell one of her furs? Claire had been outraged at the suggestion. *What about me?* Sam would have said had anyone bothered to listen. Did they think she wanted to remain gray forever? That she didn't yearn to be pretty, too?

Responsibility, that's what she would wear for the rest of her life. Every spare penny went to food.

Cyrus couldn't pay their salaries without profits, and success would elude them until Claire abdicated as leading lady, which she would never do as long as Grant remained the leading man, and so on, endlessly.

Oh drat, she didn't expect a standing ovation for being the only one with funds, or for her careful use thereof, but just once, someone could notice who scoured the shops, wrangling with the clerks for the best bargains. Grant Barton, had a kind word or a flirtatious smile for everyone else; one would think he could spare an occasional thanks for Sam.

At the least, he could cease humiliating her. Oh yes, she heard what the others whispered behind her back. Giselle must think her deaf, dumb, and blind not to notice. Not one of them bothered to mask their contempt.

And like a worm, she took it. She wished she could do something. Make a scene, walk off on her own, anything. But then, how would she ever get to Central City? She was so close to her goal now, it would be foolish to sacrifice it all for a silly thing like pride. No, she must remain ostensibly oblivious, as if their taunts could never reach her.

There was a click, she whirled and a glimpse of auburn hair catapulted her into fantasy. Jacket flung over a shoulder, waistcoat hanging open, white shirt unbuttoned at his chest, Grant seemed to be playing the part of a brigand—a dangerous one, whose eyes devoured her whole. His possession was as sensual as it was total, a lifelong affair packed into an exhilarating second of time.

As he frowned, fantasy fled and common sense limped back. How long had she held her breath? Turning to face the tracks again, she felt the heat, first and foremost, then the pounding of the distant engine. Its smoke caused the disturbance in her lungs, she insisted. And a cinder stung her eyes.

"Oh, excuse me; I didn't realize you were here."

It was more than he'd said to her in a month, but as polite and remote as if that heated gaze had never blazed between them. How absurdly like her to have imagined it had! "Don't be ridiculous, Mr. Barton. You can't be forever leaving a room merely because I am in it."

Though she refused to turn and see for herself, she thought he sounded puzzled. "Isn't that what you wanted? You said . . ."

"I said a great deal too much that day. I was tired and worn, and—and thoroughly unjust. I wish you'd forgive me."

Hearing a second click, she swallowed the rest of her plea. There he goes, she thought. Back to Claire.

"That hurt, didn't it?"

She still wouldn't turn, couldn't, but then it was hardly necessary. She could feel the heat of him burning her back. "I . . . what do you mean?"

Closer, and hotter yet. "Your apology. Knowing you, I'll wager it nearly killed you to make it."

"Oh? And just how well do you think you know me, sir?"

She felt movement behind her. He might have shrugged. "Well enough to know that you don't enjoy this scrapping any more than I do. Claire, why don't we—"

"My name is Sam."

"Dammit!" He pulled back, ever so slightly, and the warmth went with him. "No wonder you hate me, the way I'm forever mixing the two names in my mind."

It was nice to know she occupied some space there, Sam reasoned, her spirits lightening. "But I don't hate you."

"That's a start." He took her hand and spun her around to face him. "At the risk of getting my ears boxed, can I tell you now that I've actually missed our little spats?"

Sam was afraid to say anything, afraid that if she spoke, he would vanish like a dream. Lord, he was beautiful. And so close. She watched the grinning mouth but dared look no higher.

"Not only have I had to go without my daily dose of humility, my life has been downright dull of late. No stolen horses, no skulking about the streets posing as old ladies and pack animals. Ah, a smile at last. That's more the thing."

She looked at him then. She had no choice. His eyes lured hers, a flute charming a snake. How unfair of him to make her laugh. "I don't know why I made such a scene. Generally, I do my utmost to avoid them."

"Oh? You don't strike me as the sort to avoid anything."

She averted her gaze, hiding the spurt of pleasure. He was doing it again. Poking through the crevices, cracking her defenses, making her forget the purpose of this journey. Years ago, a child named Sam Eggersley had vowed to return, to learn what had happened to her parents. On the verge of her life's goal, all she could think about was how close he stood.

Why was he so suddenly quiet? Was he thinking about her parents, too? Or only her mother? A sour taste spilled into her mouth. Probing into the past, that's what she should be doing. Not watching his profile like an adoring child.

"Where are these Rocky Mountains you Americans brag about so constantly? I'd have thought

239

we'd be seeing them by now."

She nearly giggled in relief. Of course he'd be thinking about his blasted mountains. "Just wait. In another moment or so, you'll understand the boasts. We go around a bend and suddenly, there they are, towering over the city like ancient gods. They're like nothing you can imagine."

He was staring past her, his face clouded. Sam cringed. The past again. It would always be there to haunt them. "I'm sorry. It must be painful for you, being unable to remember, while here I am, rattling on as if to some tourist." She tapered off, feeling foolish.

With a half smile, he took her shoulders and spun her around. "Look. You were right."

Dramatically looming in the distance, the Rockies were all she described, and more. Painfully, she relived her last sight of them, traveling to Richmond with her stern, unsympathetic grandfather. Her little girl's heart cried out as it had then, but before sadness could claim her, Grant moved closer to rest a hand on her arm. All grief vanished in a flash.

"I see what you mean," he said softly. "Even in my dr—imagination, I never expected anything like this. It must be rugged going, way up there. I bet it takes quite a man to survive."

"It's just a matter of adapting to it. Everything's a bit different, especially the air. It's a good deal lighter. One good breath and you're intoxicated. You become light-headed and silly, but oh, so thoroughly alive. You think—you know—you can do anything."

His smile went right down into her. He was so close, mere inches away. She could feel his breath fan her cheek, his heart pounding against her back. As he dragged his eyes from the mountains to look down at her, he seemed surprised to find her there. Surprised, but not as dismayed as one might expect. Sam wondered if she would ever draw a breath again.

"Why did you do it?"

There was her breath. A sharp, painful stab of air. "I beg your pardon?"

He stepped back, rather too quickly, to lean against the rail. "Willie, Stoddard—they all insisted you had your reasons for the deception, but I remain baffled as to what they could be. It simply doesn't seem like something you would, or could, do."

She silently thanked him for that much. "I'd rather not discuss this."

"Coward."

In that instant, she almost hated him. She could lose herself in admiring Grant Barton, but she must remain wary of an inquisitive Lord Hoxton. She should be asking the questions, not he—even though they were questions to which she was no longer certain she wanted the answers. "The deception was to avoid this very scene. Marriage was the last thing I wanted, Lord Hoxton. Then, or now."

"I see." He studied his fingernails. It couldn't be that he had dirt in them; he was far too meticulous. "I recall your saying that you enjoyed yourself tremendously. Why, I wonder, would you cut such amusement short by running away?"

"I did no such thing!" But she had. Knowing this, Sam could feel her entire face burn. "Annie had sent a letter. An invitation. To come to Chicago to visit her. I just went a little sooner than I'd planned."

"This has developed into quite a visit."

"I told you, I wanted to try my hand at acting."

"But you're not acting, are you?"

This time there was no grin to take away the sting of his words. This made her more flustered, which in turn made her more resentful. "No, I am not. But whose fault is that?''

She half hoped he would flinch, but he never moved a muscle. "I had nothing to do with Cyrus's decision."

"Claire wouldn't even be here, had you not interfered. If anything had gone according to my plans, she would be safely tucked away in Richmond."

"Funny how your plans have a nasty habit of going awry, Miss Eggersley. One wonders why you persist in designing them."

She was not going to cry—at least not here, where he could witness it and no doubt later throw it back in her face. "I don't know how you can be so smug. You can hardly claim that yours and Riley's fared better."

This time he did flinch, but Sam felt no satisfaction. What had she hoped? That he would deny it? Take her in his arms, as he had once, and kiss all the ugly truths and doubts away?

"This is absurd." Her voice, she noticed, had a waspish taint to it. "I have better things to do with my time than to stand here bickering with you. If I don't arrange the luggage before we reach Denver, everyone will be screaming at me again."

"Claire, wait . . ." The arms uncrossed, one of them reaching out for her face. She could so easily melt at that touch, if he hadn't, yet again, called her by her cousin's name.

She wrenched free, her voice cracking as she spoke. "It's Sam, do you hear? I am not Claire!"

Though she heard the oath as she pushed through the door, he made no further attempt to detain her. She as still trembling as she scurried back to her seat. Fully aware of Giselle's blanketing concern, Sam stuffed loose items into a satchel. She should have started this hours ago; Claire's things would be all over the train. It would be her luck to be crawling on the floor searching for a silly pink ribbon, her posterior in a vulnerable position, when Grant returned to the car.

It hardly mattered. He would merely step over her. She was invisible, remember? Claire, her mother—his thoughts would always be on someone else.

She bit her lip to keep it from trembling. She had done it again. Left her heart out there in plain sight so he could step on it. Had it been intentional, calling her Claire? Had he been getting back at her for all the nasty things she had again said, but hadn't meant?

A hand strayed up to her cheek. She could still feel the tingling his touch had produced, as if his fingers had imprinted themselves there. Had she held her tongue . . .

Enough of that, she told herself sternly, forcing her hands back to her packing. Why didn't she forget that blasted man? She would soon be in Denver, a quick train trip away from Central City. She had too many important things on her mind to waste time thinking about what might have been.

Tomorrow, she would begin digging into the past.

The past was the last thing on Grant's mind. He was far too concerned with the present. And the future. How could he ever convince her of his good intentions if he couldn't even remember her name?

Forget her, he told himself. He could live without that shrew's scathing remarks, thank you all the same. But even as he said this, he remembered the softening in her eyes, the quickening of her breath, the way her body trembled when he touched it.

He pounded a fist into the railing. All these weeks of running away from her, from himself, and he couldn't elude the truth. He wanted her. Badly. And for all his experience, his skill and his past victories, he hadn't the slightest hope of making her want him.

Was that the attraction, then? The novelty of a woman who could resist him, he insisted, would naturally fuel his lust. Only what reason was there, then, to want to know everything that ever was or would be about her? Some inner, unknown drive to punish himself?

As the train slowed, he remembered the real Claire. She would be wondering where he was. Not that he cared; he was merely afraid she might come seeking him, and he would be tempted to throw her off the end of the train.

The silly chit must think she was glued to him. Grant didn't know which was more oppressive, her grip or her scent. Disinterest, downright rudeness—nothing seemed to discourage her. Lord help them both if she giggled one more time.

Irritably, he pushed off the railing. As he did so, his gaze went to the mountains. They were impressive, inspiring. Oh damn, could a man truly get lost in them? If he were to ride up there, could he come out, as Hoxton had done, an entirely different man, no longer knowing who or what he was?

But then, he admitted ruefully, hadn't that happened already?

Trying to calm Gus's excited yapping as she heaped their cases in one pile, Sam ignored Giselle's complaints. Claire never helped with anything; why should she behave differently today? Merely because Grant, for once, wasn't there to pay court to her? Forcing her mind to her task, Sam refused to wonder why he had yet to return from the rear of the train.

The train slowed, and as always, everything

seemed to happen at once. Between struggling to quiet the dog, dealing with a barrage of questions, and gathering their belongings, Sam had little time to think of anything but herding everyone out into the baking sunshine. With Gus to echo her, she barked out instructions, though she was forced to haul several pieces of luggage herself to speed the process.

When the last bag and body was secured, Sam took a seat of her own in the hired cab, while Gus hopped enthusiastically onto her lap. Denver at long last, she sighed as she gazed about her.

The city had done some growing since the last time she'd seen it. Compared to Chicago, or even Richmond, it still wore a provincial air, but daily, money poured into its banks and businesses from the mining centers. And now, with railroad connections to the rest of the nation, anything could happen. Denver had become Colorado's capital, and few of its residents were shy about pointing this out. The city seemed to be gathering energy, as if it knew great things could be expected of it soon.

Unfortunately, the hotel in front of which they stopped had no such pretensions. Its prosperity had come and gone, the greater portion of time spent in the going. Sam could only pray that the sheets would be cleaner than the walls. She had already abandoned hope that she need not share a room with Claire.

"Sam, just a moment. I want to speak with you."

Sam braced herself. Claire wore her butter-wouldn't-melt mouth. "I hope this won't take long. Cyrus expects me to help with the room assignments."

"But that's just it. You have to talk to him, Sam. Make him see it's silly for us to share. Why should the leading lady bed with a—a nobody, when the leading man has his own room."

"Grant sometimes shares with Willie."

Claire ignored that. "Sam, honey, use your imagination. Don't you care that people are talking about me? I mean, here I am, the star of the troupe, treated like anyone else. Make Cyrus see how he's making me suffer."

"You make him see. Just bat those lashes, and I daresay he'd see anything you want."

"Why, what a terribly nasty thing to say."

"I am hot, I am tired, and quite frankly, I have no strength left to be nice. If you and Grant wish to become roommates, you must deal with it. I have to find our dinner."

"Roommates? With Tony? Merciful heavens, wherever did you get that idea?"

"His name is Grant. And don't waste the big eyes on me. I watch you leave each night, remember? Contrary to popular belief, I am not an imbecile, Claire. I can deduce where you spend your time."

"I . . . why, I think you're jealous!"

The chit had the gall to be smug. Sam fought the urge to wrestle her down to the street. "I have neither time nor energy for such an emotion. I do, however, have more pride than to arrange sordid little trysts for the pair of you. Envy, Claire? No, what you see is anger. Rage that you can remain so immersed in yourself! Stop worrying about your own so-called suffering and think about what you might be doing to others. The tongues are already wagging. I can just imagine what will be said if I arrange for you and my supposed husband to share a room."

"Well, I never."

"No, Claire, I don't suppose you ever did."

Backing away, too upset to watch where she was going, Sam shook her head in disgust. After all these years, after all the battles she had fought on her behalf, Claire still continued to think of herself first, last and foremost. As Grandfather had consistently tried to warn her, the world was divided between the givers and the grabbers, and everyone knew who got what.

"Watch out!"

Before she could understand the warning, a hard body slammed her to the ground. Wheels clattered close to her head and she had the ugly sensation of having gone through this before.

"My God, are you all right?"

She looked up into deep, concerned blue eyes. "I think so. How silly of me to be standing in the street. One would have thought I'd learned my lesson in Chicago."

He grabbed her by the arms, hard. "What lesson?"

"What happened to Annie. To us both, I guess. I mean, we were both standing there when the cab came barreling along. I was frightened, but Annie said it was nothing. That such things happen all the time in the city."

On and on she chattered, anything to disguise how badly shaken she was, both by her narrow escape and Grant's proximity. She could feel the hard line of him along the entire length of her body. If they were in bed, she fantasized, his fingers would be sneaking to the buttons at her throat . . . .

"Oh . . . somebody, please . . . help me. I feel so dizzy, I think I might . . . I might . . . oh, Tony!"

To their right, Claire staged a most convincing swoon. She should use half that skill on stage, Sam thought, until Grant slowly rose to his feet. He hesitated briefly, his eyes searching hers. "You're certain you're all right?"

"I'm fine. Go ahead, go to her."

Again he paused, ever so slightly, until with a tightening of his lips, he went to bend over Claire. Watching him sweep the girl into his arms, Sam realized that she wasn't too tired for envy. Those arms could be cradling her, taking her upstairs, laying her onto the bed, staring into her eyes, seeing . . .

Claire moaned, ever so prettily, as she clung to his neck. Trailing behind them, Sam felt awkward and unnecessary, a discomfort that grew with the whispers preceding her into the hotel. Barely twenty feet into the lobby, Cyrus cornered her, demanding to know why she had let his star performer be injured.

Injured, my eye. Just look at her! Sam wanted to shout. Simpering up at him, milking the moment for all it was worth, while the true victim was forced to stay and explain to the panicked manager. How beautiful Claire looked, draped across Grant's arms, playing the tragic heroine. And how pleased, having gotten exactly what she wanted. What Sam wanted. Ten minutes went by, then twenty, and still Grant remained upstairs. Facing Cyrus's badgering, Sam's replies grew terse, then brusque, as she considered what they could be doing up there. Was it Claire's buttons his fingers played with instead? Or perhaps, in their eagerness, they had already gone beyond disrobing.

"—will you answer me that?"

Focusing, she discovered everyone's eyes on her. They apparently expected an answer. Good lord, what was the question?

"I'm ruined!" Cyrus ranted, pacing before her with his pudgy hands clasping his head. "I'm positively ruined."

"Not necessarily." Sam's tone dripped acid; she'd had enough of everyone else's self-preoccupation. "I doubt her injuries are that severe."

"Easy for you to say; you don't have to face my wife. Have you any idea what this booking could mean? Denver. My God, when will I ever get a chance like this again?"

"Don't worry, I'll bet anything she'll perform tonight."

Moaning, Cyrus clearly wasn't listening. Rather than waste her breath, Sam decided to find her room. She had simultaneously turned and realized just who might be in that room, when Grant materialized before her. He grinned at Sam but faced Cyrus with the solemnity of an undertaker. "I fear not, darling. Sorry, Cyrus, but the doctor says she needs a good rest. He is dispensing a sedative now."

Sam could have sworn Claire's injuries were feigned, that they were no more than another bid for attention. Could the doctor be as blind as the others? But of course, he was a man, wasn't he?

Still, she couldn't help but be disappointed in Grant. For a moment, she thought he might have seen through the ploy. But all Claire had to do was blink her big, blue eyes . . .

"Now, there's no need to be glum, Wynecote." As she glanced up, she found Grant beaming at her. "We have a perfect replacement. Have you forgotten how well my wife plays Marietta?"

"Good lord, Barton. She's too tall for the costume."

"I can find another," Sam said.

"But the billboard . . . The tickets . . ."

"Be imaginative. Explain in advance. Offer a refund if they're dissatisfied with the performance. For myself, I think we can trust Samantha to keep them in their seats."

Sam felt herself flush with surprise and pleasure, and not a little fright as Wynecote studied her. He didn't like it, the skeptical frown made that patently obvious, but she could amost hear him tallying up the sums in his brain. They needed this engagement, if they hoped to eat. "I don't know, Barton."

"Relax. Sam will be so good you'll be wondering why you haven't used her before. Isn't that right, darling?"

He winked again. Given half a chance, Sam would have kissed him. But she wasn't quick enough. Taking him by the arm, Cyrus was already leading him away.

"He did it for you, you know," came a voice behind Sam.

"My goodness, Willie, you startled me."

"Just thought you should know. Her Highness is as healthy as a horse, doctor said. It was the cap'n who suggested the stuff to make her sleep. He'll probably catch hell—big trouble for it, too, but he knows you wanted to play Marietta. I reckon he saw the chance and took it for you."

"You're not trying to tell me that he drugged Claire so I could take her place, are you?"

"Him and me, we're like this." Crossing his fingers, Willie held them out to her. "The man can't sneeze without me knowing."

"But it doesn't make sense. Why would he do such a thing? He loves Claire."

"Dunno about that. Me, I think he likes you better."

Sam tried hard not to smile. She'd been down this road before; they both knew it was a dead end. "Oh Willie, there's not a particle of truth to that and we both know it."

He shook his head. "It's true, all right. Maybe don't know it yet, but I can tell by the way he looks at you."

"He looks at me? How? How does he look at me?"

"Kinda hungry-like. Scared, almost."

This was absurd. Listening to such drivel from a twelve-year-old boy—and wanting to believe it so badly it must show on her face. "I have no time for speculation, Willie. There must be a million things to do. Where that man expects to find a costume to fit me . . ."

"I reckon he has that taken care of, too. Or he will. You gotta learn to trust him more, Miss Sam. It's hard, I know, getting past that mask of his, but underneath, he's quality too."

"What mask?"

"He's says we all wear them, to protect ourselves from getting hurt. He thinks yours must be one of the best."

"Oh he does, does he?"

"Me, I think if you two let each other see under your masks, you wouldn't need to be fighting all the time."

"Is that so? Well, I happen to think that you have too fertile an imagination, young William. Masks, indeed."

"There you go again."

Sam felt most uncomfortable, being so accurately assessed by the child. Yet somewhere inside, she felt just the teeniest bit better. He looked at her, did he?

"That's enough of this nonsense. I have far too much to do to be dawdling in a hotel lobby. I have to find our dinner."

"You shouldn't have to be dealing with that tonight. Not with your acting debit coming up."

"That's debut, please. And unfortunately, if I don't get dinner no one else will."

"I could."

Concealing her smile, Sam resisted the urge to

squeeze him tight. "You, Mr. MacPhearson, are a prince among men. I must admit, I'd love the company. I noticed a grocer on our way here but do you suppose, between the two of us, we might dig up a decent bakery in this town?"

"Bakery?"

"It's past time we treated ourselves to something special."

He grinned from freckle to freckle. "Let me guess. This something special wouldn't be hot-cross buns, now would it?"

Sam blushed. Sometimes, the boy saw entirely too much. "A favor repaid is a friend saved, young man."

"He will be tickled upside down, he will."

"If you plan to accompany me, I suggest you wipe that grin from your face."

An admonition, Sam realized as she herded him out to the street, that she herself couldn't obey. It was going to be a glorious night; she could feel it in her bones.

Grant had an altogether different feeling in his bones. He didn't like these accidents. Riley had been in Chicago. Could he have followed them here, as well?

He had this sudden, overwhelming need to see Sam safe and sound. Making a quick excuse, he left Cyrus sputtering to go in search of her.

"Tony? Tony Rawlings, you old reprobate, is that you?

"Hey Tony, it's me. Jack. Jack Parker. Don't you remember? I worked the claim next to yours and Bill's."

"Huh? Oh yes. Yes, of course. You must forgive me, Mr. Parker, but I've had an accident. I'm afraid I recall very little of those days."

"Yeah, I heard about that. That sure was a heap of bad luck followed the pair of you around. Think there's something in those tales about the Oh Susannah being cursed? Lord knows, nobody's fool enough to go near it nowadays. Gus was the only one brave enough to go up there."

Grant watched the dark head bobbing along outside the windows. Where the hell was she going? Wasn't one "accident" enough for one day?

"Heard you fell into a heap of money," Parker was saying "Reckon you got that title mess cleared up, huh?"

Confused, Grant focused on the man for the first time. Shorter than himself by a good head and a half, Jack Parker had seen better days. His tattered coat was stained in several places and dragged the unmistakable aroma of whiskey behind it. Was the man looking for money?

"I sold my half of the Oh Susannah to Bill Eggersley, Mr. Parker. As far as I knew, there was never a question about the title."

"Heck, not the claim. I meant that lordship business. Last time I talked to you, lawyers were searching for some long lost cousin that had vanished."

"Yes, that has all been cleared up satisfactorily." Grant hoped the man didn't see his bewilderment. What the hell was this about a cousin? No one had ever mentioned a problem with Hoxton gaining the title. How much else hadn't Riley told him? "I am now Lord Hoxton."

"Good for you. Nice to know one of us got what we wanted. Remember how you always used to say you'd be lording it over us one day? It's a shame poor Bill couldn't live to know this. One of the last things he said to me, you know, was that he hoped your family would recognize you one day."

And how had Hoxton repaid such friendship? Uncomfortable with that train of thought, Grant once again focused on Parker.

"I sure admired that man," he was saying, shaking his head sadly. "Everybody did. Always there if you needed him. He bailed me out of trouble more than once, I can tell you. A lot of us plain gave up, after he was killed."

"Killed? I thought it was suicide. Or an accident."

Parker leaned closer, his voice pitched soft and low. "To my way of thinking, there's been too many accidents up that way. Look at what happened to Gus Malloy."

"What happened?"

"Died. All of them on the same cliff. Bill, his wife, and now Gus. Some coincidence, huh?"

But there was no such thing as coincidence. Hadn't he had that drilled often enough into his mind? Three people, all dying on the Eggersley claim.

"Folks claim the place is cursed. There was this company from the East, must have been a big one with the money it threw around, but it stopped buying up land after Bill died. I mean, even them easterners got scared off. The few folks brave, or dumb enough, to go up there say they can sometimes still hear the stamp mills, pounding away beneath the ground. If that ain't enough to spook you, I don't know what is."

"Are you suggesting that the Oh Susannah is haunted?"

"All I do know for certain is that I ain't about to go testing my luck like Gus did. I'll stay right here in Denver, if it's all the same to you."

Grant had an ugly feeling in his gut. Even here in

Denver, he'd already seen, all was not safe. Where the hell had Sam gone? "Listen, Mr—uh, Jack, I'd love to stay and chat, but I've got to run. Business. Perhaps I can buy you a drink later?"

"Yeah, sure, I'd enjoy that."

Grant waved his reply as he dashed for the street. Dismayed at the density of the crowd he found there, he wondered how he would ever find Sam.

Sick inside, he started to the right, eyes searching every shop window. In his mind, he could see it again, the scene playing itself out slowly. He, on the curb, silently applauding as Sam at long last stood up to her cousin, and then draining of all color as he realized the carriage wasn't going to stop.

It had to have been deliberate. There was far too much time and room to swerve safely to the side. Whoever had been driving that carriage had, at the very least, meant to scare the girl.

But why? He kept coming back to that question. Lord knew, he'd had his own momentary urges to throttle that lovely neck, but, kill her? Like the Eggersleys and Gus Malloy.

Up ahead, he saw the tightly bound hair and felt relief swamp him. She emerged from the bakery, smiling broadly as she clasped a box. His first impulse was to go running up and throw his arms around her, but he thought better of it.

For what could he say? "Sorry, but I want to make certain my employers haven't murdered you yet?" Lord, what a pickle. He couldn't warn her without embroiling himself. And even if he was willing to risk that, which he wasn't, what possible motive could he offer? It sounded insane, suggesting that Hoxton would want to kill her. For what reason? A useless claim?

Ducking into the lobby, melting into the crowd,

he watched Willie and Sam bounce up the stairs. How girlishly happy she seemed. How pretty with all that color on her cheeks.

His smile faded. He knew what this opportunity meant to her. And he would not spoil it with his as-yet-groundless paranoia. Until he had some substantial proof to offer, he would stand back, watch, listen, and wait. It was all he could do.

So he fought the intense, ungovernable urge to fly up those stairs and shield her in his arms, as if by so doing he could keep her safe. Why her safety should be so vital to him, he refused to examine. Or, for that matter, why he had abandoned all he had ever hoped to accomplish in life to chase after her. Clearly, he had burned all his bridges behind him. Riley, when and if he caught up with him, would not be holding a paycheck, but more likely the long arm of the law.

Watching Sam vanish into her room, he stuffed his hands into his pockets and sighed. A fine mess you've landed yourself in now, Mr. Barton. How in the devil's name do you hope to charm your way out of this one?

Hell, the explanations could wait. Grinning sheepishly, he decided to make the most of tonight. With Sam playing Marietta to his Damion, anything could happen.

Anything at all.

16

Where was she? Worried, Grant scanned the crowd again. Sam had gone upstairs to tuck in Willie, but that had been hours ago, surely.

Another glance at his watch confirmed an absence of a mere fifteen minutes, but it seemed far longer. He must have checked that door a hundred times. She could have been gone a year.

"I declare, you pay more attention to your watch than you do to me."

"What?" Perfume clogged his nostrils. He frowned. Why hadn't Claire slept the twelve hours the doctor promised? Dressed to the teeth, she had arrived just as Sam was making her curtain calls. All five of them.

"I've explained," he snapped. "Sam did us a favor by going on in your place. What would you have us do? Cancel?"

As her face puckered up, he braced himself. She must know Wynecote's greed outweighed his lust, that her pretty face would no longer be enough. Not when her cousin could draw a larger audience.

Oh, but how they had adored Sam tonight! Small wonder, for she had been incredible. A fascinating, unpredictable creature he alone seemed to recognize. But then, that creature had been haunting his dreams too often lately.

"Why must you always bring the conversation back to Sam? She is a saint, everyone knows it, but the fact is, I am not feeling at all well and no one cares a fig.''

"That's not so. I am always distracted after a performance. What is it, your head again?" He tried to sound soliticitous but his attention had already strayed back to the door. Where the hell was Sam?

"Yes," Claire sniffled. "I feel absolutely wretched and I know I must look it, too. I just can't bear having people see me this way."

He wanted to groan. There was nothing wrong with Claire, in health or looks. She merely hoped to draw attention to herself, to have him appreciate her beauty. It was a game she often played; a rather insulting one, come to think of it. Did the woman really think he could be so easily manipulated?

Still, if playing along removed her arm from his, he would happily comply. "You look splendid, darling, though a trifle drawn. You must be tired; why don't you go back to bed?"

"Alone?"

"Of course. The doctor was most explicit about not disturbing your rest."

"Rest?" Her complexion now matched her gown. "This has been the most restful month of my life. Have you kept count of how many times you've left me in the evening so you could get an early night's sleep?"

"Well, I can't leave, now. I've invited all these people in here to celebrate. As the host of this little party, I must stay and—and mingle."

He didn't deceive her for a second, he could tell by the tightening of her lips. "Celebrate what, *darling*? Sam's success? Or her treachery? She engineered the entire thing, you know."

"I beg your pardon?"

"Isn't it odd how I was the one injured, how Sam

was the one to strut out on the stage in my place?"

How blind could a person be? Claire must live in her own little world, a convenient one, where she could see only that which she wanted to see. Otherwise, she'd know that he saw through this latest ploy, that he was fully aware of the extent of her so-called injuries. "For God's sake, how can you say such a thing after all Sam has done for you?"

"So she's tricked you as well. But then, this isn't the first time, is it?"

He wouldn't grace that with an answer. Did she think him stupid enough to forget her own involvement? Disgusted, he yanked free of her grasp.

He felt the prickling along his skin, actually saw her before his eyes were drawn to the door. Relief spread over him like a warm blanket. For a wonderful moment, as Sam's eyes searched the room, he was free to drink in the sight of her.

It was happening again, that same magic he'd felt earlier, as she approached from across the stage. She was still draped in the costume he had chosen, the scarlet silk hugging her body as he dared not. He let his eyes act for his hands, sliding up the graceful folds of the full skirt, along the narrow curve of her waist, to touch the bare white flesh of her shoulders, glistening in the light. Down his gaze traveled, inevitably drawn to the luscious breasts. As if bursting with pride, they strained against the delicate lace trim and he wondered where on earth she'd been hiding them.

Her hair, he noticed with pleasure, hadn't returned to the Claire Farnstable knot. His fingers itched to slide through it, to take her head in his hand and tug her closer. As if back onstage, they could be Damion and Marietta, alone on a balcony, he planning the thousand ways he would kiss her. It seemed the most natural thing in the world to drift to her side.

The room fell into a hush, an audience awaiting a performance. But he heard, saw and felt only Sam. She smiled, hesitantly. Sensing her shyness, he held out a hand to draw her closer. "I . . . we've been waiting for you, Mrs. Barton."

"I'm sorry. I tried to hurry, but Willie was so excited. And then, when I went to change into street clothes, I found I couldn't face the prospect of gray. I hope this gown isn't—well, a bit too much?"

A young girl facing her coming-out had more confidence. Squeezing her hand, he wished he could put her on a pedestal, higher than her cousin could reach, so she could never again doubt her loveliness. "You look how I feel. Positively splendid. Look at them. Not one of those cads can take their eyes away. Whoever chose your costume had a good eye for your—er, attributes."

"But Willie said you chose it."

"Oh he did, did he? And do you listen to everything that little yarn-spinner tells you?"

Reddening, she pulled her hand from his grasp. "Of course not. We all know where your eye rests, sir. She seems quite recovered, by the way. That must be a great relief to you."

He followed her gaze. Damn, but he had forgotten Claire. And such negligence, he knew from experience, could only spell trouble. The last thing he needed was one of her tantrums.

"Tony . . ." Claire bit her lip as she grabbed for his arm. "I mean, Grant, darling, come see your surprise. You'll just adore this."

He had no choice but to follow, but his eyes remained on Sam. She seemed upset. Damn, what had he done wrong this time? Must he forever say the wrong thing?

Blatantly pleased with herself, Claire opened the baker's box. Grant knew its contents long before the unmistakeable aroma drifted up to tempt him. "They're his favorites" Sam had once told Willie. And unless he missed his guess, this was the box they'd been carrying this afternoon.

Sam had looked away. Her cheeks were flushed, her shoulders slumped. Why didn't she step up to take the credit? Didn't she realize he'd know?

He forced a smile at Claire, wanting to box her pretty ears. How many times had this happened in the past? It was just like Sam to do such a thoughtful thing, and then sit back and let someone else take credit for it. Watching with growing exasperation, he saw her edge back to the fringe of the crowd. She looked miserable.

But this, he realized in a burst of revelation, was the real Sam. The rest—the prim and proper facade—was all defense. Any moment now, she would drift out the door, fading from sight, and no one would ever notice.

But he would. Admit it, he told himself. If Sam left, the party would go with her. "Where's that champagne?" he shouted. "Fill up the glasses. I want to propose a toast."

"But Grant, honey, don't you want . . ."

Ignoring Claire, he concentrated all his energy on trapping Sam with his gaze. *Look at me, dammit*, he coaxed her silently. She hesitated, but when the gray eyes at last met his, he thought he might have conquered the world.

Someone handed him a glass. Raising it into the air, he saluted her, his eyes holding her in place. "To my lovely and talented wife. Let's put it to a vote. I say Samantha shall be Marietta from now on."

Around them, the troupe cheered the decision. Put on the spot, Cyrus muttered that yes, well, it might be wise . . .

Drawn by Sam's soft, spreading smile, Grant ignored Claire's gasp and ensuing scowl. Her tapping foot might just as well have been his heart, reacting as the new Marietta slowly approached to take the glass he offered. For a crazy, impossible moment, he was alone with her. And he had never felt so right about things in his life.

Their fingers touched for the briefest of seconds, and the cool, electric shock startled them both. She recovered first. A wariness settled back into her gray eyes, and he slowly, painfully, remembered the crowd surrounding them.

"Well, I declare," Claire whined, "if you'd rather drink than eat, I honestly don't know why we bought these. We might just as well take them back where they came from."

With an effort, he dragged his eyes away. "Don't be silly. I'd love one. Here, everyone, help yourselves. Sam, how about you—care for a taste?"

Giving her no time to protest, he tore off a bite popped it into her mouth, happy for the excuse to touch her lips. He was swamped in a sea of emotions and he was powerless against its tide.

Get yourself under control, he tried to warn himself. One could not stroll up and touch a Samantha Eggersley. One must exercise care and patience.

Yet she seemed just as reluctant as he for him to remove his fingers, for all that she would not meet his gaze. If Claire hadn't barged in to insist she must be fed next, lord knew what might have happened.

Considering the intimacy of his gesture, Sam's quick thank-you was remotely polite. And from the

speed with which her feet edged backward, one
would think she had a hundred other, more pressing
engagements.

"I should be mingling," she mumbled.

The brilliant smile was as false as the excuse.
Hadn't he used the same on her cousin? As he
watched Sam walk away, he felt a tug at his sleeve.
"Feed yourself," he snapped at Claire, and grabbed a
bottle of champagne to go sulk in the corner.

Sam seized the first available guest to talk with.
Unable to pull his eyes away, Grant watched her,
swelling with need. Every inch of him ached for her
with a desire that would never be reciprocated, nor
even eased. How, on God's good earth, had he landed
himself in such a state?

He gulped straight from the bottle. He might as
well drink himself into such a stupor, that he
wouldn't feel a thing, no matter what she said or did
to him.

Claire materialized at his side, complaining about
Sam, his drinking, and a barrage of other peeves.
Grant let her come and go, not reacting, still watching
Sam. She was a disease, he decided, a nasty, little
parasite that had burrowed under his skin. His was a
purely physical attraction, spurred into this delirium
by her indifference. If just once he could break
through her barriers, drive her to a reciprocal lust, the
fever would go, and he would be cured. He could
then sleep in peace.

He laughed as Emma Wynecote trapped her.
Poetic justice, that. Normally, he felt pity for Cyrus's
wife, but tonight she struck him as an inveterate
prude, a prune of a female, just the sort Sam would
turn into if she didn't soon mend her ways.

"I must say I am surprised," Emma said. "You
were surprisingly good on that stage tonight."

"Why, thank you."

"For a moment there, you reminded me of someone. It's impossible, of course. Susannah would be a good twenty years your senior."

Sam smiled nervously, playing with her glass. "I'm told that quite often. That I remind people of someone else, that is."

"It must be the gown. I must say, I never expected to see you dressed so inappropriately."

"Inappropriately? Why, this was my costume. My husband chose it and I have the utmost faith in his taste. Don't you?"

That little baggage, Grant thought, amused in spite of himself. He doubted Emma's embarrassing infatuation was a secret to anyone, except perhaps her uncaring, philandering husband. Sam knew the woman would cut out her tongue before she would criticize the great Grant Barton.

"Why, yes, of course. For the stage. But here, in a room filled with men? Drinking men, at that. At least we, I am happy to see, know how a lady should behave. A disgusting habit, drinking."

Though she plainly wished to tell the woman to mind her own business, Sam would sit there the rest of the night, swallowing platitudes, if no one came along to rescue her.

Yet as Grant rose, ready and anxious to play the shining knight, Sam raised her glass with a tight smile. "Ordinarily, I might agree with you, but tonight is a special circumstance. Even we women should be permitted to drink on a special occasion, don't you think?" She drained her glass and glanced about, as if for another.

"Special occasion?" Emma sputtered. "What utter nonsense. I could understand wasting hard-earned profits had we opened in New York, or even

Boston, but not here. No, my dear girl, you can rest assured, this is merely someone's feeble excuse to misbehave. I can imagine whose, too. It's appalling, the way she flaunts herself in front of the men. Oh yes, I've caught her toying with *my* husband, too."

Sam clenched her hands in her lap. How lowering, Grant thought, that she could so easily flee from him, but she would stay until Doomsday to let this harridan provoke her. But it was no more than she deserved if she were left to suffer all night.

"Actually, the idea was mine, Emma." Sam's surprise could not be deeper than Grant's own. He had been perfectly happy, guzzling his bottle. Why rush to her side to play the smitten fool? Was he naive enough to expect a reward? "I'm sorry it took so long getting your drink, darling. How about you, Emma? It isn't every night we celebrate Sam's debut."

"Debut? I thought she was an accomplished actress?"

Careless. The alcohol must be getting to him. "Yes, of course, but she retired after the birth of our son. Er—excuse me, I'm so fond of the boy, I tend to forget he isn't actually mine."

Sam was grateful, but blatantly unwilling to be so as she took the offered glass.

"Your devotion does you credit, Mr. Barton. But I must say the lad seems more yours than hers. After all, you're far closer to me in years. She"—and here her eyes narrowed disdainfully as they focused on Sam—"seems far too young to have had a boy that age and a career too."

He decided to make the best of his opportunity by sitting on the arm of Sam's chair. Nice sensation, leaning into her. "Yes, a remarkable woman, my wife. A girl of constant surprises."

"It runs in the family." Tucking her arm in his,

Sam smiled sweetly up at him. Amazement nearly knocked him to the floor.

"How comfortable." Standing abruptly, Emma glared at Sam, who sipped her wine defiantly. "If you will excuse me, I see Cyrus. No doubt he needs me."

The man was all but drooling down Claire's chest. Feeling that unwanted tug of pity again, Grant held out the bottle. "Let him stew a bit, Emma. Join us for a drink instead."

She was obviously tempted. The stiffness left her face long enough for Grant to regret his offer. But as her gaze shifted to Sam, it tightened with contempt. "Thank you, but I was reared to know that ladies never drink, regardless of the occasion. Or the excuse."

As Emma swished off, Grant supposed she must be left her dignity, since she had precious little else. Pity, though, was not the emotion he would have chosen to inspire.

"I doubt she meant to snap that way," Sam said softly, as if she could read his thoughts. "Loneliness tends to sour your outlook. But it was awfully nice of you to try to include her."

Admiration, now, was not a bad substitute. "Nice is my middle name. For example, I came over here for the express purpose of refreshing your glass."

"I really shouldn't, but I suppose if you went out of your way . . ."

"I did."

"Then, yes, please, I'd love some. What a marvelous beverage, champagne is. It goes down so easily, doesn't it."

"I must say, Miss Eggersley, I never expected you to behave in so unladylike a fashion."

To his delight, she recognized the taunt and laughed quite naughtily. "Do you think she realizes what a prig she is? I mean, is she actually that narrow-minded, or just wearing one of those masks Willie says you're always talking about?''

''Oh? And just how often have you and that loose-lipped traitor been discussing me?''

She giggled like a girl. ''How stern you look, Mr. Barton. As if you weren't the one who drugged Claire to keep her off that stage tonight.''

''Did he tell you that, too?''

''Is it true?''

''And if it were?''

Grant braced himself, but she smiled and he felt as if her eyes devoured him in one big gulp. ''Then I suppose I should be thanking you. That was the nicest thing anyone ever did for me.''

That undid him. Had she asked, he'd have drugged the entire city of Denver for just such another smile. ''I did the troupe, not to mention the audience, a favor. You're quite an actress. I don't believe I've ever seen Marietta played with such sincerity.''

She seemed inordinately interested in the bubbles in her glass. ''I can't take undeserved credit. Marietta is—well, I rather identify with the role. I played my part on sheer emotion. You, on the other hand, played with incredible skill.''

He'd been praised often enough before, but never had it pleased him more. ''I had one of the best to teach me. There was a woman—''

''Isn't there always?''

Her grin robbed the words of their sting. His own smile went sheepish. He had a strange urge to confide in her, as if in so doing, he could purge himself of his past sins. ''She was older; very much a mother to me, but how I idolized that lady! I'd have given my last breath for her.''

"I notice you speak in the past tense."

"There was . . . trouble. When I turned to her, believing she would help, she refused to have anything more to do with me. She had no choice, I can see that now, but I was so bitter at the time, I swore I would never trust a woman again."

There was a momentary silence, as if she understood the importance of that confession. The hand that stole up to touch his arm was so warm and reassuring that he felt an inner click, as if everything had settled back into its proper place.

"I know what you mean," she said softly. "It's hard, trusting people. Yet sometimes, doesn't it seem harder to be trustworthy? I mean, we all have such good intentions, but life and its problems always get in the way."

"I can drink to that." Taking a healthy gulp, he pictured her face when she learned just how untrustworthy he was. She would learn, it was inevitable, but please, not tonight. Not when she smiled at him this way.

"For example," he said, quickly changing direction, "it had been my intention to see that you celebrate, and here I am burdening you with my life's sordid details. I've even let your glass go dry."

"Then I suppose you shall just have to refill it." Looking into him, she held out her glass. "And it was hardly a burden. It was . . . very trusting. I'm flattered."

Then flatter me, he wanted to beg. Tell me all there is to know about you. But she had lowered her eyes, ostensibly to watch him fill her glass. Her voice was low and barely audible. "I was wrong that night on the balcony. Divergent paths or not, perhaps we were destined to become friends."

Take it slow, he warned himself; *don't rush her and*

spoil this. "Let's seal that with a toast. To my good friend, Samantha—er, Barton. A very beautiful and talented lady."

She tilted her head, as if she couldn't quite trust her ears. A tiny, almost hesitant grin played at her lips. He watched, wanting to taste them.

"That is very gallant of you, sir, but you exaggerate. Friends should be more honest with each other."

Keep it light, Barton; don't think of what the words could mean. "I do not. You're every bit a lady, even if you do drink like a soldier."

She touched her glass to his. "And you're quite a gentleman, Mr. Barton, even if you drug women to get your way."

Lord help him if she knew what was on his mind now. How much champagne would it take before she was willing? Shamed by such thoughts, he took her hand to place a gentle kiss upon it.

"To us, then. The Bartons, a formidable team."

"Here, here!" someone shouted behind them. "I say we all drink to the Bartons. May they fill the house again tomorrow night."

Laughing nervously, Sam rose to join the others. Grant relinquished her hand, but not without rebellion. This was her moment—only a selfish lout would deprive her of it—but just once, why couldn't he have her to himself?

But he needed to put distance between them. He needed to regain control of himself. Yet even as he thought this, he followed in her wake. It damned near took his breath away, this need to touch her. It didn't seem to matter where, who, or what they were; he could have taken her right there on the floor.

As they drank, refilled their glasses, and drank again, Grant mentally undressed her. He spoke when necessary, laughed in the right places, but his mind pulsed with the vision of lowering her to his bed. And the fantasy grew more involved, more fevered, with every glass he drained.

Too soon, Claire returned. She snuggled close, slipping a proprietary arm through his. "Don't you think you've had enough, darling? At this rate, you'll never be able to perform."

He didn't know which had the tighter grip, her hand or his fury. There wasn't an ear in the room deaf to the double entendre.

Sam's least of all. "Nonsense," she said, laughing, though her eyes had darkened to charcoal. "He has a full day to recuperate. Besides, the man can act with his eyes closed."

"And what about you, cousin dear? Can you recover as quickly? I swear, Granddaddy would have apoplexy, if he could see the way you are behaving."

There was an awkward silence. Sam, drained of all animation, shriveled to half her size. If not for those gray eyes, silently begging him not to make a scene, he'd gladly have knocked her cousin to the floor.

"You know what they say about stones," he said instead. "I doubt there's one among us qualified to throw one."

There was a loud guffaw and a thump on his back. The conversation then spun off on who had committed the biggest and best sins, but Grant was reduced to the miserable triangle he and the two cousins formed.

Claire tightened her grip. "It's time for bed, darling."

"Have a nice sleep."

He turned his back to her, in order to better face Sam, but it was a motion done with more enthusiasm than caution. The room swayed, taking its own sweet time to right itself. With a lurch, he realized the chit was right. He was quite disgustingly drunk. Hell and damnation, not tonight!

Slowly, deliberately, and far too late, he placed his bottle on the nearby table. His eyes sought Sam's. She watched her cousin warily.

"Tony. I want to talk to you." He heard the rustle of skirts as Claire flounced to the door. There was a pause, then a hissed, "upstairs, now."

Still his eyes sought Sam's. He needed contact. Any contact. Incredible, the messages the eyes could transmit from the one area a mask never covered. I love you, his said, while hers dropped to the floor.

"You'd better go to her."

Muttering an oath, he glanced over his shoulder. Claire stood at the door, tapping her foot furiously. If she had owned a leash, she'd have had it around his neck to yank him out of the room. "I'd rather stay."

How peevish that sounded, like a small boy throwing a tantrum. Sam was clearly startled. Never one to shirk responsibility, was our Miss Eggersley, and her opinion was clear. Whatever his wants, he was to blame for the threatened tantrum. He and his indiscretion.

I never touched her! he wanted to protest. She doesn't own me and I don't owe her a thing. But even as he opened his mouth, Sam turned away and he was reminded of that long-ago night on his balcony. She would always be yards away, forever out of reach.

"Tony!"

"If I go with her now," he begged, his voice hushed and pleading, "will you wait for me?"

She turned back, clearly puzzled, looking from him to her cousin. "Why would you want me to wait?"

Because you're so damned beautiful, he wanted to tell her. The need to confess rushed over him, to bury his head in her lap and tell the whole sordid story. "We need to talk. Please, wait for me?"

Sam bit her lip, glanced at her cousin, then nodded reluctantly. Grant, who felt as if he'd been given the world, grabbed her hand to kiss it. "I'll make it quick. Give me fifteen minutes."

There was a faint smile. Of derision? Considering his condition and past record, he could hardly fault her for that. But he'd do it, dammit, if he had to drug the chit again. A prospect that gained in appeal as he followed her into a room he belatedly recognized as his own.

"Tony, darling, at last we're alone!"

Unwrapping himself, none too gingerly from her embrace, he grabbed the brandy decanter for a good stiff shot to fortify him. A healthy gulp later, he loosened his tie and braced himself for battle. "First of all, I told you not to call me Tony. My name is Grant, remember?"

"I hate that name. Ever since you started using it, you've been so different. I—I don't know you any more."

You never did, he thought wearily. He eyed the bed with longing. The urge to lie down, to close his eyes forever, was damned near overwhelming. He shook his head, hoping to pull himself together, but it only made him dizzier. He set the glass on the stand and sat on the edge of the bed.

Taking his movement as an invitation, Claire plopped onto his lap. Her eyes were steamy with promise. Ignoring his groan, she took his hand to kiss each finger. Her cloying scent made him want to gag. He needed more brandy. Only how could he get to the decanter?

He reached out for it, but she caught his hand and brought it back, smiling, then covered it with her two small hands. They were cool as they slid next beneath his shirt to his chest.

They stopped abruptly at his medallion. "This dirty old thing. Why on earth do you wear it, when you can easily have gold and diamonds?"

"I don't want gold or diamonds."

"That's what Sam said." She gave him an odd look. "That it's worth more to you than any jewel. If it's so valuable, why haven't you given it to me?"

"I can't." He brushed her hands away. "It was a gift. It's my good luck charm."

"Oh.' Claire was diverted, but in the process, he seemed to have lost a sleeve. "Speaking of good, you were awfully sweet to Sam tonight."

"Sam's a sweet girl."

"Of course she is, but I doubt that she's prepared for all this attention. I hope it doesn't go to her head."

"I've never known a more level-headed woman in my life."

"But do you? Know her, I mean?"

It was a good question. Irritated by it, he wanted to push Claire away, but the female had a death grip on his chest hair. Where the hell was his shirt?

"You see, Sam's not like us. She's a dreamer."

"There's nothing wrong with dreaming." Nothing at all. As a matter of fact, that pillow looked damned inviting.

"Here, lift your leg, darling. Dreaming might be natural, to a point, but Sam makes an art of it. I don't know how many times Granddaddy punished her. Darling, I'm only afraid she'll take you seriously. An old maid like that—why, Sam knows nothing about flirting. She's the happy-ever-after sort. I'd hate to see her hurt, wouldn't you?"

She nudged him, and he fell to his back. Her face blurred as he gazed up at her, but her words were clear and precise. She was right. He'd rather kill himself than see Sam hurt.

"She's going to marry Emery Blankfield anyway."

The fiance. How could he have forgotten? She was amusing herself, Riley had said. Lord, when he thought about it, he still didn't know what went on in that devious mind of hers.

"It's been arranged for centuries. Grandfather chose him because he's, well, he's her type. Compared to you, though . . ."

Perched above him, smug now, she ran her tongue over her lip. Grant felt like a prized plum, ripe for the plucking. "Her type," he snarled. "Just what is that?"

"Oh, Emery's sterling. He gleams with respectability. With you distracting her, Sam might forget how much she needs those things. She doesn't need what you have to offer. As fun as flirting might be, you don't want to be cruel, do you?"

He shut his eyes and ears, as she droned on about his unsuitability. Hell, Sam was no different than any other female in his life. They'd all thought him an amusement. A "pretty boy," good for fun, but not to love, and certainly not to marry. How could he expect more, he who didn't have a cent, or even a name of his own to offer? Claire was right. Sam didn't need him. No one did.

Except, perhaps, in his dreams. There, he could own his cottage in the woods, bought and paid for with hard-earned cash. A place to come home to, a cozy niche for him and the woman he loved.

He felt arms shaking him, but he clung tight to the image. Not even the thumping on his chest could dislodge it, nor the subsequent slam in the distance. He was approaching his cottage, stepping ever closer to the brown-haired angel in the doorway, who waited with a wide smile and welcoming gray eyes.

Home . . .

17

Slowly, with great restraint, Sam placed her glass on the table. She'd had enough. More than. When was it that the champagne had lost its appeal?

But that was silly; she could pinpoint the exact second. She had been sipping the bubbly wine, drinking in the magic, when Claire burst into her bubble. In a blink, the wine had soured to vinegar. The entire evening had gone sour, in fact. Fifteen minutes, he'd promised, but she had known, even then, that he'd never return.

She couldn't blame him. When Claire issued a summons, men obeyed. What was it Willie called her, her highness? Sam nearly laughed, but it would have been a rude, bitter sound, so clearly out of place in this bawdy crowd.

A hand slipped around her waist. Smiling, she wheeled to face him, but it was only Calvin Bodine. It wasn't disappointment she felt, of course, merely surprise. Heretofore, she and Grant's understudy hadn't shared ten words, yet he now behaved as if they'd been friends for years—but friendship was no longer enough. His blonde mustache twitched, but while the gleam in those bedroom eyes might sooth her damaged pride, Sam's heart could not be tempted.

She felt the disappointment so keenly that she nearly completed her humiliation with tears. Stupid fool, had she truly believed he'd come back? A man in that condition often said things he didn't mean, things he wouldn't even remember in the morning.

Yet . . . . Her heart clung to that "yet" as she said her good-nights and trudged up the stairs. Yet . . . he had he had been in a strange mood tonight. He had been gently bracing as he helped overcome her stage fright, and earlier, endearingly concerned, as if knowing she had been the one nearly injured, and not Claire. And his gaze, each time their eyes met, had been every bit as hungry as Willie claimed. He hadn't wanted to go with Claire, she insisted as she reached her door. Had he?

She froze as she heard a movement inside the room. Yanking her hand back from the knob, she wondered how gullible one woman could be. Naturally he'd ask her to wait, because he and Claire wanted the room to themselves. If she hadn't heard that noise, she would have barged in and caught them in the act.

She backed away from the door as if it could burn her. Where could she hide? She'd positively die, should he walk out now and catch her here in the hallway.

And of course, the door flew open. "There you are, Sam! I declare, do you know how long you've kept me up worrying? Why, I've imagined—well, never mind. Just come on in and climb into bed so I can get some sleep."

Too stunned to argue, Sam followed her cousin into the room. Claire continued to grumble as she threw herself onto the bed. "Nobody seems to care that I was almost killed this afternoon. It's beyond me how some people can be so inconsiderate. Sleep, the doctor said. But how is that possible when everyone else is doing—well, God only knows what they are doing."

Sam barely heard. Seating herself before the

mirror, she busied herself poking the pins back into her hair. She should have listened to her grandfather. Pin up your hair; act like a lady. But Grant had said she was a lady, even if she did drink like a soldier. Grant . . .

She spun on the seat. "Claire," she blurted out as she finally realized the significance of her cousin's tantrum, "where is Grant?"

"The man's impossible!" Claire huffed as she punched her pillow. "He actually had the nerve to fall asleep on me."

Sam suddenly felt like laughing. "I—I doubt he did so intentionally. It's been a long and busy day. And he had a great deal to drink."

"That might be his excuse tonight, but what of every other time? I'm tired of tossing and turning in frustration. If you want to know the truth, I'd rather meet the man he's impersonating. I bet this Grant Barton could teach him a thing or two about seduction. Tony, if you want my opinion, falls asleep too easily."

Sam felt a surge, as if all the blood had rushed to her head. *He falls asleep on her!* her brain chanted. His feelings can't be that deeply involved.

"Poor Claire. You must love him terribly. To keep going to him as you do."

"Lordee, you're so naive. As if love has anything to do with it. I'm not sure I even like him any more. Not with the way he grumbles about that silly play. And he teases, making jokes he knows I can't understand."

Better and better. Sam felt so good, she could have danced on her head. If Claire "didn't even like him any more," then her heart would hardly be shattered to lose him. Her pride might be damaged, and her greed, maybe, but surely love—Sam's love—had the stronger claim.

"I've got to get to sleep. I'm so tired I could scream."

"Would a glass of wine help?"

The tossing stopped. They could have doused the lamp, so radiant was Claire's smile. "Sam, you're so good to me. I don't deserve a cousin like you."

Guilt had made the offer, not Sam. At this hour, the last thing she wanted was to go in search of a bottle. "I don't think I should go back downstairs, though. They were getting rather rowdy."

"I swear, Sam, how do hope to get anything done, hiding from your shadow? Very well, if you're too scared to go downstairs, try Tony's room. He has a bottle on his dresser. And some glasses."

"His room?"

Claire's grin was not kind. "Don't have the vapors; he's asleep. Dead to the world. Though even if he weren't, I doubt you would have to worry."

The emphasis on the *you* decided her. Why not go? Most likely, Grant would never know she'd been, but if he should wake, all the better. Drunk as he was, he might think her Marietta, and he could make good on the promises his eyes had made earlier. That would show Claire who was afraid of her shadow.

Still, she couldn't resist the urge to glance over her shoulder as she approached his room. What if he was awake? *We need to talk,* he'd said. But about what?

Though it should have been locked, his door opened easily to her touch. Sam welcomed the fortifying anger. How typically thoughtless of Claire to leave the poor man to be robbed or murdered in his sleep.

But even indignation was stripped away as she stepped closer to the bed. Every thought, coherent or otherwise, concentrated on the dark head buried in the pillows. Lord, how she longed to stretch out beside him beneath the covers. She didn't need his love; she had more than enough love for them both.

The wine, she had to remind herself; you came for Claire's wine. Dragging her eyes across the room, she noticed the opened window. The poor man would catch a cold in this draft. Drawing the drapes tight, she reasoned that with all he'd had to drink, Grant would be sorry enough in the morning without facing the glare of the rising sun.

That task completed, she risked a glance at hm. Still asleep. She moved about the room, not overly cautious with noise, but he never moved a muscle. Claire was right; he was dead to the world.

Sam swallowed her disappointment. She'd better get back. She grabbed the bottle—it was brandy, but it would have to do—knowing Claire would be wondering where she was. If she delayed one minute longer, her cousin would come marching in to make a scene. Sam might as well take the next train to Richmond, for there would be no living with the troupe then. Sneers? They'd be laughing in her face.

As she reached for the glass, she brushed a small, white packet to the floor. Stooping to retrieve it, she recognized the landanum her grandfather had used. As his nurse, Sam had often administered it, frequently diluted in a glass of wine. Would it work with brandy?

Stop nagging me, she told her conscience. Hadn't Claire begged for rest? With a quick glance to the bed, she poured a generous amount into the glass. If her cousin's request coincided with this golden opportunity, wouldn't she be a fool to refuse it? It wasn't as if anyone would be hurt. She merely wanted a few moments alone with him. To watch his sleep, to memorize his face. Very well, so maybe she did have this wild hope he would waken, would somehow see how desperately she wanted him. How she loved him. Was that a sin?

She poured the brandy on top of the powder and swirled it around a little to mix it. Then she poured a good, stiff drink for herself. Throat burning, she hurried back to her room before she could change her mind. As an extra measure, she had left his door unlocked. She had no choice, now, but to go back.

Though Claire complained about the delay, about the size of the glass and the brandy not being wine, she snatched at and downed the stuff with professional ease. As she settled back on the pillows with a contented smile, Sam breathed easier. Luckily, the liquor disguised the taste of the drug.

''Is he still sleeping?''

Sam jumped. She had been imagining herself dressed in a silky negligee. As she drifted into his room, Grant waited with his arms open wide. His smile was likewise welcoming. She had glided closer, inches from his touch, when Claire's voice shattered the image to bits. ''No. I mean, yes. As you said, he's dead to the world.''

''I imagine it's the brandy. I'm feeling deliciously drowsy myself.''

''Good. I mean, now you can get your rest.''

''You're so good to me, Sam. Aren't you coming to bed?''

''No, I'm not.'' She wasn't coming to bed, and she certainly was not good. Especially considering what she planned to do. ''Not yet. I have some thinking to do.''

Claire purred into her pillow. As she drifted off, Sam walked to the window. Her heart thumped so loudly, she feared it would waken Claire, despite the sedative. For a terrified moment, she wondered what she would do if she were caught slipping from the room. How could she consider this? Had she gone clear out of her senses?

Pictures flashed across her mind. Grant, in nothing but a towel. Grant, leaning down to kiss her. Grant, standing on a far-off balcony, seeming as lost and vulnerable as she. Grant, always Grant.

Looking out at the sleeping houses, she ached with envy. All those wives, lying complacently on their side of the marital bed, knowing little and caring less about the dreams being dreamed beside them. Fools. Given the chance, Sam would listen to him every moment, every second. She would never ignore him, or even leave his bed as Claire did. Even if he never made love to her, she would hug him close every possible moment, never once forgetting the miracle of holding him in her arms.

Suddenly calm, she saw that this was a turning point in her life. Fate offered an opportunity. She could go to him now, taking a chance she might later learn to regret, or she could stay in her shell and begin her regret right now. She could listen to Samuel's warnings, gone stale with overuse, or for once in her life, she could do what *she* wanted to do.

Oh, fiddlesticks, she had no choice. Not really. All this had been decided weeks ago, the first time she looked into those too blue eyes.

Claire's light snore started her giggling. What a waste of good laudanum it would be—not to mention Grant's brandy—if she didn't go back to his room.

Feeling delightfully wicked, she dug through her cousin's trunk. Oh, she was wicked, she thought as she pulled out the negligee Claire had bought with Willie's food money. It was pink and not her style at all, but Grant would never notice in the dark. Besides, it was his other senses she hoped to impress, not his sight.

She dabbed Claire's perfume at her neck. It nearly gagged her, but it was a necessary evil. She didn't want him knowing who he actually held, did she? She wasn't exactly going with an engraved invitation. It was Claire he loved. Would think he was loving.

Have I gone straight of my mind? she thought frantically as she fingered the pink silk. What she meant to do was immoral. She should stop this, here and now.

But no, she would not be discouraged. Love did strange things to people. Even if she tried to fight, the emotion had too firm a grip. It would take her where it wanted her to go. Even into a sleeping man's bedroom.

The face of a stranger smiled knowingly from the mirror. It was centuries old, eons wise, and it knew exactly what it was doing. It wanted its man and it would lie, cheat and steal to have him.

The other Sam, the straitlaced, innocent one, drew back, somewhat shocked. She tried to warn her wicked self about what people would think, what they would say, but all her arguments were feeble ones. She wanted to go, too.

Leaving Claire deep in sleep, she blew out the lamp. Tomorrow morning, she could make hints about her cousin's sleepwalking. Should Grant mention a visitor, everyone would assume it had been Claire. Let them think, or say, whatever they chose then.

What an accomplished liar she'd become! How's this for unlacing the corset, Annie? Did you ever dream your old friend would go this far? Sam giggled, an alcohol-soaked bubbling suspiciously akin to panic.

She slipped into the hall, the giggling stilled as she approached his door. She paused as she opened it, her breath lost somewhere behind her, with her courage. More brandy, she thought desperately, I need another drink. What am I doing here?

He stirred, ever so gently, to give her the answer. Curled up like a boy, he hugged his pillow. How sweet he was in his sleep, how young and trusting, with his chestnut hair falling across his face. Drawn to him against all better judgment, Sam stepped into the room and quietly closed the door behind her. He is so beautiful, she thought. So perfect. Her poor heart ached with loving him.

A wave of tenderness, deep and consuming, formed a lump in her throat. If she pushed that hair out of his face, would he smile up at her, as Willie did each night as she tucked him in?

As she approached the bed, she tripped over a pile of clothing. Reaching out to right herself, she grabbed at the bedcovers. They slipped to reveal him inall his glory. My lord, the man was naked!

She should have been shocked. At the very least, she should have looked away. But her eyes drank him in as freely as she had the wine, touching him as her fingers could not. They tiptoed through the coarse hair of his legs, up along the smooth line of his buttocks, down the dip in his spine. Could her heart break with wanting him? Needing him? Just one, tiny stroke at the curve of his neck . . .

She must not stand in the light, where he could wake at any moment and see her. That would truly be insane. Dousing the lamp, she stood there in the dark, trying to gather courage, listening as he slept. His breathing grew shallow, as though disturbed by dreams. Was Claire in them? Or her own mother?

Enough of that. Determinedly, she moved closer but stopped again when she realized she did not know what to do. She and Giselle had talked about this moment, of course, but now that it had come, Sam felt only stage fright. Would her instincts, as her maid insisted, be enough?

They would have to be, for she wasn't about to leave now. Leaning down, she gently brushed the hair from his eyes, letting her fingers stray to his neck, down along the strong shoulders. Her breasts felt swollen, her body moist, waiting to welcome him inside. One word, one touch, and she would be his. Forever and always.

"I love you, Grant Barton," she whispered into the night. "God help me, but I love you so."

Grant heard the words through a mist. Sam? Opening his eye, he squinted into the dark, but he felt as if he'd gone blind. As he tried to raise his head, it felt heavy and thick with sleep. Damn, he must have been dreaming that same dream again.

Cool lips brushed his neck. Sam, his brain repeated with a jolt. My God, *Sam?*

He sniffed. The combination of perfume and disappointment nearly choked him. Damned cloying scent. What must he do to convince the woman she wasn't wanted?

He lay there, stiff and unyielding, willing Claire to leave. It was not in him to be rude, but if she touched him again, he'd lose his dinner all over her. As it was, the room swirled out of control.

And then, just as he could stand it no longer, as he opened his mouth to screech at her to go away, a drop of rain fell onto his cheek. Pulled by gravity, it rolled into his opened lips, its taste salty and pure. Not rain; tears. And surely not from Claire, for hers would be cool and sugary.

Bewildered, he rolled onto his back. He still

couldn't see a thing, but he sensed Sam's presence as he had earlier that night. With crystal clarity, he could see the gray eyes, deep with mystery. And though it made no sense—it had to be a dream—they seemed to want him, to love him.

"Am I dreaming?" he whispered, reaching up for her.

He felt her withdraw. Desperate now, he tugged her down to him, not about to let her escape again. She seemed so fragile, so he gentled his grip. She trembled in his arms, her heart drumming a similar beat to his own.

He shut his eyes, struggling to sober himself. As the world continued to spin, he clung to her as boat would to its anchor. She steadied him, this woman. She was his focus.

Breathing deeply, he caught the sweet spring fragrance of her hair. Definitely Sam, he grinned, for no one else would bind her hair that tight. With unsteady hands, he reached up to remove the pins, placing them on the nightstand one by one, until every last strand was free and spilling across his chest.

Though she barely breathed, she made no move to leave. Heartened, he eased his fingers through the dark tresses, fanning them out around them. He felt like a millionaire, surrounded by his wealth. Burying himself in it, he lost himself in luxury. He felt drunk with the feel and scent of her. "You're so beautiful," he told her huskily. "So incredibly lovely."

She moved now, and he thought she might be shaking her head. Before she could flee, he tilted her face upward, bringing it closer, closer, until he could paint her face with a hundred tiny, indelible kisses. She sighed as he circled ever closer to her lips.

They parted slowly, and his tongue slid in like a

hero welcomed home. Pure, sweet, and deep with promise, her mouth was more incredible than in even his most fevered dreams. His mind went wild, savoring the taste of her. He slipped over the edge, just this side of frenzy, knowing that dream or no, this time he would have her.

He shifted their bodies, bringing them together in one long line of shimmering heat. Darts of fire pricked at his manhood. She was a witch, he decided. No other woman in his life had ever been so enticingly hot. Running practiced fingers beneath the silk of her gown, he memorized every luscious curve. And with each delectable inch, his grip grew tighter, his touch more frantic.

In a haze, he heard the sharp indrawn breath. Damn his greed, he had frightened her. He shut his eyes, again fighting the wine's effect, knowing that everything depended upon him doing this right. Her passion must be released slowly, painstakingly. It must be perfect for her, this lady of his dreams.

Wishing she could see the reassurance in his eyes, he took her face in his hands, letting his fingers speak for him. As they traced gentle lines across her face, he tried to tell her how long he had hoped for this moment, how deeply he cherished it, but his tongue was locked in the wonder of it all. All he could do, he decided, was kiss her.

Drawing her close, he brushed his lips against hers. Her hands tightened at his neck. Powerful emotions surged between them, fusing them together. She opened her mouth to his tongue, sucking it in, holding him eager prisoner. Head spinning, his tongue delved deeper, caressing the soft flesh, seeking the wonderful, secret pleasure she alone could give.

To his happy amazement, she pressed her body

tight to his. Her hands dug into his hair. He wanted to hold back, to make good his intentions, but she drove him past reason. He felt like a beast released from its cage, free to roam and prowl at will. Roam and prowl, with his mate at his side.

Her hunger impressed him. Fueled him. Never in his life had he felt so strong and powerful, so alive. "You are incredible," he whispered raggedly into her ear. "I'd give anything to see you now."

She stiffened. Her hands slipped down from his neck to come between them. Cold with dread, he saw her clearly, hovering on that balcony, eyes preceding her to the door. She was about to run away again. Desperate and dizzy, he grabbed for her. "God, don't leave now. Can't you see how much I want you?"

His hands encountered air. The room tilted and swirled. "Please don't go. I swear, I'll marry you. I only want your happiness. Can't you see that?"

His answer was the click of the door. She was gone, vanished as if in a puff of smoke. She might never have been there, except for the erratic beating of his heart.

He propped himself on an elbow, intending to go after her, but all that champagne said no. Knocking his arm, and intentions, out from under him, it felled him to the mattress with a humiliating thump.

Reality came and went, and came again. Fluttering in and out of consciousness, Grant kept his ears trained to the door. It had to open again. She had seemed so real, so warm and alive.

Face facts, Barton; it was only a dream. Had he the strength, he would have punched his pillow. Lord, he felt sick. How had he come to not knowing what was real and what was not? It was nothing but another damned dream, enhanced by his intoxication and ending with the same tortured frustration as the rest of them. He should have taken Claire when she offered herself.

Yet even as he thought this, he closed his eyes and went in search of Sam. His dream Sam, who always smiled, always welcomed him home.

Against the backdrop of skittering clouds, a lone wagon clattered along Eureka Street. Watching from his window in the glamorous new Teller House, the only trace of civilization in Central City, Charles Riley followed its progress as it climbed upward, out of sight. Good. Three more days and his work here should be finished.

He let the drape fall as he turned back to his bed. he would need his sleep, for he had several busy days ahead of him. Tomorrow he must ride down to Denver to meet with that incredible fool Samuel had chosen for his granddaughter's husband. He had summoned Mr. Blankfield to Denver; now it was time the man knew how badly in debt the Eggersley bank stood, and exactly what must be done to restore it.

That would take Miss Eggersley out of the picture as her near-accidents had failed to do, but he must think of some way to deal with Barton. He had heard that drunken fool, Jack Parker, call him Tony. From the start, Riley had dreaded the day Barton would realize the significance of their resemblance. Lord knew, he easily could be a by-blow of Roger's, the way Tony's wastrel uncle scattered his seed throughout England. You couldn't deny that the lad had Roger's style and charm.

But Barton would not, damn his conniving black heart, get his greedy hands on Roger's money. It belonged to Tony, as proven in the courts. It had taken considerable effort to have Tony Rawlings declared Lord Hoxton, and no urchin from the streets of London would get a penny of the fortune Riley had worked so long and hard to build.

No, he had other plans for the lad. Mr. Barton had a hunger for the good life. And clearly he also had an under-developed conscience, or he'd never have taken this job and then so quickly switched loyalties. What fun it would be, to test just how far that greed would take him, to pull the strings until the lad danced to the proper tune.

Three more days. And then, as the saying went, he who laughs last, laughs the best.

18

Central City, 1861

Bill carved out another notch in the wood, marking the end of another day. Twenty of them, all marked by the passing of the miners as they trudged to their prison at the end of the long, hard day. Every night, Bill could hear their grumbling, but none of them ever heard his shouts. Amazing how deaf a man could be, when money did the talking.

He'd learned a heap of bitterness, these last three weeks. Soon, his captor had announced, Sam would be on her way to Richmond with his father. That had been Bill's only condition. He wasn't going to sign away his claim until his daughter was safe. And then what? It didn't take much imagination to guess what they'd do to him. The groundwork had already been laid. Suicide, the coroner had decreed, just yesterday. There was no way, now, for Bill Eggersley to just get up and walk away.

So why should he sign? Why give these greedy bastards what rightfully belonged to him? The Oh Susannah was his dream, dammit, and the way things stood, it was the only legacy he had to leave Sam.

After all, what could they do—kill him twice?

19

Grant struggled against the tide. It sucked him in, pulling him under, threatening to fling him onto the distant shore.

He came awake suddenly, his mouth as dry and scratchy as if he had indeed landed in a sand dune. What had he done to his head to cause such awful pounding?

Last night. He sat up and was instantly sorry he did so. Cushioning his head with his knees, he swore he would never drink again. But oh, the dreams the alcohol had brought him. He smiled unwillingly, as visions of Sam, lovely Sam, flashed across his mind.

How soft she'd seemed in the scarlet gown. His pulse began to pound in time with his skull. She'd looked so sweet, so alluring that he'd nearly told her the truth. Bloody fool; he had asked her to wait for him. Had she? Or had she seen how inebriated he was and run, laughing, all the way to her room?

Did it matter? Either way, he must face her this morning. But first he needed a hot, bracing cup of tea. Rising shakily, he scanned the room for his clothes. He found them in a heap on the floor. Claire. Painfully, he remembered her undressing him. Had she told Sam? Must he explain about that, too? Grumbling, he stabbed at the pile. The damned shirt had too many buttons. And where the hell was his medallion? Had Claire relieved him of that, too?

After five minutes wasted crawling about on his

knees, he spotted it on the bedside table. Cursing soundly, he hobbled over to fetch it, but the sight of the hair pins beside it stopped him cold. Once again, he felt the silky strands slide through his fingers.

There was a queer sensation in his gut as he lifted one of the pins into his hand. He sniffed, hoping to recapture her scent, but it remained an impersonal piece of metal. He must be going crazy. Could he be fantasizing like this about Sam Eggersley? Annoyingly proper Sam? The woman wore her virtue like a shield, for heaven's sake. It was sheer lunacy to imagine her taking advantage of his drunken state by hopping into bed with him. If his mind wasn't so steeped in alcohol, the idea would never have crossed it.

He set the pin down. This wasn't the first time he'd embarrassed himself by mistaking one cousin for the other. Insatiable, scent-drenched Claire. It would be just like her to return to seduce him, and then to leave in a snit. What in God's name had he said to her?

But thinking back, all he could see, feel or taste was hair. Long, soft luxuriant hair. He had called her lovely, beautiful, and then he had . . .

His limbs went cold. The ache in his head was monumental. Had he actually proposed marriage? God alone could help him then, for he had said the words to the wrong woman.

Sitting on the edge of the bed, he yanked on his boots, bruising his heels in the process. Now look where his insane dreams had taken him. Soft and alluring? Even if it *had* been Sam last night—a very big if—you could bet your last farthing she'd be her old, chilly self this morning. Hung over, and blaming him for that, too.

Standing too abruptly, he bumped into the table.

Hairpins scattered over the carpet. Muttering another oath, he stooped to retrieve them. The last one, for some reason, refused to leave his hand. He cupped it, squeezing it tight. It *was* Sam, his imagination insisted stubbornly.

Distractedly, he tucked the thing in his pocket. It was this damned July heat that caused this nonsense. That, and the lack of food. He needed some breakfast, a hearty American meal, with scalding tea.

But he remained vaguely depressed as he descended to the hotel's miserable excuse of a dining room. He doubted they could even brew a decent cup of tea. Damned bloody wilderness.

A woman appeared to take his order, her grease-stained apron and unwashed hair confirming his suspicions. He lowered his expectations, hoping his tea would at least be hot and wet. If not, the place was deservedly empty. No one need see him gag.

Like the night before, he felt the air stir. Tugged there, his gaze focused on the doorway. Sam stood in it, clad in her plaid riding habit. For an unprotected second, their eyes met.

Grant rose slowly, hopefully, but he should have spared himself the embarrassment. As expected, the brown hair was plastered to her head and her features were likewise tight and drawn. Deliberately looking the other way, she scurried to a distant table.

He sat down again, rather painfully. What a damned bloody fool he'd become. From their first encounter, he had known she was poison, and he knew that she considered him worse than poison.

She greeted the waitress pleasantly, of course. She always had a smile for everyone else. Marriage, bah! He could imagine her reaction should he go down on his knee before her. She'd clap her hands and say, "Bravo, Barton, your finest performance yet!'' Then she'd laugh herself hoarse.

His was a hopeless case. He acknowledged this, even as he edged toward her table. Last night on the stage, and later at the party, he couldn't have imagined the warmth between them. Something had leapt into her eyes, something hot and untutored and meant for him alone.

But whatever that ''something'' might have been, it wasn't there today, he realized as he seated himself at her table. After an initial, startled glance, Sam kept her gaze lowered, safely out of reach.

As his brain searched for something clever to say, the waitress bustled up and presented Sam's breakfast. Hot-cross buns? His, no doubt. And that was undoubtedly his tea, as well. He snapped at the woman to bring him another cup, and was rewarded with yet another sneer.

He was in no mood, therefore, to be diplomatic. ''It was you, wasn't it?''

The gray eyes went wide, then shuttered. ''I—I don't know what you mean.''

Of course not. He alone was aware of the dual nature of that question. Sitting, he leaned over the table to grab a bun. ''These. Why did you let your cousin take credit for them?''

''Oh. I, well—I must say, you are in a foul mood this morning. Too much celebrating last night?''

''You've changed the subject.''

The waitress timed her entrance with suspicious precision. Taking his tea with far more exasperation than grace, Grant knew he had somehow lost the advantage. This was confirmed by the tiny smile playing at those well-remembered lips.

''I know it was you, you know.''

''You do?''

Watching her lips, he was once again unsettled by

the double meaning. "It—well, it didn't seem like something Claire would think of, much less do."

"But I would?"

"I saw you coming out of the bakery."

"Oh." She must have looked at everything else in the room but him. "You convinced Cyrus to let me play Marietta. It was the least I could do."

"I see. And how often does this happen?"

"I always repay my debts."

"You know what I mean. How often do you step aside and let Claire take credit for what you do?"

Her coffee must have been hot, for she swallowed quickly and dropped the cup onto its saucer. Her hands locked in her lap. "Do you have a reason for these questions, sir?"

"I have a name, you know."

"You seem to have several."

"Dammit, Sam, I thought we were going to be friends. You did an incredibly thoughtful thing, and now, when I try to think you, you make me want to throttle you instead."

"I'm sorry." She looked at him then. So directly, he could feel her gaze touch him deep inside. "I suppose I'm not in the best of moods, either," she said. "You should have warned me about the champagne."

He should have. He would have, had he been less a cad and not so tempted by the vision of her, relaxed and loose in his arms. "I'm sorry, too. I thought you were enjoying yourself."

"I was." Her smile was sheepish, and adorable. Grant could feel those lips on his own. Taste them.

"Actually, I had a wonderful time. Until"— she looked away, down into her cup, before continuing in one breath—"this morning. I stopped Claire the second time, but the first—well, she could have gone anywhere."

Sleep walking? How foolish he felt, caught clinging to his hopes. He had known it was only a dream. Not trusting himself to speak, he stuffed a bun in his mouth.

Sam forced another smile. With the air of having completed an unpleasant task, she pushed her chair back and rose from the table. "As nice as it's been chatting with you, I must be off."

"Where are you going?" He spoke with a mouth half full. He barely stopped himself from grabbing for her.

She seemed surprised, and doubly evasive. "Just for a ride."

"I'll come with you."

"Oh . . . no, that isn't necessary. Stay and get some rest."

"The exercise will do me good."

What was it about doors that were so bloody attractive? Must she always prefer to look at them instead of at him? "It won't be exercise. There's some rugged terrain up in these hills. Your seat might be adequate for your estates, but I'd hate to see you hurt yourself up there."

All those hours he'd invested in learning to ride, the saddlesores and Riley's insults, and all so she could call him "adequate?"

She saw either the insult or his reaction, for two bright spots of color appeared on her cheeks. "Very well, if you must know, I plan to visit an old friend. I hate to be rude, but we have a great deal of catching up to do."

"And I'd be intruding?"

"Grant . . ." The word hung between them, ringing with some indecipherable plea. But she sucked in a breath, securing the barriers once more.

"I'm sorry, but yes, you would. I'll see you later."

He listened to her boots scratch the floor, but he refused to watch. Let her have her mysterious rendezvous. It mattered little to him. Nothing at all, in fact.

The sound stopped. Against all better judgment, he turned in his chair. Sam was smiling at Calvin Bodine and the lecher continued to ogle her as she passed into the lobby. Not Bodine. Lord, she had to have better taste than that. Grant rose. He was not about to let her go off with a womanizing scoundrel like Calvin Bodine.

"Morning, Barton." Leering, the damned fool blocked the door. On the other side, Grant heard the boots pause again. "You and the little woman fighting again? I thought you patched things up."

What was he talking about? What little woman?

"Quite a gal you have there. I considered trying for her myself, but not after I saw her leaving your room last night."

Oh hell, he meant Claire. "She walks in her sleep."

"Is that what they call it these days?" He chuckled. "Relax, Barton, Claire will never learn about it from these lips."

Confused, yet too proud to call him back, Grant watched him stroll away. As he stuffed his hands in his pockets, he felt and fingered the hairpin, and his pulse quickened. Sam could forget her ride. She wasn't going anywhere until he had an explanation.

But she was no longer in the lobby. His gaze went to the stairs. No, she'd already been wearing her riding habit. He hurried outside, to be stopped cold as he faced the place where she had so nearly been killed. Did another cab wait somewhere along this busy street, hoping to try again today? What a fool he was, letting his pride get the best of him—he, who had vowed not to let her out of his sight.

Think! he ordered his cluttered brain. Riding, she'd said. That meant a stable, but which one? There had to be dozens in a city this size. He wished Willie was with him; he'd know what to do. But valuable time would be lost in waking and dressing the boy.

Besides, he knew what Willie would say. Desk clerks were a mine of information; people left messages, asked questions. In Grant's mind, he again heard Sam's boots pause in the lobby. Had she asked for directions?

She had. Willie was, Grant decided as he later hurried down the street to the train depot, quite a remarkable boy. Rummaging through his pockets, he found precious little cash there. He could only pray she wasn't going far.

As he neared the depot, he heard the warning toot of a whistle. With the way his luck as running, that would be her train. Sure enough, as he approached the tracks, he saw the distinctive plaid duck into the third car. He turned immediately to the ticket booth, to face a line ten people thick. Damn.

Belching out air, the train began to crawl. Double damn! With a last desperate glance at the ticket window, Grant heaved himself onto the train. His fingers jammed against the railing, bruising them, but he managed to hoist himself up and over onto the rear car.

It took several minutes to recapture his breath. Behind him, the city of Denver diminished in size. Now where was she taking him? It wasn't enough to be dragged across the continent; was there no limit to the lengths the woman would go to escape him?

"Ticket, sir?"

Focusing, Grant saw the brass-buttoned uniform

of the conductor. "I—I'm sorry, I don't have one. I barely made it onto the train. How much do I owe you?"

"Well now, that would depend on your destination, sir."

Of course it would. Only, he hadn't the least idea whee he was going. "I had planned on taking in the sights. It might help if I knew where this train will be stopping."

The round face smiled, a friendly, proud-of-my-land smile. "From the accent, I'd say you're not from around here. Cornish?"

"English. I'm an actor. Barton's the name. Grant Barton."

"Pleased to meet you, Mr. Barton. Well, the town we're pulling into is called Golden. Named for Tom Golden, not after the ore. Once was our territorial capital and major supplier to the mining fields. Eastern railroaders thought so much of the place, they ran their tracks down from Cheyenne to it. Now, with the Kansas-Pacific line running through Denver, it's the state seat. But that's life out West for you; nothing ever stays the same."

Grant only half-listened. He was too busy watching the passengers alight. No Sam, he was relieved to note.

"But if it's sights you want, stay aboard. Clear Creek Canyon will just about take your breath away. Black Hawk's next, or you can go on up to Central City. Just opened up the track this year."

Central City. The words hit like a club to the head. Where else would Sam go? "Central City sounds fine. How much?"

He paid the named amount, feeling mighty pleased with himself. Knowing Sam's destination, he needn't be forever on guard. He could sit back and enjoy the scenery.

"Hope you enjoy your stay with us, Mr. Barton. And be sure you hold onto that railing. Some of these canyons are mighty steep. Wouldn't want you falling overboard."

The door banged shut behind him. Falling overboard? In his mind, he could see a dark-cloaked cabby snatch Sam to fling her unsuspecting body into one of these endless ravines.

They were climbing now. The engine ahead huffed out gigantic clouds of smoke, and cinders danced like fireflies about his head. Licking his lips, Grant discovered a few there and spit them out with his self-disgust. What utter rot. If Sam were in danger, a far from proven fact, his sympathies should lie with the poor cabby. Anyone tangling with Sam Eggersley was more likely to land in the ravine himself.

The tangy scent of pine mingled with the smoke, a rather pleasant combination. Grant filled his lungs with it, letting his muscles stretch and unwind slowly. The air *was* intoxicating.

He's best watch his breathing. Danger or no, he would need all his wits just to deal with Sam. If only he knew what went on in that active little mind of hers.

There no time like the present to find out, he supposed. Taking one last gulp of air, he went through the door into the next car. She wasn't there; that would be too easy. Two lovely ladies smiled eagerly as he wound down the aisle. He winked from habit, feeling little interest, though at one time their adorable giggles would have drawn him like a bee to honey. What was wrong with him? Why not stay there, where he was clearly wanted, instead of blundering into where he just as plainly was not?

Sam glanced up as he entered the next car, but

quickly looked away. Ignoring her upraised nose, he fell into the seat beside her. "Good morning, Miss Eggersley."

"What are you doing here?"

"I decided to play truant, too. I didn't want to be around when Cyrus discovers you're not there for rehearsal."

"Oh." She sounded deflated. "I forgot. Do you think he will be terribly cross?"

"Likely dock us a day's pay, but since he isn't paying us anyway, does it matter? Considering the scenery, I daresay it's worth a tantrum or two."

She sighed, turning to gaze out the window. "You know, I'd forgotten how much I missed this."

Sitting beside her, seeing only hair, Grant wondered what she might do if he put his arms around her, not passionately, but with tenderness. Damn, *had* that been Sam last night?

Before he could ask, though, he had to put her in a friendlier mood. "You could have warned me," he tried to joke, gesturing at an ill-kept pair now entering the car. "I feel a trifle over-dressed."

One would think he had leprosy, the way she glared. "Those men are miners. They work in their clothes."

"And I do not?"

"I did try to warn you. It's a different world up here. Men, and their clothing, need to be as rugged as the terrain."

"Must you be so nasty?"

"Must you follow my every move?"

"Yes, dammit! We've got to talk about last night."

As she went white, he turned coward. Just what could he say next? Pardon me, but was that you in my bed last night? She'd only deliver some scathing remark, to which he'd feel compelled to reply in kind, and then they'd be back to where they always were. Nowhere.

"You needn't explain," she said quickly, her gaze trained on the window. "I retired soon afterward. I never expected you to return. Not in your condition."

As predicted, that brought them nowhere. And it hurt to look at her. Forcing his gaze away, he watched the pine-covered cliffs that extended above and below their limited view. Cascading over the rocks and branches strewn in its way, a lively stream raced along on its own little path. Just like this elusive woman beside him. Always in the opposite direction.

Must everything remind him of the blasted female? His mind waded through the contradictions. If Bodine were right, and that had been Sam coming out of his room, why had she been there? Spying, as Riley maintained? Stealing? But what? All he had of any value was his medallion.

But she had been reaching for his chest. Sam knew it was valuable to him; Claire had mentioned that. But it still made no sense. What would Sam want with his medallion? And why hadn't she struggled when he pulled her into his arms? Would a thief, or even a spy, have such hungry, tempting lips?

No, it must have been Claire. She had smelled like her. She had certainly shown Claire's eagerness. Until the end. The way their lovemaking had come to such an abrupt end was vintage Sam. Riley would claim she had been amusing herself yet again.

Leaning back, he decided his abused brain needed a rest. For a few minutes, he could close his eyes and let the rocking motion soothe him. To hell with her if he fell asleep.

Not five minutes later, the air stirred. He was instantly alert. Through lowered lids, he watched

Sam slip past. Silly, to feel so disappointed, when it was so like her to sneak off that way.

He waited a few minutes before going after her. This time, he didn't even see the two giggling females. He overtook Sam as she stepped onto the rear platform. Her eyes went wide with the look of a cornered animal. Unnerved, he grabbed for her, thinking wildly that she might be desperate enough to jump.

He should have known better. Sam rounded on him, gray eyes glittering. "Stop following me."

He dropped the arm, embarrassed to have lost control again. "You flatter yourself. Did it never occur that I too might want an unobstructed view?"

She glanced at the bruise already forming on her wrist, but wisely said nothing. Biting her lip, she turned away to face the cliffs.

They were deep into a dark and awe-inspiring canyon, where the sheer walls seemed to squeeze the train between them. Had he spoken, she'd never have heard him, for the coughs from the engine echoed against the rock. Beside them, the river thundered past. He moved closer, remembering the conductor's warning. Did Sam know about the danger, or who presented it? Was she now running to or from them? And how in hell would he ever help her if she kept him forever in the dark?

As if to ridicule him, the train broke out into sizzling sunshine. The coolness of the canyon slipped into her memory as rock gave way to grass-covered, rolling hills. Odd, he'd have sworn they were up in the mountains by now.

He was nearly foolish enough to mention this, when the train passed by a gap, affording a view downward. Way down. With a jolt, he saw he was now perched on the peaks he had seen from his hotel window. The realization was enough to take his breath away.

And it had, quite literally. Hidden from the light back in the canyon, the air had a crystal, piercing quality, but here, in the relentless summer sun, it seemed to have vanished. Disoriented, he breathed with conscious care.

Sam caught him at it. "Take it easy. Don't push yourself until you adjust to the lighter air."

Her indulgence irked him. "We can't be that high up."

"Actually, Denver is a mile above sea level and they say Central City is a good three thousand feet above that."

Miss Smug and Superior. Did she consider his breathing as inadequate as his seat? "Success, I've been told, is merely a matter of setting one's mind to a goal and keeping it there. If I want to play the cowboy, it will take more than air to stop me."

"This is rugged country; I would not suggest overstepping your limits."

How accommodating of him to amuse her so. "And what would you know about my limits?"

"One does not go out and *be* a cowboy. It takes years of hard work and practice."

Grant could feel the perspiration at his collar. How dare she use his own words against him. "I spent some time here," he snapped, resuming the role he'd come to hate. "I helped your father find the Oh Susannah, remember?"

"Of course I remember. You're the one with the defective memory, not me."

The collar felt even tighter. "I employ others to remind me of what I need to know. It's a pity my attorneys weren't in my room last night. Perhaps they could have explained who visited me. And why."

Her eyes went dark, her cheeks scarlet. As she wheeled, she nearly tilted them both off balance. Stunned, Grant watched her tug on the door, which stubbornly resisted her pull. Roughly brushing her face with one hand, she planted her feet. With all her weight behind her, she tugged again and the door broke loose, all but toppling her to the floor.

Before he could recover sufficiently to offer assistance, or even to laugh, she was gone, making for the other end of the train. He leaned back, half sitting on the rail, running a hand through his hair. Bloody, impulsive fool. If it had, indeed, been Sam in his room, he'd just lost all hope for a repeat performance tonight.

It embarrassed him, this impulse to go groveling after her. If she had been his midnight visitor, she must have been there for more than a hug and tickle. What had she been planning, before he reached out and grabbed her?

Unconsciously, his hand went to the medallion. It hung heavy on his neck. Was that why Sam was forever looking at his chest, and not his face? Was there some value in the faded bronze that he could not see?

Stroking it, he realized how little he had thought of the sun-filled room in the last few weeks. What had happened to his drive to find it? Sam Eggersley, that's what. She'd cost him his past, his future, everything. And what had he to show for it? Fairy dust, for that was all his dreams would ever be.

He sought the comfort of his memories. Going back to the cheery room, he found a woman this time, bending down to fold him in her arms. She smelled wonderful, like roses, and her love covered him in a scented cloud. How warm and secure he had felt in that grasp. Had she been his mother?

In a painful flash, he saw her clearly. Winged brows, auburn hair hanging about her shoulders, she now smiled with unbearable sadness. Salty tears dropped onto his cheeks as she hugged him, so tight it hurt. More than anything, he wanted to dry those tears, to make her smile again, but he had known even then that there was nothing he could do. She would leave him. Sooner or later, everyone left him.

As the handle jiggled behind him, he jumped. His mind whispered, "Sam?" He turned hopefully, but it was only the conductor. "Still here, Mr. Barton? With the fare you paid, you know, you are entitled to a seat."

"I beg your pardon?"

"Just funning with you. Actually, I prefer standing out here myself. Some pretty country we have hereabouts, eh?"

"Yes, very."

"Though not as pretty as our girls. But you would know best. I saw you talking with one of them. Spitting image of her mother, Sam Eggerlsey's grown to be."

"Oh?"

"Sure is good to see her again. There wasn't a prospector in these hills that wasn't a little in love with her mama. The minute Susie strolled onto that stage, I imagine we all saw ourselves up there with her. She brought a little magic into our lives, Susannah Eggersley did."

After his own experience on stage last night, Grant readily understood. It must run in the family, that magic.

The conductor laughed. "She might look like her mama now, but I still picture Sam in those pigtails, trying to save every stray that came to town. It was a sad day for us all when her grandfather came to take her away. The Malloys had planned on keeping her with them. Darned near broke Molly's heart, saying good-bye to her. It'll do her good, having Sam back again, especially after losing Gus that way."

Molly Malloy must be the friend Sam meant to visit. Traces of yesterday's conversation with Jack Parker returned to unsettle him. Gus Malloy had dropped off the same cliff as Sam's parents. Some coincidence. Only there was no such thing as coincidence, Riley had insisted. Just a wise man, moving his pawns.

"I reckon poor Molly's been alone too long. Been talking crazy lately, about ghosts and what-not haunting the Oh Susannah mine."

In light of what Parker had said, she was not alone. What the devil was going on here?

"Train's slowing," the conductor said abruptly, as if jolted awake. "We'll be coming into Black Hawk soon. After that is Central City."

Yes, there was less determination in the chugging now. Perhaps even fewer cinders, though the smoke was just as thick. Grant watched the distant stacks belch noxious yellow fumes into the air. "Is this an industrial center? What do they produce, iron? Textiles?"

The man smiled. "Gold's the only industry here. What you see are smelters. They refine the ore to make it worth digging."

"They make quite a noise."

"That's the stamp mills. Bars of iron that smash the rock to split the ore free. You'll find quite a few in Black Hawk, since they work with water and there's plenty of it here. Time was, folks came all the way from Nevadaville to process their finds."

Grant thought of the rudimentary procedures used in his youth in the tin mines and shook his head.

"Amazing, the machines modern science can create."

"I suppose. I miss the old days, though. All the small claims have been swallowed up by those big Eastern companies. There was a lot more neighborliness when us prospectors combed the hills."

"But the machines must work faster."

"Yeah. And the gold is so deep now you can't get at it without them. The thing is though, them Easteners are ruining our mountains. For them, profit means stripping the land and spitting waste back. They say the ore is here and has to come out, but once it's gone, they take off for the next field, leaving deserts in their wake, while us that live here have to deal with it. Without the trees, the hills burn come summer, and flood in the spring. I hate what they've done to this beautiful land. The way town after town has been abandoned, it's no wonder poor Molly's seeing ghosts."

Peering through the smoke, Grant understood. Twenty years ago, the hills must have been covered with pine, as cool and fresh as the canyons behind them. Now they lay scorched in the sun, as yellow as the air hanging above them. Twenty years from now, with the stacks lying dormant, the gingerbread houses hugging the hills would be abandoned too, their warped boards taking on the same yellowish hue, the same air of desolation.

"What about Central City?" he wondered aloud. "Is it the same there?"

"We could have quit four years back, when the town burned to the ground, but Central folks don't hold much with ghosts. We built ourselves right back up. We have our traditions to uphold. Did you know President Grant himself came to visit us, back in '73? We wanted to make his trip special, so we lined the sidewalk with silver bricks. Gold was too common, you see."

Grant grinned. The town seemed to have a sense of humor, and a flair for the flamboyant. In fact, it sounded like his kind of place. He pictured himself, strolling in like the lgendary gunslinger, everyone, even Sam, pausing to admire his confidence.

"If you'll excuse me," the conductor broke into his thoughts, "I'd best be getting back to work. Nice chatting with you, Mr. Barton. Tell our Sam I was asking after her, will you?"

Grant gave a dumb nod as the man slid quietly through the door. "Our" Sam, was it? Grant had a vision of a thousand open arms, swallowing her up, keeping him away. As always, he was the outsider, the one who didn't belong.

"Black Hawk," the conductor bellowed in the car ahead. "Next stop, Central City."

Grant straightened his cuffs, preparing to return to his seat, but he was distracted by the sight of a building lying across the tracks ahead. He hoped the engineer knew his job, for they were headed right for the middle of it. And while the train had slowed, it would never stop in time. Grant looked over the rail, wondering if he should jump, when he saw that the train meant to pass right through a large opening in the center of the building. Typical Yankee ingenuity, he thought with a grin as they pulled to a stop inside. Why waste a perfectly good structure when you could just cut a hole in its side and have a train depot!

His chuckles died off as he spotted the plaid riding habit, scooting off the car ahead. He went for the door, but with a jerk, the engine started up and began to crawl forward. Sam ran for the door. The train hissed, began its coughing, and picked up speed. Swearing under his breath, Grant vaulted the rail, only to land on his backside on the tracks. His cussing became more prolific as he brushed his seat. He had ruined a perfectly decent pair of trousers, of which he was in poor supply, and for what? So Sam could elude him yet again? He'd be damned if he'd be trapped into any more acrobatics. If she wanted them, she'd have to hire a trained bear.

There was no sense in hurrying to the door; she'd already be gone. And there was less sense in letting her make a fool of him again. He would let her play her endless games, since he knew where to find her. She'd go straight to the nearest livery, obviously, and since the town as nowhere near the size of Denver, he should have little trouble finding the place.

Unfortunately, though, Sam stayed one step ahead of him. As he approached the stable, she burst through the doors, knees digging into the flanks of a splendid gray mare. She did not stop to wave.

There was no reason he could not find himself an equally good horse. Marching inside, Grant pounded on the desk. Gray mare, indeed. Was she, like her cousin, hoping to match her wardrobe?

He tapped on the desk, then pounded again. Where was everyone? He was in a hurry, dammit. As he raised his hand a third time, a large gentleman with huge side whiskers and the inevitable baggy trousers sauntered into view with a hard-to-ignore grin. Irritated all the more, Grant barked out that he wanted the man's best horse, and he wanted it at once.

A bushy eyebrow shot up, emphasizing the twinkle in his eyes. "Aye, do you now? And what would the likes of ye be doing with me best horse, Mr. Rawlings?"

Could he truly resemble the man so? "What do you think I'd be doing? I wish to ride, obviously."

"Oh, and where would ye be going?"

"Do you grill all your customers so?"

The man grinned. "No, but then all me customers

ain't an English milord, are they?''

"Look, will you hire out a horse or not? I don't have all day to stand here playing games with you.''

"You pay me fee and I'll give ye a horse.''

As the man went on to quote a price, Grant blanched. Even before he'd wasted his cash on that train ticket, he'd never have come close to paying it.

As if aware of his dilemma, the eyes twinkled even more. "Will ye be paying cash, or should I be setting up an account?''

"Yes.'' Grant seized on the idea before the wretch changed his mind. "By all means, set up an account.''

The man chuckled as he ambled back to the horses. Tapping his foot, Grant counted the seconds as they wasted away. Just as he could stand it no more and was ready to storm into the stables after him, the owner re-emerged, dragging an ungodly nag. "This is your best mount?''

The whiskers twitched. "It is.''

"But I just saw Sam—young lady leave with a fine-looking mare.''

"That was me next-to-last horse. This be me last. At this hour of the day, ye can hardly be expecting different.''

This hour of the day? Did the people of Black Hawk all hire their horses at daybreak? Ready to spit, Grant would have argued further had he not caught another twitch of the whiskers. The man obviously wasn't about to offer anything better, and Grant hadn't the time to search for another livery. Rather than give this fool added amusement, he'd take the wretched beast.

Hopping on the nag's back, he ignored the muffled laughter and turned toward the street. Serve the fool right if his "last" animal never made it back at the end of the day.

He turned in the direction Sam had gone, following the road to its end. Now which way? Glancing around, he noticed a small boy perched on a picket fence. "Son, did you happen to see a young lady in a plaid riding habit?"

Again, the shuttered look. "Don't rightly know what plaid is. We don't dress so fancy-dancy hereabouts."

As he gave his damaged suit a disdainful glare, Grant wished again that he had brought Willie. "Never mind. I—uh, need to find my aunt. She lives up there somewhere. Her name's Molly. Molly Malloy."

The boy looked at him long and hard before shrugging his indifference. "Head up to that ridge. On the other side, you'll find a path through the woods. Follow it to where it forks. Take the left path; the right only leads to an abandoned mine."

"That wouldn't, by any chance, be the Oh Susannah?"

The boy's eyes took on a speculative gleam. "Folks hereabouts stay away from that place. Smarter, that way."

But the question was addressed to a retreating back, for the boy hopped down and ran in the opposite direction. Shaking his head, Grant turned the horse toward the ridge. It grunted and refused to budge. He dug his heels into its flanks, but as if it had a bit too much of Samantha Eggersley in its make-up, the stubborn nag resisted all attempts to move it. He might as well hae hired himself a mule.

Hot, tired, and still hung-over, Grant was angry enough to spit. Some cowboy he'd make. How could he disprove his inadequacies if the damned horse wouldn't go?

Fifteen minutes later, he was reduced to pleading

into its ear. Using his gentlest whisper, he explained how vital it was to catch up with Sam before she hurt herself, how he deserved to look like more than the comic hero in her eyes. He was amazed at the results his wooing produced. Within moments, the horse had been coaxed into a trot. Interesting. With the same gentle tone, could Miss Eggersley be likewise coerced?

I must be mad, he thought. Talking to animals, chasing off to the back of beyond, all in the hopes that the shrew would be nice to him. Lord, one false step by this wobbling beast and he'd have a good deal worse than torn trousers.

Sam had been right about the terrain, he had to grant her that. But he was not about to knuckle under to it. He could hold his own. Guiding the nag along the narrow ridge, skirting holes, debris and seemingly every obstacle known to man, he was proud of his reserves of strength. As she said, it was only a matter of adapting, and he was determined to prove that he was as adaptable as she.

He wished he'd see her, though. With every inch he climbed, each step further into this God-forsaken land, his uneasiness grew. Perhaps it was those stamp mills, pounding their unholy rhythm, but Grant had the fanciful notion that Parker's ghosts might be lurking in the air around him.

He reined in the nag, squinting for a sign of Sam. The air became increasingly thin. His clothes, torn and worn, clung to his frame in a wrapping of sweat. At this moment he would gladly have sold his soul for a cool grass of water, if not for a healthy American sandwich.

To his relief, the path the boy described ducked into a cool thicket of pines. He followed it gratefully, unbuttoning his shirt to the breeze. The first stream he found, he swore, he would stop for a long, reviving drink.

Well into the trees, he heard the tempting gurgle of water but he dared not leave the path until he found Sam. He wound through the trees, his patience sorely tried by the horse's lack of speed. Where the hell was that fork?

They came upon it suddenly. The Malloys' place lay to the left, he remembered, but curiosity drew him to the right, toward the mine. And the cliff. He made his intentions clear to the horse, but it whinied, making its protest equally plain. Not even his most seductive tone, Grant soon discovered, could convince it to take another step.

He dismounted with an oath, deciding to follow the path on foot. Until the butt of a rifle jabbed his stomach. Grunting, he looked up to find an ominous, muscular lout behind it.

"Why don't you and that sorry animal turn around and go back the way you came?"

From the strength of the voice, this definitely wasn't one of Parker's ghosts. "Isn't this the path to the Oh Susannah mine? A young man down in Black Hawk told me—"

"You're trespassing. Owners had to abandon the mine, but they don't want no fools wandering in and getting themselves hurt."

How considerate, Grant thought, staring pointedly at the gun. Apparently they hadn't stopped to consider the injuries the weapon could inflict. Or had they?

The only owner, as far as he knew, was Sam. Was she behind this? What could she be up to now, that she didn't want him snooping around?

"I am with Miss Eggersley," he bluffed. "She is expecting me. I'm surprised she didn't mention me when she passed by.''

The gun went higher, and closer. "Nobody passes by me. Not this Eggs person, and not you. I got my orders, see?''

"Commendable." Heartened that Sam had nothing to do with this, Grant was determined to learn who did. "I'll be certain to tell your employers what a fine job you're doing up here. Who did you say they were?''

"Didn't. Just who are you to be asking?''

"The name is . . .'' No, he couldn't use Hoxton's name, or his own. What about that fiance—what did Claire say his name was? ''. . . uh, Blankfield. Emery Blankfield. Miss Eggersley's betrothed. Her family owned the Oh Susannah, you see, and she wanted to see it again. I was to have met her here.''

"Well, I ain't seen her. And I can't let her in, not until she clears it with Dr. Charles. And he's down in Denver on business for his lordship.''

Warning bells seemed to be going off all over his brain. Dr. Charles, as in Charles Riley? And in Denver? Was it one of his non-existent coincidences that he had been in Chicago, too, when that other runaway carriage had nearly run Sam down?

"This good doctor—please refresh my memory. Is he short, bald, and wearing a perpetual scowl?''

The man tried not to smile. "That's him.''

"Splendid. As I thought, I know the fellow. I'll go speak with him, then.''

As he turned, the lout grabbed for his arm. "Don't forget to tell him about what a fine job I'm doing. The name's Bull. Bull Atkins.''

"Oh, that I will, Mr. Atkins. That I will.''

20

Sliding from the mare, Sam searched the trees behind her. Yes, she had lost him. Relieved, she hugged the animal's side, fighting for breath. As much as she hated to admit it, she was exhausted. This was rugged terrain, indeed.

And he had done far better than she had anticipated. Heavens, but he had been persistent in his pursuit! If she hadn't ridden through these hills in her childhood, she might never have eluded him. Why, she wondered, was he so determined to follow her?

He knew. He hadn't believed her lie about Claire sleepwalking. She pushed away from the mare, embarrassed to find herself clinging to it. Like Claire, she was letting herself get hysterical. He'd only been teasing. If he thought she had been in his room last night, he would have avoided her entirely.

She tried to recall his exact words but all she could remember was the anger in his eyes as he gazed at her. And her humiliating retreat. What a comic picture she must have presented, fighting with that door. She deserved his laughter; she was a fool.

Whatever could have gotten into her last night? For one weak moment, she let herself relive the too-brief time in his arms. Hugging herself, she went dizzy with the longing. Why did he have to remind her that it was Claire he thought he held? Dear God, he truly did mean to marry *her*?

Dabbing at her eyes, she secured the mare to the

nearest tree. It was the lack of sleep, she insisted, that brought her so close to tears. Lord, but she was tired. How on earth would she ever accomplish all she hoped to do? There was Molly to visit, the mine to inspect, and of course, the cabin . . . .

She thought longingly of her childhood bed. What she wouldn't do to curl up into a ball with her favorite teddy bear and just drift off into a deep, dreamless sleep.

Enough of that, she told herself sternly as she walked to the door. She had come here to look the place over, to find clues that the younger Sam wouldn't have recognized. Somewhere, there must be proof that her father hadn't killed himself.

But as she stepped over the threshold, time seemed to stop for her. As if it were yesterday, she could picture her father sitting before the fire mending her teddy bear, talking to it as he made his repairs, the way the doctor talked to Sam. And Mama would be smiling from the kitchen, the aroma of her fresh-baked cookies driving Papa from his work and to the kitchen to steal a bite and a kiss.

Running her hands along the wood of the chair he had sat in, Sam felt the tears well in her eyes. So many times, he had sat here and listened as another miner talked about giving up. Never, Bill Eggersley had said. A man should hold on to his dream, for what else did he have?

She rose from the chair, the tears blinding her. She wandered through the rest of the house, feeling, not seeing, as the past came alive again. She could picture her father, that last day before he left, shoulders slumped as if in surrender. All evening long, she had waited for him to return. And then, when it got too dark to see her nose on her face, she had gone out looking, despite Molly's protests, and she would have stayed out all night long if the sheriff hadn't come to drag her home. He was out there, she had told them. And deep inside, she felt he still was, somewhere, just waiting for her to find him.

As she entered her bedroom, she faced the much longed-for bed. Propped on a pillow by the headboard was her teddy bear. She grabbed it to hug to her chest. Its right arm was stitched, where her grandfather had torn it when he snatched it from her hands. Molly must have picked it up, repaired it, and brought it home where it belonged.

And now she was home, too. She sank to the bed, the bear still clasped in her arms, waiting for the past to catch up with the present. So hard, when everywhere she looked, she found traces of her mother. From the pink organdy curtains and spread, to the fine furniture her wages had bought, Sam could feel her mother's strength and love flood through her. *Oh Mama, I'm so sorry I failed you that day,* she whispered softly, wishing her mother could hear. If she had known, she would have stayed with her baby brother for the rest of her life. But she had hid under this bed, like the coward she was, until it was too late.

Curling into a ball, she was that child again, the same little girl who had cried, night and day, wishing the pain and guilt would go away. Praying that her father would forgive her, that he would be his old self again. Then he could prove them all wrong, and magically appear to save her. See, he would say; my Sam is a good girl.

But it was not Bill Eggersley she saw as she closed her eyes and drifted off to sleep. She was in a field of snow, pristine white, wherever the eye could see. She was following a flake, always out of reach, until she tripped and fell . . . .

Emery Blankfield wanted to weep with frustration. Where was Samantha Lynn? He had been told she would be here, all day, visiting this Molly Malloy person. That was not the sort of name with which he wanted his future wife aligning herself, especially not after he'd seen this ramshackle hut. When his intended did put in appearance, she would hear from him about the futility of continuing this relationship. Imagine if his employers back in Richmond learned of this!

Emery Blankfield had pretensions, and a burning ambition. the first of these was to be rich and respected. To do this, though, he must first acquire the Eggersley wealth and influence. Upon entering law school, it had been made painfully clear that the best of everything went to those who were allied with the proper names. The right wife could open doors otherwise closed to a carpetbagger's son, and while Miss Eggersley might not be the belle of last year's season, she was accessible. And wealthy enough for a man of even his expectations. Or so he'd thought.

Emery hated being poor. With money, he could have whistled old Samuel's edicts down the wind and followed his heart instead. How much tidier things would have been had Claire Farnstable inherited the Eggersley fortune. Had there been any justice to this world, it would be at her lap that he would be kneeling tonight, her hand he would be leading to the altar in the morning.

But Claire, as lovely as she was, had less to her name than he had. Perhaps, with the utmost care, he could one day claim her as his mistress.

Ah, what heaven, to hold such a treasure in his arms. Daydreaming, he leaned back—and fell through a rotting board. They called this a porch? Greedily, he thought of the fine Eggersley mansion. A few more days and he could look forward to sitting on that porch, if not tall, at least proud, nodding his head as Richmond's elite passed by.

Drat that woman; where was she? He didn't have all day. Arrangements had to be made. Carefully selecting a board that had not succumbed to the weather, he made himself as comfortable as he could for his vigil. He would wait all night, if necessary, but he wished his saddle sores would lessen. Especially since improvement in the local livestock seemed unlikely. Wretched animal, he sneered at the one he had hired today. It had to be the worst piece of horse-flesh in creation.

As he attempted to fan himself with his hat, he noticed the dust on it. What was wrong with that woman, forcing him out here into this wilderness? He'd heard of playing hard-to-get, but this was absurd.

Thank heavens for that letter, warning that perhaps his intended had other plans—even pretensions of becoming Lady Hoxton. When he'd met with that Bavoure fellow early this morning, Emery had been shocked, and appalled, to learn the extent of Samantha Lynn's financial difficulties. How dared she run off like that, without telling him about the severe problems at the bank? Going to visit an old friend of her father's, indeed. Did she think him stupid?

If so, she would soon learn otherwise. Thanks to his clever manipulations with Bavoure, the bank would be saved. Three days he'd been given, to convince the woman to marry and leave with him. Three days to recoup a fortune.

He would do it, too, Emergy vowed. One did not let a goose this golden slip from one's grasp.

As he continued through the woods, Grant's overriding thought was that Sam was in danger. He had to find her. Find her and somehow get her as far away from Colorado as he possibly could. After all, there had been no attempts on her life in Richmond all those years. It was only now, here so close to the mine, that Hoxton saw her as a threat.

What a fool Grant had been to believe that nonsense about the hopeless romantic. The discreet compliments, the lingering touches, had all been planned from the start. He'd been hired to distract, not court her. They wanted poor Sam so flustered, she would never notice how her father's partner, and "very good friend" had been robbing her blind.

But stubborn as she was, Sam had thwarted them at every turn. More than a little proud of her, Grant wondered how he could ever have listened to Riley's accusations. If she had been playing with him, hell, maybe he deserved it, for linking himself with the likes of Hoxton.

He came to the crest of a hill. Pausing, he saw a cabin cozily set in a nest of pines. It was so like the cottage of his dreams that his heart flopped. He noticed the mare beside it, flicking flies with its tail. There was no sign of Sam. Was she waiting inside for him, or more likely, would she order him away?

Wincing, he turned his gaze to the other valley. Through the trees, he could see abandoned mining equipment, rustling in the sun. Underneath, he felt that ghostly pounding. It was certainly an eerie place, he thought, but then a pair of legs wandered across his line of vision. Definitely not a ghost. As a second pair of ragged, baggy trousers passed, he remembered Sam sneering that miners worked in their clothes. Miners, working?

But the mare whinned down below, recapturing

his attention. First things first. As if Riley stood at his
shoulder, he could feel him moving his pawns. The
queen was in danger. Grant must get her out of here,
back to Richmond if possible. And then, he would
have a look at that mine.

His mind made up, he spurred the horse forward.
Unfortunately, he failed to take into account the
steepness of the incline. When he finally did, the
horse was already skidding downhill, far beyond his
control, and he spent each inch of that perilous
descent praying for survival.

Seeing level ground loom before him, Grant
pulled at the reins, speaking in his most coaxing tone
as he prepared to dismount. He planned to slip off
midstride as he'd seen the locals do, only the damned
horse refused to slow down. It thundered past the
cabin, Grant sawing on the reins, until it surrendered
quite some distance down the path.

But it did so far too abruptly. Only quick reflexes
saved him from flying over the beast's head, and he
was forced to alight far more gingerly than had been
his original intent.

Standing beside it, refusing to be shaken, he
returned its glare twofold. If he could master this
monster, he knew, there was nothing he couldn't do.

He released the reins to lean down and brush the
dust from his poor trousers. As he did, the blasted
animal took advantage by galloping away.

Well, it was good to know, even too late, that it
was capable of such speed. But, he would not demean
himself by giving chase. Nor would he admit he had
neglected to secure it, he thought as he walked back
up to the cabin.

As he neared it, he heard a whimper. Senses
suddenly alert and concentrating on Sam, he forgot
his anger and inched toward the cabin. Damn, he

wished he had a weapon of some sort. A pair of those imagined six-shooters would certainly be welcome.

Drawing on his acrobatic skill, he silently edged around the cabin. His only weapon, unfortunately, was the element of surprise. Stepping over a stout limb, he decided he might as well take it with him. Lumber made a more convincing deterrent than his fists.

He crept up to the porch. As his hand tightened on the door knob, he realized he could easily kill, if one hair on that beautiful head had been touched.

Ever so carefully, he eased the door open. Peering inside, he found the room empty. He let the branch drop an inch as he listened for Sam. Nothing. Could she be . . . ?

Grim now, he slipped into the cabin. He faced a large room, simply but nicely furnished. A braided rug of assorted grays was encircled by a grouping of chairs, with cushions the same plaid as Sam's riding habit, all facing the large stone fireplace on the far wall. Directly opposite, raised slightly above the rest of the room, was the kitchen. The small, square table, covered by a faded yellow cloth, was flanked on all sides by similarly cushioned chairs. Yellow-checked curtains framed a window looking out over the valley, while skirts of the same material disguised the shelves of supplies behind it. Oh yes, he thought wistfully; it was just the sort of place to fit his dreams. Just the kind of place that would be forever beyond his reach.

How nice it would be, though, to spend a day here. Just the two of them, playing house, lying naked before he fire so thoughtfully set and waiting to blaze . . . .

It hit him then, how the entire place seemed ready and waiting. As if someone had known Sam would come and wanted everything to be perfect for her. All that was missing was a chilled bottle of champagne. She had said she was meeting a friend. Had she meant a lover?

He lowered the limb. He felt ridiculous, rushing in here, ever the comic hero, just to interrupt a tryst. Women often whimpered in the throes of passion. He should have recognized the sound.

Yet, as he turned to go, there was another whimper. No female he had ever held uttered such a desolate sound. If that bastard was hurting her . . .

Acting on sheer impulse alone, he charged through the door to the right, club poised above his head. Sam lay on the bed, arms clutching a ragged stuffed bear. She was alone, and fast asleep.

A wave of tenderness gripped him. Without thinking, he dropped the branch and approached the bed. Half of him wanted to let her sleep, to take his pleasure in watching her, but another whimper convinced him this would be selfish at best. "Sam," he whispered as he gently shook her shoulders. "Come on, wake up."

She sat up, suddenly, her eyes wide and frightened. "Papa. Oh Papa, they have Mama. And Devon."

"It's all right; it was only a dream."

"No, they killed her. I saw the footprints in the snow. And Dr. Charles."

Grant felt suddenly cold. All too clearly, he could remember Riley's interest in those footprints. God help her, what had Sam seen?"

His grip tightened on her shoulders. "Who is this Dr. Charles, Sam?"

Clearly confused, she tried to focus. "Our family doctor. I never liked him, though. He was always scowling. Like . . . like . . ." She squinted, as if half of her tried to remember and half wanted to forget.

"Never mind, I know who you mean. Tell me where did you see these footprints?"

"On the ridge. By the mine. They went clearly up to the cliff where I found Mama . . . ."

"My God, Sam. I never realized . . ." She had to have been a baby. What a horror for a child, to find her mother's lifeless body. He understood, now, the haunted look behind those gray eyes. And he cursed Hoxton with all his might for not warning him of this.

He opened his arms and gathered her close. She fell against him, weeping softly, and the sounds of her sobs tore at his heart. He understood everything now. Her prickliness, her reluctance to trust, and her determination to return here. Someone had killed her parents, and she would not rest until she learned who.

And he, by God, was going to help her. Cradling her head against his chest, he tried to find a way to tell her this, only to be distracted by the alluring scent of her hair. He had an overwhelming urge to bury himself in its wealth. As he stared at the pins imprisoning it, he wondered what she would do if he reached down to remove them, one by one. And once they joined the one in his pocket, would she be as eager as she'd seemed the previous night?

He stopped himself there, disgusted. Friends supported one another; they didn't take advantage of a moment of weakness. He gazed into the tear-soaked eyes, drowning in them. He wanted far more than friendship, he acknowledged. He wanted to love her.

The thought stunned, then ultimately soothed him. He did love her. How ironic, that it should happen this way. All those women throwing themselves at him, and he had to choose one so far out of his reach. And still it didn't matter. He loved her.

Disobedient, his fingers inched up to her hair. As the brown curls cascaded to her shoulders, the gray eyes mirrored the fright in his. He was making a commitment here. And he wasn't the least bit drunk.

So be it. The choice had long since been taken from his hands. Resigned, he let the emotion spread, filling him, fulfilling him. It brimmed into his eyes and floated out to hers, until an answering spark sprang to life in the mysterious gray depths. As he watched, hoping, her body quivered. Each breath she drew grew longer and deeper. Then, miraculously, her lips parted.

He fell on her mouth, as hungry as he had ever been. She clung to his neck, her tongue countering his eagerly, with a greed to match his own. He needed to kiss her everywhere, all at once, but he could not bear to leave her mouth. So warm. So sweet. My God, how could he stop now?

As if in mutual consent, they both drew back slightly to draw a ragged breath. Her gaze faltered, and then dropped away. Poor, unsure-of-herself Sam. Didn't she know? Couldn't she see how he adored her?

He took her face in his hands. Time seemed to hang there between them, as if lending a bit of itself for them to recognize the inevitable. Heart literally in his throat, Grant took her chin in one hand and forced her to look at him. Before she could pull away, he kissed her. Tenderly. Reverently. Her lips went soft, pliant, and he parted them with his tongue. One hand held her tight, while the other clasped the back of her head. Lost, he delved within her mouth, taking his time, exploring every inch, savoring the deep, flavorful recesses there. His bones melted, his muscles seemed to flow with his blood. *Sam!* his stunned brain kept repeating. No dream, this time. It was good and truly Sam.

And through it all, a dark, primitive pulsing grew within him. He tried to ignore it—he must—but it grew more insistent with every second. Take her, it hissed, a serpent tempting him to ruin. The urging snaked through his body, infecting every inch, until he was burning for her. He had to feel her skin.

Scooping her into his arms, he whirled around to place her on the bed. With a hand on each side of her head, he used his lips to silence any protest. God, she was beautiful. And she was his.

Reluctantly breaking away from her mouth, he slipped open each button of her bodice. Creamy breasts, hiding beneath the coarse fabric, lay temptingly just beyond his touch.

Holding her breath, Sam watched him slowly undress her. Patience, he schooled himself; don't frighten her. The layers of female clothing might have slowed a less determined man, but Grant moved practiced fingers through the buttons and ties until at last they touched skin.

Both breasts broke free in one, fluid motion. In a trance, he reached for one, needing to restrain his eager fingers. It took all his will to force them to trail slowly over the budding nipple.

As proud as he was of his restraint, the movement drew a tiny gasp of alarm. He pulled his gaze away, up to her face, "What is it? Have I hurt you?"

She shook her head, her hair rustling back and forth on the pillow. "I—I'm frightened."

He hated himself. What was wrong with him, taking advantage of a moment of weakness this way? Muttering an oath under his breath, he started to leave her, but a hand shot out to cover his. Her eyes entrapped him, swallowed him. "Not of you. Of this. I—I've never . . . ever . . . I don't know what to do."

"You needn't do a thing." He laughed shakily as he smoothed the hair from her face. "For once, let someone else worry about what must be done. I've spent my life learning how to please a woman; trust me to put it to good use."

He kissed her forehead, then both cheeks, hoping to dispell the last of her doubts. Inside he was trembling, awed by the trust she placed in him. Did he deserve her trust? Yes, dammit; he must. For if Sam trusted him, and he failed her, he could only hurt himself.

He kissed her again, long and deep, wondering how any of it could be real. They must be caught in a play, their words and actions predetermined by the script. How else could she be so warm and eager beneath him? She was a witch, this woman, her fiery tongue weaving her magic around him. Losing himself to it, he held her close, so close, letting her soft, sweet fragrance calm his fears. *I love her*, he thought with wonder. *My God, I actually love her.*

And with such acknowledgement came desire. A strong, hot gust of it, burning through his brain. He needed to touch her, taste her, know her. Forcing his tongue from her mouth, he kissed her chin, nibbled her neck, and drew a long, hot line down to the crevice of her breasts. Pausing there, he drew in air like a diver ready to submerge.

As he took her breasts in his hand, he felt a surge of power. He shut his eyes to steady himself, but his hand continued to caress the soft flesh. Lowering his lips slowly, he fought to control the greed of his tongue as it sought the blossoming nipple. He could control his greed no longer. As his tongue licked the eager flesh, his sigh of pleasure echoed across the room.

There was another surge, and this time he let it

carry him away. Grasping the other breast, he captured them both for his mouth's delight. He nuzzled them, licked them, sucked them to shivering erection. God, she tasted so good. It was all he could do not to devour her whole.

Long slender fingers entwined themselves in his hair. She moved them in a lazy, circular motion, the tempo building with his desire, until with a groan, she pulled his lips to her mouth. His tongue was sucked in and held a happy captive. Yes, she was a fiery witch, his Sam. Consumed by the sudden need, he drew back to look at her, his breath shallow and quick.

Like a glutton, he filled his mind with the sight of her. Eyes glazed with passion, she stared back at him, as if feeding upon his need. As if she absorbed his love and sent it flowing back to him, deeper and stronger than ever.

With a new urgency, he ran his hands down her sides, pushing the unwanted remains of her clothing to the side. Reality went with them. All that existed was he and this fantastic woman. And he would make love to her with every acquired skill, as she so miraculously wanted him to do.

But the she smiled at him, that shy little-girl smile, and his control slipped further. He could so easily crush those delicate limbs. Holding back, fighting the throbbing urgency in his groin, he stroked her soft, warm flesh. God give him strength; he must wait for her.

But again, she surprised him. Reaching up, her hands fumbled with the buttons of his shirt. He watched, amazed, as her smile lost its shyness. Slipping the sleeves from his arms, she became seductive and wise, a woman lost to passion. Fascinating, incredible Sam. God, he worshipped her.

His fingers joined with hers, desperate now to

discard anything that stood between them. All their clothing flew to the floor. With infinite care, he set her face to face beside him. He edged his body closer and as their skin touched, he swore he could hear the tension between them crackle through the air.

He gripped her, fighting the impulse demanding release. He wanted to fill her up with himself, to become such an integral part of her being that she would never again be satisfied without him. Let that Blankfield try to wed her. Grant Barton must be all she would ever see, or feel, or dream.

Yet, more than this, he longed to please her. Her smile, her happiness, became his only goal. To erase that haunted look, deep within her eyes, would bring meaning to his life at last.

But his hands continued without him, not caring much for loftly ideals. Hers either, it would seem, for they traveled in unconscious imitation over his chest, sending darts of fire downward as they teased the tiny nipples. Heat followed wherever they crept, around to his back, down, over the tightening muscles of his buttocks. As she traced teasing circles on the sensitive flesh, he moaned deep within his throat.

Dizzy now, he slid his hands along her thighs, down to the knees, his fingers creeping ever upward . . . beautiful. Up, so slowly it hurt . . . incredible. To the sweet, welcoming warmth between them . . . ah, Sam . . . .

All the blood he owned rushed to his groin. Gripping her, he opened her lips with his tongue, pouring his love into her. He could not stop. Their joining was inevitable. He had known it, that first time the gray eyes touched his soul.

His fingers stroked her, teasing, enflaming, until she too moaned softly, and began digging her nails into his back. Their scents mingled, a heady combination drawing his mouth everywhere, each touch and taste urging him on. It seemed he could never get his fill. He would never want to. Sam whimpered as she clung to him, her body arching to meet him.

Inside, his passion rose up in a flood, threatening to drown them both. It was time, he decided; it had to be, for he could resist her no longer. Poised above her, reveling in the heat created between them, he took her mouth with aching tenderness. He prayed that she was ready for him, that she would forgive him if she was not.

Easing between her legs, he sank down into the cushioned warmth of her, every nerve pulsing with his need. "This may hurt," he rasped, hoping to reassure her, "but it will pass quickly."

She tried to return his smile, the result touching him in a buried, vulnerable place. Oh yes, the commitment had been made. All that remained was to possess her. To give himself completely to this lady of his dreams.

The slight resistance gave way. Her slender body tensed. Her pain became his own. "Trust me," he begged. "Oh Sam, I swear. I will never willingly hurt you again."

She answered by grasping his neck and pulling his mouth to hers. Grant's world spun out of tilt, twisting off into a crazy, spiraling orbit. Hazily, he felt her legs lock across his thighs, joining them in a way that could never be undone. It was sheer agony to withdraw, but oh, how acute was the pleasure as he thrust himself deeper yet. He shuddered with it. His tempo quickened, grew desperate.

Poised above, each muscle tensed and concentrated, he was a a mighty hunter, Sam, his elusive quarry. All his life, he had tracked her, her scent taunting him, only to have her vanish without a trace. And now here she was, so close—so miraculously close—smiling, luring him ever onward, until he could feel her essence in every shining detail, hovering there just within his grasp.

"Oh, Grant," she gasped, fingers biting into his back. "Oh!"

"Hold on." Passion exploded in a thousand twinkling lights. He sucked it in, making it his own, all so he might pour it without end into her quivering body. He had her. His Sam. All that magic and mystery lay shimmering in his hands.

His tongue was thick and swollen as he kissed her. Had he his way, he'd have gone on, thrusting and throbbing forever, but Nature had her own designs. Enough, she decreed, as he slowly withdrew, his entire being already aching with the loss. How at home he had felt inside her. As if he'd finally found where he belonged.

He sank down into the dark, sweet luxury of her hair, still unable to believe his fortune. Had the dream, for once, truly held? By all that was good and right, could this actually be his angel, clinging to him, raining tiny kisses on his sweat-soaked shoulder? Perhaps a new chapter had opened in his life. For the first time since those prison bars had clanked shut behind him, he felt clean and whole again.

For somehow, Sam was his. There was no need for a written or spoken pledge; these past few precious moments had sealed it. Whatever the future brought, whatever its uncertainties, the magic could not be undone. He felt like laughing, like crying. Hell, he was delirious with happiness.

He turned to Sam, expecting to share this special moment in their lives, and all the joy in him froze.

"My God, what have I done!" she hissed with

piercing intensity as she bolted up and scrambled out of the bed.

21

Sam refused to look at the bed she had so hastily abandoned. Inside and out, she still trembled from the sensations Grant had aroused. It wasn't fair that he should hold such power over her. It wasn't safe.

And what a cad he was to take advantage of a moment of weakness. Fighting the tears that stung her eyes, she went in search of her clothes. He must have seen she was distraught, disoriented from her nightmare. Yet he had used that soothing voice, those tender hands, not to comfort and console, but to make her fall into his lap like a ripe plum.

And oh, how willing she had been! She was. All he had to do was run those practiced hands along her traitorous flesh and she would whimper, "yes, yes, anything you want."

She scrambled into her clothes. They provided small defense, and too late now, but she must be dressed before she faced him. Otherwise, how could she pretend indifference? Eggersley pride demanded that he mustn't see how this—this mistake—had affected her. Or how desperately she longed to jump back beside him in that bed.

"Dammit, Sam. Look at me."

She wouldn't. Couldn't. "I think we should be going."

She heard the creak of the springs, then his muttered oaths as he gathered his clothes. She had made him angry. Again. But perhaps it was best this way.

Her fingers fumbled with her buttons. She couldn't stop them from shaking.

"Here, let me."

She gasped as cool fingers brushed hers aside to fasten the button of her skirt. The scent of their mingled bodies clung to him, wafting up to tempt her again. No! She wheeled around, attempting to break free, but lost her balance. His hands went to her waist to steady her. In a panic, she pushed him away. "No. Don't touch me."

"What the hell is the matter with you?"

"Nothing."

"Nothing? You're acting as if we hadn't just—"

"I said, nothing." She pulled free of his grip, working at the button herself. "I am trying to be sensible. And to—thank you for satisfying my curiosity. It was a pleasant experience."

"Pleasant?" His eyes narrowed. "Don't you mean, amusing?"

She blinked. Her eyes hurt dreadfully. "Pleasant, amusing, call it what you like. You mustn't fear I took it seriously. I know this sort of thing happens all the time."

"Damn you." The words were quiet, but pierced her like a blade. "You and your bloody games." Wearily, he raised both hands in a gesture of surrender. "You win. You can be happy, if you were out to make me feel like a damned fool. I truly thought, this once, there was something special between us."

"Special, Lord Hoxton? the way it is with Claire?"

"I swear to you, I've never touched her."

"I'm not blind, you know. Or stupid. I was there last night. I heard you ask her to marry you."

He was not light on his feet as he moved away. As he finished dressing, Sam hugged herself hard, fearing that if she didn't, she just might unravel completely. What a fool she was, blurting out that she had been in his room! No wonder he was embarrassed. What did she expect? Any denial from him now would be as false as her hopes.

"You can believe it or not, but I swear to you, I've never touched your cousin. Or any other woman since I met you. God knows, I should have, just to ease the frustration, but for some bizarre reason, I can't seem to get your face out of my mind."

"My face?" She could feel the hysteria bubbling up inside her. "Don't you mean my mother's?"

"What the hell are you talking about?"

The blank expression on his face infuriated her. "Everyone takes great delight in reminding me how like her I am! Isn't it her face that you see?"

"Oh, for God's sake, I don't even know the woman."

"I was there!" she all but screeched. "I heard the whispers. Lord, my grandfather jammed it down my throat at every possible opportunity. I know that you loved her."

He cursed softly, then dropped with an angry motion to the bed. Grunting, he yanked on his boots. She knew she should do the same, but an overwhelming lethargy gained control. She should have lain there on that bed, warm and secure at his side for as long as the illusion lasted. Talk about biting off your nose to spite your face. Pride only left a sour taste in the mouth.

Sam had never felt more miserable. *Tell me I'm wrong*, she pleaded silently. Tell me it's me that you love. At least say that you like me.

As if he had heard, he sighed, brushing off his trousers as he rose to his feet. "Obviously, nothing I say is going to convince you. But before we put an end to this farce, can I at least know why you came to my room last night?''

She was mortified. Looking away, she tried to find a lie to satisfy him, but again he seemed to read her thoughts.

''Don't bother denying it. Bodine saw you there.''

The lethargy had full control now. She sat down on the other side of the bed with her hands in her lap; her eyes traced the floral pattern of the rug. ''Claire sent me. She couldn't sleep. She knew there was a bottle of brandy in your room.''

''Oh? And she waited patiently all that time?''

''I—I came back. A second time. I forgot to lock your door. That was when . . . when you heard me. You were tossing off your covers and I—I tried to tuck you in. Like I do with Willie.''

''And do you jump into his bed, too?''

''I didn't jump. I was pulled.''

''Dammit, you weren't forced today. Why do you always leave me?''

''How could I stay, when you were saying such untimate things to me . . . to her . . . I mean, when you thought I was Claire.''

''I see.''

No, he didn't. But then, neither did she. All she could do was feel. And it hurt.

Standing before her, he tilted his head. His voice, so gentle, nearly undid her. ''And today, the excuse was your mother. You'll have to make up your mind, Sam. You, Claire, your mother; I can sleep with only one woman at a time.''

Wondering what he meant, she looked up into the probing blue eyes. He seemed as bewildered and hurt as she. She trembled again, all those pent-up emotions battling to break loose. Shame came first. Small wonder the man was confused; smaller yet if he was disgusted. In the blink of an eye, she had gone from a pliable wretch to a brazen hussy and then to this screeching shrew. I'm not like this, she tried to plead, but speech was beyond her. Why didn't he say something? Anything.

"Should we expect anyone else?"

Three women in one bed is quite sufficient, she started to snap, but as she glanced up, she found him inching toward the window, the lean body coiled for action. His face went tight with concentration, and she realized he didn't mean last night. "You mean, here? Why, no."

"I think we have company." His harsh whisper sent shivers along her spine.

"Company?"

In two strides, he stood before her, placing a finger over her lips. "Someone's outside. I'll go see who. You wait here."

As if to stun her into obedience, he pulled her close. His kiss was deep and fierce, almost ruthless. "We will finish this, but for now, stay on that bed until I call for you."

She couldn't have moved if she'd wanted to. Long after he had passed through the door, she sat on the bed, touching her lips. Her mind spun off in a hundred dizzy circles. Finish this? We? What on God's good earth could he possibly mean by that?

Cussing like a sailor, Molly Malloy hobbled toward Bill's cabin. Damned heathens, messing with her hills. That was dynamite she'd heard yesterday. Nobody could tell her it was a ghost. There was too much nonsense going on in these parts, too much dying that shouldn't be done.

As always when she thought of Gus, an awful aching made itself at home in her chest. Easygoing

Gus, who'd never harmed a soul; nobody could make her believe *he* had tried to kill himself.

She sure was glad Sam was coming home. It hadn't been the same here without Gus. She'd have moved to town, if not for keeping Sam's place up. Now she was getting too old, too worn, to keep the two places going much longer.

Thinking of the Eggersleys put a different kind of ache in her gut. A mountain of memories were tied up in that family. It was a downright tragedy, losing them. First Susie, the baby, then Bill. And she could remember Sam, tears streaming down her cheeks as they packed her off on that train with her heart-shrivelled grandfather. Enough to break a heart. From where she stood, Molly figured, they'd all been robbed.

Sam. With so many years gone by, would she recognize the girl? Girl; she was a woman grown by now. A stiff and formal one, from the sound of her letters. Time changed folks, they said. What if she and Sam had nothing to say to each other any more? Spoiled by the Eggersley money, would Sam remember how it was to go without? Molly looked down at her dress. Like herself, it was clean and decent, but they'd both seen better days. Would Sam take one look at her old Molly and sniff with contempt?

The devil take her, then. There was no sense placing much stock in this reunion. It was a waste of time, wishing things back to the way they was. Only, whose idea had it been to cut off the good times so soon? One minute, life was so full, the days slipped by unnoticed, then poof! Time was crawling and Molly was left with nothing but memories and solitude.

Mounting the porch, Molly let her mind slide back to the happier years. She could hear Susie's laughter, even now. How Bill had worshipped that woman. He'd gone to his grave mourning her. Such a waste, all of it, with poor little Sam paying the most.

Molly sniffed. You're a silly old woman, she told herself. A body can't live in the past. She gave the doorknob an extra shove, then burst into the room to hear a very male voice hiss, ''I told you to stay out of sight.''

The owner of the voice stood in the center of the room, a downright good-looking rogue, legs spread apart like a gunslinger, one arm poised at shoulder level with a stout club, the other shielding the woman behind him. Molly didn't know who was more surprised, but he was certainly the more embarrassed. The club dropped and a head of brown curls peeked over his shoulder. Molly blanched. Saints preserve her! Was that Susie's ghost?

''Molly!'' the girl shrieked, pushing the gentleman aside in her haste. ''Molly Malloy, is it truly you?''

Before Molly could reply, a pair of arms encased her. Tears glistened in her eyes as she squeezed back. It was a right nice feeling, hugging a body again.

Behind them, the man stared with puzzled eyes. Looking at him now, Molly thought he seemed familiar. He reminded her of Tony a bit, though his one had a stronger chin. He seemed sturdier all the way around, in fact. ''Sure it's me. Who else would clean this place? What I gotta know is, who's he?''

Sam followed her gaze, wiping at her eyes and laughing like her mother. ''It's all right, Molly. He's—he's a friend.''

His smile was so fatuous that Molly knew at once where that heart lay. Right in the girl's palm, no doubt with a good dozen others. Pride swelled in her massive bosom. Sam had grown into quite a beauty.

"Friend, huh? Well, since I haven't gotten to laying in supplies here yet, why don't the two of you pick yourselves up and come down to my place for some lunch? You hungry, Mr.—er . . ."

"Barton. Grant Barton."

Reluctantly, Molly warmed to that ready grin. Sam's gaze told her that whatever Barton felt was being returned double. They were still mighty awkward with each other, though.

"Grant Barton is a stage name. Actually, he is Lord Hoxton, an old friend of my father's. Oh, maybe you remember, Molly—Papa's partner, Tony Rawlings?"

As he shifted uneasily, Molly schooled her face to total blankness. He might look close enough to be kin, but this man was no more Tony Rawlings than she was. The real Tony might have been a good generation younger than she, but that hadn't stilled the fluttering in Molly's chest every time he set out to charm her. She'd baked more cookies for that boy than anyone else—at least until Susie had come to join her husband and Tony had crawled away to lick his wounds.

"Please, call me Grant." He stepped forward, taking her calloused hand as if it were a gold nugget. He had a bit of Tony in him after all, she thought. "As a matter of fact, Mrs. Malloy, I'm famished."

"If I'm to be calling you Grant, then you can just stop this Mrs. Malloy nonsense. The name's Molly."

Sam beamed at his side. "I just knew you two would like each other."

She might like him, just a bit, but Molly didn't give her trust readily. In her experience, beautiful men generally turned out to be scoundrels. And it seemed too great a coincidence that a man claiming to be Tony Rawlings was acting like a schoolboy in love with Susannah Eggersley's lovely daughter.

As they made small talk, Molly watched him carefully. He had a way about him, no doubt about that. And she was kinda partial to the way he kept making excuses to touch Sam, the way his eyes followed her every move. If it was just an act for her benefit, it was a darned good one.

As they stepped outside, Sam went straight for her horse and mounted. Looking down, she seemed surprised to find Molly and Grant on foot. "Oh. Aren't we riding? Grant, where is your horse?"

"I sent it back where it belonged. It wasn't worth the trouble; anyway, I'd rather walk. And just what are you grinning at?"

"Nothing. Don't you have a horse either, Molly?"

"Soldier pulled up lame, a month back."

"Oh. Well then, here, take mine."

Molly shook her head. Circumstances had given her the opportunity to be alone with this boy and she aimed to take advantage of it. "No, you can go on ahead and light up my stove for me."

"But you shouldn't have to walk while I—"

"Go on with you; I've been walking in these hills half my born days. Be a good girl and do as you're told."

Sam didn't want to go. Molly could see that in the set of her shoulders, but she *was* a good girl, and she probably suspected Molly had her reasons. With a reluctant, almost silly, smile she kicked the horse and trotted off.

No sooner was she out of sight than Molly gave Grant the full force of her stare. "I might as well warn you, mister. I knew Tony Rawlings like the back of this hand. I don't know who you are, but you ain't him."

He faltered, just a second, and then once again fell

into step beside her. "So why didn't you tell Sam?"

"Don't reckon I know. A hunch, maybe. You're in love with her, ain't you?"

Again, he halted involuntarily. "You don't mince your words, do you Molly?"

"Never held much with avoiding the issue. Are you?"

A powerful lot of emotion went into his sigh. "I am."

"Beats me why you're lying to her, then. I reckon you have your reasons, and I ain't saying they're any business of mine, but I swear to you, son, if just once I catch you hurting that girl, you'll wish you never met Molly Malloy."

Considering the way he towered over her, the man had every right to laugh. He frowned instead. "Do you think I enjoy it this way? I'd gladly tell the truth, only then Sam wouldn't let me near her. Who'd protect her then?"

"You saying Sam's in danger?"

"I don't know. I think so."

It was a remarkable conversation, one a younger Molly might have scoffed at, but then she'd seen too much since this so-called civilization came to her Rockies. "Just be warned, then. Sam's like kin to me, so I'll be looking out for her. And I can land a load of buckshot like anyone else can a bullet. I don't miss and I don't wait for explanations."

"Thanks for the warning. I'll see to it that we remain on the same side."

"You even smile like Tony. Any relation?"

His eyes rolled upward. "Heaven forbid. That man is the source of all my trouble."

He went silent, deep in thought, and Molly was content to let him be. He'd implied something about Tony she wasn't prepared to hear. She'd stayed up all night talking to that boy, convincing him to leave out of respect for Susie and Bill. He wouldn't—couldn't, dream of hurting their little girl.

Could he?

Between the heat and Sam's preoccupation, the horse wandered. It took a low, rumbling snore to jolt them both back onto the path. The horse whinnied, as if in answer, and Sam blinked furiously.

Half-consciously, she noticed the air of neglect hanging about Molly's cabin and vowed something would be done about it before she left town. The focus of her attention, however, was the dozing form on the porch. Sliding from the horse, she approached cautiously. There was something painfully familiar about the pinstripes on that suit. She could feel the chains of the past tighten around her throat.

Emery Blankfield, in Colorado? This was pushing credibility one step too far. None of this day could be real. It must be God's punishment for the fiasco last night.

Only, no matter how she blinked or pinched her skin, Emery and his snores failed to disappear. Her eyes bored into him, willing him to evaporate. Any minute now, Grant would appear on the path. It wasn't that she was ashamed, exactly, but he would take one look at Emery, lying so ingloriously dead to the world, and instead of being properly humbled, Grant would laugh himself hoarse.

It was a terrible thing to do, but she nudged him with her boot. "Wake up. Emery, darn you, wake up."

"Huh?" He sat up, squinting owlishly, his hat tilted at a drunken angle. Jaw dropping in a most unattractive fashion, he focused on her face.

And it was this way, of course, that Grant found

them. At the precise moment of recognition, just before Emery lunged into her arms. "Samantha Lynn! Darling! Where the devil have you been? I've been waiting for hours."

She had to catch him, or let him fall flat on his face, but she didn't have to hold him. With awkward, embarrassed haste, she pushed him away. Grant stared.

Sam spoke through clenched teeth. "I'd like to present my good friend, Molly Malloy. Molly, this is Mr. Emery Blankfield, my grandfather's—er, associate."

"How'd ya do, Blankstone."

"Blankfield. Samantha Lynn, my precious, we must go somewhere where we can—"

"And this is," she interrupted deliberately, "this is—"

"Grant Barton." Grant's frown deepened as he stepped forward to offer a hand. "Sam and I are associates, also."

She hated him for that. We're lovers, she wanted to scream, but Molly watched her with those all-seeing eyes.

"Man's right. We should all get out of the sun to talk. You had any lunch, Blankfoot?"

"Blankfield. No, I have not. As a matter of fact, I have been sitting on this porch for hours. Have you any idea how hot and dusty it is here?"

"Reckon I do, considering it's my home. Come on in, Sourpuss. I'll get you a glass of water."

The pinstripes seemed to stretch, up and outward. "I have no intention of going inside that—that structure. Come, Samantha Lynn. You and I have a great deal to discuss. You will be so pleased, when you learn how I have managed your affairs."

"I can manage my own affairs." And then,

realizing the double entendre, she began to giggle. She looked at Grant, hoping he might share her humor, but he stared as if she had grown another head. She wasn't handling this well at all.

"Forgive me, dearest, but it is painfully clear that you cannot." He took her by the elbow to nudge her off the porch. "You left your finances in dreadful disorder."

"That bank was failing for years before Sam gained control."

Both she and Emery turned to Grant in surprise. "She told you about the bank?" Emery squeaked. "You?"

"Emery, this is—" Once again, she started to say that he was Hoxton, her father's friend and partner, but Grant gave an almost imperceptible shake of his head. "A very close friend of the family."

Emery caught the smile that passed between them, but Sam didn't care. She'd tell a thousand lies, for a smile like that. And a thousand more, for every step he took closer to her.

"I must say, I am disappointed in you, Samantha. To find you, here of all places, looking like a—a—goodness gracious, what have you done to your hair?"

Unconsciously, her hand went up to it. A hazy recollection of hair pins, scattered across her bedroom floor, brought a sunset to her face. "I decided to wear it down today."

"Something she should do more often," Grant purred close beside her. "I find it exceedingly attractive."

"Quite so," he sniffed, "but hardly proper. A female of Samantha Lynn's position must not risk gossip. I feel it my duty to stress more caution."

"When I am in the company of a beautiful

woman, caution is the last thing on my mind."

Sam could taste the tension in the air as Grant's hand went casually to her shoulder. She moved the tiniest bit closer. His grip tightened reassuringly. How warm it felt. How wonderful.

"Beauti—" Emery caught himself, as if belatedly realizing how skepticism might harm his suit. He eyed Sam with an odd new glint. "Well, yes, I see what you mean. Still, if Samantha is to be my wife, she has a position to maintain. We mustn't lose sight of that."

The hand dropped from her shoulder. "No, I suppose not."

Emery smirked. "Well, as I said, I have wonderful news. I have solved all our financial problems."

"You what?"

The smirk vanished. Even Emery seemed to sense that she was not pleased. "Precious, we will be married in no time at all. Since you were not nearby, I took it upon myself to take advantage of this marvelous opportunity. Mr. Bavoure promised—"

"Bavoure?"

"Yes. A splendid fellow, though a trifle glum. I met with him early this morning. He has given us the chance to save the bank. But we must hurry back to Richmond. There is so much to do."

"Wait. You're going too fast. I know that name. Bavoure." Sam searched her memory. Yes, there had been a Mr. Bavoure, just before her parents had died, trying to buy— "Oh, Emery, what have you done?"

"You are not to worry your pretty head; I will deal with it all. You concentrate on becoming my lovely wife."

She barely heard him. Could the silly fool have sold her land? Legally? Somehow, she must see those papers. "This Mr. Bavoure; is he nearby? I mean, can I see him myself?"

"Whatever for?"

Whatever for, indeed! "I wish to thank him, of course. It's not every day that you find a gentleman so—so, generous."

"He might still be in Denver, but I doubt he'll see you. He prefers to discuss business with gentlemen."

How like Emery. Overlook the condescension, she told herself, linking her arm with his. Charm him. She was determined to meet this Bavoure, for she sensed he must be the key to her parents' deaths. "He would if you asked him, I bet. You're so clever at these things. If anyone can manage it, it must be you."

"Oh, I don't know," Grant muttered at her side. "You seem to be doing awfully well yourself."

Emery didn't hear him. He was too busy tugging her arm. "Let us go, then. We're wasting time, sitting around here chatting. We have a great many things to do, my love. At least you've brought a decent horse."

Molly was clucking like a mother hen. "Now just you wait a cotton-picking minute, son. That girl came here for some lunch. Look at her—all skin and bones. The least you can do is let her have a bite to eat."

"I will find her a decent restaurant in Denver." Emery shuddered as he looked at the cabin. "We haven't time to stay."

"And what about him? You just gonna leave him here?"

All eyes turned to Grant, whose own gaze was focused on Sam. She felt odd, as if a single glance could turn her bones to jelly.

"And why not? Who is he, anyway? Samantha Lynn, I demand to know why you are traipsing about the woods with him."

Sam felt torn. For two cents, she'd have pushed Emery's pudgy hands away and told him what he could do with his demands. But she knew she must do the sensible thing. "Grant kindly escorted me here to visit Molly. I told you about the Malloy's, how they're like family to me."

"Heaven forbid. And he—is he like family, too?"

"Well, in a way. Grant is here with Claire. They're all but engaged."

Emery tightened his grasp, forcing her to look at him. "Claire is with you? Here, in Colorado?"

"Temporarily." Grant's smile was as tight as Emery's grip.

Sam flinched. "Grant doesn't have a horse. We can't just leave him here."

"And what do you suggest? That I give him mine?"

"No, of course not, but couldn't we double up?" Behind her back, she crossed her fingers. She would be able to explain everything, if she and Grant shared the horse. And what heaven it would be, riding to Black Hawk with him behind her. Just like in her dreams.

"I suppose, if we must. But I shall sit in the front and direct the horse. You ride like a maniac."

"No," Grant said quickly. "You two seem to have a great deal to discuss. I wouldn't dream of intruding. Besides, I find I'd much rather stay and have this lunch that Molly has so graciously offered."

So would I, Sam thought as Emery pulled her away. As he helped her alight, she cursed him silently. He had ruined everything in his greed. Because she had to straighten out the mess he had made, she and Grant might never get to talk about their afternoon together.

Turning back to where he stood with Molly, she

tried to establish a link between them. "You will be back for tonight's performance, won't you?"

He raised one eyebrow. "I don't know. But then, you should have no trouble finding someone to replace me."

His gaze fixed rather pointedly on Emery, who was sputtering again. "Samantha Lynn, what is this? What performance?"

She never heard him. She felt as cold as Grant suddenly seemed. How accommodating of Emery, appearing like that to take her off his hands. Considering her earlier hysteria, he no doubt feared she'd cling to his knees and refuse to let go. In fact, she had that most childish urge right now. "I thought we had a great deal to discuss."

"Apparently not."

"I see. Very well, Emery, let's go."

She meant to be as distant and aloof as Grant was, but she felt the betraying sting of tears. To hide them, she spun the mare toward the road. Without looking back, she dug her heels into its flanks and raced away.

"Maniac!" she could hear Emery sputter behind her. But what Grant might have said, she would likely never know.

22

Grant scowled as he watched them leave. What could she see in that toad? Respectable, my eye. Emery Blankbrain was a damned, stupid snob.

He watched until she disappeared from sight. She was gone again, in yet another panicked escape. Was it commitment that frightened her off, or just him? The Sam he thought he knew would have no patience with a self-glorifying prig like Blankfield.

"What the devil is she up to now?" he muttered.

Molly chuckled at his side. "I might have an answer to that, boy. But first, you come in and help me light that stove. I have a stew to heat up that'll just about knock you out of those boots."

"Molly, you are a woman after my heart."

"Go on with you now. We both know that's already taken." She patted his arm. "Now, no scowling. We'll put a remedy to all this, but you can't think straight without a good meal in your belly. Come on, let's go eat some lunch."

Grinning in spite of himself, Grant followed her into a homey-looking room. Molly gestured to one of the split-log chairs set before a stone fireplace, but as tempting as the faded gold cushions seemed, Grant insisted that he was here to earn his meal; he would light her stove.

He was mighty ignorant of wood stoves, as Molly teased him, but he was a quick study, as he explained to her. Soon enough, their stew was warmed, their coffee hot, and they sat companionably at the hand-built table in the center of the room.

"You've got some appetite, boy."

Grant grinned sheepishly at the empty pot. "I've finished your stew, haven't I? Sorry. We've been eating make-shift meals for weeks and well, I can't remember when I've enjoyed a meal more."

"No need for apologies. It does my heart good to see you eat up. It's been some time since my cooking ws so appreciated. Besides, I wasn't criticizing your appetite. I like that in a man."

"I'm glad someone does."

Molly chuckled. "I got just one question for you, boy. You aim to let Sam go off and marry that fool?"

"I do not."

"Good, 'cause she don't want to."

"You could have fooled me."

"Heck, you're so crazy, mixed-up in love, any-body could fool you." Suddenly solemn, Molly leaned across the table. "Sam tell you why she came to Colorado?"

"Not exactly. But I assume she's trying to learn what happened to her parents."

Molly nodded. "The day before Susie died and the walls to the Oh Susannah collapsed, the only other family left on this hill sold out their claim. The whole mountain, except for Bill's mine, belonged to one company. All bought and paid for by Mr. Charles Bavoure."

"*Charles* Bavoure? Can you describe him?"

Molly tilted her head. "He wasn't a real colorful character. Let me think. He was short, a bit heavy, and had a headful of gray hair—beard, whiskers, side-burns. Could hardly see the man's face for all that hair."

Grant thought of Riley's shiny dome. Of course,

that was many years ago. He could have lost all his hair in the meantime.

"Had a strange habit," Molly continued. "Kept saying, *we* want this, or *we* will offer that. Almost like he couldn't separate himself from whoever it was that owned the company."

"Did he scowl a great deal?"

"Wasn't exactly what I'd call a friendly guy."

"Sam spoke of a Dr. Charles. Were they anything alike?"

"Dr. Charles? Funny, I'd forgotten about him. Never understood why the Eggersleys took the baby to that man, for all Tony swore by him. He was always spouting off orders, but Devon never got better. Nondescript guy. All I can remember about him was his hair. It never seemed real, that black thatch. Like if he turned too fast, his hair and head would go in different directions."

A wig? As false as the gray hair and whiskers? It was hard to credit that a man could wander through a town the size of Central City as two separate people, but then, as a former actor, Riley would be a master of disguise. "I have worn many guises in my life," he had once bragged to Grant. Charles Riley, Dr. Charles, and now Charles Bavoure; they were all circling around the dangerously unaware Sam.

"Molly, what's going on up at the Oh Susannah?"

"Huh?"

"Yesterday, a man named Jack Parker told me that no one comes near the mine any more because they're afraid of ghosts. And on the train today, the conductor said that you've been hearing them, too."

She waved a hand through the air. "I put that story out to keep the danged fools away. Well-meaning, most of them were, but I got sick of people gawking and moaning, so I started acting crazy.

Nothing scares folks away like crazy old women and ghosts. Thing of it is, though"—she leaned even closer—"there is something odd going on up in these hills. Started right before Gus . . ."

"I'm sorry. I didn't mean to stir up bad memories."

"Ghosts don't lie down, boy, until they're set to rest. I reckon Gus's memory will haunt me, no matter what I do. Least until I find out who killed him."

"Then you think he was murdered?"

"You tell me. He went out of this house as hale as a horse, investigating that pounding in the ground. They brought him back in a wooden box. Fell off a cliff, they said. Nowadays, only the occasional gang of kids come this way, on a dare, but they get sent packing faster than you can sneeze by them big guards up there."

"There's more than one?"

"At least four, three as big and mean as they come. The fourth a skinny, crazy-looking devil. I don't know what's on the other side of the mountain. I can't get around like I used to, and after Gus—well, some of the starch has gone right out of me."

"Does Sam know any of this?"

She shrugged. "I doubt it. I was afraid to put it in my letters; you can never tell who might read them. And then hers seemed so stiff, like—well, kinda like that fool, Blanknose."

Grant grinned. "Ah yes, the Miss Farnstable pose. I know it well."

"The thing was, I planned to tell her all this today. To warn her. That cliff has claimed too many of the people I love."

"And I ruined it. Sorry, Molly, but at the time, I thought I was the only one she had looking out for her."

She placed a weathered hand reassuringly over Grant's. "No, boy, I'm glad you're here. It was him, I didn't want knowing. Why she didn't just send him packing, I'll never know."

Grant sighed. "That makes two of us. You don't suppose she'd actually marry him, do you?"

"Not if you ask her first."

"Thanks, but we both know I can't do that. Not when she thinks I'm someone else."

"Why don't you just tell her the truth, then?"

"Come on, Molly, you must know how she hates liars. I remember her saying that once she's caught a man lying, she never trusts him again. And at the moment, she needs to trust me. It just might save her life."

Molly shivered. "Sounds like you got a plan."

"I do. But I'll need your help. Can you trust a liar?"

She looked him square in the eye. "Sometimes, lying is the only way out of things. Heck, you don't live in these hills without learning to trust your instincts, and mine are telling me you're the man for her. That ain't to say I can't be meaner than a hungry bear when I'm made a fool of, but I'm willing enough to listen to this plan."

It was a reluctant endorsement, but better than none. "I want Sam out of here. Far away, possibly back in Richmond."

"That ain't gonna be easy."

"I know. That's why I need your help. She might be more easily persuaded if you go with her."

"Me?"

"Tell her you need to see a decent doctor. That after Dr. Charles, you don't want anyone local. We must convince her to leave. By tomorrow, she must be out of the area."

"You seem mighty anxious to have her gone."

"Not at all. I hate the thought of letting her out of my sight. I hope I'll be able to join you, but Sam simply must leave Colorado. There have already been two attempts on her life."

"Somebody's tried to kill her? How? And who?"

"Twice a runaway carriage nearly ran her down. As to who, my guess would be this Mr. Bavoure."

Molly gripped his hand hard. "Then why the devil did you let her go with that fool to meet him?"

"Because Bavoure won't agree to any meeting. Believe me, he's not about to let Sam see him. Not when she can recognize him. Charles Bavoure, Dr. Charles, and Tony Rawling's valet, Riley, seem to be all one and the same."

"Who are you, boy? How do you know all this?"

Who was he? Just another pawn, in Riley's game of chess. "Just someone they hired, to distract Sam. I won't bore you with the sordid details; I think Sam deserves to hear the truth first, but I can swear to you that I hadn't the least idea of their true intentions at the time."

"Which were?"

"Which were to rob her blind. It's my guess that Hoxton learned that there was gold in the Oh Susannah, but not until after he'd sold his share to Bill. He used Riley, as this Bavoure, to buy the mine legally, but when his former partner refused to sell, he was forced to use more desperate methods."

"So all along, Bill was right about that claim," Molly mumbled. "A crying shame he couldn't live to enjoy it."

"None of this can be proved. Not yet. And since my position is so tenuous, I don't dare expose them just yet. Not until I find that proof. It shouldn't be hard, though; Riley's a bit over-confident. I saw miners crawling all over the Oh Susannah today. One look inside that mine, and I should have all the proof we need.''

''Ah, so that's what those wagons are. I hear them rolling past the cabin all hours of the night. Criminal, that's what it is, taking Sam's gold.''

''It won't be Sam's much longer, if Riley has his way. You heard Blankfield. He must have sold the mine to him. Since the deeds won't be legal until Sam becomes his wife and relinquishes her property to his dubious care, he will stand on his head to push that marriage.''

''And you sit here while that fool is sweet-talking her? Heck, he has all that way to Denver.''

''They won't get married today. I know my Sam. Once she gets an idea in her head, she doesn't let go, and she wants to see this Bavoure. By the time she learns that she can't—well, I imagine I'll have a chance to do my own sweet-talking tonight.''

''You're too good-looking by half, boy. Smile at Sam like that and Blankfield don't stand a chance. Me either. I hope I'm not wrong, lining up with the likes of you.''

Grant stood, his smile rueful. ''I'll be honest with you, Molly. I don't have much to offer her. I'm not rich, like Hoxton, or even respectable, like Blankfield. But given half a chance, I'll do my best to make her happy.''

''But you've got to tell her the truth.''

He shrugged, jamming his hands into his pockets. ''Yes, eventually. In the meantime, though, I can keep her safe. In fact, I'm going down to the depot right now to arrange for that trip to Richmond. Can I count on your help?''

''Buy your tickets. I'll be there.''

''Bless you. I suppose I'd best be going. You

wouldn't happen to know how much—oh, damn! I haven't a penny; Sam has it all.'' Pulling out his empty pockets, he felt like a fool. Was this how he planned to keep Sam safe?

"Not smart of you, son, sending your horse away like that.''

"I didn't send it; it ran away. And you can stop that laughing, Molly Malloy. Do you want to tell me how I'm expected to get back to Denver? Walk?''

"You're Hoxton, ain't you? A rich milord like you don't carry money around. You put everything on account.''

As he had done with the horse. After all, he need no longer fear that Riley would track them down. And it did seem only fitting that Hoxton should pay for what he'd done to Sam. "You're a devious old bird, Molly Malloy. If my affections weren't already engaged, I think I might let myself fall in love with you.''

"Never mind that nonsense; you just take care of Sam.''

"I'll be off, then. I've got quite a walk ahead of me, getting down that hill.''

Following him to the door, she pointed to a dirt track in front of the cabin. "Just follow this road to the first farm you see. If you tell Abe Busby that Molly sent you, he'll loan you a horse to get to town. Come to think of it, he sold his claim to Bavoure, too. Might be he can give you a better description than I did.''

"Thanks. For everything.'' Standing on the porch, Grant felt a odd reluctance to leave. A premonition almost, as if he migh never see her again. "I don't suppose I could convince you to come down to Denver with me now?''

She shook her head. "I've got some odds and ends

that need doing. But don't you worry. I'll be there bright and early in the morning."

"Not too bright. I don't plan to leave until later in the day. I have a few odds and ends of my own. I'll leave your tickets for you at the depot in Central City."

"I can pay my own way."

From the look of the place, Grant rather doubted that. "This one is on Hoxton. Quite frankly, I think it is the least he can do."

"You sure about him? The Tony I knew—"

"The Tony you knew is gone. There was an accident. He was badly disfigured—perhaps mentally, as well as physically. He has almost no recollection of the past."

"I reckon that was one instance when my instincts failed me, then. Don't you be the second, hear?"

"I'd rather face Hoxton's entire empire than your buckshot. You keep that rifle loaded, Molly. We may need it yet."

He laughed, but the words continued to bang against his skull as he walked to the Busby farm. It all seemed so impossible. Thugs, guarding a treasure. Riley, skulking about making death threats. And he, for pity's sake, playing the hero. Was he out of his mind?

Abe Busby was more than happy to let him borrow a horse, for he recognized "old Tony" right away. Funny he should ask about that Bavoure fellow, though; didn't Bavoure work for him?

Seizing the opportunity, Grant said no, he did not, but he'd like to know who the man did work for. Reckon they'd know in the land office, Busby offered as he scratched his scraggly beard. They kept darned good records in this town.

So when Grant at last rode into Central City—if not armed with sixshooters, then certainly with a predatory glint in his eye—the sight of the land office caught his attention at once. He took a few precious minutes to hand the horse to a friend of Abe's, since his conscience wouldn't let him lose two animals in one day, but his feet couldn't move fast enough to test Abe Busby's boast.

There was an elderly lady at the desk, and he gave her his most charming smile. She preened, then gladly spent the next hour or so scouring every document in the place. Bavoure's signature lay on a great many deeds, but if Hoxton owned this Falcon Mining Company, there was nothing there to prove it.

He smiled and thanked the woman for her help, but his disappointment must have shown. Smiling like a mother who has just bandaged her son's knee, she told him that he might possibly learn who owned the company at the bank. After all, they kept good records in this town.

He was extremely conscious of his torn trousers as he sat at the manager's desk. He wasn't dealing with a woman this time, and this man certainly would not be coerced by his boyish grin. Still, Riley had trained him well and he fell into the pose with polished ease.

Explaining that he was Anthony Rawlings, Lord Hoxton, he went on to admit that his horse had thrown him somewhere up in the hills, leaving him with no way home and precious little cash.

As he told his story, punctuating it with spurts of temper, the poor man blanched. He all but fell over himself in his haste to arrange for the suitable funds. As various clerks scrambled about for the money, the manager gave a sickly smile, apologizing for not having recognized Lord Hoxton sooner. But one

would assume his lordship's business manager, Mr.
Bavoure, would take care of such details. Oh indeed,
yes, he was in town. He'd been in the bank not thirty
minutes before.

This was so embarrassing, Grant admitted with
forced sheepishness, hoping to hide his own surprise.
If at all possible, he'd prefer that Bavoure never
learned of the escapade, for he would never be permitted to hear the end of it. He left the bank a good
deal richer, and reasonably certain that Riley would
never learn he'd been there.

Taking no chances, he rushed to the train depot
and jumped on the first train to Denver. Better to
purchase the tickets for Richmond there. He sat in a
daze, barely seeing the scenery as it pased by. His
mind couldn't absorb all he had learned. Riley and
Hoxton were clever devils. If this were indeed a game
of chess, then somehow, he must remove the queen
from their grasp.

The major drawback to this, though, was that it
would give them exactly what they wanted. Sam
would hate that, would hate him for it. But damn, did
she think he would let her stay here and risk her
being killed?

He would need to tell her one more lie. It was
necessary, to get her on that train without him. He
hated to let her out of his sight, but the only way to
stop those bastards was to get into that mine. Without
concrete proof to give the sheriff, it would become a
case of his word against Hoxton's, and considering his
record, he knew who would land in jail. No, it was
better to do it this way. With any luck, he needn't test
the law at all. Then he could go after Sam to explain.
But if anything went wrong, Sam must be safely out
of the way.

He thought of her as she had been this afternoon,

so soft and warm and loving. Whatever it took, he vowed, he would keep her from harm. Even if he must give her away.

But not tonight. Absentmindedly, he pulled out his medallion, rubbing it for luck. Give him just one more night and he would sweet-talk her until he was blue in the face, romance her more than Hoxton could ever have imagined. He would give her a night so filled with love, she could never marry Blankfield. For though Grant might never share her life, he would haunt her dreams, long after he sent her away. She might come to resent him, but after tonight, she would never, ever forget him.

With a sigh of satisfaction, Riley slid the papers back into the pouch. Tomorrow he could register these deeds at the land office. It required a wedding to make them valid, but Riley had the utmost faith in Blankfield's greed, or he would never have summoned him here to Colorado.

Placing the pouch in the wall safe, he rewarded himself with a fine cigar. Another job well done. As he poured himself a snifter of brandy, he chuckled. He always did his work well. He wouldn't be where he was if he didn't have an eye for the main chance.

He leaned back in his chair before the fire, exhaling smoke, to savor the triumph. How easily the girl had been led away from that Malloy woman. All to see Charles Bavoure. She would meet him eventually, but she would be Mrs. Emery Blankfield before she did. And then it would be too late.

With a frown, he thought of Barton. Blankfield claimed he was too attentive, that Miss Eggersley seemed overly susceptible to his charm. Opportunist. To think Riley had encouraged him at the start. Well, now he must find some way to divert that charm. The right words, placed on Blankfield's tongue, should sway Samantha Lynn not to trust the cad.

Yes, he thought smugly; another job well done. From now on, he could treat himself to the best of everything. This cigar, the brandy, this roaring blaze . . .

A log dropped, and it was as if the fire whispered, "Andrea." Riley wriggled in the chair. In his mind, he could see her again, the reddish glints of her brown hair alive in the fire's glow. How he had yearned to run his fingers through those shining tresses, to . . .

He leaned forward, squinting into the flame, as if it could bring her back to life. Not the way she was, but the way he wanted her to be. In love with him. Not the gracious lady being kind to a servant, but so madly in love that she would step into that fire for him.

But she had loved her profligate husband, Roger. Riley's hand tightened around the stem of his glass. He had been nothing but a tutor to Andrea's orphan nephew, Tony Rawlings. No matter how Andrea and Riley enjoyed their lively, intelligent conversations, he might as well have vanished whenever Roger, the wastrel heir to the Hoxton fortune, deigned to pay his wife a visit.

Everyone stopped to pay court to him. The old lord was worst of all. He'd insist that Andrea dress up her son, young James, and parade him about as if he were some gilded toy while Riley and Tony were completely ignored.

He could not blame the lad. If not for the fact that he was Roger's son, Riley might have liked James. He had Andrea's eyes and hair, and a lively, inquisitive mind. His only fault was that he made poor Tony seem a pale copy in comparison. Everyone fawned over him. Everything fell into the younger boy's lap—the attention, the love, and eventually, too, the Hoxton estates.

For Riley, who had been neglected since the day he was born, the injustice of it became more and more intolerable. There was an affinity between him and Tony; they were a pair of have-nots amidst all that plenty. Bit by bit he began to shield the boy, to arrange events so Tony would have the life he deserved, the life they both deserved.

Except for Andrea. Riley wriggled again, embarrassed to remember how he had behaved. It had been the first, and last, time he had let anyone make such a fool of him. But Roger's many and increasingly prolonged absences had drawn them together, and he had truly thought, that night when he went to console her in her bedroom, that Andrea knew the truth. That someone would have told her that her husband had not been alone when he crashed that carriage over the cliff.

"You are mistaken," she had said softly as he told her, repeating herself with each accusation, her pitch rising with his anger, until she was nearly screeching and he was red with rage. Taking her in his arms, he had kissed her, swearing breathlessly that it was all right, that he would take care of her and James, that they could be married as soon as was decently possible.

She had laughed. A horrible, gurgling sound that made him go a little insane. Roger was worth ten of him, a hundred! She spat in his face. Riley's rage went cold, for her laughter proved what he should have known already; that Andrea had always seen him as a nobody, not fit to lick her boots, and for all her smiles and false gentleness, she was as hateful as the rest.

Something clicked inside. Even before the echo subsided, his hands had gone around her throat, tightening, tightening . . .

The stem of the snifter cracked, and brandy trailed down his wrist. He never felt it. Smiling, he prided himself on his coolness that night. Another man, horrified by what he had done, might have panicked and lost his life. Not he. His clever brain had analyzed everything and known instantly what must be done. Losing no more than a minute or two, he dressed the body in a cloak and bonnet, and shoved it through the window to drop three stories below. He had no need to disguise the bruises, for he would arrange everything to appear as though a distraught Lady Hoxton had driven the family carriage over a cliff, in a conscious imitation of her husband's death.

A nice touch. An ideal one, had not the drowsy James woken from a bad dream and discovered the tutor in his mother's room.

Again, Riley's wits had not failed him. Encouraging the boy to dress, he told him that he was to join his mother on an unexpected trip. Adoring his mother as he did, the boy did not think to object, and he had fallen into the trap like the spider's hapless fly. He had understood in the end, though, and perhaps that bewildered, hurt look in his eyes had been why Riley had spared him.

It was a dreadful mistake. One he would regret for years. For though the boy was easily sold to one of his former colleagues in London, only to die years later from abuse and overwork, his ghost had remained to haunt and thwart him. Until they found his body, the old lord decreed, his grandson would remain his heir.

And though Lord Hoxton had died a few years later of a broken heart, his decree had not. The battlefront merely moved to the courts. Tony would have given up, but Riley would not allow it. Not when they had come so close. Not when the Hoxton name and fortune, by means of the malleable Tony, were almost his.

But a small fortune was needed for that fight, a fortune that Tony could not lay his hands on. In those early days, they tried many business ventures, but since Tony was always too busy pursuing his silly dream of becoming an actor, none of them showed sufficient return for their needs.

Then Susannah Myers had waltzed into their lives. An actress could hardly become Lady Hoxton, but as an entertainment, Riley thought she might be good for the boy. Her reputation was good, her outlook strong, and lord knew, Tony idolized her. But she, fickle bitch, had chosen someone else. Just like Andrea.

Yet a heartbroken Tony had been easy to control. They had began to make some headway in their fight—when that fateful letter came from Bill Eggersley. Leaving only a note, Tony had flown off to Colorado to join him. Naturally concerned, Riley had investigated the claim himself, and the results of the engineer's report had floored him. Here was the fortune they required. He did not, however, intend to share it.

Yet even as he made his plans, Tony arrived on his doorstep, ever the weak fool, having played the gentleman by selling his share to Bill. Riley had nearly killed him, but he had not gotten where he was by giving way to panic. There was always a way, if a man was wise enough to look for it.

So he went to Colorado and used his acting skills to pose as a doctor to gain the Eggersley's trust. Bill had never met Riley in England and Susannah had never taken any notice of her former beau's valet.

Every chance he could, he kept Bill in that cabin, nursing his sickly son, while he and his workers blasted in from the other side of the mine. Somehow, and someday soon, Bill's absence must become a permanent thing.

The opportunity had come unexpectedly. No doubt hoping to make up for lost time, Bill had been working late on Christmas Eve, his workers having gone home to their families long since. With that invention of his pounding away, it had been an easy matter to saw the timbers at the entrance. Unfortunately, Bill had nearly reached the entrance when the beams collapsed. He'd been trapped, but not, damn him, buried in the depths of the mine.

Susannah had come in time to find him. Riley caught her, just as she emerged from the cave. She had spun out of his grasp, screaming that she must run for help, but it wasn't until he again caught up with her that they both seemed to realize what he must do. And when she had breathlessly asked why, he had smiled, appreciating her quiet dignity in the face of the inevitable; and told her simply that he did it for Tony.

But as he kissed her, rather brutally, and then pushed her and her baby off the cliff, he had known that he had done it for himself. From the first moment he had seen Susannah Eggersley, he had known she was just like Andrea, and he had wanted to kill her, too.

Now, a third woman had come into his life to taunt him. He hadn't lied to Barton; he had known Samantha at once. A man didn't gaze into that face without recognizing her mother, no matter how skillfully she tried to disguise herself. Nor could she hide the childish gray gaze that had stared into him on a long-ago day on the ledge, he fleeing and she rushing toward the scene of the crime. He had kept her heavily sedated for days afterward, until Samuel came to spirit her away, but he had known even then that he must eventually kill her, too. This time, he must not let a frightened child's face deter him.

With a deep sigh, he tried to sip his brandy. He looked down to see the broken glass in his lap, and scowled in annoyance. He had no time to lose himself to useless reflections of the past. Or threats.

Speaking of which, he must deal with his new overseer. Standing abruptly, he grabbed another glass and slowly, methodically, sipped his brandy. Calmed by the drink, he admitted that while it had been a mistake to allow himself to be blackmailed into giving the man a job, he needn't make a career out of it. There was more than one way of paying the man off. Accidents happened in the mines all the time. Riley had no use for a man who couldn't be exclusively loyal to him. As Clanton—and later Barton—would all too soon learn.

Draining the glass, he smiled. He would make the arrangements at once. Oh yes, he could work his way out of any situation. He always had and always would.

23

Easing the door shut behind him, Grant stepped into the wings. Out on the stage, he could hear Sam's strong, clear voice. She was doing a good job. Without him. It stung, but he was proud of her. She was a strong girl, Sam, for all her outward fragility. One way or another, she would always land on her feet.

Bodine came on, plodding through his lines. Forced into carrying the scene for them both, Sam was visibly irritated. While her anger did not bode well for his plans, Grant liked knowing that he couldn't be so easily replaced, after all.

Especially as he would have given his soul to have this last chance to be on that stage with her. But he had been delayed at the depot; the fool there had been new and unable to make the necessary connections, and then to top it off, Emma Wynecote had strolled in to catch him with the tickets in his hands. Her eyes had widened with curiosity, but he had smiled and scurried off, having no time or desire, to waste on explanations for her.

"Tony darling, there you are! Goodness, I thought maybe you had gone off to lick your wounds. I don't know why I should worry about you, though. When Calvin told me how you two-timed me with Sam last night, why, I broke down and cried."

He knew it was Claire by the drawl and the over-powering scent of her perfume; he didn't waste time scowling at her. Not even his blackest look could stop her now.

She gave his arm a squeeze. "But isn't it the most romantic thing? I mean, coming all the way from Virginia for her like that? And did you see the ring? I never thought Emery had it in him."

"What are you talking about?"

"The wedding, silly."

"What wedding?"

"Sam's. Emery told me himself. First thing tomorrow, he's marching her off to Justice Pearce. Of course, they'll have a proper ceremony in Richmond, so all the right people can attend, but he couldn't damage her reputation by traveling all the way back home without the blessings of matrimony."

He yanked out of her grasp. "Sam never agreed to it."

"He said she did. After all, he did save the bank for her. For us all. Without Grandaddy's bank, we would all likely starve. And you know Sam; she'd never let that happen."

No, she wouldn't. Being a lawyer, Blankfield must have presented his case well. And being who she was, Sam would have seen this marriage as the only alternative, a necessary sacrifice. He almost wished that Riley had stayed in Denver, that Sam had seen him. Knowing how stubborn she was, it might be the only way to stop her. Or was it?

"Why, Tony, where are you going? Don't you want to stay and congratulate Emery and Sam?"

If he stayed, he'd likely kill that sneaking lawyer. "I have things to arrange. Tell Sam I'll see her later. We have certain things we must discuss."

"But, Tony, what about us?"

He turned on a heel, having taken all he could stand. "And which us is that?"

"Oh Tony, how can you be so cruel?"

"Brace up. I daresay you can find someone to

console you. How about Bodine? He's been ogling you for weeks.''

He left her then, and far from broken-hearted. Even before he reached the door, he knew, her gaze would be on the stage, considering the possibilities.

Besides, he had far more important things to occupy his mind. Somehow, he must stop that wedding.

Sam let herself into her room, too weary for words. What a strain that performance had been. What a disaster. Calvin Bodine was no Grant Barton. That had been painfully clear.

Thinking of Grant brought tears to her eyes. It was bad enough he hadn't been on time for the performance, but when Emma asked her where her husband planned to go with those train tickets he'd bought, anger turned to shock. She had made it through the performance, but now, without the role to distract her, she was falling apart. Just like that, he had left. No word, no good-bye. Tony Rawlings had returned to rule his empire and Grant Barton had vanished for good.

She sat on her bed, stunned into stupidity. She should have expected this. But she hadn't, and now she didn't know what to do next. Quit the troupe, of course. The snickers would be unbearable.

She leaned back, giving way to self pity, and felt a tickling at her ear. Turning, she saw the pink petals. She gasped. A single, fragile rose lay in the center of her bed. Damion, she thought, but then cursed herself for being a fool.

Sitting abruptly, she tore at the envelope. A farewell gesture? A pat on the head, a ''be a good girl, now,'' for adults don't make a scene. Did he truly think so little of her?

The note was brief. "Meet me in my room," it said, signed by "your devoted Damion." As her outrage cooled, so did her hopes. It wasn't from Grant at all. Emery had watched the performance tonight. And while he had disapproved, warning that no wife of his would prance about half-naked on a stage, he had been reluctantly impressed by that balcony scene. It would be just like him to think such a cheap trick would persuade her. He must be getting desperate, to go to the bother of securing the rose. Especially after that engagement ring.

She had refused it, naturally, with a few choice words about his and her grandfather's stubborn blindness, but Emery hadn't been daunted in the least. No doubt he was out there now, scouring Denver for a judge to marry them in the morning.

She felt so weary of it all, too weary to fight. It was easier to sit back and let Emery arrange everything, so she needn't feel a thing any more. It bothered her that he had yet to explain which property he had sold to save the bank, but he was a lawyer, wasn't he? He was trained to know how to negotiate such matters. His greed, if nothing else, should get her the best deal.

Yet, something inside her balked. After an afternoon of love with Grant, however shallow it might have been on his side, how could she settle for a life with Emery? She shuddered, just thinking of his pinstripes. And besides, she had her investigating to do. At the very least, she must spend some time with Molly.

Setting the rose firmly on her desk, she reached for her notepaper. She would make this all crystal clear to him. Better yet, perhaps she should speak to him in person. She would go to his room as he requested—he must be desperate, indeed, to suggest so improper a meeting—and she would tell him there would be no marriage. Now, or ever. And if the bank failed, well, she had begun her acting career. She had a way to feed her ever-growing family.

She marched to the door, head held high, but just as she reached for the knob, it swung inward. "Oh, drat," Claire said as she breezed into the room. "I had hoped you'd be with your beau."

Sam opened her mouth to deny that Emery was anything at all to her, but Claire sailed past, obviously agitated. Holding onto the door, Sam waited as Claire circled the room, fingering objects. She recognized the signals. In her usual roundabout way, Claire wanted to ask a favor.

"Oh, look at this. What a nice flower. It must be from Emery."

"The note was unsigned. Perhaps I have a secret admirer."

Claire smiled indulgently as she sniffed the rose. "Emery has made no secret of his admiration. How lucky you are to have him. Unlike Tony, his sort stays around."

"You obviously want something from me. What is it?"

The lips pursed. "All right, I wanted to do a little entertaining."

"So?"

"So? Be a pet, and find somewhere else to be." She gave a quick exasperated flutter of the hands, clearly meant to shoo Sam away.

Sam had time to feel surprise before Calvin Bodine brushed past her into the room. "Hey, wait. I don't mind her being here. Three's more fun. Now that hubby's left us, maybe I can replace him in more ways than one."

Even as Sam was deciding that he made a worse

man-about-town than he did a Damion, Claire was advancing toward her, hands upraised. Startled, Sam edged backward, and she was out in the hallway, listening to the click of the lock, before she knew what had happened.

Too late, she realized what the ingrate had done to her. Puffing up to what seemed three times her normal size, she grabbed the door to kick and pound and screech at it, when a soft "Sam?" wheeled her around.

Deflated, she faced Grant. He wore a pair of dark trousers and a white silk shirt, unbuttoned at the collar, surely not the clothes of a man who meant to travel. He watched her intently, his eyes never leaving her face. She felt foolish suddenly, and awkward.

"What are you doing here?" she blurted out. "Emma said she saw you at the depot, buying tickets."

He muttered something under his breath. "Can I assume, then, that Claire didn't tell you I wanted to talk tonight?"

"With me?"

He seemed almost angry as he took a step forward. Instinctively, she inched back. He muttered another oath.

"Yes, with you." His hands went into his pockets. "Those tickets I bought weren't for me. They were for you."

"I'm not going anywhere."

"Hear me out first, please?" He tried a grin. Leaning back against the doorframe, he might almost have seemed relaxed and at ease, if not for the tiniest tic, right above his eye. "It's Molly, Sam. I think she needs you."

"I don't understand. What does Molly need? And

what does this have to do with train tickets?''

"This hallway isn't exactly the best place for discussing this. Why don't we just go into my room and—''

"I—I couldn't.''

A hand came out of a pocket to run through his hair. "Just for a drink. Nothing else, I swear it.''

For Sam, who had yet to recover from the shock of seeing him there, the words made no sense. "I was just on my way to Emery.''

"I see.'' The hand went back in the pocket. There was no pretense of being at ease now. He looked miserable.

Sam once again cursed herself for a fool, even as she opened her mouth to speak. "But I was in no hurry. If it's—well, truly important, I suppose I could come in for a minute or two.''

He smiled. His entire face lit up. Holding out a hand to her, he seemed as eager as a boy. "You won't regret this, Sam. I'll see to it that you don't.''

She felt shy as she placed her hand in his. It felt almost as if they had just met, as if they hadn't shared that wonderful interlude in the cabin. And yet, somehow, it felt at the same time as though she had known him forever.

As her hand touched his, the magic began. Sounds were muted, the light went mellow, and it was as if the curtain had gone up to reveal a new world. When he opened his door, standing aside so that she might enter before him, the illusion swallowed her whole.

A sole candle burned on a table in the center of the room. That, and a gentle fire in the grate, bathed prosaic objects in a golden glow. To the right, the bed beckoned, its covers drawn back invitingly. On the bedstand stood a silver bucket, holding champagne, the tiny drops of condensation glistening as they slid down its sides.

"Oh!" she blurted out, the magic slipping somewhat. "Why didn't you warn me that you were expecting someone else?"

She jumped as his hand touched her shoulder. He pulled it back sharply and his voice seemed strained. "I'm not expecting anyone else. Didn't you get my message?"

"Message?"

"With the rose. Or didn't you get that either?"

"*You* sent the rose?" It was a struggle to take that in. "I—I was certain it was Emery."

He winced, then shrugged to hide it. "Not this time." Quietly shutting the door behind them, he strode past her into the room, forcing a laugh. "Though I imagine he sends you flowers all the time."

"Actually, Emery thinks flowers are a monumental waste of money."

"I see." His voice was flat, noncommittal, as he absentmindedly chipped away at the label on the champagne. "Does he disapprove of drinking as well?"

"Liquor is the devil's handmaiden." Sam bit her lip. She should be wearing pinstripes, so pompous did she sound. As if she agreed. "Emma Wynecote would be proud of him."

There was a faint smile, but it quickly withered as he glanced about the room. "I guess I should apologize for all this, then. It makes things incredibly awkward, doesn't it? I don't suppose you'd consider staying for that drink?"

"Champagne?"

He winced. "When I ordered this, I remembered only you saying you loved it. I forgot how you felt the following morning."

"No, please. Pour me a glass. I'm—I'm terribly thirsty." Stop fiddling with the cork, she wanted to tell him. Look at me. Hungrily, like Willie claims you do. "Oh, drat. You might as well know the sordid truth. I love champagne. And no matter how expensive they are, I adore flowers."

Almost as much as I adore you.

She could have spoken aloud, for he looked up then, deep into her eyes, as greedily as she had ever dared hope. Frightened, exhilarated, and thoroughly weak in the knees, she prayed he would take her in his arms.

But the cork chose that moment to pop, exploding between them, and the resulting stream of champagne claimed his attention. His laugh was strained, and slightly breathless. Had he felt it, too? Or was there something in this softened light that fueled her imagination? She had to be dreaming, didn't she?

"I wanted to impress you. I wanted you to walk into this room and never want to leave."

Definitely a dream. "It's . . . everything's lovely."

She reached for the glass he offered, willing their fingers to touch, but he seemed determined to prevent it. As always, his lips said one thing, his body, another.

"I had a bit of a feast, too, but I'm afraid the food's gone cold."

"I'm not very hungry."

His smile went sour. "The best-laid plans . . . damn, I don't suppose you'd care to dance?"

"Without music?"

"My dear Samantha, where there is a beautiful woman, there is always music."

She tingled, right down to her toes, as he slowly,

deliberately, took her glass away. He stepped close, pressing his body into hers. Humming softly, he began to sway, leading her in ever widening circles about the room, breathing the love song from *Marietta* into her ear.

This can't be happening, she marveled as she laid her head against his chest and listened to the frantic rhythm of his heart. Did he feel it, too? As if they were back in the cabin, the day still before them, she gave herself to the luxury of loving him. Take the moment, she told herself. If you can't have a lifetime, take the here and now.

"Oh God, Sam, I want you." His voice was husky, urgent. "If you can't, or won't, tell me now. One more moment of this, and I won't be able to stop."

Her mind whirled, even though they had since stopped moving. "But . . . I mean, I have to talk to Emery . . . ."

She did not know what she meant, but he couldn't have been more decisive in releasing her. Sam felt a chip of her heart break off. When would she ever learn to shut her mouth?

Grant sat on the bed, grabbing the bottle to scratch at its label as if he had nothing better to do. "I might hate it, and him, but I do understand. If you gave your word, I respect you too much to ask you to break it."

With a tight smile, he set the bottle down. Resting his chin on his hands, he smiled up at her with Willie's boyish sincerity. "I still think he's a fool, though. If you were mine, you'd have flowers twice a day."

Mine? Didn't he know? Too dazed to speak, to move, Sam watched him. An awful fluttering made itself at home in her chest. This was Grant, her Grant, so lonely and alone, pleading with her. He's just a man, she thought with increasing awe. And for whatever reason, or however temporarily, he needs me. Me. He truly does.

The fluttering stilled. She felt calm now, certain, and her feet moved to take her beyond caution, to the only place she had ever wanted to be. Standing before him, she held him with her gaze as she removed the pins from her hair, letting it drop in one dramatic motion to her shoulders. "I made no vow to Emery," she told him. "And I don't remember telling you to stop."

He took her face in his hands, as though it were the most precious thing he had ever held there. Awestruck, she reached up to brush his cheek. His skin was so smooth, so deliciously scented, he must have shaved only moments ago. For this? For her?

He pulled her into his lap with exquisite tenderness. Wanting to cry, to laugh, Sam opened her lips to his kiss. As his mouth made love to hers, she felt herself come to life, her body's secrets unfolding beneath his touch. Did he understand what his fingers could do? The power he held over her?

In a daze, she felt clothing drop to the floor. Grant kissed the flesh as he revealed it, sending a thousand delicious quivers along her spine. Yes, her brain repeated; yes. Reality became one grand sensation. Light, feathery brush strokes against her skin. Soft, enervating puffs of air at her ears. Magic stirred within her at the deep, drugged mingling of their tongues. Warmth, liquid and flowing. Heat, burning and speading. Building. Consuming. Blossoming, blooming, opening up just for him. Everywhere she looked, everything she touched, was love. Pure, sweet and perfect.

Like a child in a candy shop, she was greedy to

taste it all. His arms, the hair at his chest, each beautiful line of his face. She ran her hands in long, lazy strokes along his limbs, so firm and strong as they held her close to him. In his embrace, she felt released, reborn, a woman made for making and taking love. There seemed nothing she wouldn't do for his pleasure, nothing she wouldn't take for her own.

She became a wild thing. Drunk with passion, consumed by it, she gloried in her new-found freedom. All that mattered was his magnificent body, his skillful hands, his—oh, yes, his incredible tongue.

He took her face in both hands as he lowered himself into her. Gazing at her that way, he seemed so beautiful, so loving, that she groaned deep within her throat. She gripped his back, unwilling, unable to let go. As he moved within her, so at home there, she marveled at the sheer perfection of it. Grant, here, loving her. She clung to him, to the moment, knowing that she had been only half alive until now, only half aware of what life could offer.

She buried her face in his shoulder to kiss his neck, tasting the salty sweetness of him. So good. He answered by grasping her, and his soft, seductive stroking took on a life of its own. Matching her hunger, he gripped her to him.

Her hands slid into his hair, tightening. She went dizzy with the passion, the pleasure. My God, it felt so good, so right, so—

The world exploded. Taken by surprise, Sam cried out with every spasm that ripped through her body. Her mind chanted his name, her arms held him tight. And as the near-unbearable pleasure subsided, she found herself giggling, ever so giddily, with her body trembling out of control.

She opened her eyes to find him watching her,

half smiling and half questioning. "I didn't hurt you, did I?"

She loved him so much she wanted to cry. "No. Oh, no."

"Do you have any idea how beautiful you are?"

Another time she might have argued, but tonight was special. No one could be smiled at like that and not feel beautiful.

His voice was dreamy. "Lying here, the candlelight glowing on your skin—oh, God, Sam, I could swallow you whole."

"You very nearly did."

"It's your own fault, wretch. You turn me into an animal. Whenever I get close to you, I lose all control."

"I don't mind."

"Careful. You're playing with fire. Hasn't anyone ever explained the facts of Nature to you? If we continue this way, my dear, you just might find yourself with a baby."

He held her, kissing her hair, stroking her back, but she was only half conscious of this. "A baby," she sighed, softening deep inside. She could almost picture it, its soft blue eyes blinking up at her. "I think it would be wonderful. Especially if he had your eyes."

He pulled away to look at her, head leaning on his elbow. "You have the most marvelous knack for catching me off balance."

"Don't laugh at me."

"I wasn't laughing. I was thinking. Dreaming. You'd make a wonderful mother."

She was afraid to move. Afraid that if she shifted, even an inch, the spell would break.

"I don't know how to say this."

"You don't have to explain. I understand."

"No, you don't." He sat up against the headboard. He didn't look at her, but he took her hand, gripping it hard. "I've been alone most of my life. My childhood was ugly enough to convince me that I was better off on my own. Yet, through it all, I kept dreaming of someday going home. To my own place, a snug little cottage in the woods. And waiting for me at the door, always, was the gentlest, sweetest, most incredibly lovely woman in the world. At the time, I imagined it to be my mother, but she had your face, Sam. She smiled at me with your eyes."

She stared at his profile, feeling his sincerity, his insecurity, as if it reached out to touch her. The hand holding hers felt cold, so cold.

"That's it. Until today, I never had the nerve to take it further. Dreams are such fragile things. It seems the more we try to hold onto them, the more easily they shatter and break."

"Sometimes they're stronger if two people share the same one."

He squeezed her hand and kissed it hard. "Could we, Sam? You and me, do you think we could share a dream?"

She prayed for wisdom. Please, God, make me say the right thing. "I do."

"Would you cosider saying those words to a justice of the peace?"

"I . . . what do you mean?"

"I mean, will you marry me?"

"Me? Are you certain?"

"God help me, I've never been more certain of anything in my life." He leaned down to take her face in his hands. "I love you, Sam. I want to spend my life with you. Say the word and the deed will be done."

"Done?"

He slid down beside her. "I spoke with a justice

earlier. As long as we're there before midnight, he'll marry us tonight."

"Now? So soon? But this is all so sudden."

He tried to smile. "I have to make an honest woman of you, don't I? Hell, Sam, you're not in love with Blankfield, are you?"

"Emery?"

"I doubt he would be pleased to hear such disbelief in your tone."

"No, but he'll be even less pleased when he hears what we have done. He had his heart set on my grandfather's bank, you know."

"He can have it. I'll take just you, if you'll let me."

It was crazy and impulsive, but she had to take the chance. "Oh Grant, let's go find that judge before anything stops us."

He looked like a little boy who had just captured the prize. Touching that grinning face, she thought her heart would explode, it was so full of him.

"In a minute. There's something else we need to discuss."

She sobered instantly. She should have known better. Nobody got everything their heart had ever wanted without paying dearly for it. What could he want?

Pulling away, he rolled off the bed. He snatched his shirt and stabbed his arms into it. "I talked to Molly after you left. She's not feeling well and I think it frightens her. She kept talking about wanting to see the ocean before she died."

Sam sat up, the color draining from her face. "Molly's dying?"

"No! I mean, it's not quite so drastic. She's pining, I think. Hoping a change of scene might help her forget her husband's death, I bought us all tickets for Richmond."

"Richmond?" All at once, reality came rushing back. "I—I can't go back there. I have things to do here."

"I'm sorry." He poked his legs into his trousers. "I assumed you would feel duty-bound to go with her, since she practically raised you. Oh well, we'll just have to disappoint her. She might be a mountain lion in these hills, but I can't see her crossing the continent alone."

"She truly wants to see the ocean?"

He threw her clothes on the bed, but he wouldn't look at her. "It was all she could talk about. But don't you worry about that. You do what you want. There will be time to take her in the future."

Sam felt torn. She had waited so long to get to Central City, but this was Molly. Dear, loving Molly. "No, you're right. My plans can wait. We'll go to Richmond; I can always return later."

He looked at her then. What she saw in his eyes made the sacrifice worthwhile. "God, I love you."

She hobbled on her knees to the edge of the bed to fling her arms around him. He kissed her, long and hard, running his hands up and down her naked back. Passion stirred again, but before it could gain control, he pushed her away, ever so gently, and spoke huskily in her ear.

"Oh no, you little witch. The next time you seduce me, I intend to be married."

"Me, seduce *you*?" She threw a pillow at him. "Who had the cozy room and champagne waiting?"

"It was all in a good cause, I assure you." For once, he did not fall into the playful mood. "Come on, Sam, get dressed. We don't have much time."

Bewildered, Sam did as he asked, but the sudden change in mood disturbed her. A distance seemed to have been set between them. Grant seemed aloof, evasive almost. Hurt by this, she nearly blurted out that perhaps they shouldn't get married after all, but as he took her hand to lead her out of the room, she felt his need, his desperation, and wisely kept silent.

It was a strange wedding, all the same. Grant seemed nervous, far more than even a bridegroom should be. He kept glancing over his shoulder, as if afraid someone would burst through the door to stop them. And when it came time to sign their names, he was so flustered he wrote Grant Barton. When she tried discreetly to point this out to him, he muttered an oath, as if upset with her interference, and roughly scratched out a Tony Rawlings instead.

There was another awkward moment when it came time to present the ring and he had none to give her. By this time, the poor justice was so skeptical, Sam would not have blamed him for refusing to complete their vows, but the words were said and before she knew it, she was Grant's wife.

They were both a little dazed as they walked from the poor man's house, and their silence was not a comfortable one. He's likely regretting the impulse, she thought miserably. Is he wondering what to do with me now?

Grant kept them at a brisk clip all the way to their hotel room. Even after the door had closed and he automatically began to undress, he still didn't speak. Poised on opposite sides of the bed, they seemed like strangers again. Confused and more than a little frightened, Sam spoke without thinking. "Why, exactly, did you marry me?"

He turned so abruptly, she thought he might lose his balance. "I beg your pardon?"

"It can't have been for companionship. You haven't spoken one word to me since we said I do."

He drooped. It was the only word for it. "I'm sorry. I have things on my mind."

"We don't have to stay married. If I leave right now, we can have the vows annulled."

"No!" He reached across the bed for her. "Dammit, don't leave me."

He pulled too hard. They both toppled onto the bed. To her utter amazement, he began to laugh. "Oh, poor Sam. I'm not doing this right at all, am I?"

"What is so funny?"

"Everything. Nothing. Damn, I wanted to make this night perfect and I've only succeeded in making you angry."

"I'm not angry."

"Yes, you are. I can tell. You get very tight around the lips. They should be open, you know. Welcoming me. Hmmmm, yes, much better."

She couldn't stop him. Even if she were angry, as he claimed, a single touch from those lips could make her his slave. Hazily, she watched her clothing drop again to the floor. Lying naked and happy in his arms, she knew he was right. All of her should remain open to him.

For she belonged to him now. And he to her. As if their bodies knew and understood this, there was no urgency now to their lovemaking. Like a thick, sweet syrup, the tender emotions flowed between them. Slowly, tenderly, he took her again with him, up, up, up to that wondrous place where the world no longer mattered. Where nothing did, as long as they held each other in their arms.

"There," he sighed as he held her trembling body tight to his own. "Now you are good and truly mine."

"Did we actually get married?"

"Please Sam, no regrets. I promise I'll make it up to you. We'll have a decent ceremony, with a thousand people if you want. And a ring."

"Now you sound like Emery."

"God forbid. I shudder every time I think of how close you came to marrying that fool."

"For the last time, I had no intention of marrying Emery."

"Then why that meeting up at Molly's?"

"I was as surprised as anyone to find him there. My lord, you weren't jealous, were you? Of Emery?"

"I wanted to punch him in his self-righteous jaw. Especially after the way you went off with him."

He'd been jealous. How utterly delightful. "In answer to your question, I have no regrets. None at all. But I thought you did. You seemed so angry." Propping her hands on his chest, she grinned down at him. "You know, tight about the lips when they should have been open, welcoming me?"

His own grin was reluctant as he ran his fingers through her hair. "I wasn't angry at you, Sam. Just preoccupied. And resentful. There are matters I must deal with in the morning. I hate to waste that time when I'd much rather be with you."

"I'll come with you. Maybe I can help."

"I don't want you worrying your—"

"If you say anything about my pretty little head, I'll pop you in the nose. I intend to be your wife, not an ornament."

"I know. I want that, too. But just this once, I have to do it on my own. I promise you, as soon as it's done, you're the first person I'll come to to talk about it."

She smiled. "We'll have plenty of time. All the way home."

"I hope so."

The smile faded. "What do you mean?"

"I have every intention of being on that train

tomorrow, but sometimes—well, I can't always control matters. If I'm not at the station for some reason, I want you to go ahead without me."

"I don't want to go without you."

He closed his eyes, as if in pain. "Promise me, for Molly's sake, you'll be on that train? I swear, I'll catch up with you as soon as I can. Do you think I want to miss a single moment of our honeymoon?"

"No, but . . ."

He put a finger to her lips. "Get on the train, Sam. For me."

She felt uneasy, but when he pleaded like that, she couldn't refuse. If something was worrying him, what kind of a wife would she be to make it worse?

"I want you to wear this." He reached down for the chain at his neck. "Every time you start to doubt, look at it and say, Grant loves me."

"I can't take your medallion. It's your good-luck piece."

"And you're my wife. Hell, if I can't give you a bloody ring, the least I can do is give you my protection. I love you, Sam. Whatever happens, you've got to believe that."

The bronze felt heavy on her chest, but good. So good. *I am his wife. Out of all those other women, he chose me. Grant loves me,* she thought to herself. *If he could give me his medallion, he truly must.*

"Come now, lie down here beside me and let's get some sleep. Tomorrow is going to be another busy day."

Snuggling into his chest, she thought of what the day would bring. All those people to be told. "Oh, my goodness. I suppose we'll have to tell Cyrus we'll be leaving."

"Let me deal with Cyrus. You just pack your clothes."

"There's not much to pack. Quite frankly, I'm so sick of gray gowns I'd just as soon leave the lot of them here."

"That's fine with me. Just don't bother yourself with Claire. Willie and Giselle will get her packed, if she decides to go."

"They know about us?"

"Willie does. Who do you think helped me arrange this? In his own words, he always wanted a mother with gray eyes."

That made her smile. "You seem to have taken care of everything."

"I hope so. Damn, I hope so."

The words were muttered so softly, she told herself she imagined his urgency. He loves me, she chanted instead, rubbing the medallion for good luck as she drifted off to sleep. Grant loves me.

24

The Oh Susannah Mine
June, 1861

In the dark, Bill could hear arguing. One voice was his captor's but the other was too soft and indistinct. "You fool!" he heard Bavoure shout. "After all I've done for you!"

Bill stood and limped to the bars. His leg was getting so stiff, he doubted he'd ever walk properly again. Not that it mattered. As soon as those two finished fighting, he was a dead man. They knew he'd never sign. Not now that Sam was with his father. That had been a mistake, telling him that. Now, Bill had nothing left to lose.

Seeing this, Bavoure must have brought in reinforcements. But whoever it was didn't seem to want to go along. Bill enjoyed that thought. He didn't like Bavoure. He'd hate to think the man would get what he wanted.

The shouting grew louder, yet less distinguishable. Bavoure was in quite a state. Bill hoped it wouldn't make him vicious when his dying time came. If he had to go, he'd rather his death was quick.

There was a bang, a thud, and then quiet. Holding onto the bars, Bill prayed for courage. Let me die like a man, he pleaded. At least let me take my pride and dignity to the grave.

"Bill? Dammit, Bill, where the hell are you?"

The whisper was followed by a rush of footsteps. Both cut through the silence with urgent force. Bill gripped the bars, certain his mind was playing tricks with him. Was he crazy, expecting miracles, after all that had happened to him?

Maybe he'd been too long in the dark. For there stood Tony, his miracle come to life, and he couldn't believe in him. Prison did things to the soul. It made holes there that could never be filled, warped a mind so it didn't know what to think any more.

"Bill?"

He'd lost some weight, since Bill had seen him last, but Tony was still a good-looking devil. *How could you do this to me?* he wanted to ask, but didn't have the heart. If Tony could betray him—or God, poor Susie—what was there left to believe in?

Bill was unable to move. None of this made sense. "You're not in this with him?"

"Not this. I only learned of it this morning. Had I known—my God, Susie . . ."

The word trailed off. The pain seemed to echo and rebound off the stone. "He killed my cousin and aunt, too. All for that damned title. If and when we get out of here, I plan to make things right. How could I live with myself otherwise?"

"I should have known better. I've never had a better friend than you."

They fell into each other's arms, two men awkwardly expressing emotion they could no longer control. Bill felt a tear on his cheek and he let it stay there. Hell, Tony had a few, too.

"We'd better get moving," Tony said shakily as they broke apart. "Is there another way out besides that cliff?"

"This shaft opens into the shack. It's a long way, though. You go on ahead."

"Don't be silly."

"If you run, you can go get help. I'll only hold you back, with this bum leg."

"I'm not leaving you to that monster. Lean on me. We haven't the time for arguments."

It seemed strange, Tony taking charge. Maybe being Lord Hoxton wasn't a bad thing, after all. "All right. I can't say I'm not happy for the help. Sure is good to see you back again."

"I should never have left. Susie knew, I think. She tried to warn me. She had a bad hunch about my inheritance."

"I know. She had a hunch about Bavoure, too. I can't believe we never suspected he and Doc Charles were the same man."

"Don't feel bad. He was a trained actor. He tricked even my grandfather. We thought he was an impoverished gentleman, turned tutor. I didn't know the truth until today."

"He faked those engineering reports. Do you know what that means? We were right. All along, we were right about our gold."

"You were right, Bill. I was always the weak coward."

They had reached the shack. Breaking away as they passed through the curtain, Bill shook his head. "That's Riley talking. No weak coward would risk his neck to save a friend."

But before Tony's smile could ripen, Riley emerged behind them, brandishing a gun. "What a touching reunion. You may not be a coward, Tony, but you were ever the fool. Alone, you might have escaped. Now you both must die."

"You'll lose everything," Tony reminded him. "Without me, you are nothing."

"We'll just see, won't we?"

The gun went off. Tony dropped, shock stripping his face of color, his chest a deep, dark red. Bill gaped until the second explosion sent a painful echo ripping through his brain.

My God, he thought in awe as he too fell to the dirt. Losing consciousness, he heard Riley's laughter. Amidst the smell of kerosene, he felt the heat of a roaring blaze.

He had time enough to see the shack engulfed in a prison of flame, before the world went black.

25

Opening one eye, Grant cursed himself. He hadn't meant to fall asleep, but Sam had been so warm and soft beside him that he'd allowed himself just a few minutes more. Only now, every minute was precious if he was to get up to the mine and back again to meet that train.

Ever so gently, he removed his arms from her sleeping body. She snuggled closer, groping for him. Don't do this, he silently pleaded with her. God knows how I want to stay, but I must go. It's the only chance I have to save your inheritance.

Holding his breath, he eased himself free. As he stood in the chilly pre-dawn air, gazing down at her, he knew this was the hardest thing he had ever done. So many things could go wrong. So easily, his prize could be lost. Throat tightening, he had the sudden urge to wake her, to sit her down and tell her the truth. All of it.

And what good would that do? Tell Sam the truth and she wouldn't get on that train. She would find a horse, a better one than he could hire, and ride up to that mine ahead of him. No, he wasn't taking chances with her life. This was the right thing to do, the only thing. He'd give her up before he'd let her die.

His wife. Each time he thought of how easily, how eagerly she had married him, a silly smile spread across his face. She loved him. Her body told him so.

And what happens, Barton, when she learns the

truth? *Blankfield is a fool*, he argued with himself. I couldn't stand by and let him bully her into that marriage. He would have sold off everything she cared about, all to that snake Riley, and all for a bank she despised. All right, so maybe I don't have much money, or respectability, but by all that's good and right in the world, I'll find a way to keep her.

And he'd better start now. Glancing at his watch, he saw that it was fast approaching three in the morning. The train for Richmond left in less than twelve hours. Dressing quickly, he told himself to relax, that he had plenty of time, but a nagging sense of premonition snaked through him. So many things could go wrong.

Yanking on his boots, he wondered if he would have time to stop in at Molly's to tell her about her dying wish to see the ocean. No, there wasn't time. He could leave a note, with her train ticket. When she picked it up in Central City, she would have the long ride to Denver to get her story straight.

Proud of himself, he reached for the notepaper. Scribbling the note to Molly, he decided to write one to Giselle, as well. His wife wasn't going off to Richmond in those gray rags. With Hoxton paying, Giselle should be able to find some decent, ready-made clothing somewhere in this city. It was the least that Sam deserved. He wished he had the time to buy her a decent ring.

He leaned down carefully to rub the bronze one last time. It was the lightest touch, a caress, but as his hand inadvertently brushed the skin of her breasts, a wave of longing stripped away his resolve. *I want to spend every waking moment with this woman*, he thought desperately.

She moved, just slightly, and a slow, lazy smile transformed her face. Grant thought his heart would burst. *I have to leave*, he told himself over and over, but his body refused to obey. One more moment, it insisted. One more touch.

A brisk wind stirred outside the window. It seemed to call to him, its urgency clear. Cursing Riley with all his might, Grant pulled himself away from his sleeping wife to reach for his new gun. As he strapped it under his jacket, he wasn't certain he could use it, but thinking again of his adversary, it was reassuring to have it tucked against his chest.

He hurried out of the room and through the lobby. How eerie the place seemed with no one stirring. It was the same outside. The wind came in gusts, pushing bits of paper and debris before it, and Grant himself felt as if it nudged him down the street. Get moving, it seemed to say, as if it felt the same foreboding he did. Up ahead, the mountains loomed larger than ever. Dark specters against the cloud-filled skies. Come to us, they coaxed, let's test what sort of man you are.

Just what he needed: rain. Grumbling, he set off for the train depot. He'd heard about these mountain storms. Violent weather for a violent day.

He shook off that thought, not much liking it, and concentrated instead on the task at hand. With any luck at all, he would get his look at the mine, alert the sheriff, and be back down to Denver before the first raindrop fell.

But there were no passenger trains running at this hour, he was told at the depot. Whether it was his swearing, or his blatant urgency, the stationmaster took pity. Pointing to a train beginning to move on the other side of the tracks, he told Grant that if comfort wasn't an issue and he was prepared to jump, that freighter was going up to Central.

Accustomed by now to jumping on and off trains,

Grant was soon on the caboose climbing into the hills. The trip was awe-inspiring in the early morning dark. Deep shadows stretched across the canyons, moving at the wind's command. The pine and smoke mingled with a new scent now, and Grant wondered if it might be fear. The plants and animals of these mountains knew. Nature was preparing to unleash her fury. Anyone not prepared to meet it had best get out of the way.

Several rough-looking characters waited at the Central City depot to load their cargo onto the train. Grant could see only the word Falcon, but it was enough. Those heavy bags, he'd wager, held gold. From the Oh Susannah mine.

He'd better hurry. If he could get to the sheriff in time, that load might be confiscated before it left Denver, and Sam would get her gold.

There was definitely no time to visit Molly. Grasping his note, he went straight to the ticket window. It was too early, he should have realized. Nothing was open.

He would leave it with the owner of the livery stable, he decided. That is, if he could rouse the man at this hour. The stable was closed, but he coaxed the poor man from his breakfast, proving his urgency with an over-generous tip. The owner saddled a horse and promised to leave the envelope for Molly at the ticket window as soon as it opened.

As Grant rode up the mountainside he tried to ignore thunderclouds poised so close above him, but inside, his uneasiness built. It became outright dread as he stood on the ledge above the Eggersley cabin. This was the entrance to the mine, he realized with a sickening lurch. All the old fears came bounding back as he realized he must now go into it.

Dropping from the horse, he made himself

breathe slowly. This wasn't Cornwall. He was no longer a boy. He was a man, and though she might not know it yet, his wife depended on him. He would go into that stinking hole in the ground, dammit, and he would get her the proof she needed.

Tying his horse to a tree, he slipped through the woods. The place was blanketed in an unearthly quiet. How like Riley to intimidate even the wind into silence.

It was almost too easy to get beyond the burnt remnants of the shack. Though the tunnel was boarded over, it took only one pull for the makeshift barrier to come away like a door.

Replacing it, Grant faced the shaft. His breaths came short and shallow. Half hopefully, he glanced behind him, but there was no one to stop him. They were all asleep, no doubt, not expecting a prowler so early in the day.

Grimly determined, he forced himself inside. He'd forgotten how dark a mine could be. Dolt. He could break a bone, wandering about in these tunnels without a light.

Even as he convinced himself that it was wiser to return later with a lamp, he saw the distant glow. There was no hope for it now, he must go on.

His fists remained clenched as he inched along that shaft. His mind relived the horrors of the tin mine. Michael Clanton, always at him with that strap, screeching at him, his threats pushing him deeper and deeper into the bowels of the earth.

At first, as Grant stared into that vast hole where the lamps made eerie shadows against the walls, he thought he'd dreamed his way into the past. The picks and shovels, the carts laden with ore, all those weary, dirt-stained faces; he could be in Cornwall.

The machinery, though, was out of place. Those

great iron bars must be a stamp mill. When engaged, it would make the pounding Grant had heard. Built into the stream that ran through this cavern, it would dispose of its waste through the cut in the rock up ahead. Through that tubing? No, the tube was attached to the strange contraption next to it. A smelter? A crude one, but ingenious, all the same. By processing the ore at the site, Riley had rid himself of the curious middle man, thereby insuring that his theft remained unnoticed.

Before he could completely appreciate this strategy, the foreman began to scream at his crew again. Grant leaned back against the cold stone, trying to recover his balance. the slight build, the jet-black hair; he'd know that face anywhere. Hadn't he spent a lifetime fleeing from it?

Grant blinked twice, but the vision would not go away. Clanton, in Colorado? He might lack the strap, but from the looks on those miners' faces, not the power to terrify. Grant knew exactly how they felt. His throat went tight, and a cold sweat broke out across his face.

He backed away, thinking only of escape, and in the action tripped over a rail. Sitting in the dirt, his wits returned. Whatever Clanton was doing in the Oh Susannah had nothing to do with Jamie Clanton, presumed dead nearly twenty years ago. He must be working for this Charles Bavoure, more commonly known as Charles Riley.

Not bothering to brush his trousers, he hurried back the way he had come. All he had to do was direct the sheriff here, and it would end any threat Riley might pose. He knew his former "step-father." Clanton would not meekly shoulder the blame. By noon, he would be singing like a canary.

A quick visit to the authorities and Grant would

be back to Denver long before the train left for Richmond. It wouldn't be easy, telling Sam the truth, but from now on, there would be nothing but honestly between them. He had such plans for them. He—

"My, my, look what we have here."

Stopped in his tracks, Grant faced the two shadowy figures blocking the tunnel. Like Clanton, Riley's voice was distressingly familiar.

"What a coincidence," Riley drawled, clearly enjoying himself. "Two Lord Hoxtons, here in one place. We can't have that, now, can we? One of you, I fear, will have to go."

Molly hauled her faded carpetbag onto the train. Heavy load, that bag, and she was plumb wore out lugging it behind her. Especially the way she had hurried down from her place. There was a storm brewing in these hills. And she sure as shootin' didn't want to get caught out in the middle of it.

So she rushed down to town, right onto the train. She had her own tickets, bought and paid for last night. She didn't like owing anybody anything. She felt better when she did things for herself.

As the train pulled off, Bob Harden waved from the ticket window. Seemed to be something in his hand, but Molly was too distracted to pay much heed. She was too busy hoping that the boy knew what he was doing, packing them all off to Richmond.

For the fiftieth time that day, Sam glanced out the lobby window. Where was he? One more hour and Grant would miss the train. Perhaps she should just go to the depot. The way the sky looked, it might rain any minute and she'd hate to get her new clothes soaked.

She pressed her hands to her chest. Feeling the bronze, her smile grew wider. He was the most wonderful husband ever. He would come to the train on time. She just knew it.

But to be on the safe side, she rubbed the medallion, just as he had told her to do. Grant loved her. He, who could have any woman in the world, had chosen her as his wife. Was it any wonder she walked three feet above the ground?

He was her shining knight. For it was by his order, Giselle had explained, that all the hated gray had been banished forever. She now wore a pretty cotton frock of yellow and white, with a purse and bonnet to match. She pictured him, rushing to make that train. She would be waiting on the platform, and when his eyes met hers, they would shine with love and admiration . . . .

'I say, Samantha Lynn, I am delighted. All packed and ready to go? Splendid.''

It took several seconds to focus, but when she did, she groaned. Emery. She had forgotten all about him. It was dreadfully awkward, but she must find a way to tell him. It would be even more uncomfortable if he accompanied them home on the train.

He never gave her a chance to speak. "Don't just stand there. I told Justice Pearce we would be at his home within the hour. Where is your cousin?"

"Claire is staying. I can't go with you either." She giggled. It was cruel, and most unseemly, but she could picture the judge's face when she arrived, for the second time, to wed yet another confused man.

"I fail to see what is so amusing. Time is wasting.''

She giggled again. Wasting? No, the time was gone. Thank God, it was gone. Never again could Emery pester and bully her.

"What on earth is wrong with you?"

"Nothing. Absolutely nothing. Oh Emery, I have never been so right in my life."

"Samantha Lynn, I demand you stop this laughing at once."

The outburst merely set her off on another peal. "But that's the wonderful part. You can't demand anything of me. I don't have to listen to you anymore."

He seemed uncharacteristically unsure of himself. "Don't be ridiculous. As your husband—"

"You are not my husband. I already—"

"I soon will be."

"No, you will not. I already have one."

"I have no time for this senseless bickering. Come now, the judge is waiting."

He never even heard me, Sam marveled, more than ever aware of her reprieve. All these years, he had yet to listen to a word she'd said. Watching him stoop to lift her bags, she bristled with exasperation. She would never get rid of him. She could be an old woman with two hundred grandchildren and he'd still be expecting her to marry him.

Behind Emery, she saw Molly push through the door. Thinking only of escape, she snatched her bag from his hands. "Get it through your head, Emery. Forget the bank. I am going to Richmond, but I am not going with you. And I won't ever marry you because I simply can't."

"What are you saying?"

"What I've been trying to say, had you bothered to listen, is that I am already wed. Grant and I were married last night."

His jaw dropped, most likely in shock, but Sam was not about to wait for him to deliver another lecture. Slipping an arm through Molly's, she steered them both out the door.

"Sorry about this," she whispered, "but Emery is being his most difficult. Let's wait for the others at the depot."

"Others?"

"Grant had some business to attend to, and Willie and Giselle are off running errands. Claire, I'm happy to say, chose to remain behind with the Wynecotes."

"Whoa, girl, slow down. Who is Willie and who is Giselle?"

"Oh Molly, there's so much to tell you. He married me. Last night, he just swept me off my feet and made me his wife."

Molly stopped. "Hell's bells, girl. You didn't marry that fool?"

Laughing, Sam tugged her forward. "Oh, no, not Emery. Grant."

Molly almost smiled. "Now, if that don't beat all. Never figured him for the marrying kind. I can see now why you're glowing so. But heck, why are we going to the depot? If you think I'm going to come between you two on your honeymoon . . ."

Sam grabbed her hands. "Stop that right now. You're going to see your ocean and that's final."

"What are you talking about? I can't abide the sea. That's why I came to these mountains."

"I don't understand. Grant said—"

"Samantha Lynn!" A pudgy hand clamped on her arm. "Thank goodness I caught up with you before you made a fool of yourself. You must not marry that riffraff. I forbid it."

"Don't you ever listen? It's too late to forbid me anything. I *am* married. Last night."

"That's impossible."

"No Emery, *you* are impossible." Turning her back to him, she pulled Molly with her down the street. She didn't enjoy the thoughts she was having. The doubts.

"Don't you see?" Emery persisted, following her down the street. "I can help you. Admit you made a mistake and I will find a way to have it annulled."

She didn't falter a step. "No. I'm not a child; I am well past legal age. You can't annual anything without my consent."

"Without your—" He tripped, but never once lost his persistence as he stumbled after her. "Oh, do be sensible. He's good-looking, I'll grant you that, but what do you know about him? He can't possibly keep you in the style to which you are accustomed. Not on an actor's salary."

He's Hoxton, she wanted to throw in his face, but Grant clearly hadn't wanted him to know that. "We'll manage."

"I hadn't wanted to hurt you, but I think you should know that it isn't you he wants. It's your father's mine."

That stopped her. She halted so suddenly, poor Molly went sprawling ahead. "That's not true."

"No? Then tell me, why did this marriage proposal pop up so suddenly? He didn't ask for your hand before I arrived on the scene, now did he? It was my talk of selling the mine that made him act so precipitously."

She didn't answer. She couldn't. But she didn't need to; he would read her answer in her face.

"You should know, also, where he spent yesterday afternoon."

"He was with Molly."

His smile was condescending. "For a time, perhaps, but he also paid a visit to the land office in Central City. I think he wanted to know exactly where to find the Oh Susannah."

Molly gripped her arm. "Now don't you go jumping to any conclusions until the boy can speak for himself."

"But where, may I ask, is he? I hope you don't expect him to be on that train. He hasn't the least intention of going to Richmond. He merely wants you out of the way so he can investigate the mine."

"What about you, Emery? What do you want?"

He had the good grace to turn red. "I—I made a promise to your dying grandfather, as you must remember, and I—"

"Spare me. I've had about all the lies I can stomach for one day."

Molly's grip tightened on her sleeve. "Where do you think you're going, girl?"

"Let me go, Molly. I'm going back to the hotel to change. It's time I did what I came here to do. What a fool I am, to be so easily distracted. Promise me, indeed. The ocean, indeed. I'll be damned if I'll get on that train!"

Coming slowly awake, Grant thought he heard a train whistle. Sam's train, he thought groggily. Whatever happened to him, at least Sam would be safe.

Above him, he could hear them arguing. There must have been some drug in that brandy Riley had so amiably offered. He should have known better than to drink it. But he had felt so skittish, being back down in the mine and facing Hoxton, that he hadn't had time to regain his wits. Hell, he hadn't even remembered the gun, until one of Riley's guards had removed it from his chest.

He tried to move and tasted dirt. Where had they dumped him? He pursed his lips to spit, but his mouth felt as if it had been stuffed with cotton. His whole head did. Nothing seemed to work right and it hurt to keep his eyes open.

His ears worked, though. Hoxton's anger came across clear and loud. "If I'd had any idea what you were doing, Riley," he said, "I have stopped it long ago. Framing Barton for that crime was one thing. I went along with it, since we planned to free the man later, but I cannot condone theft and murder. If you don't cease at once, I must go to the law."

Ultimatums, Grant could have warned him, were not the way to motivate Riley. But before he could will his mouth to speak, there was a thud, a groan, and a second, more immediate thud to his right. Forcing one eye open, Grant found Hoxton's scarred and lifeless face sprawled in the dirt before his own.

Two Hoxtons might be an inconvenience, but Riley had disposed of one. Perhaps there was hope for Grant, after all.

26

Sam's hopes were just about gone. Her investigations in town had confirmed her worst fears. Just as Emery had claimed, Grant had been in town yesterday, in the land office. The bank, too. the bank manager had been reluctant to talk, saying that Lord Hoxton's employee, that stern Mr. Bavoure, wasn't supposed to know about his lordship's visit.

Following Grant's trail, Sam realized that he and Bavoure must have been working together, buying up all the land, until one, or both, got greedy. They were a pair of snakes, the two of them, each trying to cut the other out. Did Emery realize yet that Bavoure had been using him? Grant obviously had. That was why he had countered with his own proposal. How eagerly, how stupidly, she had fallen into his trap. Oh, Grant, why?

But he wasn't Grant; he was Tony Rawlings—the fiend who had betrayed, and possibly killed, her parents. All along, he'd been cheating and lying and she had been stupid enough to believe him.

After speaking to the livery stable owner, she hired a horse and cantered up the mountainside. She found a horse at the top of the ridge. Sliding to the ground, she noticed it carried the same impersonal saddle as her own hired mount. It must be Grant's horse, but why on earth would he leave the animal tied here? Could he be afraid of Charles Bavoure?

The wind whistled in the pines overhead.

Shivering, Sam looked up at the clouds skittering across the sky. It was a strange day, and getting awfully dark. From the feel of the air, the storm could break any moment. Maybe she should look for cover.

Uneasily, she glanced down at the cabin. The memories brought a flood of tears, which she brushed away angrily. The way he touched her, the gentle way he spoke, she'd have sworn that he loved her. How could she be so wrong?

She pulled out the medallion, gazing at it as if the falcon's lines could explain the mystery. You are my wife, Grant had said as he presented it, sounding so proud, so happy. Was he truly so good an actor?

"Miss Eggersley, what a delightful surprise. Bull said we had company, but I didn't believe him."

She spun around to face Charles Riley, and again her hopes were dashed. Though Grant might forgive her intrusion, his valet would not.

"Now, now, you needn't look so timid. If you're here to see the mine, I'll happily show it to you. Your father was right, by the way. There is a fortune in the Oh Susannah. Or, more accurately, there was."

Sam had time to wish she had let Willie come along. At the least, he could have run for help. They would kill her, she thought in a sudden panic. Just as they had her parents.

Unconsciously, she rubbed the medallion. With a hawkish gleam, Riley grabbed it. "Where did you get this?"

"Grant—I mean, Lord Hoxton gave it to me."

"Did he now? And where did he get it?"

"I don't know. A lady he once knew gave it to him, he said."

Riley's scowl deepened. "All those wasted years," he muttered. "With this, I'd have convinced that old fool his grandson was dead."

For a moment, his eyes grew so dark, Sam thought he might kill her, there and then. But with a muttered oath, he yanked the chain over her head. "Clanton!" he shouted over his shoulder. "Get your worthless hide up here."

A thin, angry-looking man shuffled up to them. He wore a perpetual squint, as if daylight hurt his eyes. "What do you want now?" he snarled, and Sam thought Riley might explode.

"You unmitigated ass. Do you see this? You told me it was buried. You told me the boy was dead."

"I thought he was. He could have been."

"Damn your soul. This changes everything. Stop gawking and get back to work, you fool."

"Work? Hell, it's quitting time. I was only sticking around until I got paid."

Even Sam edged back at the sight of Riley's face. "If you value your life, you'll do as I tell you. Work the men double. I want everything cleared out tonight."

"Tonight? Are you crazy?"

"Speak that way to me again and we shall see who is crazy. Get to work. Now. Bull, where in damnation are you?"

"Here, boss. You want me to hurt him?"

Sam was not surprised at the speed with which Clanton moved. She herself jumped as Riley turned to her. "Come with us. Now."

He turned and started down the hill. Whether it was the shadow hitting his face, or his tone of voice, Sam's refusal withered away. So that was why he had always seemed so familiar. With black hair and a mustache, yes, it was Dr. Charles. The very same man who had stood on this ledge, swearing to a frightened child that he hadn't seen her parents that night.

He turned with an irritated frown. As Bull yanked her forward, she fell into step with a fatalistic resignation. The doctor's anger had confused her then, but now she understood. He had wanted to kill her, too. That he hadn't meant only that the inevitable had been postponed.

Her fear grew as Riley stepped over the lifeless body inside the tunnel. Sam, unable to do the same, had to be forced ahead by a complaining Bull.

Lighting a lamp, Riley looked down, as if surprised to find the body there. "Hoxton is still here? Damn that Clanton, he was told to dispose of him."

Her heart did a flop, but then she saw the scars. "That isn't Grant. I mean, Tony."

"Oh yes, you never met the actual Lord Hoxton, did you? Your Grant, I am afraid, was only an imposter."

Was? Sam prayed her knees would hold her. "There were two of them?"

"More or less. Barton wasn't worth the fee we paid him. He was a convicted felon; did he mention that? But no, pinching a lover's jewelry is hardly a romantic crime and wooing you was what he was hired to do in exchange for his freedom. And a great sum of money."

"No."

"Oh, yes. He was in this with me from the start."

Dragged along by Bull, Sam felt her anger spurt. "What a pity he was too clever for you. How angry you must have been when he eluded you in Chicago."

To her dismay, he chuckled. "Clever? Oh yes. He used that incident to gain your trust. You don't truly think I would be fooled by such a ridiculous performance, do you?"

She wouldn't cry. "But he still out-manipulated you. Seduce, yes, but I doubt you expected him to marry me.''

"No. But truly, my dear, you mustn't be so naive. You can't hold him to that vow. Not when he signed the wrong name.''

She blinked, furiously. "No? He intends to remain Lord Hoxton, doesn't he? Now that the real one is dead.''

"Make no mistake, the boy can be quite ruthless. If he can prove himself reasonable, I'd like to continue using his talents. The effort is wasted, otherwise, all that careful grooming.''

"Of course. Without a Hoxton, you lose everything.''

"Not everything. You see, I've always known his lordship would one day regain his memory. I have prepared for that.''

He paused to point the lamp down a dark and narrow shaft. "This is as far as your father dug. He was remarkably close to the vein, but then, so were we. You can see where we burrowed in from one side of the mountain. If not for my tight schedule, I'd enjoy showing you the workings themselves. A marvelous invention, your father's smelter. Not as sophisticated as the ones in Black Hawk, but then, not as large, either.''

"Papa never finished building that smelter.''

"Oh, but he did, I assure you.'' His smile, in the flickering lamplight, was almost demonic. "What a joy it was, taking what he refused to sell me.''

"My lord, you are Charles Bavoure, too!''

He smiled again; then, directing the lamp ahead, he started down the right fork. "An incredibly stubborn man, your father. Down here is where I incarcerated him.''

"Then he didn't die on that cliff!''

"No. A clever touch, planting his hat and coat

there. A pity no one listened to you. Bill might have been spared the anguish of hearing us rob his claim."

Sam ground her teeth. She could kill this gloating fiend, she realized. With her bare hands. "You don't expect me to believe you worked the claim all this time without detection?"

"Unfortunately, no. After Tony's accident, your wretched grandfather put an end to my exploits by posting guards at the mine. But by then, we had gained the Hoxton title, so we barely felt the loss."

"What are you doing here now, then?"

"How could I resist? Your grandfather let his affairs go, upon his illness. I knew you, a mere female, couldn't possibly fill his shoes. I seized the opportunity, and I might have gone on for some years if not for his lordship. The fool had the gall to question me, after all I had done for him."

"And so you killed him?"

"Not I, my dear. Barton did." His eerie laughter echoed off the walls.

Sam felt suddenly deathly cold. "Grant would never do such a thing," she said, as if hoping to convince herself, but she knew Riley was right. A less naive woman would have known a man like Grant could never love her. He was as bad as any of the men Samuel had warned her against. Worse. For she had loved him, and and he had known it. "He could never commit murder."

"Ah, but I beg to differ. Here, you can hear for yourself, if you keep silent. I warn you, don't get your hopes too high. Either way, I am certain he will agree that you are dispensable."

When she would have gone for him, Bull gripped her arms. And before she could protest, his large, fleshy hand covered her mouth. She thought of biting him, but Riley ducked through the iron bars ahead.

She had no choice but to let Bull drag her into the room.

Though he'd been awake for some time, Grant's mouth still felt like cotton. He still couldn't see, either, but the drugs were not to blame. A tight and rather rancid cloth covered his eyes. What in God's name were they afraid he'd see?

The cloth muffled his hearing, too, since it was tied over his ears. His legs ached, but there were few positions open to him, sitting in the dirt. He had long since ceased struggling against the ropes. Bull must have been in the navy, the way he had secured them, and they felt a good six feet thick. No, his only hope was to bluff his way out of this. Use the old Barton wit and charm. It had rarely failed him in the past.

He sat up, his back scraping stone, as he heard voices, indistinct and indistinguishable. He had convinced himself that he must be hearing things, when he was startled by a vicious kick to his aching legs. "All right, Barton. Let's discuss what we're going to do with you."

"I can't hear a thing with this putrid cloth over my ears."

He felt hands at his head. Mean hands, enjoying their work. "There, that better?"

"A bit. Aren't you going to take it off my eyes?"

"All in good time. For the present, though, I must decide what to do with you."

Grant had been practicing in the dark for hours and had all his arguments waiting. Once the man trusted him, he could make good his escape. Then he would go straight to the law and Sam. "It's not like you, Riley, to show so little insight. I am indispensable now. You can't have the Hoxton empire without a Hoxton, after all."

"Perhaps I don't need the Hoxton empire. With
what I have deposited in my accounts, I can start an
empire of my own. From this mine alone, I can live in
luxury for the rest of my days."

He should have anticipated that. "Perhaps, but
how can you abandon the set-up you have here?
That's some processing plant."

"I have the blueprints. I can always rebuild elsewhere."

"And live in obscurity? What fun would you
have, without all that Hoxton power and influence?"

"A valid point. You surprise me, Barton. I hadn't
thought you'd be so astute."

"I have several more attributes that might
surprise you."

"Yes, I've noticed. I was impressed by the
calculated risk you took. A man of your experience,
resorting to marriage?"

"You know about that?"

"Come now, this is a small town. A British noble-
man can't stroll into town and not expect to be
gossiped about. A shame, though, that you used a
dead man's name."

"As you said, a calculated risk. I couldn't let you
and Blankfield walk off with everything, could I?"

"No, I suppose not. But it will never hold up in
court."

He hated that chuckle. "Who will contest it? I *am*
Hoxton now. Listen, I merely wish to enjoy the
benefits of my wife's wealth. You can still run the
bloody Hoxton empire."

"I do like your train of thought—to a point. But
you see, your new wife is not exactly malleable.
Sooner or later, she is bound to learn what we've
done. You really must get rid of her."

He said it as if he had suggested inviting her over

for tea. He was so matter-of-fact, displaying no emotion at all. Try as he might, Grant couldn't quite match Riley's tone. "I've taken care of that. She's on her way to Richmond this very minute. I tricked her into escorting Mrs. Malloy back to Virginia."

"Devious lad. Having gained her land, you had no further need of her."

"Precisely. Hanging about, she would only get in the way."

"Good plan, but what I had in mind was of a more permanent nature. More in terms of what happened to his lordship."

"You want me to kill her?"

"Squeamish?"

"No. Of course not. I can do what needs to be done."

He heard the sharp, indrawn breath. It was not Riley's. "Who was that? Who else is here?"

"Oh, I'm sorry. Did I neglect to mention that we had company? But how rude of me; I imagine you'd like to see."

Too suddenly, the cloth fell from his face. As his eyes adjusted, he focused on Sam. "You bastard," he snarled. "You scheming, heartless bastard."

"Come, Barton, a good player loses graciously. Surely you understood from the start that I had no intention of letting you win? Oh, you were good. I especially liked your move in Chicago, but the game is quite over. For you both."

"You won't get away with this."

"You disappoint me. If all you can manage is cliches, I'd just as soon use this cloth to quiet you."

Before Grant could move, the gag filled his mouth. He nearly retched at the taste of it. If Riley didn't kill him, this rag would.

He looked up at Sam, who stared with the same

lifeless eyes that Hoxton had. Oh God, what she must think? Recalling his words, he saw how surely they had damned him.

Never had he felt such rage, such powerlessness. He strained against the gag, but his words were garbled. I love you, he tried to tell her with his eyes, but she pointedly looked the other way.

She would never believe him now, he realized bitterly. She would never even listen to him again. Even if they survived, he had lost her for good. And Riley had planned it from the start. No doubt it was his idea of revenge. And fun.

"Let's not dally here. Have you set that charge, Bull?"

"Dougherty did."

"Good. Why don't you say good-bye to your—er, husband, my dear? Make it quick. I do detest sloppy farewells."

"What are you going to do to him?"

"What should have been done twenty years ago. Don't grieve. This will keep the rest of the female population from making your mistake. One should never trust a rogue, you know."

"He doesn't deserve to die."

"Incredible. Barton, do you hear this foolish child? After all you've done, still she champions you. I don't believe she grasps the truth yet. My dear girl, no one deserves to die. It is simply what happens when you get in the way."

"Like my parents? And Gus?"

"I offered Malloy good money to keep his mouth shut, but he was determined to play the meddling fool."

"How hateful you all are! I hope the money you've stolen brings you nothing but heartache."

"Come, child. You're getting maudlin. Cease the

theatrics and follow me. We have things to do.''

He turned to go, but Grant's eyes remained on Sam. With a jerking motion, she broke free of Bull's grasp and came to kneel before him. She knows I tried to save her, he thought in a surge of hope. If he had to die, at least he could do so knowing she believed in him. He smiled, his love rushing up in a mighty, soul-saving flood.

But she spat at him. She looked at him long and hard and spat in his face. ''Damn you, Grant Barton. I wish I had never met you.''

Numbed, he watched her stand and leave. She held her head with dignity. She stood tall and proud, as she trampled the remnants of his dream into the dirt. *We came so close*, he protested silently as she left him for the last time. For a moment there, they'd held the world in their hands.

The bars clanked shut and he stopped struggling. It no longer seemed to matter. Nothing did. He closed his eyes, but for once, he couldn't find her. The dream was dead. Soon he would be too. Only the hero got the girl, and he'd proven, too conclusively, how far short he fell of the ideal.

It was dark, and cold, but it wouldn't remain so for long. Dougherty had set the charge. It didn't take a genius to figure out his fate. His and that of anyone else Riley no longer needed. Grant wished it would happen soon. He wanted it over and done with, so he needn't live with this ache. She'd damned him. Her last words, and she had damned him.

Slumping against the wall, he further embarrassed himself with a groan. It seemed he hadn't lost all feeling after all; his legs hurt like hell.

''Cap'n, is that you?''

The harsh whisper was unrecognizeable, but only one person called him cap'n. And only one animal could yelp like that.

He sat up, kicking the dirt with his boots and making noise enough to drown out Gus. "In here, sir," he heard Willie whisper. "I told you Gus would find him."

There was a gratifying clink of a key in the lock. "There he is. On the back wall."

In the dark, he could make out three forms. Gus bounded in first to furiously lick his face. Willie followed to work at his gag. The third didn't move, except to tremble. Grant could feel his agitation, vibrating in the air between them.

"I can't do it," Willie hissed. "Down, Gus. Ain't you gonna help me, sir?"

"Oh. Yes. I'm sorry, son. But the memories . . ."

The voice trailed off as he kneeled beside them, but Grant needed no more for identification. What he did need to know was whether to feel relieved, or wary. "So you're alive, Lord Hoxton. Where did you get the key?"

"What? Oh, it was easy enough. A single key unlocks everything in this mine. Riley gave me one to pacify me. though I don't think he expected me to use it for this."

"No, I didn't either. But what are you doing here?"

His hands shook so much, Grant doubted the ropes would ever be untied. "Trying to stop him. As he would have been stopped years ago, if he hadn't burned us in that shack. If that stranger hadn't dragged me to safety . . ."

"Does this mean your memory has returned?"

"I owe you an explanation, son." He stood as the ropes fell free. "But if you don't mind, I would rather find Sam first."

"Riley's got her. They went that way."

"To the cliff? My God, Barton, you must stop him."

Grant rubbed his wrists. "Me? What about you? You're the one who brought her to this."

"Don't you think I know that? Go on, we haven't the time to argue. I promise, I will come as soon as I can, but I can't run as fast as you with this limp."

Grant had to trust him. If he didn't go right now, Sam would die. And whatever her opinion of him, he didn't want that.

He ran. It wasn't easy in the dark, and he tripped twice, but he picked himself up and ran again. His fingers itched, as if they could already feel the flesh of Riley's throat.

He burst through the entrance just as a flash of lightning crackled across the sky. Counting, as he'd been taught in his youth, he waited for the accompanying thunder. Ten miles away. He'd better find Sam and get her to shelter.

It was then that he heard the voices. Definitely Riley, and certainly gloating. Stall him, he silently begged of Sam, as he hurried to catch up, but he should have known it wasn't necessary. Egotist that he was, Riley relished this opportunity to boast of his exploits.

". . . so perfect. You do recognize the cliff, don't you? And once again the husband will be blamed, though this time, I needn't conceal the entrance. The Oh Susannah and all its headaches will cease to exist the moment I set off that charge. As if mimicking the coming explosion, another bolt of lightning ripped aross the sky.

"No one will believe all these coincidences. You won't get away with this."

"Try not to be redundant, my dear. Learn from Barton's example that no one tells me what I will or

427

won't do."

"But Grant—" There was another crash of thunder. "Relatives will wonder where he is and send someone looking for him."

"Why do you think he was chosen? The boy is an orphan; I made certain of that."

"As you did with me. That's a nasty habit you have."

Riley chuckled. "I must say, whatever your other faults, you and Barton were never dull. This has been one of the best games I've played in years. Here, why not take this medallion back? No, don't argue; you know you want it."

Grant prayed Sam would take the medallion. But he couldn't hear her reply over the thunder. The last bolt had been only five miles away. This storm was traveling fast.

"Sensible girl. Lends a nice touch, don't you think? The authorities will be so confused. I wish I could remain to watch them sort out who was who, but alas, this game is over. I must be off to the next."

"You must be mad, if you think I'll step off this cliff."

"How amusing. That's exactly what your mother said. Andrea called me insane, too. But I'm not, you know. I'm just a wise man, planning my coincidences."

"You can't make me jump."

Crouching behind a boulder, Grant waited for the right moment to attack. Surprise was the only advantage he had.

"Apparently you have forgotten Bull."

"Bull? Wait—where are you going?"

"I do wish I could help, my dear, but someone must deal with the mine. Do not dally, Bull, unless you wish to land in the ravine with her. I can't predict what that explosion might do."

The sky seemed to blaze everywhere at once as Grant launched himself out into the open. In front of a wagon, some distance away, Riley spoke to soothe the pair of skittish horses, while directly ahead, Bull forced the struggling Sam closer to the cliff.

Bull, he should have realized, had twice his strength, and Riley had his gun. Though the thunder drowned out the sound, he felt a sharp sting graze his arm. *The bastard's shot me*, he thought in a daze. And God help them, he was about to do it again.

He dove, catching Sam at the knees. The air went bursting out of her as they landed in the dirt. Poor Bull, reaching down to recapture his prey, caught Riley's bullet in the center of his skull. With a horrific screech, he tumbled backwards over the cliff. "Oh, my God," Sam gasped beneath him.

Stunned and winded, Grant shielded Sam with his body as he waited for the third shot. He hoped she wouldn't suffocate, but he knew Riley too well to hope he wouldn't make sure they were dead. Dead bodies don't talk, and they didn't come looking for revenge.

He heard a growl. He tensed, thinking the maniac had come closer for a better shot, but as he glanced up, he saw Gus leap onto the wagon, straining for the man's throat. Missing this, he settled instead for the arm holding the gun.

A scene from hell, Grant thought as he rose to help the dog. The storm blew harder, while the huge black horses pranced frantically. One more shot, or a lightning bolt, and they would rear.

"Looks to me like you lose!" Grant shouted to taunt Riley into a foolhardy shot. "But then, the dog owes you a beating."

True to form, Riley's face went dark with rage and he shot. And as Grant had hoped, Gus diverted his aim. Unfortunately, the bullet went into the dog, staining his coat a deep crimson, and a triumphant Riley tossed him to the ground.

It was, however, enough to spook the team. Whinnying with more furor than the storm, they raised their forelegs high into the air. It was an awesome sight, those dark, terrified creatures, scraping their hooves against the electrified sky. And when they dropped down, the earth rumbled with thunder.

Grant had time to see Riley's startled expression as he was forced back into the seat, but as the next shaft lightened the sky, it was on the wagon he focused. For there, as bright and commanding as the heavens themselves, were the words, The Falcon Mining Company, and directly beneath was the same falcon that was emblazoned on his medallion.

He turned to Sam, who had scrambled up to follow him, and yanked the medallion from his hand. "Did you see—" he started, but got no further as a fearsome scream shattered the air.

They both stared over the cliff. It was too dark to see, but they could hear the crash of the wagon. The horses, thank the stars, screamed no more.

Grant stood for a long, dazed moment, letting the rain run down his face, cleansing him. It seemed impossible, and far too easy, but Riley could never again manipulate his life.

"My God," Sam said shakily beside him. Drenched to the boots, hair and clothes clinging to her skin, she looked like a drowned cat, but Grant had never seen anything more beautiful in his life. *We're alive!* he wanted to shout as he lifted her up and spun her around. *You and me, Sam; we made it.*

But she was shivering, from far more than the cold, so he merely removed his jacket to slip over her shoulders. She looked up at him with those wide gray eyes.

"Don't you dare touch me."

He dropped his hands, feeling as if she'd slapped him. "Sam . . ."

"Run. Go on. I'll give you that much, but I won't lie to the sheriff for you."

He had to shout over the force of the wind. It whipped against his trousers, as if it too wanted him gone. "You don't believe I did any of those things, do you? I had to lie to save you. You've got to believe me!"

"Believe you?" Her shout was high and shrill. "I tried that once. It nearly got me killed."

"I can prove it to you. The medallion—"

"Take the filthy thing. I don't want it. My wife, you said. But I wasn't yours, any more than the medallion ever was."

Grant watched her with dismay. In his way, Riley had gotten the last laugh after all. She wouldn't listen now.

As the lightning flashed, dangerously close, he could see the wagon's insignia as if it had been branded into his brain. The Hoxton falcon. Bit by bit, the pieces fell together. Riley's intense dislike of him, his likeness to Hoxton, the memories of his past. Was it mere coincidence, or had he at last found his sunlit room?

Clanton would know. If he had to beat the man senseless, Michael Clanton would tell the world what he and Riley had done to Tony's cousin. Once Clanton spoke out, Hoxton himself would be coerced into telling the truth. Then Sam would listen.

Taking her chin in his hand, he forced her to look at him. "I've got to go back to the mine. I want you to keep this," he told her, squeezing the medallion into her hand. "Keep it close, for one day I will return for it. Do you understand?"

Their gazes linked, and for a brief moment, the

softened gray eyes told him that she did. No matter what had happened, or what might occur in the future, she would always love him.

That didn't mean, of course, that she would trust him. Much too soon, she stiffened and pulled her eyes away. "Go," she said quietly, her tone flat. "Before they lock you away for good."

"I'll be back, Sam. I promise you."

Turning her back, she proved what she thought of his promises. She'd rather stay out on the edge of the cliff in this storm than listen. "Get yourself to shelter. This storm could be dangerous."

She didn't move, but then, she wouldn't. Not until he left. Cursing under his breath, he started running. He hated leaving her like that, but he had to get to Clanton before the scurvy bastard escaped from him, too.

To his immense relief, he ran into Willie and Hoxton on his way down. "I'm glad to see you, Willie. Sam's up there. She needs you."

Willie paled, then bolted. Hoxton touched his arm. "We should take you to a doctor, Barton. You're bleeding."

"It's nothing. I must go after Clanton. With Riley dead, he's all I have left to prove who I truly am."

Hoxton nodded. "He's inside. Good luck, and—Barton? I just want you to know, I'm here to help in any way I can."

"That's rich. You, help me?"

"Try to believe me. I never knew what that monster was doing."

"Nor did I. Very well, as soon as I return, let's you and I sit down for a good long chat."

"What about Sam?"

"Forget it," he flung over his shoulder. Sam was his wife, dammit. Hoxton had lost his mind for certain, if he thought Grant would give her over to him now. "As she will no doubt tell you herself, she is no Susannah."

Numb, Sam went to the dog. Poor Gus. How valiantly he had rescued her. But where were her tears? Didn't the poor thing deserve her tears?

"Sam? What happened to Gus?"

She turned to see Willie, climbing up the way Grant had gone. "He tried to save me." Her voice had a hollow ring. Funny, she hadn't stopped to consider it before, but Grant had saved her life, too.

"Was it Fatso? Did he shoot the both of them?"

Both? Vaguely, she remembered the blood on Grant's arm. Had he been injured, rescuing her?

As Willie bent down, Gus twitched and whimpered. She dropped to her knees. "Gus? Oh Gus, you wonderful mutt; you're alive."

"We'll fix him, Sam. You and me, just like before."

She hugged the boy close, tears now mingling with the rain. This time, there would be no Grant to catch them sneaking Gus scraps. She had sent him away. Forever.

She heard the scratching noise behind them and turned. She thought, I never actually saw Riley in that wagon as it went over. Could he have jumped?

Her heart went to her throat as a shadowy form limped closer. Through the rain, she watched the dark boots, then the muddy trousers, and in the next flash of lightning, saw the scarred features of Hoxton's face. He was alive?

"Sam? Oh, my darling, are you all right?"

She stood, shakily. It was impossible, but that voice had soothed her to sleep on many a restless night. This man had taught her to hold tight to her dreams.

"Papa," she said softly, taking one slow step after another. "Papa, my God, is it truly you?"

He gathered her in his arms, trembling as he held her. "All these years. My baby, all these years."

She clung to him. "I knew you weren't dead. I knew it."

"Oh baby, I wanted to come to you, but I couldn't."

"It doesn't matter. You're here now. And you're alive."

As a bolt crashed down close to where they were standing, he laughed giddily. "I won't be, if we don't get out of this storm. Come, let's help the boy move his dog to that cave over there."

Sam was laughing, too, more out of reaction than humor, as they carried poor Gus to shelter. Bending over him, determining that his injury was not fatal, she explained to them both what had happened to Riley.

"And when I saw you, Papa, I thought sure it was him. I mean, it seemed too easy that he would die that way."

"I know what you mean. He did terrible things to us all, Sam. And lately, I'm afraid I helped him. I am so ashamed. From the moment I was dragged from that burning shack, I was clay in his hands. He used my amnesia to convince me I was Tony, that I must depend on his judgment. When I came here yesterday, I remembered at last, and realized the full extent of his lies."

"His and that snake, Grant Barton."

"Oh no. Sam, you must understand. Barton was as much a victim as we were."

"He was a thief, Papa. Even Cyrus Wynecote knew he had taken that lady's jewels."

"We planted those jewels on him. I am to blame. Riley was against it, but the first time I saw him on a London stage, his resemblance to Tony set off an alarm in my mind. I got it all mixed up, of course, hiring him to court you in my stead, but somehow I knew I had to protect you. We used him dreadfully. Barton could either work for us, or rot in prison. But still, we underestimated him. He defied us, you know, by running away with you."

"But Riley said—"

He put a hand over her lips. "Riley lied. Repeatedly. It may take us years to sort out the mess the man made."

Sam hugged herself. In her mind, she could see Grant pleading, the frustration in his eyes as Riley placed the gag over his mouth. And then her spit, running down his face.

"He wanted my money. He said himself that all he ever wanted was the—"

She never did finish. There was a monstrous blast, far too fierce to be thunder, and then a low, slow rumbling shook the ground. "Dynamite!" her father shouted, sheltering her with his arms. As the stones and debris fell around them, Sam followed the implications as they sifted into her brain. Only one person would have set that charge. Only one wanted the Oh Susannah destroyed. Riley must have jumped from the wagon, after all. And he would escape, untouched, with everything!

Even as the rage filled her, her mind stumbled on another unpalatable truth. The mine. Grant had gone into the mine. To his death.

"My God," she said one last time, before dropping, unconscious, against her father's chest.

27

There was an invigorating nip to the air as Grant eased his horse along the path. For the start of April, it had been unusually warm today, but as the afternoon waned, so did the heat. Sniffing, he smelled the pine smoke as the local stoves were lit. In another hour, he would need an overcoat.

But by then, he should reach his destination. Picturing it in his mind, he felt the familiar ache. So many months it had taken. Thousands of frustrating, spirit-dimming hours, chasing the wrong dream. For the sunlit room hadn't been cheery at all, merely filled with hollow echoes from the past. His dream had always been here in Colorado. With Sam.

Suddenly, he felt as nervous as a boy. Would she smile and welcome him? Or, like last time, would she order him away? How long ago that night now seemed. It could have been centuries ago that he had left her alone on that cliff. All to follow Clanton.

It was a mistake he had recognized the moment he caught up with the wretch and saw him loading his pockets with Eggersley ore. And then Grant had compounded his error by confronting Clanton with the past. He had blanched, and then predictably bolted. When Grant would have tackled him, wrestling him into the stream, the entire mine had gone beserk as a blast ripped it open at the seams.

Grant had time to think, "damn that Riley," before Clanton was jolted free of his grasp. With timber and stone falling about their ears, the stream, no doubt fed by the storm, became a raging torrent. Grant spied Clanton, bobbing up ahead, as they both plunged through the crack in the wall.

That was all he remembered. He had woken, bruised and groggy, on a sandy bank farther down the mountain. Ears still ringing from the blast, he had looked up at the toothless smile of his rescuer before going under again for what the doctor later told him was four-and-a-half days.

It had taken the Hoxton legal contingent less than that to locate him, though. Barely had he regained consciousness than they were at his bedside with forms to sign. Clanton's body could not be found, but a certain Mr. Bill Eggersley had explained the entire affair to the authorities and a full investigation was now under way. If he would kindly sign on the dotted line, they would happily represent him in any claims upon the Hoxton properties, since it seemed highly likely that the title would revert to him.

Bill Eggersley? The dazed Grant had questioned. Oh yes, they had clucked; that was dreadful affair but it could be dealt with later. A message from a Miss Eggersley? Why no, there was not.

So he'd followed their advice and sailed to England. The chaos waiting him there was worse than he'd been led to believe. Riley had directed a fortune into his own account, where the money could not be touched. There was nothing left of the Hoxton empire except a mountain of debts. Short of the permanent fixtures on the venerable walls, Riley had stripped the legal heir of everything else.

As always when he thought of the man, Grant suffered a helpless rage. He didn't mind losing the wealth, though a shilling or two would certainly help at the moment, but he could kill the man for what he had done to him and Sam.

Beneath him, his horse pranced, infected by his own uncertainties. Only minutes more. How would she look? Would her hair be up and tightly bound, or would she be smiling at the door, the fire lit and waiting, the fresh-baked hot-cross buns on the table?

There it was again, the ache that had driven him here prematurely. Though he still had little to offer her, he'd found he couldn't endure the fight alone. He needed Sam. Nothing made sense without her. Not a day slipped past that he didn't ache for the scent of her hair, the sound of her laughter.

As he saw puffs of smoke in the distance, his hands tightened on the reins. A good omen, surely. Digging his heels into the horse's flank, he could taste the soft, sugary magic of her mouth. With any luck at all, she would soon be in his arms.

But as he crested the hill and reined the horse in, he was forced to suppress his hopes. Once, long ago, he had teased her that she hadn't exactly a line of suitors at her door, but there seemed to be a goodly number of men there today. As they buzzed about, taking advantage of the fading afternoon sunlight to pound another plank or add one more shingle, the additions to the cabin took on an ominous look. Two bedrooms should have been sufficient for Sam and her father, even including Willie. But it looked as if the cabin had tripled in size.

One of the workers, clearly Willie, hopped across the roof. But it was the woman who shouted at him that drew Grant's resentful gaze. Even from this distance, there was no mistaking the priggishness of that pose. Had she had opted for comfort and respectability after all?

Queasy, now, he would have turned and fled, had Molly not appeared behind him.

"Well, will you look who we have here?" Molly

said to cover her astonishment. Heavens, but she had
forgotten what a handsome devil he was. From the
auburn hair to the gleaming boots, he was every inch
the British aristocrat. "Thought you'd forgotten all
about us, your lordship."

He flinched. Good. Served him right, after what
he'd done to Sam. "I thought you and I had settled on
first names, Molly."

She might have melted at his wistful tone, if he
hadn't broken Sam's heart. Sam had been putting on a
show, but Molly noticed how her eyes lit up at every
knock on the door. "That was when I thought I could
trust you. What are you doing here? Ain't your
lawyers handling things?"

"I came to see Sam." He dropped from the horse
in a slow, almost resigned motion. "I see I'm too
late."

He gripped his mount's reins as he gazed down
the hill. Molly felt a spurt of pity, but it was Sam's
heart she had to think of, to protect. "You sure are.
Time to come and see Sam was months ago. Never did
tell her the truth, did you?"

"I tried. She wouldn't listen." He sighed. "I see
they're adding on to the cabin."

"Yeah, well, that's Blankbrains for you. If he had
to live in these heathenish hills, he insisted on having
his own room."

"I see."

He didn't move. Molly thought she could blow at
him, and like a feather, he would just float away.
"Not that I'll mind having that new kitchen to cook
in. There's so many mouths to feed, I don't know how
Sam does it."

"How does she? Where does the money come
from?"

"You ain't getting it. Whatever Bill took from

your estate, he had coming. You should just leave. Sam's too busy to see you anyway—too busy with all those papers your lawyers made her sign.''

''What papers? What are they up to now?''

Molly eyed him. ''That assumed identity nonsense. Shame on you, boy. You, of all people, going after Bill for damages done to the Hoxton name.''

He groaned. ''I swear, I knew nothing about this.''

''Sam is fit to be tied. She don't need any more heartache right now.''

''It will be stopped. Immediately.'' With a sigh, he reached for his horse. Molly thought he meant to leave, but he merely took something from his pocket to put in the saddlebag. ''Won't be needing that,'' he said grimly, as if making a big decision. ''Or this, either. Have any use for a rose, Molly?''

She took the delicate flower, eyes misting. Heck, what if her first impression had been the right one? Bill still believed in the boy. ''This mean you're not gonna see her?''

''Dammit, I did not come all the way from England to turn back now. Whether or not she'll listen, I'm telling Sam the truth.''

He started down the hill. Falling into step behind him, Molly didn't want to smile. But hell, how could she stop herself? Even if he was a rogue, he was the best-looking one her sore old eyes had ever seen.

Silent as they made the descent, he didn't say a word until Blanknose came running at them. Then he cursed, a long string of obscenities that made Molly feel even better.

''What is *he* doing here? Molly, if you sent for him—''

''Calm down; he came on his own. You seen

Sam?''

"I forbid him to see her. He is not to upset her again."

"I'll make that decision, Emery." To Molly's relief, Bill rolled up in that fancy chair Sam had ordered for his "bad days." "Why don't you finish your work on the roof?"

"Mr. Eggersley," Barton was saying next to her. "It seems I owe you a great deal. Without your intervention, no one would have listened to me."

"It was the least I could do. And if it's any consolation, I never meant you harm. You see, my conscience knew only that Sam needed protection, and I always felt you were the best man for the job."

"Thank you. I once thought so, too."

They looked each other over, both a bit too sad and defeated for Molly's way of thinking. She was about to open her mouth to say something, when that nice Mr. Stoddard strolled out of the house. "Ah, there you are, sir. And—oh, my, Mr. Barton? What a pleasure this is. We had quite given up on ever seeing you again."

"Stoddard? Is this where you've been? I thought you'd want to return to your family in England. I made the arrangements, but you couldn't be found."

"Why, how kind of you, sir. But you see, Miss Samantha had written, concerned that I might need employment. Her father and I—well, it's proven a mutually satisfying relationship."

"Does she have you reading yet?"

Stoddard chuckled. "Quite so, sir. And a good many other things, as well."

"As much as I'd like to keep you here chatting, Barton," Bill spoke up, "I assume you came to see my daughter?"

"May I?"

"Go right in. She should be in the second room to the right. But when you're done, please, I'd like to talk to you."

With a grim nod, Grant turned to the house. He looked as if he was walking into a noose, Molly thought. Chuckling, she hoped Sam would go easy on him.

Grant stood outside the shut door and knew better. With or without Sam's cooperation, this would be the hardest thing he had ever done. Getting her to listen would be bad enough, but then to leave her? With a toad like Blankfield?

Thinking of the lawyer renewed his anger, which was good, because he needed all the strength he could muster. He raised his hand to knock, hard, before he persuaded himself to turn and walk away.

If the soft, "come in" nearly undid him, then the sight of her, dwarfed by towering piles of papers on that mammoth desk, just about broke his heart. She seemed so tired, her hair slipping out of its knot to flow down over her slumped shoulders. Lines of worry creased her forehead.

"Sam," he tried, but could manage no more as she swiftly, devastatingly, looked up into his eyes.

It all came back in a rush. All those precious moments they'd had together, how bright the future had once seemed. She loved him still, she couldn't hide that, no more than she could hide her swollen belly as she rose from her chair to greet him.

He had to look away. To marry Blankfield was one thing, but to so quickly have his child? There was no hope now.

She stopped abruptly, still on her side of the desk. Her eyes were granite gray. "I never thought to see you again, Lord Hoxton. Have you run out of females in London?''

How could he have thought that voice soft and gentle? The only softness, he realized, was in his own head. ''Miss Farnstable, I presume?''

His sarcasm flew past her. ''I thought we had settled that long ago. Claire is the one with the beauty, remember? I am the one with the mine. Speaking of which, exactly what is it you want of me this time?''

''I came for my medallion. I told you I would, remember?''

She bit her lip. He thought perhaps she'd misplaced it and was afraid to tell him so, but her hands went quickly to her neck. In rapid, jerking motions, she took it from under her blouse and thrust it across the desk. ''Here. Take it. Now you can have everything you always wanted. The title, the money—''

''What money?'' He didn't like the sound of his own laughter. ''There isn't a penny. Riley diverted it all to his own accounts.''

''I see. So that is why you are bothering my father.''

''No, dammit. I had nothing to do with that. You know how lawyers are.'' She should; she was married to one.

''He's been through an ordeal. I warn you, I won't allow you to punish him any further.''

Grant slammed his fist on the desk. ''I told you, dammit, I had nothing to do with it. The minute I return to London, I will dismiss every last one of those money-hounds.''

''You're going back?'' She seemed to shrink. ''When?''

''Tonight.'' He felt suddenly smaller as well. What a helpless, hopeless fool, standing there staring at her, wanting her so much it must show in every line of his body. "There doesn't seem to be much reason for me to stay."

"Molly is making stew. Surely you can stay for dinner?"

"I'm afraid it would be awfully awkward, don't you think?"

She lowered her eyes. "Yes, I suppose. Willie will be disappointed, though."

Why did she do this? To torture him? "It can't be helped."

"No, of course it can't. You're the great Lord Hoxton now, aren't you? It would be demeaning to eat with a menagerie like us. And was it also beneath your dignity, my lord, to scribble off a quick note to let us know you were alive?"

"Dammit Sam, I wrote to your father."

"Over a month later. And through your lawyers. They're a cold, calculating bunch. But then, so are you."

To his amazement, he saw tears, huge, heavy drops, dripping down her cheeks. "Listen, Sam . . ."

"No, you listen." She came around the desk to stand before him. The gray eyes flashed fire. "You broke that boy's heart, Grant Barton—I mean—"

"I kept the name. Despite my lawyers' protests. I found I was weary of changing identities. And James brought back too many memories of my years with Clanton."

"Well, whoever you are, Willie believed in you. He still believes your nonsense about being a real family."

At least someone did. "Good, since I have every intention of adopting him, once I clear up the mess Riley made of my life."

"You what?" Her voice raised in pitch with every

word. "After all this time, you plan to just waltz in here and take him away from me?"

He eyed her belly. "You have other compensations."

"You bastard." She came at him, and he was so stunned at her loss of composure that he let her pound at his chest. "All these months of hoping and waiting."

"Waiting?" He grabbed her hands, feeling a bit hysterical himself. God spare him, but he wanted to pull her close and kiss her. "What kind of a fool do you take me for? Molly let me know how little I was welcomed here. Oh, and how could I forget the proud little papa? He ordered me off your land, you know. But how silly of me. It's his land now, isn't it? All these wonderful additions; I doubt Blankfield is so pleased with his nuptial arrangements now."

To his dismay, she began to laugh. Holding her hands between them, he wondered if he should slap the hysteria away.

"Oh Grant, I didn't realize . . ."

He tugged her closer. "Dammit Sam, how could you? You belonged to me."

"I know."

The soft reply undid him. *You're still mine,* he swore silently, as he leaned down to take her lips. He kissed her long and hard, as a drowning man takes in the last few precious gulps of air. He couldn't leave her, he knew. Not ever again.

"Oh Sam, why couldn't you wait for me? Why couldn't you believe in me?"

"I did."

Holding her tight, afraid to let her go, his mind raced with plans. "We'll find a way. Whatever it takes, Sam, you'll stay with me. If I have to fight him with my fists, Blankfield won't have you."

She shook her head. "Oh Grant, you're as bad as Emery. Didn't you listen? I said I did."

He pulled away to look at her. "What?"

"I did wait. And I did believe in you. I fought it, but then I have always fought against you."

"You waited?"

"Of course. As I repeatedly told Emery, I was already married. He gave up quickly enough when he realized he could then pursue Claire. They were married last month."

"Then the baby . . ."

"Is yours. Ours, actually. And I might warn you, due any day."

He stared into her eyes, afraid to believe, yet needing to very much. Something in her smile reassured him. "Good God, Sam, why didn't you tell me?"

Her hand went up to gently stroke his cheek. "I couldn't write something like this in a letter. I thought, when he comes, then I'll tell him. But then you were here, and you were so angry, and I was so hurt and confused and frightened . . ."

"I almost left. You would have let me go, thinking . . ."

"No." She bit her lip, trying not to smile. "If you must know, I was just about to attach myself to your leg. I wasn't about to let you leave this room without saying what must be said."

"Oh, and what was that?"

"I love you, Grant Barton. You silly man, I love you."

Solemnly, almost afraid to breathe lest he break the spell, Grant slipped the medallion back over her neck. "My wife," he whispered softly, and she fell into his arms. Holding her, stroking her hair, he swore he would never let her get away from him again.

"One of my less obnoxious attorneys drew up a form. If we both sign it, Sam, it will validate our marriage. I brought a proper ring, this time. And a rose. I had it all planned out how I'd go down on my knee, but then, when I thought you'd married that toad, I left everything on the horse."

"You wonderful man. All I want is you."

"And all I want is you, Sam. You're all I've ever wanted."

She answered by drawing his head down to hers. Running his hands along her love-swollen frame, Grant savored the knowledge that he had at last come home.

When they finally broke apart, she sighed with great contentment. "I imagine the others are extremely curious by now. I suppose we should go tell them. Especially Willie. And Gus, or he'll never stop barking."

"Not just yet. For the moment, I just want to fill myself with the sight of you."

"Oh Grant, I missed you so. Do you know how beautiful you are when you smile at me like that?"

"That's funny; I was about to say the same thing."

"Pinch me. Prove that I'm not dreaming."

"Not on your life." For the only dream he had ever cared about stood before him, living and breathing and welcoming him home. He, Grant Barton, with a home and family all his own. Here was all the wealth he'd ever sought. Here, in this woman. His woman. "Sam, my love, this is how it feels when your dreams come true."